The World's Greatest Short Stories

A SELECTION *from the* WORLD'S GREATEST SHORT STORIES

ILLUSTRATIVE OF THE HISTORY OF SHORT STORY WRITING

WITH CRITICAL AND HISTORICAL COMMENTS
By SHERWIN CODY

EDITOR OF "A SELECTION FROM THE BEST
ENGLISH ESSAYS," AND AUTHOR OF "THE ART OF
WRITING & SPEAKING THE ENGLISH LANGUAGE"

SECOND EDITION

CHICAGO · A. C. McCLURG
& COMPANY · *MCMIII*

Contents

to Write Fiction," London), the critics were about equally divided between brief commendation of the volume and lengthy condemnation of the idea of analyzing and teaching the art of fiction at all. But a great change has been wrought since then. The University of Chicago established a course in short story writing. Numerous magazine writers offered themselves as expounders of the art ; and the confessions of successful novelists and short story writers were freely recorded. The author of the volume above referred to soon realized what small scope there was for a volume professedly written to instruct the professional writer, but how large and important was the work of assisting the general reader to a more intelligent reading of fiction. Only by raising the critical standard of the great body of readers can the standard for writers of fiction be raised. So almost from the start this volume has been working itself out.

The first definite list of the world's masterpieces of short story writing which came in the editor's way was one suggested during an hour's chat with Mr. W. E. Henley, in 1895. Among the young writers in London at that time, Mr. Henley (for a number of years editor of the *National Observer*) was considered the best judge of a really good short story, and the best critic. Kipling, Barrie, Gilbert Parker, Arthur Morrison, H. D. Lowry, Kenneth Grahame, and many others were proud to acknowledge him as their teacher and master, in some cases their discoverer. Mr. Henley's opinions have been supplemented by suggestions from Arlo Bates, Edmund Gosse, Brander Matthews, and contributors to various discussions of the short story which have occurred in the public prints.

On some of the stories all competent judges will agree, on a few a majority will agree, and on the remainder hardly any critic will agree with any other critic as to relative rank. For the purposes of this volume the editor feels that he is in duty bound to follow his own best judgment, not expecting or even hoping that every one will agree with him in his omissions and inclusions, but trusting that as a whole the volume will not be deemed altogether unworthy.

All will probably agree in placing " Patient Griselda," " Aladdin's Lamp," " Rip Van Winkle," " A Passion in the Desert," and " The Gold Bug " among the world's masterpieces. From Dickens Mr. Henley would have selected " Barbox Brothers " in " Mugby Junction; " but the editor has chosen " A Christmas Carol " (using the shorter version arranged by Dickens himself for his American readings) because it is so indisputably great in its good humor and its appeal to the heart, though otherwise full of faults, and " A Child's Dream of a Star " because it so well represents the element of pathetic sentiment, in which Dickens particularly excelled, and because the story is very short and at the same time popular. Very short stories were not common in the old days, though to-day they are so universal. "A Princess's Tragedy," which forms a chapter in "Barry Lyndon," was suggested by Mr. Henley, and is here presented as unquestionably one of the finest short stories Thackeray ever wrote. "Barry Lyndon" as a novel has never been popular, and, so far as the editor is aware, the story of "The Princess's Tragedy" has not before been set forth for what it is really worth. Seldom do we find such an example of the power of restraint in a simple narrative of intensely tragic character. Some critics select "The Birthmark" as Hawthorne's masterpiece, but the popular verdict has fixed unalterably upon "The Great Stone Face," and the editor profoundly agrees with the choice. The best stories of Maupassant ("Boule de Suif" and "La Maison Tellier") are not suitable for English publication; but nearly all the critics agree that "La Ficelle" ("The String") is a genuine masterpiece. "The Necklace" has been included because it illustrates in so simple and obvious a manner the various elements in an artistic story, and thus forms a suitable paradigm for the study of constructive fiction. "The Man Who Would Be King" is the universal choice of the younger friends of Mr. Kipling in London, though "Without Benefit of Clergy" and "Drums of the Fore and Aft" contend with it in popularity. Most critics grant the superior art of "A Window in Thrums," and the chapter selected is a short story enchanting in its humor. "On the Stairs," by

Arthur Morrison, is not a great story, but it illustrates admirably the clever technic of the younger
writers.

It will be observed that but three selections have
been made from current or comparatively recent
writers. The editor regrets that he cannot include
Stevenson's "A Lodging for the Night" or "Will
o' the Mill," Miss Mary E. Wilkins's "The Scent
of Roses" or "The Revolt of Mother," Edward
Everett Hale's "The Man Without a Country,"
Bret Harte's "The Luck of Roaring Camp," and
one or more selections from Thomas Hardy's
"Life's Little Ironies." Stockton's "The Lady
or the Tiger?" is an admirable example of an
interesting type, but scarcely a great story. Of
stories by foreign writers, apologies for omission
are due above all to Turgenieff, who may be
spoken of as a "current" writer, in the sense that
excellent translations are only lately making him
known to English readers. His short stories excel
those even of Tolstoi.

"The Great Stone Face," by Nathaniel Haw-
thorne, is used by special arrangement with and
permission of Messrs. Houghton, Mifflin, & Co.,
the authorized publishers of Hawthorne's works.
Similar acknowledgments are due to Messrs. G. P.
Putnam's Sons for Irving's "Rip Van Winkle," to
Messrs. Little, Brown, & Co. for Arthur Morrison's
"On the Stairs," and to Messrs. Harper & Brothers,
the first publishers of a translation of the stories by
Maupassant used in this book.

one can say that a genius may not arise who will violate all the assumed laws of novel-construction, and yet produce a story as successful as any that has ever been published. Of the fixed arts, such as sculpture, painting, and music, we can make no such statement as that; and now it would be untrue of short story writing.

In works of art there are always two things to be distinguished,—the subject-matter, and the form into which that matter is wrought by the hand of the artist. The artistic work of a genius is rated great, as the general public counts greatness, according to the depth and variety of the knowledge of human nature displayed. Knowledge of human nature is the gold which is to be worked into a form of beauty, it is the diamond which is to be cut and polished. Art is that which forms the gold into a thing of use and beauty; it is that which reveals the natural beauty of the diamond to the ordinary observer. A good form, a true art, displays the precious object to the best advantage. Art alone— that is, skill in displaying knowledge of human nature to advantage — is of no value unless there is knowledge to be displayed. But a little set forth with skill is of more practical utility than a great deal presented badly, or without art; we may even imagine that a lack of art might debar the greatest genius the world has ever seen (so far as real knowledge of human nature is concerned) from making the least impression on his fellow men. So after all, art — or skill in shaping

and presenting — is as absolutely essential as original knowledge of human nature. Those two are
the essential principles of human progress, without
whose marriage there can be no children of the
imagination; indeed no growth of the human soul
in the things of beauty, in the joys and sorrows of
the emotions of the mind, in that whole section of
human existence which we have marked out and
roughly named "the realm of art."

The absolute equality and complete interdepend-
ence of these two great forces in the movements
of the world's thought, popularly referred to as art
and genius, have been but imperfectly recognized
by the majority of critics. We have the staunch
defenders of genius, who say that "the poet is
born, not made," — which is perfectly true if regarded simply as a way of emphasizing one side
of the question, — and we have the devotees of
Art, who invariably write the word in capitals, and
seem to believe that there is nothing else in life.
The fact is, both genius and art are utterly barren
unless united, and the greatness to which they give
birth is usually measured by the harmony and
completeness of their union.

Though in a perfect work of art subject-matter
and form are so perfectly blended that we think of
neither separately, yet for critical purposes it is
well to keep them rigidly separated; and one or
two preliminary remarks on each will facilitate our
study.

First, the world grows in knowledge of human

nature and the philosophy of life as steadily as in other directions, and a story of transcendent interest to one age becomes the merest commonplace to the next. In time the world will outgrow even Shakespeare, as it has in part already outgrown Virgil and Homer; but the historical student views these men in the light of the effect their works have had upon the world in its progress. It is impossible to measure them with perfect accuracy until their influence is largely a matter of the past. The fact is, we cannot understand genius till we have grown up to it, and of course then it has ceased to become the light and inspiration that it once was; and the brilliancy of the light that is still our inspiration we are not in a position to measure critically. We must remember this in reading the present volume. Very likely the common reader will find the stories that are known to be the greatest a little tiresome, because these stories are so old that the world has outgrown them; and he will like best some of the more modern stories which the judicious critic would place very low. The editor of this volume has tried to make it of value both to the historical student and to the common reader; and this effort has fallen in naturally with the logical plan of the book.

So much for the subject-matter: let us now turn to the art side.

There are two kinds of art, conscious and unconscious. When the knights-errant of genius cry, "The poet is born, not made," they by no means intend to imply that form is nothing: they are thinking, "Genius invents its own forms unconsciously, which are far superior to the forms selected by the conscious artist who is uninspired by genius." They ignore the conscious artist who *is* inspired by genius, for there is nothing at all incompatible between conscious art and genius. The fact is, however, that the history of nearly every special art is that at first its forms are unconscious, or, let us say, experimental; and as in its evolution it draws near to perfection and its possibilities are realized to the full, very nearly all its practitioners become conscious artists. Moreover, as soon as the possibilities of an art are realized to the full, that art begins to decline, and new arts arise to take its place. So it happens that we are likely to find the unconscious artists associated with the rise of an art, and the conscious artists associated with its decline; but at the height of the progress we find one great conscious artist who overshadows all others, conscious or unconscious. Such an artist in dramatic poetry was Shakespeare.

Short story writing is but a branch of the larger art of fiction which comprehends the novel, and though short story writing has become a conscious art, we find no supreme artist in it who is also a supreme genius. Novel-writing as an art is still in the unconscious stage, and we may yet have our Shakespeare of fiction. In the history of short story writing Maupassant is probably the supreme

conscious artist, but he is a genius of no such
calibre as Poe or Hawthorne. Poe probably
comes nearer than any other story-writer to
being our great conscious artist and genius combined ; but Poe's powers as a story-writer are too
limited in scope to entitle him to any position
which we may call supreme. Hawthorne was also
a conscious artist in part, and his field of success
is just that portion of the great field which Poe
left untouched. Together they mark the beginning of the modern conscious and fixed art of
short story writing. Hence we may claim this art
as fairly American; and this justly encourages us
to hope that the future perfect form of the novel
will spring from America.

The peculiarity of the unconscious artist is that
he perfects some one phase of the complete art.
A collection of the best works of the unconscious
period will give us in striking form all the different
elements of the complete artistic story. In it we
find pure types of character-study, of lofty atmosphere, of moral instruction, of plot. For this
reason a collection of masterpieces of short story
writing, such as the present volume, affords the
best possible examples for study of the constructive side of fiction, as well as the historical side.
Observing the unconscious steps by which the
world learned the art of short story writing, we
may not unnaturally conceive that these are the
steps by which the individual learns the conscious
art. What the editor conceives these steps to

be, alike in the historical progress of the art and in the evolution of the individual artist, will be indicated in the introductions to the successive stories.

SHERWIN CODY.

CHICAGO,
January, 1902.

I

PATIENT GRISELDA

Then every one who wished to be amused crowded
into the main room of the tavern, and the distinguished traveller became the popular novelist.
Boccaccio did not originate a single story in the
Decameron. He merely retold in the choicest
Italian the stories he heard at the inns as he
journeyed about.

In those days when there were no newspapers,
few theatres, and fewer books, life must have been
dull indeed. The arrival of a traveller at the village inn was like a breath of fresh air admitted
into a close room. Such conditions gave zest to
travelling. The man who could tell a story was
sure of an eager audience wherever he went, and
if he liked the clatter of applause, he knew there
was no better way to get it than this. So the professional traveller became the professional story-
teller. He got up his stories with all the art he
could muster, and would go a long distance out of
his way to hear a good tale, that he might tell it afterwards himself. In this way certain stories became
widely popular, and they came to be told with great
skill. The tellers studied their audiences, they
learned what interested their hearers, what touched
their emotions, and so became adepts in the art of
playing on the feelings of their fellows.

No form of literary art ever had so democratic
an origin as fiction. Just fancy what the literary
critics of to-day, even, would say to a collection of
one hundred bar-room yarns! And when poetry,
history, and philosophy were the only recognized

forms of literary art, how much more contemptible would these gossiping tales appear to be!

The Decameron is the beginning of the modern love-story. For the first time woman held the place of chief interest. Most of the stories are so grossly immoral and vulgar that they are unreadable to-day; but that only illustrates the general advancement in public taste and morals. In Boccaccio's time any of his stories might be told in a lady's drawing-room with perfect propriety.

By long odds the most popular of Boccaccio's hundred tales is that of Patient Griselda, and strangely enough, it is the most highly moral story of them all. Chaucer heard it from the poet Petrarch and used it in his Canterbury Tales. Soon after its publication it appeared in France in thirty different forms.

In this story we have a simple tale, of a purely narrative character. Prose has its rhythm as well as music and poetry, and in " Patient Griselda " we find a long, gentle undulation (which the translator has endeavored to imitate in the English), and a total absence of the staccato-like variations of the more modern short story. There is no strained sentiment, no special attempt at " atmosphere," and the speeches of the various characters vary in style in no respect from the narrative portions of the story. The whole, however, presents an example of chaste simplicity which has never been surpassed, and seldom equalled. Our ideas of women have so far advanced that we have no patience with Griselda's conduct, and on that account find the story a trifle tiresome; but any modern writer who would revert to the gentle and unruffled method of story-telling employed by Boccaccio would be astonished at the power he would find in such a style.

PATIENT GRISELDA

[Rewritten in English by the Editor]

LONG ago there was a certain marquis of Saluzzo, Gualtieri or Walter by name, who seemed to have made up his mind to remain a bachelor. He did nothing but hawk and hunt, and never dreamed of encumbering himself with a wife and children. In that he was no doubt very wise; but his subjects did not view the matter in the same light, and often urged him to marry, that he might not be left without an heir, or they without a lord. They said they stood ready to provide a lady from such a family that she would not be likely to disappoint their hopes, nor give him reason to be dissatisfied with their choice.

"Worthy friends," he replied, "you ask me to do a thing I had fully made up my mind never to venture upon, considering how difficult it is to find the kind of person one would wish for a wife. You must admit there is a great abundance of the kind one would *not* wish; and I know of no lot more miserable than to be tied to a disagreeable woman.

"The idea of judging a woman's temper by her family, or in that way choosing a wife that will please me, strikes me as quite a ridiculous fancy. Apart from the fact that one never knows who their fathers are, we know very well how few daughters resemble either father or mother.

"For all that, as you are so anxious to see me noosed, I will agree. But that I may have no one to blame but myself should it turn out amiss, I will choose for myself; but I swear, let me marry whom I will, unless you show her the respect due to my wife, you shall know, to your sorrow, what a responsibility you assume in urging me to marry against my inclination."

The worthy deputation of citizens bowed low and replied that they were satisfied, provided only that he would make the trial.

Now the marquis had already taken a fancy to a poor country girl who lived in a small village not far from his palace. Thinking that he might live as comfortably with her as with any one, he decided to look no farther, but make her his wife. So he sent for her father, who was a very poor man, and told him what he purposed to do. Then he summoned his subjects and said to them:

"Gentlemen, it was and is your desire that I take a wife. I do it rather to please you than out of any liking I have for matrimony. You will remember that you promised to be satisfied with my choice, whoever she might be, and to pay her due respect. I am now ready to fulfil my side of the bargain, and I expect you to do likewise. In a near-by village I have found a young woman after my own heart. I intend to marry her and bring her home in a few days. See that you honor my nuptials and respect her as your sovereign lady, that I may be as well satisfied with the fulfilment of your promise as you have reason to be with that of mine."

The people declared themselves well pleased, and renewed their promise to accept her as their mistress, whoever she might be. So everything was made ready for a noble feast, and the prince invited all his relations and the great lords from all the surrounding provinces. He also had a number of rich dresses made on a model that seemed to be about the size of his intended spouse, and provided a girdle, a ring, and a fine coronet, with everything requisite for a bride.

When the appointed day arrived, about the third hour he mounted his horse, attended by all his friends and vassals.

"My lords and gentlemen," he said, "we will now go for my new spouse."

So they rode into the next village, and when they came near the father's house, the marquis saw his bride carrying water in great haste, that she might be ready to go with some of her friends to see the new marchioness.

He called her by her name Griselda, and asked where her father was. She replied modestly:

"My gracious lord, he is in the house."

So the marquis alighted, and commanding them all to wait, went alone into the cottage, where he found Giannucolo, Griselda's father.

"My good man," said he, "I am come to marry thy daughter; but I should like first to ask her a few questions before thee."[1] He then asked if she would try, to the best of her ability, to please him and not be uneasy at any time, whatever he might say or do; and more to the same effect. To all she answered "Yes."

He then led her out by the hand and made her strip before them all, and ordering up the rich dresses he had provided, clothed her completely and set the coronet upon her disordered hair, to the amazement of all.

"Behold," said he, "the person I have chosen for

---

[1] This form was used with inferiors. The forms "you" and "yours" were employed toward superiors.

my wife, provided she will accept me for her husband."
Then turning toward the abashed girl he asked:

"Will you have me for your husband?"

She replied, "Yes, if it so please your lordship."

"Well said!" he exclaimed. "I take you for my wife."

In this public manner he married her, and mounting her on a palfrey led the way back to the palace. The wedding was celebrated with as much pomp and grandeur as if he had taken to wife the daughter of the King of France; and apparently the young bride had exchanged both her mind and her behavior with her garments. She was good-looking and amiable, and had the bearing rather of a lord's daughter than a poor shepherd's, a fact that astonished every one who had previously known her. As for her husband, he found her so obedient and obliging in every way that he thought himself the happiest man in the world. To her subjects, likewise, she was so gracious and considerate that they all honored her and loved her, praying for her health and happiness, and declaring that after all Gualtieri was a shrewder fellow than they had given him credit for being. Who else would have discovered so many virtues under so mean a dress?

Before they had been married long she proved to be with child, and she gave birth to a daughter, for which he made great rejoicings.

But now the marquis developed a new fancy. He made up his mind to make trial of his wife's patience by long and intolerable sufferings. He spoke harshly to her, and affected to be weary of her. He told her his subjects murmured at her mean parentage, and at the idea of her being the mother of his daughter.

She listened to these unkind words without a change of countenance, and quietly replied:

" My lord, pray dispose of me as you think most proper for your honor and happiness. I know that I am meaner than the meanest of your people, and that I was quite unworthy of the dignity to which your favor was pleased to raise me."

This pleased the marquis. But shortly afterwards his servant appeared before Griselda and said :

" Madam, I must either lose my life or obey my lord's commands. Now he has ordered me to take your daughter and —— " He said no more, but hung his head and acted in such a distraught way that she supposed he had orders to destroy the child. She lifted it tenderly from the cradle and kissed it again and again, gave it her blessing, and, though her heart was ready to burst with a mother's love, she laid it in the servant's arms.

" Take it," said she, " and do with it what thy lord and mine has commanded ; but please, please, leave it not to be devoured by fowls or wild beasts, unless that be his will."

The result of this experiment was a great surprise to the marquis ; but he sent the child to Bologna to be educated in secret.

Soon Griselda was with child again, and brought a son into the world. Not long after its birth the marquis determined upon a further trial of his wife's patience. So he said to her :

" Since thou hast brought me this son, I can no longer live with my people ; for they are so indignant that a poor shepherd's grandson is to succeed and be their lord after me, that I must dispose of this child as I did of the other, or run the risk of being driven out of my dominions. Then I must send thee away and take a wife more suitable to my position."

" My lord," said she, with resignation, " study your own

ease and happiness without the least regard for me ; for nothing will bring me happiness but that which is pleasing to yourself."

Accordingly the son was sent to Bologna, though under such circumstances as to give the impression that he had been destroyed.

The marquis was greatly pleased with the results of his experiment, and declared to himself that there was not another woman in the world equal to his wife. He had often observed her great fondness for her children, so he knew that it was no want of affection that led her to part with them so readily.

The people, being as much deceived as Griselda herself, and supposing the children had been put to death, blamed the marquis to the last degree, and began to think him the most cruel and monstrous of men. They likewise showed their compassion for the lady. But when they went to condole with her for the loss of her children, she said :

"It was not my will, but his who begot them."

Several years went by, and the marquis determined to make a last trial of the patience of his humble wife. He announced to his people that he had come to the conclusion that he had acted foolishly and like a young man in choosing Griselda, as he had done, and that he meant to petition the pope for a dispensation to divorce her and marry another more suitable to his rank. There were many who blamed him bitterly for this action ; but he gave them no heed.

Griselda heard this announcement, and prepared herself to go back and tend her father's cattle while some other lady occupied the place of honor that had been hers for so many years. She grieved in secret over this last calamity, but determined to bear it as resolutely as she had borne the loss of her children.

Counterfeit letters of dispensation arrived, as if from the pope, and the marquis said to his wife:

"Woman, by the pope's leave I may dispose of thee and take another wife. As my ancestors have been all sovereign princes of this country, and thine only peasants, I intend to keep thee no longer, but to send thee back to thy father's cottage with the same portion which thou broughtest me, and afterwards to make choice of one more suitable in quality to myself."

Griselda had difficulty in restraining her tears, but she said calmly:

"My lord, I was always sensible that my servile condition would in no way accord with your rank and descent. For what I have been, I own myself indebted to Providence and you. I consider it as a favor lent me. You are now pleased to demand it back; I therefore willingly restore it. Behold the ring with which you espoused me; I deliver it to you. You bid me take the dowry back which I brought you. You will have no need for a teller to count it, nor I for a purse to put it in, much less a sumpter horse to carry it away, for I have not forgotten that you took me naked, and if you think it decent to expose that body that has borne you two children, I am content; but I would entreat you, as a recompense for my virginity, which I brought you and do not carry away, that you would be pleased to leave me one shift over and above my dowry."

Though ready to weep, he put on a stern countenance, and said:

"Thou shalt have one only, then."

All the people begged him to allow her at least one old gown to keep her body from shame, but in vain. So she left the palace with no covering but her shift, and returned weeping to her father's house, to the great grief of all.

Poor old Giannucolo had not thought the prince would keep her long, so he had laid her old garments away ready for use on an occasion like this. As for Griselda, she went courageously about the affairs of her father's household.

The marquis gave out that he was going to marry a daughter of the Count of Panago. When the time of the wedding drew near he sent for Griselda and said to her:

"I have no woman to set my house in order. As thou art familiar with all the details of my establishment, I wish thee to make what provision is required, invite what ladies thou wilt, and when the marriage is ended, get thee home to thy father's again."

"My lord, I am ready to fulfil your commands," she answered quietly.

So she went in her coarse dress to the palace, and with her own hands swept out the rooms and set them to rights; she cleaned and scrubbed like the meanest servant, and directed affairs in the kitchen till all was in readiness. She also invited the ladies of the neighborhood in the name of the marquis, and on the day named, meanly clad as she was, she received them in the most genteel and cheerful manner imaginable.

In the meantime the children had been living at Bologna with a kinswoman of the marquis. The girl was twelve, an extremely pretty creature, and the boy was a bright little fellow of six. The marquis now sent to his kinswoman to bring them with a retinue to Saluzzo, and to give it out all along the way that she was bringing the young lady to be married to him.

They reached Saluzzo about dinner-time after several days' travel. The news of their coming had been spread abroad, and they found the whole country assembled and waiting to see the new marchioness.

The young lady was graciously received. Griselda went cheerfully to meet her, saying :

" Your ladyship is most welcome."

The ladies of the neighborhood had begged the marquis that Griselda be allowed to stay in a room by herself, or else have some suitable clothes to wear. But he turned a deaf ear to all their entreaties. However, when the young lady appeared, nearly every one agreed that the prince had made a good choice. Griselda in particular commended her highly.

" What thinkest thou of my bride ? " asked the prince.

" My lord, I like her extremely well," she answered. " If she be as prudent as she is fair, you may be the happiest man in the world with her. But I most humbly beg that you will not take those heart-breaking measures with this lady that you did with your former wife, because she is young, and has been tenderly educated, whereas the other was inured to hardships from a child."

Gualtieri rejoiced exceedingly in this last evidence of Griselda's humility and sweetness of temper. So he made her sit down beside him and said:

" Griselda, it is now time for you to reap the reward of your long patience, and for those who have reputed me cruel and unjust, a monster by nature, to know that what I have done has been merely to show them how a wife ought to behave. I was apprehensive that I might have endangered my ease and quiet by marrying; but now I know they are secure as long as we live together. I had a mind to prove you by harsh words and seemingly harsh acts. You have not transgressed my will in any particular, and I know that I have met with that happiness which I desired. All shall be restored to you in one hour which was taken away in many, and with it such sweet recompense as I can bestow.   Accept this young lady and her brother as your children and mine.   They are the same that you and many others thought I had cruelly murdered.

"In me you see a husband who loves and values you above all things, and one who feels that no person in the world can be happier in a wife than I in mine."

He thereupon embraced her with affection, while she wept for joy.   They then went to their daughter, who was very much astonished, and tenderly saluted her and her brother.

All the women rose from the table overjoyed at the news they heard, and leading Griselda away to her chamber, clothed her as became a marchioness.   But even in her rags she seemed of that estate.

Joy and satisfaction reigned on every side, and the feasting went on for many days.   The marquis was judged a wise man, though his treatment of his wife had been intolerable ; and Griselda was admired as a woman beyond compare.

In a few days the Count da Panago returned home with his retinue.   The marquis took Giannucolo from his drudgery and maintained him as his father-in-law.   So for the rest of his life the old peasant lived in respect and honor.

In view of an instance like this, must we not admit that divine spirits may descend from heaven into the meanest of cottages ; while royal palaces shall give birth to such as seem rather adapted to the care of animals than the government of men?   Who but Griselda could, not only without a tear, but even with seeming satisfaction, undergo the most unheard-of trials at the hands of her husband?   Many women there are who, if turned out of doors naked as Griselda was, would have found means to procure fine clothes for themselves, adorning at once their own persons and their husbands' brows (with frowns).

NOTE. — There is probably not one woman in a hundred in modern times who, if she were treated as Griselda was, would not invoke the courts. Yet there are some who will bear almost anything for the sake of peace. One cannot help the suspicion that Griselda was deeper than she seemed, and knowing more of her husband's nature and purposes than appears in the story, was acting a diplomatic and exceedingly shrewd part in refusing to be provoked. Viewed in this light, she is a striking example of the power of modesty and non-resistance to give dignity, and finally authority and power, to one from the lowliest social rank. Yet even if we take this view, there is nothing in the story that would for a moment lead us to question Griselda's simplicity and ingenuousness of nature. If she was as wise as a serpent, she was as pure and generous-minded as a child. — EDITOR.

II

ALADDIN, OR THE WONDERFUL LAMP

ALADDIN,
OR THE WONDERFUL LAMP

FROM

"*THE ARABIAN NIGHTS' ENTER-TAINMENTS*"

INTRODUCTORY

THE ORIGIN OF THE MODERN ROMANCE

AS the modern love story had its beginning in the Decameron, so the modern romance had its beginning in the Arabian Nights. Strangely enough, the stories of the Arabian Nights were collected in almost the same way and at the same time as the stories of the Decameron. But while the love stories were Italian, the Arabian Nights' Entertainments were Oriental. The Arabs are a nation of free-booters and merchants. Both are travellers, and we have already seen how easily the distinguished traveller in the old days merged into the distinguished story-teller. The wonderful tales of the genii were invented to give excitement to an evening at the tavern. Most of them are at the same time tales of travel, and in their very setting we see the signs of their bar-room origin.

So low was the origin of modern fiction that the matchless tales of the Arabian Nights are even to this day looked on with contempt by the Oriental critic and philosopher. But in them we see the dreams of the common people, and we realize what an important part dreams have in the spiritual economy of life. We must hope; we must escape from the drudgery of the lot in which we toil; we must rest our hearts, or they will break! Romance takes us out of ourselves and makes us free spirits for the hour. It is one of the greatest blessings of life; and the fact that the mere printed pages of a book can do this to-day shows the marvellous advancement of the average intelligence in modern times.

There is a popular misconception to the effect that any wild fancy may constitute a " fairy story." The truth is, however, that a tale of this kind requires as profound a knowledge of human nature as any form of fiction. Take for granted the existence of genii and fairies, with their peculiar and unnatural powers, and we can go no farther in the way of license. Everything that is said and done must be as strictly logical, as well worth doing, and as instructive and dramatic as in the most realistic fiction. It is by no means easy to assume a little license without being constantly

tempted to assume more; but restraint here as
elsewhere is the invariable sign manual of the
master.

ALADDIN, OR THE WONDERFUL LAMP

IN one of the large and rich cities of China there once
lived a tailor named Mustapha. He was very poor.
He could hardly, by his daily labor, maintain himself and
his family, which consisted only of his wife and a son.

His son, who was called Aladdin,[1] was a very careless
and idle fellow. He was disobedient to his father and
mother, and would go out early in the morning and stay
out all day, playing in the streets and public places with
idle children of his own age.

When he was old enough to learn a trade, his father
took him into his own shop, and taught him how to use
the needle; but all his father's endeavors to keep him to
his work were vain, for no sooner was his back turned, than
the boy was gone for that day. Mustapha chastised him,
but Aladdin was incorrigible, and his father, to his great
grief, was forced to abandon him to his idleness; and
was so much troubled about him, that he fell sick and
died in a few months.

Aladdin, who was now no longer restrained by the fear
of a father, gave himself entirely over to his idle habits,
and was never out of the streets or away from his companions. This course he followed till he was fifteen
years old, without giving his mind to any useful pursuit
or the least reflection on what would become of him.
As he was one day playing, according to custom, in the

---

[1] Aladdin signifies "The Nobility of the Religion." — Lane,
vol. ii. p. 285.

street, with his evil associates, a stranger passing by stopped to observe him.

This stranger was a sorcerer, known as the African magician, as he had been but two days arrived from Africa, his native country.

The African magician, observing in Aladdin's countenance something which assured him that he was a fit boy for his purpose, inquired his name and history of some of his companions, and when he had learnt all he desired to know, went up to him, and taking him aside from his comrades, said, "Child, was not your father called Mustapha the tailor?" "Yes, sir," answered the boy, "but he has been dead a long time."

At these words the African magician threw his arms about Aladdin's neck and kissed him several times, with tears in his eyes, and said, "I am your uncle. Your worthy father was my own brother. I knew you at first sight, you are so like him." Then he gave Aladdin a handful of small money, saying, "Go, my son, to your mother, give my love to her, and tell her that I will visit her to-morrow, that I may see where my good brother lived so long and ended his days."

Aladdin ran to his mother, overjoyed at the money his uncle had given him. "Mother," said he, "have I an uncle?"

"No, child," replied his mother, "you have no uncle by your father's side or mine." "I am just now come," said Aladdin, "from a man who says he is my uncle and my father's brother. He cried and kissed me when I told him my father was dead, and he gave me money, sending his love to you, and promising to come and pay you a visit, that he may see the house my father lived and died in." "Indeed, child," replied the mother, "your father had no brother, nor have you an uncle."

The next day the magician found Aladdin playing in another part of the town, and embracing him as before, put two pieces of gold into his hand, and said to him, "Carry this, child, to your mother; tell her that I will come and see her to-night, and bid her get us something for supper; but first show me the house where you live."

Aladdin showed the African magician the house, and carried the two pieces of gold to his mother, who went out and bought provisions; and considering she wanted various utensils, borrowed them of her neighbors. She spent the whole day in preparing the supper; and at night, when it was ready, said to her son, "Perhaps the stranger knows not how to find our house; go and bring him, if you meet with him."

Aladdin was just ready to go, when the magician knocked at the door, and came in loaded with wine and all sorts of fruits, which he brought for a dessert. After he had given what he brought into Aladdin's hands, he saluted his mother, and desired her to show him the place where his brother Mustapha used to sit on the sofa; and when she had so done, he fell down, and kissed it several times, crying out, with tears in his eyes, "My poor brother! how unhappy am I, not to have come soon enough to give you one last embrace!" Aladdin's mother desired him to sit down in the same place, but he declined. "No," said he, "I shall not do that; but give me leave to sit opposite to it, that although I see not the master of a family so dear to me, I may at least behold the place where he used to sit."

When the magician had made choice of a place and sat down, he began to enter into discourse with Aladdin's mother. "My good sister," said he, "do not be surprised at your never having seen me all the time you have been married to my brother Mustapha of happy memory. I have been forty years absent from this country, which is my native place, as well as my late brother's; and during that time have travelled into the Indies, Persia, Arabia, Syria, and Egypt, and afterward I crossed over into Africa, where I took up my abode. At last, as it is natural for a man, I had a desire to see my native country again, and to embrace my dear brother; and finding I had strength enough to undertake so long a journey, I made the necessary preparations and set out. Nothing ever afflicted me so much as hearing of my brother's death. But God be praised for all things! It is a comfort for me to find, as it were, my brother in a son, who has his most remarkable features."

The African magician perceiving that the widow wept at the remembrance of her husband, changed the conversation, and turning toward her son, asked him, "What business do you follow? Are you of any trade?"

At this question the youth hung down his head, and was not a little abashed when his mother answered, "Aladdin is an idle fellow. His father, when alive, strove all he could to teach him his trade, but could not succeed; and since his death, notwithstanding all I can say to him, he does nothing but idle away his time in the streets, as you saw him, without considering he is no longer a child; and if you do not make him ashamed of it, I despair of his ever coming to any good. For my part, I am resolved, one of these days, to turn him out of doors and let him provide for himself."

After these words, Aladdin's mother burst into tears; and the magician said, "This is not well, nephew; you must think of helping yourself, and getting your livelihood. There are many sorts of trades; perhaps you do not like your father's, and would prefer another; I will endeavor to help you. If you have no mind to learn any handicraft, I will take a shop for you, furnish it with all sorts of fine stuffs and linens; and then with the money you make out of them you can lay in fresh goods, and live in an honorable way. Tell me freely what you think of my proposal; you shall always find me ready to keep my word."

This plan just suited Aladdin, who hated work. He told the magician he had a greater inclination to that business than to any other, and that he should be much obliged to him for his kindness. "Well, then," said the African magician, "I will take you with me to-morrow, clothe you as handsomely as the best merchants in the city, and afterward we will open a shop as I have suggested."

The widow, after his promise of kindness to her son, no longer doubted that the magician was her husband's brother. She thanked him for his good intentions; and after having exhorted Aladdin to render himself worthy of his uncle's favor, served up supper, at which they talked of several indifferent matters; and then the magician took his leave and retired.

He came again the next day, as he had promised, and took Aladdin with him to a merchant, who sold all sorts of clothes for different ages and ranks, ready made, and a variety of fine stuffs, and bade Aladdin choose those he preferred, which he paid for.

When Aladdin found himself so handsomely equipped, he returned his uncle thanks, who thus addressed him: "As you are soon to be a merchant, it is proper you should frequent these shops, and be acquainted with them." He then showed him the largest and finest mosques, carried him to the khans or inns where the merchants and travellers lodged, and afterward to the sultan's palace, where he had free access; and at last brought him to his own khan, where, meeting with some merchants he had become acquainted with since his arrival, he gave them a treat, to bring them and his pretended nephew acquainted.

This entertainment lasted till night, when Aladdin would have taken leave of his uncle to go home; the magician would not let him go by himself, but conducted him to his mother, who, as soon as she saw him so well dressed, was transported with joy, and bestowed a thousand blessings upon the magician.

Early the next morning, the magician called again for Aladdin, and said he would take him to spend that day in the country, and on the next he would purchase the shop. He then led him out at one of the gates of the city, to some magnificent palaces, to each of which belonged beautiful gardens, into which anybody might enter. At every building he came to, he asked Aladdin if he did not think it fine; and the youth was ready to answer when any one presented itself, crying out, "Here is a finer house, uncle, than any we have yet seen." By this artifice, the cunning magician led Aladdin some way into the country; and as he meant to carry him farther, to execute his design, he took an opportunity to sit down in one of the gardens, on the brink of a fountain of clear water, which discharged itself by a lion's mouth of bronze into a basin, pretending to be tired. "Come, nephew," said he, "you must be weary as well as I; let us rest ourselves, and we shall be better able to pursue our walk."

The magician next pulled from his girdle a handkerchief with cakes and fruit, and during this short repast he exhorted his nephew to leave off bad company, and to seek that of wise and prudent men, to improve by their conversation; "for," said he, "you will soon be at man's estate, and you cannot too early begin to imitate their example." When they had eaten as much as they liked, they got up, and pursued their walk through gardens separated from one another only by small ditches, which marked out the limits without interrupting the communication; so great was the confidence the inhabitants reposed in each other. By this means the African magician drew Aladdin insensibly beyond the gardens, and crossed the country, till they nearly reached the mountains.

At last they arrived between two mountains of moderate height and equal size, divided by a narrow valley, which was the place where the magician intended to execute the design that had brought him from Africa to China. 'We will go no farther now," said he to Aladdin; "I will show you here some extraordinary things, which, when you have seen, you will thank me for; but while I strike a light, gather up all the loose dry sticks you can, see, to kindle a fire with."

Aladdin found so many dried sticks, that he soon collected a great heap. The magician presently set them on fire; and when they were in a blaze, threw in some incense, pronouncing several magical words, which Aladdin did not understand.

He had scarcely done so when the earth opened just before the magician, and discovered a stone with a brass ring fixed in it. Aladdin was so frightened that he would have run away, but the magician caught hold of him, and gave him such a box on the ear that he knocked him down. Aladdin got up trembling, and with tears in his eyes, said to the magician, "What have I done, uncle, to be treated in this severe manner?" "I am your uncle," answered the magician; "I supply the place of your father, and you ought to make no reply. But, child," added he, softening, "do not be afraid; for I shall not ask anything of you, but that you obey me punctually, if you would reap the advantages which I intend you. Know, then, that under this stone there is hidden a treasure, destined to be yours, which will make you richer than the greatest monarch in the world. No person but yourself is permitted to lift this stone, or enter the cave ; so you must punctually execute what I may command, for it is a matter of great consequence both to you and me."

Aladdin, amazed at all he saw and heard, forgot what was past, and rising, said, "Well, uncle, what is to be done? Command me : I am ready to obey." "I am overjoyed, child," said the African magician, embracing him. "Take hold of the ring and lift up that stone." "Indeed, uncle," replied Aladdin, "I am not strong enough ; you must help me." "You have no occasion for my assistance," answered the magician ; "if I help you, we shall be able to do nothing. Take hold of the ring, and lift it up; you will find it will come easily." Aladdin did as the magician bade him, raised the stone with ease, and laid it on one side.

When the stone was pulled up, there appeared a staircase about three or four feet deep, leading to a door. "My son," said the African magician, "descend those steps and open that door. It will lead you into a palace, divided into three great halls. In each of these you will see four large brass cisterns placed on each side, full of gold and silver ; but take care you do not meddle with them. Before you enter the first hall, be sure to tuck up your robe, wrap it about you, and then pass through the second into the third without stopping. Above all things, have a care that you do not touch the walls so much as with your clothes ; for if you do, you will die instantly. At the end of the third hall, you will find a door which opens into a garden planted with fine trees loaded with fruit. Walk directly across the garden to a terrace, where you will see a niche before you, and in that niche a lighted lamp. Take the lamp down and put it out. When you have thrown away the wick and poured out the liquor, put it in your waistband and bring it to me. Do not be afraid that the liquor will spoil your clothes, for it is not oil, and the lamp will be dry as soon as it is thrown out."

After these words the magician drew a ring off his finger and put it on one of Aladdin's, saying, "It is a talisman against all evil, so long as you obey me. Go, therefore, boldly, and we shall both be rich all our lives."

Aladdin descended the steps, and, opening the door, found the three halls just as the African magician had described. He went through them with all the precaution the fear of death could inspire, crossed the garden without stopping, took down the lamp from the niche, threw out the wick and the liquor, and, as the magician had desired, put it in his waistband. But as he came down from the terrace, seeing it was perfectly dry, he stopped in the garden to observe the trees, which were loaded with extraordinary fruit of different colors on each tree. Some bore fruit entirely white, and some clear and transparent as crystal; some pale red, and others deeper; some green, blue and purple, and others yellow; in short, there was fruit of all colors. The white were pearls; the clear and transparent, diamonds; the deep red, rubies; the paler, balas rubies [1]; the green, emeralds; the blue, turquoises; the purple, amethysts; and the yellow, sapphires. Aladdin, ignorant of their value, would have preferred figs, or grapes, or pomegranates; but as he had his uncle's permission, he resolved to gather some of every sort. Having filled the two new purses his uncle had bought for him with his clothes, he wrapped some up in the skirts of his vest, and crammed his bosom as full as it could hold.

[1] Balas rubies are rubies of the brightest color.

Aladdin, having thus loaded himself with riches of which he knew not the value, returned through the three halls with the utmost precaution, and soon arrived at the mouth of the cave, where the African magician awaited him with the utmost impatience. As soon as Aladdin saw him, he cried out, " Pray, uncle, lend me your hand, to help me out." " Give me the lamp first," replied the magician; " it will be troublesome to you." " Indeed, uncle," answered Aladdin, " I cannot now, but I will as soon as I am up." The African magician was determined that he would have the lamp before he would help him up ; and Aladdin, who had encumbered himself so much with his fruit that he could not well get at it, refused to give it to him till he was out of the cave. The African magician, provoked at this obstinate refusal, flew into a passion, threw a little of his incense into the fire, and pronounced two magical words, when the stone which had closed the mouth of the staircase moved into its place, with the earth over it in the same manner as it lay at the arrival of the magician and Aladdin.

This action of the magician plainly revealed to Aladdin that he was no uncle of his, but one who designed him evil. The truth was that he had learnt from his magic books the secret and the value of this wonderful lamp, the owner of which would be made richer than any earthly ruler, and hence his journey to China. His art had also told him that he was not permitted to take it himself, but must receive it as a voluntary gift from the hands of another person. Hence he employed young Aladdin, and hoped by a mixture of kindness and authority to make him obedient to his word and will. When he found that his attempt had failed, he set out to return to Africa, but avoided the town, lest any person who had seen him leave in company with Aladdin should make inquiries after the youth. Aladdin being suddenly enveloped in darkness, cried, and called out to his uncle to tell him he was ready to give him the lamp; but in vain, since his cries could not be heard. He descended to the bottom of the steps, with a design to get into the palace, but the door, which was opened before by enchantment, was now shut by the same means. He then redoubled his cries and tears, sat down on the steps without any hopes of ever seeing light again, and in an expectation of passing from the present darkness to a speedy death. In this great emergency he said, "There is no strength or power but in the great and high God;" and in joining his hands to pray he rubbed the ring which the magician had put on his finger. Immediately a genie of frightful aspect appeared, and said, "What wouldst thou have? I am ready to obey thee. I serve him who possesses the ring on thy finger; I, and the other slaves of that ring."

At another time Aladdin would have been frightened at the sight of so extraordinary a figure, but the danger he was in made him answer without hesitation, "Whoever thou art, deliver me from this place." He had no sooner spoken these words, than he found himself on the very spot where the magician had last left him, and no sign of cave or opening, nor disturbance of the earth. Returning God thanks to find himself once more in the world, he made the best of his way home. When he got within his mother's door, the joy at seeing her and his weakness for want of sustenance made him so faint that he remained for a long time as dead. As soon as he recovered, he related to his mother all that had happened to him, and they were both very vehement in their complaints of the cruel magician. Aladdin slept very soundly till late the next morning, when the first thing he said to his mother was, that he wanted something to eat, and wished she would give him his breakfast. "Alas! child," said she, I have not a bit of bread to give you; you ate up all the provisions I had in the house yesterday; but I have a little cotton which I have spun; I will go and sell it, and buy bread and something for our dinner." "Mother," replied Aladdin, "keep your cotton for another time, and give me the lamp I brought home with me yesterday; I will go and sell it, and the money I shall get for it will serve both for breakfast and dinner, and perhaps supper too."

Aladdin's mother took the lamp and said to her son, "Here it is, but it is very dirty; if it were a little cleaner I believe it would bring something more." She took some fine sand and water to clean it; but had no sooner begun to rub it, than in an instant a hideous genie of gigantic size appeared before her, and said to her in a voice of thunder, "What wouldst thou have? I am ready to obey thee as thy slave, and the slave of all those who have that lamp in their hands; I, and the other slaves of the lamp."

Aladdin's mother, terrified at the sight of the genie, fainted; when Aladdin, who had seen such a phantom in the cavern, snatched the lamp out of his mother's hand, and said to the genie boldly, "I am hungry, bring me something to eat." The genie disappeared immediately, and in an instant returned with a large silver tray, holding twelve covered dishes of the same metal, which contained the most delicious viands; six large white bread cakes on two plates, two flagons of wine, and two silver cups. All these he placed upon a carpet and disappeared; this was done before Aladdin's mother recovered from her swoon.

Aladdin had fetched some water, and sprinkled it in her face to recover her. Whether that or the smell of the meat effected her cure, it was not long before she came to herself. "Mother," said Aladdin, "be not afraid; get up and eat; here is what will put you in heart, and at the same time satisfy my extreme hunger."

His mother was much surprised to see the great tray, twelve dishes, six loaves, the two flagons and cups, and to smell the savory odor which exhaled from the dishes. "Child," said she, "to whom are we obliged for this great plenty and liberality? Has the sultan been made acquainted with our poverty, and had compassion on us?" "It is no matter, mother," said Aladdin, "let us sit down and eat; for you have almost as much need of a good breakfast as myself; when we have done, I will tell you." Accordingly, both mother and son sat down and ate with the better relish as the table was so well furnished. But all the time Aladdin's mother could not forbear looking at and admiring the tray and dishes, though she could not judge whether they were silver or some other metal, and the novelty more than the value attracted her attention.

The mother and son sat at breakfast till it was dinner-time, and then they thought it would be best to put the two meals together; yet, after this they found they should have enough left for supper, and two meals for the next day.

When Aladdin's mother had taken away and set by what was left, she went and sat down by her son on the sofa, saying, "I expect now that you should satisfy my impatience, and tell me exactly what passed between the genie and you while I was in a swoon;" which he readily complied with.

She was in as great amazement at what her son told her, as at the appearance of the genie; and said to him, "But, son, what have we to do with genies? I never heard that any of my acquaintance had ever seen one. How came that vile genie to address himself to me, and not to you, to whom he had appeared before in the cave?" "Mother," answered Aladdin, "the genie you saw is not the one who appeared to me. If you remember, he that I first saw called himself the slave of the ring on my finger; and this you saw called himself the slave of the lamp you had in your hand; but I believe you did not hear him, for I think you fainted as soon as he began to speak."

"What!" cried the mother, "was your lamp then the occasion of that cursed genie's addressing himself rather to me than to you? Ah! my son, take it out of my sight, and put it where you please. I had rather you would sell it than run the hazard of being frightened to death again by touching it; and if you would take my advice, you would part also with the ring, and not have anything to do with genies, who, as our prophet has told us, are only devils."

"With your leave, mother," replied Aladdin, "I shall now take care how I sell a lamp which may be so serviceable both to you and me. That false and wicked magician would not have undertaken so long a journey to secure this wonderful lamp if he had not known its value to exceed that of gold and silver. And since we have honestly come by it, let us make a profitable use of it, without making any great show, and exciting the envy and jealousy of our neighbors. However, since the genies frighten you so much, I will take it out of your sight, and put it where I may find it when I want it. The ring I cannot resolve to part with; for without that you had never seen me again; and though I am alive now, perhaps, if it were gone, I might not be so some moments hence; therefore, I hope you will give me leave to keep it, and to wear it always on my finger." Aladdin's mother replied that he might do what he pleased; for her part, she would have nothing to do with genies, and never say anything more about them.

By the next night they had eaten all the provisions the genie had brought; and the next day Aladdin, who could not bear the thoughts of hunger, putting one of the silver dishes under his vest went out early to sell it, and addressing himself to a Jew whom he met in the streets, took him aside, and pulling out the plate, asked him if he would buy it. The cunning Jew took the dish, examined it, and as soon as he found that it was good silver, asked Aladdin at how much he valued it. Aladdin, who had never been used to such traffic, told him he would trust to his judgment and honor. The Jew was somewhat confounded at this plain dealing; and doubting whether Aladdin understood the material or the full value of what he offered to sell, took a piece of gold out of his purse and gave it him, though it was but the sixtieth part of the worth of the plate. Aladdin, taking the money very eagerly, retired with so much haste that the Jew, not content with the exorbitancy of his profit, was vexed he had not penetrated into his ignorance, and was going to run after him, to endeavor to get some change out of the piece of gold; but Aladdin ran so fast, and had got so far, that it would have been impossible to overtake him.

Before Aladdin went home, he called at a baker's, bought some cakes of bread, changed his money, and on his return gave the rest to his mother, who went and purchased provisions enough to last them some time. After this manner they lived, till Aladdin had sold the twelve dishes singly, as necessity pressed, to the Jew, for the same money; who, after the first time, durst not offer him less, for fear of losing so good a bargain. When he had sold the last dish, he had recourse to the tray, which weighed ten times as much as the dishes, and would have carried it to his old purchaser, but that it was too large and cumbersome; therefore he was obliged to bring him home with him to his mother's, where, after the Jew had examined the weight of the tray, he laid down ten pieces of gold, with which Aladdin was very well satisfied.

When all the money was spent, Aladdin had recourse again to the lamp. He took it in his hands, looked for the part where his mother had rubbed it with the sand, and rubbed it also, when the genie immediately appeared and said, "What wouldst thou have? I am ready to obey thee as thy slave, and the slave of all those who have that lamp in their hands; I, and the other slaves of the lamp." "I am hungry," said Aladdin, "bring me something to eat." The genie disappeared, and presently returned with a tray and the same number of covered dishes as before, set them down, and vanished.

As soon as Aladdin found that their provisions were again expended, he took one of the dishes and went to look for his Jew chapman; but as he passed by a goldsmith's shop, the goldsmith perceiving him, called to him, and said, "My lad, I imagine that you have something to sell to the Jew, whom I often see you visit; but perhaps you do not know that he is the greatest rogue even among the Jews. I will give you the full worth of what you have to sell, or I will direct you to other merchants who will not cheat you."

This offer induced Aladdin to pull his plate from under his vest and show it to the goldsmith; who at first sight saw that it was made of the finest silver, and asked him if he had sold such as that to the Jew; when Aladdin told him that he had sold him twelve such, for a piece of gold each. "What a villain!" cried the goldsmith. "But," added he, "my son, what is past cannot be recalled. By showing you the value of this plate, which is of the finest silver we use in our shops, I will let you see how much the Jew has cheated you."

The goldsmith took a pair of scales, weighed the dish, and assured him that his plate would fetch by weight sixty pieces of gold, which he offered to pay down immediately.

Aladdin thanked him for his fair dealing, and never after went to any other person.

Though Aladdin and his mother had an inexhaustible treasure in their lamp, and might have had whatever they wished for, yet they lived with the same frugality as before, and it may easily be supposed that the money for which Aladdin had sold the dishes and tray was sufficient to maintain them some time.

During this interval, Aladdin frequented the shops of the principal merchants, where they sold cloth of gold and silver, linens, silk stuffs, and jewelry, and, oftentimes joining in their conversation, acquired a knowledge of the world, and a desire to improve himself. By his acquaintance among the jewellers, he came to know that the fruits which he had gathered when he took the lamp were, instead of colored glass, stones of inestimable value; but he had the prudence not to mention this to any one, not even to his mother.

One day as Aladdin was walking about the town, he heard an order proclaimed, commanding the people to shut up their shops and houses, and keep within doors while the Princess Buddir al Buddoor, the sultan's daughter, went to the bath and returned.

This proclamation inspired Aladdin with eager desire to see the princess's face, which he determined to gratify by placing himself behind the door of the bath, so that he could not fail to see her face.

Aladdin had not long concealed himself before the princess came. She was attended by a great crowd of ladies, slaves, and mutes, who walked on each side and behind her. When she came within three or four paces of the door of the bath, she took off her veil, and gave Aladdin an opportunity of a full view of her face.

The princess was a noted beauty; her eyes were large, lively, and sparkling; her smile bewitching; her nose faultless; her mouth small; her lips vermilion. It is not therefore surprising that Aladdin, who had never before seen such a blaze of charms, was dazzled and enchanted.

After the princess had passed by and entered the bath, Aladdin quitted his hiding-place and went home. His mother perceived him to be more thoughtful and melancholy than usual; and asked what had happened to make him so, or if he was ill. He then told his mother all his adventure, and concluded by declaring, "I love the princess more than I can express, and am resolved that I will ask her in marriage of the sultan."

Aladdin's mother listened with surprise to what her son told her; but when he talked of asking the princess in marriage, she laughed aloud. "Alas! child," said she, "what are you thinking of? You must be mad to talk thus."

"I assure you, mother," replied Aladdin, "that I am not mad, but in my right senses. I foresaw that you would reproach me with folly and extravagance; but I must tell you once more, that I am resolved to demand the princess of the sultan in marriage; nor do I despair of success. I have the slaves of the lamp and of the ring to help me, and you know how powerful their aid is. And I have another secret to tell you: those pieces of glass, which I got from the trees in the garden of the subterranean palace, are jewels of inestimable value, and fit for the greatest monarchs. All the precious stones the jewellers have in Bagdad are not to be compared to mine for size or beauty; and I am sure that the offer of them will secure the favor of the sultan. You have a large porcelain dish fit to hold them; fetch it, and let us see how they will look when we have arranged them according to their different colors."

Aladdin's mother brought the china dish, when he took the jewels out of the two purses in which he had kept them, and placed them in order, according to his fancy. But the brightness and lustre they emitted in the daytime, and the variety of the colors, so dazzled the eyes both of mother and son that they were astonished beyond measure. Aladdin's mother, emboldened by the sight of these rich jewels, and fearful lest her son should be guilty of greater extravagance, complied with his request, and promised to go early in the next morning to the palace of the sultan. Aladdin rose before daybreak, awakened his mother, pressing her to go to the sultan's palace, and to get admittance, if possible, before the grand vizier, the other viziers, and the great officers of state went in to take their seats in the divan, where the sultan always attended in person.

Aladdin's mother took the china dish, in which they had put the jewels the day before, wrapped it in two fine napkins, and set forward for the sultan's palace. When she came to the gates, the grand vizier, the other viziers, and most distinguished lords of the court were just gone in; but notwithstanding the crowd of people was great, she got into the divan, a spacious hall, the entrance into which was very magnificent. She placed herself just before the sultan, grand vizier, and the great lords, who sat in council, on his right and left hand.

Several causes were called, according to their order, pleaded and adjudged, until the time the divan generally broke up, when the sultan, rising, returned to his apartment, attended by the grand vizier; the other viziers and ministers of state then retired, as also did all those whose business had called them thither.

Aladdin's mother, seeing the sultan retire and all the people depart, judged rightly that he would not sit again that day, and resolved to go home; and on her arrival said, with much simplicity, "Son, I have seen the sultan, and am very well persuaded he has seen me, too, for I placed myself just before him; but he was so much taken up with those who attended on all sides of him that I pitied him, and wondered at his patience. At last I believe he was heartily tired, for he rose up suddenly, and would not hear a great many who were ready prepared to speak to him, but went away, at which I was well pleased, for indeed I began to lose all patience, and was extremely fatigued with staying so long. But there is no harm done; I will go again to-morrow; perhaps the sultan may not be so busy."

The next morning she repaired to the sultan's palace with the present, as early as the day before; but when she came there, she found the gates of the divan shut.[1] She went six times afterward on the days appointed, placed herself always directly before the sultan, but with as little success as the first morning.

On the sixth day, however, after the divan was broken up, when the sultan returned to his own apartment, he said to his grand vizier: "I have for some time observed a certain woman, who attends constantly every day that I give audience, with something wrapped up in a nap-

[1] Sir Paul Ricaut says that the divan is not held on two successive days.

kin; she always stands up from the beginning to the breaking up of the audience, and affects to place herself just before me. If this woman comes to our next audience, do not fail to call her, that I may hear what she has to say." The grand vizier made answer by lowering his hand, and then lifting it up above his head, signifying his willingness to lose it if he failed.

On the next audience day, when Aladdin's mother went to the divan and placed herself in front of the sultan as usual, the grand vizier immediately called the chief of the mace-bearers, and pointing to her bade him bring her before the sultan. The old woman at once followed the mace-bearer, and when she reached the sultan, bowed her head down to the carpet which covered the platform of the throne, and remained in that posture until he bade her rise; which she had no sooner done than he said to her, "Good woman, I have observed you to stand many days from the beginning to the rising of the divan; what business brings you here?"

After these words, Aladdin's mother prostrated herself a second time; and when she arose, said, "Monarch of monarchs, I beg of you to pardon the boldness of my petition, and to assure me of your pardon and forgiveness." "Well," replied the sultan, "I will forgive you, be it what it may, and no hurt shall come to you; speak boldly."

When Aladdin's mother had taken all these precautions, for fear of the sultan's anger, she told him faithfully the errand on which her son had sent her, and the event which led to his making so bold a request in spite of all her remonstrances.

The sultan hearkened to this discourse without showing the least anger; but before he gave her any answer, asked her what she had brought tied up in the napkin. She took the china dish which she had set down at the foot of the throne, untied it, and presented it to the sultan.

The sultan's amazement and surprise were inexpressible, when he saw so many large, beautiful, and valuable jewels collected in the dish. He remained for some time lost in admiration. At last, when he had recovered himself, he received the present from Aladdin's mother's hand, saying, "How rich, how beautiful!" After he had admired and handled all the jewels one after another, he turned to his grand vizier, and showing him the dish, said, "Behold, admire, wonder! and confess that your eyes never beheld jewels so rich and beautiful before." The vizier was charmed. "Well," continued the sultan, "what sayest thou to such a present? Is it not worthy of the princess my daughter? And ought I not to bestow her on one who values her at so great a price?" "I cannot but own," replied the grand vizier, 'that the present is worthy of the princess; but I beg, of your majesty to grant me three months before you come to a final resolution. I hope, before that time, my son, whom you have regarded with your favor, will be able to make a nobler present than this Aladdin, who is an entire stranger to your majesty."

The sultan granted his request, and he said to the old woman, "Good woman, go home, and tell your son that I agree to the proposal you have made me; but I cannot marry the princess my daughter for three months; at the expiration of that time come again."

Aladdin's mother returned home much more gratified than she had expected, and told her son with much joy the condescending answer she had received from the sultan's own mouth; and that she was to come to the divan again that day three months.

Aladdin thought himself the most happy of all men at

hearing this news, and thanked his mother for the pains she had taken in the affair, the good success of which was of so great importance to his peace, that he counted every day, week, and even hour as it passed. When two of the three months were passed, his mother one evening, having no oil in the house, went out to buy some, and found a general rejoicing, — the houses dressed with foliage, silks, and carpeting, and every one striving to show their joy according to their ability. The streets were crowded with officers in habits of ceremony, mounted on horses richly caparisoned, each attended by a great many footmen. Aladdin's mother asked the oil merchant what was the meaning of all this preparation of public festivity. "Whence came you, good woman," said he, "that you don't know that the grand vizier's son is to marry the Princess Buddir al Buddoor, the sultan's daughter, to-night? She will presently return from the bath; and these officers whom you see are to assist at the cavalcade to the palace, where the ceremony is to be solemnized."

Aladdin's mother, on hearing this news, ran home very quickly. "Child," cried she, "you are undone! the sultan's fine promises will come to nought. This night the grand vizier's son is to marry the Princess Buddir al Buddoor."

At this account, Aladdin was thunderstruck, and he bethought himself of the lamp, and of the genie who had promised to obey him; and without indulging in idle words against the sultan, the vizier, or his son, he determined, if possible, to prevent the marriage.

When Aladdin had got into his chamber, he took the lamp, rubbed it in the same place as before, when immediately the genie appeared, and said to him, "What wouldst thou have? I am ready to obey thee as thy slave; I, and the other slaves of the lamp." "Hear me," said Aladdin; "thou hast hitherto obeyed me, but now I am about to impose on thee a harder task. The sultan's daughter, who was promised me as my bride, is this night married to the son of the grand vizier. Bring them both hither to me immediately they retire to their bedchamber."

"Master," replied the genie, "I obey you."

Aladdin supped with his mother as was their wont, and then went to his own apartment, and sat up to await the return of the genie, according to his commands.

In the meantime the festivities in honor of the princess's marriage were conducted in the sultan's palace with great magnificence. The ceremonies were at last brought to a conclusion, and the princess and the son of the vizier retired to the bedchamber prepared for them. No sooner had they entered it, and dismissed their attendants, than the genie, the faithful slave of the lamp, to the great amazement and alarm of the bride and bridegroom, took up the bed, and by an agency invisible to them, transported it in an instant into Aladdin's chamber, where he set it down. "Remove the bridegroom," said Aladdin to the genie, "and keep him a prisoner till to-morrow dawn, and then return with him here." On Aladdin being left alone with the princess, he endeavored to assuage her fears, and explained to her the treachery practised upon him by the sultan her father. He then laid himself down beside her, putting a drawn scimitar between them, to show that he was determined to secure her safety, and to treat her with the utmost possible respect. At break of day, the genie appeared at the appointed hour, bringing back the bridegroom, whom by breathing upon he had left motionless and entranced at the door of Aladdin's chamber during the night, and at Aladdin's command transported the couch with the bride and bridegroom on it, by the same invisible agency, into the palace of the sultan.

At the instant that the genie had set down the couch with the bride and bridegroom in their own chamber, the sultan came to the door to offer his good wishes to his daughter. The grand vizier's son, who was almost perished with cold by standing in his thin under-garment all night, no sooner heard the knocking at the door than he got out of bed, and ran into the robing-chamber, where he had undressed himself the night before.

The sultan having opened the door, went to the bed-side, kissed the princess on the forehead, but was extremely surprised to see her look so melancholy. She only cast at him a sorrowful look, expressive of great affliction. He suspected there was nothing extraordinary in this silence, and thereupon went immediately to the sultaness's apartment, told her in what a state he found the princess, and how she had received him. "Sire," said the sultaness, "I will go and see her; she will not receive me in the same manner."

The princess received her mother with sighs and tears, and signs of deep dejection. At last, upon her pressing on her the duty of telling her all her thoughts, she gave to the sultaness a precise description of all that happened to her during the night; on which the sultaness enjoined on her the necessity of silence and discretion, as no one would give credence to so strange a tale. The grand vizier's son, elated with the honor of being the sultan's son-in-law, kept silence on his part, and the events of the night were not allowed to cast the least gloom on the festivities on the following day, in continued celebration of the royal marriage.

When night came, the bride and bridegroom were again attended to their chamber with the same ceremonies as on the preceding evening. Aladdin, knowing that this would be so, had already given his commands to the genie of the lamp; and no sooner were they alone than their bed was removed in the same mysterious manner as on the preceding evening; and having passed the night in the same unpleasant way, they were in the morning conveyed to the palace of the sultan. Scarcely had they been replaced in their apartment, when the sultan came to make his compliments to his daughter, when the princess could no longer conceal from him the unhappy treatment she had been subject to, and told him all that had happened as she had already related it to her mother. The sultan, on hearing these strange tidings, consulted with the grand vizier; and finding from him that his son had been subjected to even worse treatment by an invisible agency, he determined to declare the marriage to be cancelled, and all the festivities, which were yet to last for several days, to be countermanded and terminated.

This sudden change in the mind of the sultan gave rise to various speculations and reports. Nobody but Aladdin knew the secret, and he kept it with the most scrupulous silence; and neither the sultan nor the grand vizier, who had forgotten Aladdin and his request, had the least thought that he had any hand in the strange adventures that befell the bride and bridegroom.

On the very day that the three months contained in the sultan's promise expired, the mother of Aladdin again went to the palace, and stood in the same place in the divan. The sultan knew her again, and directed his vizier to have her brought before him.

After having prostrated herself, she made answer, in reply to the sultan: "Sire, I come at the end of three months to ask of you the fulfilment of the promise you made to my son." The sultan little thought the request of Aladdin's mother was made to him in earnest, or that he would hear any more of the matter. He therefore took counsel with his vizier, who suggested that the sultan should attach such conditions to the marriage as no one of the humble condition of Aladdin could possibly fulfil. In accordance with this suggestion of the vizier, the sultan replied to the mother of Aladdin: "Good woman, it is true sultans ought to abide by their word, and I am ready to keep mine and make your son happy in marriage with the princess my daughter. But as I cannot marry her without some further proof of your son's being able to support her in royal state, you may tell him I will fulfil my promise as soon as he shall send me forty trays of massy gold, full of the same sort of jewels you have already made me a present of, and carried by the like number of black slaves, who shall be led by as many young and handsome white slaves, all dressed magnificently. On these conditions I am ready to bestow the princess my daughter upon him; therefore, good woman, go and tell him so, and I will wait till you bring me his answer."

Aladdin's mother prostrated herself a second time before the sultan's throne, and retired. On her way home she laughed within herself at her son's foolish imagination. "Where," said she, "can he get so many large gold trays, and such precious stones to fill them? It is altogether out of his power, and I believe he will not be much pleased with my embassy this time." When she came home, full of these thoughts, she told Aladdin all the circumstances of her interview with the sultan, and the conditions on which he consented to the marriage. "The sultan expects your answer immediately," said she; and then added, laughing, "I believe he may wait long enough!"

"Not so long, mother, as you imagine," replied Aladdin. "This demand is a mere trifle, and will prove no bar to my marriage with the princess. I will prepare at once to satisfy his request."

Aladdin retired to his own apartment and summoned the genie of the lamp, and required him to prepare and present the gift immediately, before the sultan closed his morning audience, according to the terms in which it had been prescribed. The genie professed his obedience to the owner of the lamp, and disappeared. Within a very short time, a train of forty black slaves, led by the same number of white slaves, appeared opposite the house in which Aladdin lived. Each black slave carried on his head a basin of massy gold, full of pearls, diamonds, rubies, and emeralds. Aladdin then addressed his mother: "Madam, pray lose no time; before the sultan and the divan rise, I would have you return to the palace with this present as the dowry demanded for the princess, that he may judge by my diligence and exactness of the ardent and sincere desire I have to procure myself the honor of this alliance."

As soon as this magnificent procession, with Aladdin's mother at its head, had begun to march from Aladdin's house, the whole city was filled with the crowds of people desirous of seeing so grand a sight. The graceful bearing, elegant form, and wonderful likeness of each slave, their grave walk at an equal distance from each other, the lustre of their jewelled girdles, and the brilliancy of the aigrettes of precious stones in their turbans, excited the greatest admiration in the spectators. As they had to pass through several streets to the palace, the whole length of the way was lined with files of spectators.   Nothing, indeed, was ever seen so beautiful and brilliant in the sultan's palace, and the richest robes of the emirs of his court were not to be compared to the costly dresses of these slaves, whom they supposed to be kings.

As the sultan, who had been informed of their approach, had given orders for them to be admitted, they met with no obstacle, but went into the divan in regular order, one part turning to the right and the other to the left.   After they were all entered, and had formed a semicircle before the sultan's throne, the black slaves laid the golden trays on the carpet, prostrated themselves, touching the carpet with their foreheads, and at the same time the white slaves did the same.   When they rose, the black slaves uncovered the trays, and then all stood with their arms crossed over their breasts.

In the meantime, Aladdin's mother advanced to the foot of the throne, and having prostrated herself, said to the sultan, "Sire, my son knows this present is much below the notice of Princess Buddir al Buddoor; but hopes, nevertheless, that your majesty will accept of it, and make it agreeable to the princess, and with the greater confidence since he has endeavored to conform to the conditions you were pleased to impose."

The sultan, overpowered at the sight of such more than royal magnificence, replied without hesitation to the words of Aladdin's mother : " Go and tell your son that I wait with open arms to embrace him ; and the more haste he makes to come and receive the princess my daughter from my hands, the greater pleasure he will give me."   As soon as Aladdin's mother had retired, the sultan put an end to the audience ; and rising from his throne ordered that the princess's attendants should come and carry the trays into their mistress's apartment, whither he went himself to examine them with her at his leisure. The fourscore slaves were conducted into the palace; and the sultan, telling the princess of their magnificent apparel, ordered them to be brought before her apartment, that she might see through the lattices he had not exaggerated in his account of them.

In the meantime Aladdin's mother reached home, and showed in her air and countenance the good news she brought to her son. "My son," said she, "you may rejoice you are arrived at the height of your desires. The sultan has declared that you shall marry the Princess Buddir al Buddoor. He waits for you with impatience."

Aladdin, enraptured with this news, made his mother very little reply, but retired to his chamber. There he rubbed his lamp, and the obedient genie appeared. "Genie," said Aladdin, "convey me at once to a bath, and supply me with the richest and most magnificent robe ever worn by a monarch." No sooner were the words out of his mouth than the genie rendered him, as well as himself, invisible, and transported him into a hummum [1] of the finest marble of all sorts of colors; where he was undressed, without seeing by whom, in a magnificent and spacious hall. He was then well rubbed and washed with various scented waters. After he had passed through several degrees of heat, he came out quite a different man from what he was before. His skin was clear as that of a child, his body lightsome and free; and when he returned into the hall, he found, instead of his own poor raiment, a robe, the magnificence of which astonished him. The genie helped him to dress, and when he had done, transported him back to his own chamber, where he asked him if he had any other commands. "Yes," answered Aladdin, "bring me a

---

[1] A Turkish word for a bath.

charger that surpasses in beauty and goodness the best in the sultan's stables; with a saddle, bridle, and other caparisons to correspond with his value. Furnish also twenty slaves, as richly clothed as those who carried the present to the sultan, to walk by my side and follow me, and twenty more to go before me in two ranks. Besides these, bring my mother six women slaves to attend her, as richly dressed at least as any of the Princess Buddir al Buddoor's, each carrying a complete dress fit for any sultaness. I want also ten thousand pieces of gold in ten purses; go, and make haste."

As soon as Aladdin had given these orders, the genie disappeared, but presently returned with the horse, the forty slaves, ten of whom carried each a purse containing ten thousand pieces of gold, and six women slaves, each carrying on her head a different dress for Aladdin's mother, wrapt up in a piece of silver tissue, and presented them all to Aladdin.

He presented the six women slaves to his mother, telling her they were her slaves, and that the dresses they had brought were for her use. Of the ten purses Aladdin took four, which he gave to his mother, telling her, those were to supply her with necessaries; the other six he left in the hands of the slaves who brought them, with an order to throw them by handfuls among the people as they went to the sultan's palace. The six slaves who carried the purses he ordered likewise to march before him, three on the right hand and three on the left.

When Aladdin had thus prepared himself for his first interview with the sultan, he dismissed the genie, and immediately mounting his charger, began his march, and though he never was on horseback before, appeared with a grace the most experienced horseman might envy.

The innumerable concourse of people through whom he passed made the air echo with their acclamations, especially every time the six slaves who carried the purses threw handfuls of gold among the populace.

On Aladdin's arrival at the palace, the sultan was surprised to find him more richly and magnificently robed than he had ever been himself, and was impressed with his good looks and dignity of manner, which were so different from what he expected in the son of one so humble as Aladdin's mother. He embraced him with all the demonstrations of joy, and when he would have fallen at his feet, held him by the hand, and made him sit near his throne. He shortly after led him amidst the sounds of trumpets, hautboys, and all kinds of music, to a magnificent entertainment, at which the sultan and Aladdin ate by themselves, and the great lords of the court, according to their rank and dignity, sat at different tables. After the feast, the sultan sent for the chief cadi, and commanded him to draw up a contract of marriage between the Princess Buddir al Buddoor and Aladdin. When the contract had been drawn, the sultan asked Aladdin if he would stay in the palace and complete the ceremonies of the marriage that day. "Sire," said Aladdin, "though great is my impatience to enter on the honor granted me by your majesty, yet I beg you to permit me first to build a palace worthy to receive the princess your daughter. I pray you to grant me sufficient ground near your palace, and I will have it completed with the utmost expedition." The sultan granted Aladdin his request, and again embraced him. After which he took his leave with as much politeness as if he had been bred up and had always lived at court.

Aladdin returned home in the order he had come, amidst the acclamations of the people, who wished him all happiness and prosperity. As soon as he dismounted, he retired to his own chamber, took the lamp, and summoned the genie as usual, who professed his allegiance. "Genie," said Aladdin, " build me a palace fit to receive the Princess Buddir al Buddoor. Let its materials be made of nothing less than porphyry, jasper, agate, lapis lazuli, and the finest marble. Let its walls be massive gold and silver bricks laid alternately. Let each front contain six windows, and let the lattices of these (except one, which must be left unfinished) be enriched with diamonds, rubies, and emeralds, so that they shall exceed everything of the kind ever seen in the world. Let there be an inner and outer court in front of the palace, and a spacious garden; but above all things, provide a safe treasure-house, and fill it with gold and silver. Let there be also kitchens and storehouses, stables full of the finest horses, with their equerries and grooms and hunting equipage, officers, attendants, and slaves, both men and women, to form a retinue for the princess and myself. Go and execute my wishes."

When Aladdin gave these commands to the genie, the sun was set. The next morning at daybreak the genie presented himself, and, having obtained Aladdin's consent, transported him in a moment to the palace he had made. The genie led him through all the apartments, where he found officers and slaves, habited according to their rank and the services to which they were appointed. The genie then showed him the treasury, which was opened by a treasurer, where Aladdin saw large vases of different sizes, piled up to the top with money, ranged all around the chamber. The genie thence led him to the stables, where were some of the finest horses in the world, and the grooms busy in dressing them; from there they went to the storehouses, which were filled with all things necessary both for food and ornament.

When Aladdin had examined every portion of the palace, and particularly the hall with the four-and-twenty windows, and found it far to exceed his fondest expectations, he said, "Genie, there is one thing wanting, a fine carpet for the princess to walk upon from the sultan's palace to mine. Lay one down immediately." The genie disappeared, and Aladdin saw what he desired executed in an instant. The genie then returned, and carried him to his own home.

When the sultan's porters came to open the gates, they were amazed to find what had been an unoccupied garden filled up with a magnificent palace, and a splendid carpet extending to it all the way from the sultan's palace. They told the strange tidings to the grand vizier, who informed the sultan, who exclaimed, "It must be Aladdin's palace, which I gave him leave to build for my daughter. He has wished to surprise us, and let us see what wonders can be done in only one night."

Aladdin, on his being conveyed by the genie to his own home, requested his mother to go to the Princess Buddir al Buddoor, and tell her that the palace would be ready for her reception in the evening. She went, attended by her women slaves, in the same order as on the preceding day. Shortly after her arrival at the princess's apartment, the sultan himself came in, and was surprised to find her, whom he knew as his suppliant at his divan in such humble guise, to be now more richly and sumptuously attired than his own daughter. This gave him a higher opinion of Aladdin, who took such care of his mother, and made her share his wealth and honors.

Shortly after her departure, Aladdin, mounting his horse, and attended by his retinue of magnificent attendants, left his paternal home forever, and went to the palace in the same pomp as on the day before. Nor did he forget to take with him the Wonderful Lamp, to which he owed all his good fortune, nor to wear the Ring which was given him as a talisman. The sultan entertained Aladdin with the utmost magnificence, and at night, on the conclusion of the marriage ceremonies, the princess took leave of the sultan her father. Bands of music led the procession, followed by a hundred state ushers, and the like number of black mutes, in two files, with their officers at their head. Four hundred of the sultan's young pages carried flambeaux on each side, which, together with the illuminations of the sultan's and Aladdin's palaces, made it as light as day. In this order the princess, conveyed in her litter, and accompanied also by Aladdin's mother, carried in a superb litter and attended by her women slaves, proceeded on the carpet which was spread from the sultan's palace to that of Aladdin. On her arrival Aladdin was ready to receive her at the entrance, and led her into a large hall, illuminated with an infinite number of wax candles, where a noble feast was served up. The dishes were of massy gold, and contained the most delicate viands. The vases, basins, and goblets were gold also, and of exquisite workmanship, and all the other ornaments and embellishments of the hall were answerable to this display. The princess, dazzled to see so much riches collected in one place, said to Aladdin, " I thought, prince, that nothing in the world was so beautiful as the sultan my father's palace, but the sight of this hall alone is sufficient to show I was deceived."

When the supper was ended, there entered a company

of female dancers,[1] who performed, according to the custom of the country, singing at the same time verses in praise of the bride and bridegroom. About midnight Aladdin's mother conducted the bride to the nuptial apartment, and he soon after retired.

The next morning the attendants of Aladdin presented themselves to dress him, and brought him another habit, as rich and magnificent as that worn the day before. He then ordered one of the horses to be got ready, mounted him, and went in the midst of a large troop of slaves to the sultan's palace to entreat him to take a repast in the princess's palace, attended by his grand vizier and all the lords of his court. The sultan consented with pleasure, rose up immediately, and, preceded by the principal officers of his palace and followed by all the great lords of his court, accompanied Aladdin.

The nearer the sultan approached Aladdin's palace, the more he was struck with its beauty; but when he entered it, came into the hall, and saw the windows enriched with diamonds, rubies, emeralds, all large, perfect stones, he was completely surprised, and said to his son-in-law, " This palace is one of the wonders of the world; for where in all the world besides shall we find walls built of massy gold and silver, and diamonds, rubies, and emeralds composing the windows? But what most surprises me is, that a hall of this magnificence should be left with one of its windows incomplete and unfinished." "Sire," answered Aladdin, " the omission was by design, since I wished that you should have the glory of finishing this hall." "I take your intention kindly," said the sultan, " and will give orders about it immediately."

After the sultan had finished this magnificent enter-

---

[1] These were the " Nautch girls," attached to this day to all Eastern courts.

tainment, provided for him and for his court by Aladdin, he was informed that the jewellers and goldsmiths attended; upon which he returned to the hall, and showed them the window which was unfinished. "I sent for you," said he, "to fit up this window in as great perfection as the rest. Examine them well, and make all the dispatch you can."

The jewellers and goldsmiths examined the three-and-twenty windows with great attention, and after they had consulted together, to know what each could furnish, they returned, and presented themselves before the sultan, whose principal jeweller, undertaking to speak for the rest, said, "Sire, we are all willing to exert our utmost care and industry to obey you; but among us all we cannot furnish jewels enough for so great a work." "I have more than are necessary," said the sultan; "come to my palace, and you shall choose what may answer your purpose."

When the sultan returned to his palace, he ordered his jewels to be brought out, and the jewellers took a great quantity, particularly those Aladdin had made him a present of, which they soon used, without making any great advance in their work. They came again several times for more, and in a month's time had not finished half their work. In short, they used all the jewels the sultan had, and borrowed of the vizier, but yet the work was not half done.

Aladdin, who knew that all the sultan's endeavors to make this window like the rest were in vain, sent for the jewellers and goldsmiths, and not only commanded them to desist from their work, but ordered them to undo what they had begun, and to carry all their jewels back to the sultan and to the vizier. They undid in a few hours what they had been six weeks about, and retired, leaving Aladdin alone in the hall. He took the lamp, which he carried about him, rubbed it, and presently the genie appeared. "Genie," said Aladdin, "I ordered thee to leave one of the four-and-twenty windows of this hall imperfect, and thou hast executed my commands punctually; now I would have thee make it like the rest." The genie immediately disappeared. Aladdin went out of the hall, and returning soon after, found the window, as he wished it to be, like the others.

In the meantime, the jewellers and goldsmiths repaired to the palace, and were introduced into the sultan's presence; where the chief jeweller presented the precious stones which he had brought back. The sultan asked them if Aladdin had given them any reason for so doing, and they answering that he had given them none, he ordered a horse to be brought, which he mounted, and rode to his son-in-law's palace, with some few attendants on foot, to inquire why he had ordered the completion of the window to be stopped. Aladdin met him at the gate, and without giving any reply to his inquiries conducted him to the grand saloon, where the sultan, to his great surprise, found the window, which was left imperfect, to correspond exactly with the others. He fancied at first that he was mistaken, and examined the two windows on each side, and afterward all the four-and-twenty; but when he was convinced that the window which several workmen had been so long about was finished in so short a time, he embraced Aladdin and kissed him between his eyes. "My son," said he, "what a man you are to do such surprising things always in the twinkling of an eye! there is not your fellow in the world; the more I know, the more I admire you."

The sultan returned to the palace, and after this went

frequently to the window to contemplate and admire the wonderful palace of his son-in-law.

Aladdin did not confine himself in his palace, but went with much state, sometimes to one mosque, and sometimes to another, to prayers, or to visit the grand vizier or the principal lords of the court. Every time he went out, he caused two slaves, who walked by the side of his horse, to throw handfuls of money among the people as he passed through the streets and squares. This generosity gained him the love and blessings of the people, and it was common for them to swear by his head.[1] Thus Aladdin, while he paid all respect to the sultan, won by his affable behavior and liberality the affections of the people.

Aladdin had conducted himself in this manner several years when the African magician, who had for some years dismissed him from his recollection, determined to inform himself with certainty whether he perished, as he supposed, in the subterranean cave or not. After he had resorted to a long course of magic ceremonies, and had formed a horoscope by which to ascertain Aladdin's fate, what was his surprise to find the appearances to declare that Aladdin, instead of dying in the cave, had made his escape, and was living in royal splendor, by the aid of the genie of the wonderful lamp!

On the very next day, the magician set out and travelled with the utmost haste to the capital of China, where, on his arrival, he took up his lodgings in a khan.

He then quickly learnt about the wealth, charities, happiness, and splendid palace of Prince Aladdin. Directly he saw the wonderful fabric, he knew that none but the genies, the slaves of the lamp, could have per-

[1] There is a trace of this custom in Joseph's swearing to his brethren, "By the life of Pharaoh, ye are spies!"

formed such wonders, and, piqued to the quick at Aladdin's high estate, he returned to the khan.

On his return he had recourse to an operation of geomancy to find out where the lamp was — whether Aladdin carried it about with him, or where he left it. The result of his consultation informed him, to his great joy, that the lamp was in the palace. "Well," said he, rubbing his hands in glee, "I shall have the lamp, and I shall make Aladdin return to his original mean condition."

The next day the magician learnt, from the chief superintendent of the khan where he lodged, that Aladdin had gone on a hunting expedition,[1] which was to last for

---

[1] "But even in the East, where the qualities of the chetah appear to be best appreciated, and his faculties to be turned to most account, it would seem that he is not employed in hunting by all classes of the people indiscriminately ; but, on the contrary, that he is reserved for the especial amusement of the nobles and princes of the land rather than used for purposes of real and general advantage. In this respect, and, indeed, in many others, as will be seen by the following brief account of the mode in which the chase with the hunting leopard is conducted, it bears a close resemblance to the ancient sport of hawking, so prevalent throughout Europe in the days of feudal tyranny, but scarcely practised at the present day, except by the more splendid slaves of Asiatic despotism. The animal or animals — for occasionally several of them are employed at the same time — are carried to the field in low chariots, on which they are kept chained and hooded, in order to deprive them of the power and temptation to leap forth before the appointed time. When they are thus brought within view of a herd of antelopes, which generally consists of five or six females and a male, they are unchained and their hoods removed, their keepers directing their attention to the prey, which, as they do not hunt by smell, it is necessary that they should have constantly in sight. When this is done, the animal does not at once start toward the object of his pursuit, but, seemingly aware that he would have no chance of overtaking an antelope, winds cautiously along the ground, concealing himself as much as possible ; and when he has nearly reached the unsuspecting herd, breaks forth upon them un-

eight days, of which only three had expired. The magician wanted to know no more. He resolved at once on his plans. He went to a coppersmith, and asked for a dozen copper lamps; the master of the shop told him he had not so many by him, but if he would have patience till the next day, he would have them ready. The magician appointed his time, and desired him to take care that they should be handsome and well polished.

The next day the magician called for the twelve lamps, paid the man his full price, put them into a basket hanging on his arm, and went directly to Aladdin's palace. As he approached, he began crying, "Who will exchange old lamps for new ones?" As he went along, a crowd of children collected, who hooted, and thought him, as did all who chanced to be passing by, a madman or a fool, to offer to exchange new lamps for old ones.

The African magician regarded not their scoffs, hootings, or all they could say to him, but still continued crying, "Who will exchange old lamps for new ones?" He repeated this so often, walking backward and forward in front of the palace, that the princess, who was then in the hall with the four-and-twenty windows, hearing a man cry something, and seeing a great mob crowding

awares, and after five or six tremendous bounds, which he executes with almost incredible velocity, darts at once upon his terrified victim, strangles him in an instant, and takes his fill of blood. In the meanwhile the keeper quietly approaches the scene of slaughter, caresses the successful animal, and throws to him pieces of meat to amuse him and keep him quiet, while he blinds him with the hood, and replaces him on the chariot, to which he is again attached by his chain. But if, as is not unfrequently the case, the herd should have taken the alarm, and the chetah should prove unsuccessful, he never attempts to pursue them, but returns to his master with mortified and dejected air, to be again let slip at a fresh quarry whenever a fit opportunity occurs." — Tower Menagerie, pp. 66, 67.

about him, sent one of her women slaves to know what he cried.

The slave returned, laughing so heartily that the princess rebuked her. "Madam," answered the slave, laughing still, "who can forbear laughing, to see an old man with a basket on his arm, full of fine new lamps, asking to exchange them for old ones? The children and mob crowding about him, so that he can hardly stir, make all the noise they can in derision of him."

Another female slave, hearing this, said, "Now you speak of lamps, I know not whether the princess may have observed it, but there is an old one upon a shelf of the Prince Aladdin's robing-room, and whoever owns it will not be sorry to find a new one in its stead. If the princess chooses, she may have the pleasure of trying if this old man is so silly as to give a new lamp for an old one, without taking anything for the exchange."

The princess, who knew not the value of the lamp and the interest that Aladdin had to keep it safe, entered into the pleasantry, and commanded a slave to take it and make the exchange. The slave obeyed, went out of the hall, and no sooner got to the palace gates than he saw the African magician, called to him, and showing him the old lamp, said, "Give me a new lamp for this."

The magician never doubted but this was the lamp he wanted. There could be no other such in this palace, where every utensil was gold or silver. He snatched it eagerly out of the slave's hand, and thrusting it as far as he could into his breast, offered him his basket, and bade him choose which he liked best. The slave picked out one and carried it to the princess; but the exchange was no sooner made than the place rang with the shouts of the children, deriding the magician's folly.

The African magician stayed no longer near the palace,

nor cried any more, " New lamps for old ones," but made the best of his way to his khan. He had accomplished his purpose, and by his silence he got rid of the children and the mob.

As soon as he was out of sight of the two palaces, he hastened down the least-frequented streets ; and having no more occasion for his lamps or basket, set all down in a spot where nobody saw him ; then going down another street or two, he walked till he came to one of the city gates, and pursuing his way through the suburbs, which were very extensive, at length reached a lonely spot, where he stopped till the darkness of the night, as the most suitable time for the design he had in contemplation. When it became quite dark, he pulled the lamp out of his breast and rubbed it. At that summons the genie appeared, and said, " What wouldst thou have? I am ready to obey thee as thy slave, and the slave of all those who have that lamp in their hands ; both I and the other slaves of the lamp." " I command thee," replied the magician, " to transport me immediately, and the palace which thou and the other slaves of the lamp have built in this city, with all the people in it, to Africa." The genie made no reply, but with the assistance of the other genies, the slaves of the lamp, immediately transported him and the palace, entire, to the spot whither he had been desired to convey it.

Early the next morning, when the sultan, according to custom, went to contemplate and admire Aladdin's palace, his amazement was unbounded to find that it could nowhere be seen. He could not comprehend how so large a palace, which he had seen plainly every day for some years, should vanish so soon and not leave the least trace behind. In his perplexity he ordered the grand vizier to be sent for with expedition.

The grand vizier, who, in secret, bore no good will to Aladdin, intimated his suspicion that the palace was built by magic, and that Aladdin had made his hunting excursion an excuse for the removal of his palace with the same suddenness with which it had been erected. He induced the sultan to send a detachment of his guard, and to have Aladdin seized as a prisoner of state. On his son-in-law's being brought before him, he would not hear a word from him, but ordered him to be put to death. The decree caused so much discontent among the people, whose affection Aladdin had secured by his largesses and charities, that the sultan, fearful of an insurrection, was obliged to grant him his life. When Aladdin found himself at liberty, he again addressed the sultan : "Sire, I pray you to let me know the crime by which I have thus lost the favor of thy countenance." "Your crime !" answered the sultan, "wretched man ! do you not know it ? Follow me, and I will show you." The sultan then took Aladdin into the apartment from which he was wont to look at and admire his palace, and said, "You ought to know where your palace stood ; look, mind, and tell me what has become of it." Aladdin did so, and being utterly amazed at the loss of his palace, was speechless. At last recovering himself, he said, "It is true, I do not see the palace. It is vanished ; but I had no concern in its removal. I beg you to give me forty days, and if in that time I cannot restore it, I will offer my head to be disposed of at your pleasure." "I give you the time you ask, but at the end of forty days, forget not to present yourself before me."

Aladdin went out of the sultan's palace in a condition of exceeding humiliation. The lords who had courted him in the days of his splendor, now declined to have any communication with him. For three days he wandered about the city, exciting the wonder and compassion of the multitude by asking everybody he met if he had seen his palace, or could tell him anything of it. On the third day he wandered into the country, and as he was approaching a river, he fell down the bank with so much violence that he rubbed the ring which the magician had given him so hard by holding on the rock to save himself, that immediately the same genie appeared whom he had seen in the cave where the magician had left him. "What wouldst thou have?" said the genie, "I am ready to obey thee as thy slave, and the slave of all those that have that ring on their finger; both I and the other slaves of the ring."

Aladdin, agreeably surprised at an offer of help so little expected, replied, "Genie, show me where the palace I caused to be built now stands, or transport it back where it first stood." "Your command," answered the genie, "is not wholly in my power; I am only the slave of the ring, and not of the lamp." "I command thee, then," replied Aladdin, "by the power of the ring, to transport me to the spot where my palace stands, in what part of the world soever it may be." These words were no sooner out of his mouth, than the genie transported him into Africa, to the midst of a large plain, where his palace stood, at no great distance from a city, and placing him exactly under the window of the princess's apartment, left him.

Now it happened that shortly after Aladdin had been transported by the slave of the ring to the neighborhood of his palace, one of the attendants of the Princess Buddir al Buddoor, looking through the window, perceived him and instantly told her mistress. The princess, who could not believe the joyful tidings, hastened herself to the window, and seeing Aladdin, immediately opened it. The noise of opening the window made Aladdin turn his head that way, and perceiving the princess, he saluted her with an air that expressed his joy. "To lose no time," said she to him, "I have sent to have the private door opened for you; enter and come up."

The private door, which was just under the princess's apartment, was soon opened and Aladdin conducted up into the chamber. It is impossible to express the joy of both at seeing each other after so cruel a separation. After embracing and shedding tears of joy, they sat down, and Aladdin said, "I beg of you, princess, to tell me what is become of an old lamp which stood upon a shelf in my robing-chamber."

"Alas!" answered the princess, "I was afraid our misfortune might be owing to that lamp; and what grieves me most is, that I have been the cause of it. I was foolish enough to exchange the old lamp for a new one, and the next morning I found myself in this unknown country, which I am told is Africa."

"Princess," said Aladdin, interrupting her, "you have explained all by telling me we are in Africa. I desire you only to tell me if you know where the old lamp now is." "The African magician carries it carefully wrapt up in his bosom," said the princess; "and this I can assure you, because he pulled it out before me, and showed it to me in triumph."

"Princess," said Aladdin, "I think I have found the means to deliver you and to regain possession of the lamp, on which all my prosperity depends; to execute this design, it is necessary for me to go to the town. I shall return by noon, and will then tell you what must be done by you to insure success. In the mean time, I shall disguise myself, and I beg that the private door may be opened at the first knock."

When Aladdin was out of the palace, he looked round him on all sides, and perceiving a peasant going into the country, hastened after him; and when he had over-taken him, made a proposal to him to exchange clothes, which the man agreed to. When they had made the exchange, the countryman went about his business, and Aladdin entered the neighboring city. After traversing several streets, he came to that part of the town where the merchants and artisans had their particular streets according to their trades.[1] He went into that of the druggists; and entering one of the largest and best fur-nished shops, asked the druggist if he had a certain powder, which he named.

The druggist, judging Aladdin by his habit to be very poor, told him he had it, but that it was very dear; upon which Aladdin, penetrating his thoughts, pulled out his purse, and showing him some gold, asked for half a dram of the powder; which the druggist weighed and gave him, telling him the price was a piece of gold. Aladdin put the money into his hand, and hastened to the palace, which he entered at once by the private door. When he came into the princess's apartment, he said to her, "Princess, you must take your part in the scheme which I propose for our deliverance. You must overcome your aversion to the magician, and assume a most friendly manner toward him, and ask him to oblige you by partaking of an entertainment in your apartments. Before he leaves, ask him to exchange cups with you, which he, gratified at the honor you do him, will gladly do, when you must give him the cup

[1] This location of persons of one trade in one part of a town was once common in England. Hence the "Draper's Lane" and "Butcher's Row," found in many large towns; and the "Old Jewry," "Lombard Street," and "Cheapside," of London.

containing this powder. On drinking it he will instantly fall asleep, and we will obtain the lamp, whose slaves will do all our bidding, and restore us and the palace to the capital of China."

The princess obeyed to the utmost her husband's instructions. She assumed a look of pleasure on the next visit of the magician, and asked him to an entertainment, an invitation which he most willingly accepted. At the close of the evening, during which the princess had tried all she could to please him, she asked him to exchange cups with her, and giving the signal, had the drugged cup brought to her, which she gave to the magician. He drank it out of compliment to the princess to the very last drop, when he fell backward lifeless on the sofa.

The princess, in anticipation of the success of her scheme, had so placed her women from the great hall to the foot of the staircase, that the word was no sooner given that the African magician was fallen backward, than the door was opened, and Aladdin admitted to the hall. The princess rose from her seat, and ran, overjoyed, to embrace him; but he stopped her, and said, "Princess, retire to your apartment; and let me be left alone, while I endeavor to transport you back to China as speedily as you were brought from thence."

When the princess, her women, and slaves were gone out of the hall, Aladdin shut the door, and going directly to the dead body of the magician, opened his vest, took out the lamp which was carefully wrapped up; and when he rubbed it, the genie immediately appeared. "Genie," said Aladdin, "I command thee to transport this palace instantly to the place whence it was brought hither." The genie bowed his head in token of obedience, and disappeared. Immediately the palace was transported into China, and its removal was only felt by two little shocks, the one when it was lifted up, the other when it was set down, and both in a very short interval of time.

On the morning after the restoration of Aladdin's palace, the sultan was looking out of his window and mourning over the fate of his daughter, when he thought that he saw the vacancy created by the disappearance of the palace to be again filled up.

On looking more attentively, he was convinced beyond the power of doubt that it was his son-in-law's palace. Joy and gladness succeeded to sorrow and grief. He at once ordered a horse to be saddled, which he mounted that instant, thinking he could not make haste enough to the place.

Aladdin rose that morning by daybreak, put on one of the most magnificent habits his wardrobe afforded, and went up into the hall of twenty-four windows, from which he perceived the sultan approaching, and received him at the foot of the great staircase, helping him to dismount.

He led the sultan into the princess's apartment. The happy father embraced his daughter with tears of joy; and the princess, on her side, afforded similar testimonies of her extreme pleasure. After a short interval, devoted to mutual explanations of all that had happened, the sultan restored Aladdin to his favor, and expressed his regret for the apparent harshness with which he had treated him. "My son," said he, "be not displeased at my proceedings against you; they arose from my paternal love, and therefore you ought to forgive the excesses to which it hurried me." "Sire," replied Aladdin, "I have not the least reason to complain of your conduct, since you did nothing but what your duty required.

This infamous magician, the basest of men, was the sole cause of my misfortune."

The African magician, who was thus twice foiled in his endeavor to ruin Aladdin, had a younger brother, who was as skilful a magician as himself, and exceeded him in wickedness and hatred of mankind. By mutual agreement they communicated with each other once a year, however widely separate might be their places of residence from each other. The younger brother not having received as usual his annual communication, prepared to take a horoscope and ascertain his brother's proceedings. He, as well as his brother, always carried a geomantic square instrument about him. He prepared the sand,[1] cast the points, and drew the figures. On examining the planetary crystal, he found that his brother was no longer living, but had been poisoned; and by another observation, that he was in the capital of the kingdom of China; also, that the person who had poisoned him was of mean birth, though married to a princess, a sultan's daughter.

When the magician had informed himself of his brother's fate, he resolved immediately to revenge his death, and at once departed for China; where, after crossing plains, rivers, mountains, deserts, and a long tract of country without delay, he arrived after incredible fatigues. When he came to the capital of China, he took a lodging at a khan. His magic art soon revealed to him that Aladdin was the person who had been the

[1] Reml or Raml signifies "sand prepared," or a preparation of sand on which are marked certain figures serving for a kind of divination, which we call Geomancy, and the Arabs and Turks Kikmut al Reml. These, disposed in a certain number on many unequal lines, are described also with a pen on paper; and the person who practises divination by this art is called Rammal. — D'Herbelot, art. Raml.

cause of the death of his brother. He had heard, too, all the persons of repute in the city talking of a woman called Fatima, who was retired from the world, and of the miracles she wrought. As he fancied that this woman might be serviceable to him in the project he had conceived, he made more minute inquiries, and requested to be informed more particularly who that holy woman was, and what sort of miracles she performed.

"What!" said the person whom he addressed, "have you never seen or heard of her? She is the admiration of the whole town, for her fasting, her austerities, and her exemplary life. Except Mondays and Fridays, she never stirs out of her little cell; and on those days on which she comes into the town she does an infinite deal of good: for there is not a person who is diseased but she puts her hand on him and cures him."

Having ascertained the place where the hermitage of this holy woman was, the magician went at night, and plunging a poniard into her heart, killed this good woman. In the morning he dyed his face of the same hue as hers, and arraying himself in her garb, taking her veil, the large necklace she wore round her waist, and her stick, went straight to the palace of Aladdin.

As soon as the people saw the holy woman, as they imagined him to be, they presently gathered about him in a great crowd. Some begged his blessing, others kissed his hand, and others, more reserved, only the hem of his garment; while others, suffering from disease, stooped for him to lay his hands upon them; which he did, muttering some words in form of prayer, and, in short, counterfeiting so well, that everybody took him for the holy woman. He came at last to the square before Aladdin's palace. The crowd and the noise were so great that the princess, who was in the hall of four-and-twenty windows, heard it, and asked what was the matter. One of her women told her it was a great crowd of people collected about the holy woman to be cured of diseases by the imposition of her hands.

The princess, who had long heard of this holy woman, but had never seen her, was very desirous to have some conversation with her; perceiving which, the chief officer told her it was an easy matter to bring the woman to her, if she desired and commanded it; and the princess expressing her wishes, he immediately sent four slaves for the pretended holy woman.

As soon as the crowd saw the attendants from the palace, they made way; and the magician, perceiving also that they were coming for him, advanced to meet them, overjoyed to find his plot succeed so well. "Holy woman," said one of the slaves, "the princess wants to see you, and has sent us for you." "The princess does me too great an honor," replied the false Fatima; "I am ready to obey her command," and at the same time followed the slaves to the palace.

When the pretended Fatima had made her obeisance, the princess said, "My good mother, I have one thing to request, which you must not refuse me; it is, to stay with me, that you may edify me with your way of living, and that I may learn from your good example." "Princess," said the counterfeit Fatima, "I beg of you not to ask what I cannot consent to without neglecting my prayers and devotion." "That shall be no hindrance to you," answered the princess; "I have a great many apartments unoccupied; you shall choose which you like best, and have as much liberty to perform your devotions as if you were in your own cell."

The magician, who really desired nothing more than to introduce himself into the palace, where it would be a much easier matter for him to execute his designs, did not long excuse himself from accepting the obliging offer which the princess made him. "Princess," said he, "whatever resolution a poor wretched woman as I am may have made to renounce the pomp and grandeur of this world, I dare not presume to oppose the will and commands of so pious and charitable a princess."

Upon this the princess, rising up, said, "Come with me, I will show you what vacant apartments I have, that you may make choice of that you like best." The magician followed the princess, and of all the apartments she showed him, made choice of that which was the worst, saying that was too good for him, and that he only accepted it to please her.

Afterward the princess would have brought him back again into the great hall to make him dine with her; but he, considering that he should then be obliged to show his face, which he had always taken care to conceal with Fatima's veil, and fearing that the princess should find out that he was not Fatima, begged of her earnestly to excuse him, telling her that he never ate anything but bread and dried fruits, and desired to eat that slight repast in his own apartment. The princess granted his request, saying, "You may be as free here, good mother, as if you were in your own cell: I will order you a dinner, but remember I expect you as soon as you have finished your repast."

After the princess had dined, and the false Fatima had been sent for by one of the attendants, he again waited upon her. "My good mother," said the princess, "I am overjoyed to see so holy a woman as yourself, who will confer a blessing upon this palace. But now I am speaking of the palace, pray how do you like it? And before I show it all to you, tell me first what you think of this hall."

Upon this question, the counterfeit Fatima surveyed the hall from one end to the other. When he had examined it well, he said to the princess, "As far as such a solitary being as I am, who am unacquainted with what the world calls beautiful, can judge, this hall is truly admirable; there wants but one thing." "What is that, good mother?" demanded the princess; "tell me, I conjure you. For my part, I always believed, and have heard say, it wanted nothing; but if it does, it shall be supplied."

"Princess," said the false Fatima, with great dissimulation, "forgive me the liberty I have taken; but my opinion is, if it can be of any importance, that if a roc's egg were hung up in the middle of the dome, this hall would have no parallel in the four quarters of the world, and your palace would be the wonder of the universe."

"My good mother," said the princess, "what is a roc, and where may one get an egg?" "Princess," replied the pretended Fatima, "it is a bird of prodigious size, which inhabits the summit of Mount Caucasus; the architect who built your palace can get you one."

After the princess had thanked the false Fatima for what she believed her good advice, she conversed with her upon other matters; but could not forget the roc's egg, which she resolved to request of Aladdin when next he should visit his apartments. He did so in the course of that evening, and shortly after he entered, the princess thus addressed him: "I always believed that our palace was the most superb, magnificent, and complete in the world : but I will tell you now what it wants, and that is a roc's egg hung up in the midst of the dome." "Princess," replied Aladdin, "it is enough that you think it wants such an ornament ; you shall see by the diligence which I use in obtaining it, that there is nothing which I would not do for your sake."

Aladdin left the Princess Buddir al Buddoor that moment, and went up into the hall of four-and-twenty windows, where, pulling out of his bosom the lamp, which after the danger he had been exposed to he always carried about him, he rubbed it ; upon which the genie immediately appeared. "Genie," said Aladdin, " I command thee, in the name of this lamp, bring a roc's egg to be hung up in the middle of the dome of the hall of the palace." Aladdin had no sooner pronounced these words, than the hall shook as if ready to fall ; and the genie said in a loud and terrible voice, "Is it not enough that I and the other slaves of the lamp have done everything for you, but you, by an unheard-of ingratitude, must command me to bring my master, and hang him up in the midst of this dome ? This attempt deserves that you, the princess, and the palace, should be immediately reduced to ashes ; but you are spared because this request does not come from yourself. Its true author is the brother of the African magician, your enemy whom you have destroyed. He is now in your palace, disguised in the habit of the holy woman Fatima, whom he has murdered ; at his suggestion your wife makes this pernicious demand. His design is to kill you, therefore take care of yourself." After these words the genie disappeared.

Aladdin resolved at once what to do. He returned to the princess's apartment, and without mentioning a word of what had happened, sat down, and complained of a great pain which had suddenly seized his head. On hearing this, the princess told him how she had invited the holy Fatima to stay with her, and that she was now in the palace; and at the request of the prince, ordered her to be summoned at once.

When the pretended Fatima came, Aladdin said, "Come hither, good mother; I am glad to see you here at so fortunate a time. I am tormented with a violent pain in my head, and request your assistance, and hope you will not refuse me that cure which you impart to afflicted persons." So saying, he arose, but held down his head. The counterfeit Fatima advanced toward him, with his hand all the time on a dagger concealed in his girdle under his gown; which Aladdin observing, he snatched the weapon from his hand, pierced him to the heart with his own dagger, and then pushed him down on the floor.

"My dear prince, what have you done?" cried the princess, in surprise. "You have killed the holy woman!" "No, my princess," answered Aladdin, with emotion, "I have not killed Fatima, but a villain who would have assassinated me if I had not prevented him. This wicked man," added he, uncovering his face, "is the brother of the magician who attempted our ruin. He has strangled the true Fatima, and disguised himself in her clothes with intent to murder me." Aladdin then informed her how the genie had told him these facts, and how narrowly she and the palace had escaped destruction through his treacherous suggestion which had led to her request.

Thus was Aladdin delivered from the persecution of the two brothers, who were magicians. Within a few years afterward, the sultan died in a good old age, and as he left no male children, the Princess Buddir al Buddoor succeeded him, and she and Aladdin reigned together many years, and left a numerous and illustrious posterity.

NOTE. — In regard to the art with which this story is constructed, let us note one or two points. First, though we get an impression of boundless power, a perfect riot of possibility, on examination we are struck with the restraint shown by Aladdin. He really does but one thing, namely, woo and win the princess, and he makes use of the lamp only to attain and keep her. Before he sees her he seems to think of nothing more than to get food for himself and his mother. After he has obtained the princess and built his palace, we may almost imagine he never so much as calls up his genie till it is absolutely necessary in order to protect himself. Many a man in history has risen by perfectly natural means from a position of humble birth to rule an empire, and, like Aladdin, he has in so doing put off the manners of a peasant and taken on those of a king. Second, we know that every rise to power creates enemies, who are typified in the magician and his brother. Doubtless Aladdin did not appreciate all his good fortune till he had lost it and was threatened with the loss of his head also. Third, all power has its limit, and in this story that truth is illustrated by the discovery that even the genie of the lamp, all powerful as he seems to be, has his master, the mysterious roc. Had Aladdin been foolish enough, in a fit of vanity, to insist on having the roc's egg, we can imagine his complete and final downfall; but as soon as he learns the truth he abandons his request, as any wise person would do. — EDITOR.

III

RIP VAN WINKLE

RIP VAN WINKLE

By WASHINGTON IRVING

INTRODUCTORY

WHAT THE SHORT STORY OWES TO THE ESSAY

THAT intangible something known as "prose style" was a contribution to English literature made by the essayists, whose art rose with Addison, Steele, Swift, Goldsmith, and Johnson, reached its climax in Lamb, with special developments in Macaulay and De Quincey, and has since sunk into desuetude. Most readers know the stories of the " Decameron " and the " Arabian Nights " only in translations, in which any beauties of language in the originals may be supposed to have been partly lost; but it may be observed that in neither do we have so much as a single line of description, either of scenes or of characters. The facts are stated without embellishment, and the characters are known only by their actions. All the wonders of Aladdin's palace do not so much as excite a single metaphor or an ejaculation of surprise. Both stories are the purest possible types of simple narrative.

In " Rip Van Winkle " we have a modern Arabian Nights wonder story, but it is splendidly clothed with all the art of one of the most accomplished of the essayists. It has description, it has humor, it has character-drawing, all lacking in the earlier stories; and at the same time the actual wonders shrink almost to insignificance beside those of Aladdin's lamp. All the essay-writers who were really contributors to the development of the language were also more or less story-writers, — Addison, with his Sir Roger de Coverly; Swift, with his Gulliver; Lamb, with his story of the origin of roast pig. Emerson and Carlyle, who were great philosophers, but in no sense story-writers, made little or no contribution to English style.

As the powers of fiction expanded, it absorbed not only the best in the art of the essayist, but also much that had before belonged to poetry; and as fiction has grown, poetry has dwindled. The beginning of both these tendencies we find in " Rip Van Winkle," not in the construction and development of the story, but in the language with which the plot is clothed. The words flow in melodious rhythm; the whimsicalities and light, pleasing fancies of the essayists appear at every turn, and we also note the touches of poetic beauty in descriptions of the mountains which no mere essayist would venture upon. Here we have in concrete form the progress in story-writing of a hundred years (following the appearance in English of the Arabian Nights), bringing us down to the time of Sir Walter Scott, whose influence on the novel (but not on the short story) was so revolutionary.

RIP VAN WINKLE

A POSTHUMOUS WRITING OF DIEDRICH KNICKERBOCKER

> By Woden, God of Saxons,
> From whence comes Wensday, that is Wodensday,
> Truth is a thing that ever I will keep
> Unto thylke day in which I creep into
> My sepulchre —— CARTWRIGHT

[The following Tale was found among the papers of the late Diedrich Knickerbocker, an old gentleman of New York, who was very curious in the Dutch history of the province, and the manners of the descendants from its primitive settlers. His historical researches, however, did not lie so much among books as among men; for the former are lamentably scanty on his favorite topics; whereas he found the old burghers, and still more their wives, rich in that legendary lore so invaluable to true history. Whenever, therefore, he happened upon a genuine Dutch family, snugly shut up in its low-roofed farmhouse, under a spreading sycamore, he looked upon it as a little clasped volume of black-letter, and studied it with the zeal of a book-worm.

The result of all these researches was a history of the province during the reign of the Dutch governors, which he published some years since. There have been various opinions as to the literary character of his work, and, to tell the truth, it is not a whit better than it should be. Its chief merit is its scrupulous accuracy, which indeed was a little questioned on its first appearance, but has since been completely established; and it is now admitted into all historical collections as a book of unquestionable authority.

The old gentleman died shortly after the publication of his work; and now that he is dead and gone, it cannot do much harm to his memory to say that his time might have been much better employed in weightier labors. He, however, was apt to ride his hobby his own way; and though it did now and then kick up the dust a little in the eyes of his neighbors, and grieve the spirit of some friends, for whom he felt the truest deference and affection, yet his errors and follies are remembered "more in sorrow than in anger," and it begins to be suspected that he never intended to injure or offend. But however his memory may be appreciated by critics, it is still held dear by many folk whose good opinion is well worth having; particularly by certain biscuit-bakers, who have gone so far as to imprint his likeness on their New-Year cakes; and have thus given him a chance for immortality, almost equal to the being stamped on a Waterloo Medal, or a Queen Anne's Farthing.]

WHOEVER has made a voyage up the Hudson must remember the Kaatskill mountains. They are a dismembered branch of the great Appalachian family, and are seen away to the west of the river, swelling up to a noble height, and lording it over the surrounding country. Every change of season, every change of weather, indeed, every hour of the day, produces some change in the magical hues and shapes of these mountains, and they are regarded by all the good wives, far and near, as perfect barometers. When the weather is fair and settled, they are clothed in blue and purple, and print their bold outlines on the clear evening sky; but sometimes, when the rest of the landscape is cloudless, they will gather a hood of gray vapors about their summits, which, in the last rays of the setting sun, will glow and light up like a crown of glory.

At the foot of these fairy mountains, the voyager may have descried the light smoke curling up from a village, whose shingle-roofs gleam among the trees, just where the blue tints of the upland melt away into the fresh green of the nearer landscape. It is a little village, of great antiquity, having been founded by some of the Dutch colonists in the early times of the province, just about the beginning of the government of the good Peter

Stuyvesant (may he rest in peace!), and there were some of the houses of the original settlers standing within a few years, built of small yellow bricks brought from Holland, having latticed windows and gable fronts, surmounted with weathercocks.

In that same village, and in one of these very houses (which, to tell the precise truth, was sadly time-worn and weather-beaten), there lived, many years since, while the country was yet a province of Great Britain, a simple, good-natured fellow, of the name of Rip Van Winkle. He was a descendant of the Van Winkles who figured so gallantly in the chivalrous days of Peter Stuyvesant, and accompanied him to the siege of Fort Christina. He inherited, however, but little of the martial character of his ancestors. I have observed that he was a simple, good-natured man; he was, moreover, a kind neighbor, and an obedient, hen-pecked husband. Indeed, to the latter circumstance might be owing that meekness of spirit which gained him such universal popularity; for those men are most apt to be obsequious and conciliating abroad, who are under the discipline of shrews at home. Their tempers, doubtless, are rendered pliant and malleable in the fiery furnace of domestic tribulation; and a curtain-lecture is worth all the sermons in the world for teaching the virtues of patience and long-suffering. A termagant wife may, therefore, in some respects, be considered a tolerable blessing; and if so, Rip Van Winkle was thrice blessed.

Certain it is, that he was a great favorite among all the good wives of the village, who, as usual with the amiable sex, took his part in all family squabbles; and never failed, whenever they talked those matters over in their evening gossipings, to lay all the blame on Dame Van Winkle. The children of the village, too, would shout with joy whenever he approached. He assisted at their sports, made their playthings, taught them to fly kites and shoot marbles, and told them long stories of ghosts, witches, and Indians. Whenever he went dodging about the village, he was surrounded by a troop of them, hanging on his skirts, clambering on his back, and playing a thousand tricks on him with impunity; and not a dog would bark at him throughout the neighborhood.

The great error in Rip's composition was an insuperable aversion to all kinds of profitable labor. It could not be from the want of assiduity or perseverance; for he would sit on a wet rock, with a rod as long and heavy as a Tartar's lance, and fish all day without a murmur, even though he should not be encouraged by a single nibble. He would carry a fowling-piece on his shoulder for hours together, trudging through woods and swamps, and up hill and down dale, to shoot a few squirrels or wild pigeons. He would never refuse to assist a neighbor even in the roughest toil, and was a foremost man at all country frolics for husking Indian corn, or building stone fences; the women of the village, too, used to employ him to run their errands, and do such little odd jobs as their less obliging husbands would not do for them. In a word, Rip was ready to attend to anybody's business but his own; but as to doing family duty, and keeping his farm in order, he found it impossible.

In fact, he declared it was of no use to work on his farm; it was the most pestilent little piece of ground in the whole country; everything about it went wrong, and would go wrong, in spite of him. His fences were continually falling to pieces; his cow would either go astray, or get among the cabbages; weeds were sure to grow quicker in his fields than anywhere else; the rain always made a point of setting in just as he had some out-door work to do; so that though his patrimonial estate had dwindled away under his management, acre by acre, until there was little more left than a mere patch of Indian corn and potatoes, yet it was the worst conditioned farm in the neighborhood.

His children, too, were as ragged and wild as if they belonged to nobody. His son Rip, an urchin begotten in his own likeness, promised to inherit the habits, with the old clothes, of his father. He was generally seen trooping like a colt at his mother's heels, equipped in a pair of his father's cast-of galligaskins, which he had much ado to hold up with one hand, as a fine lady does her train in bad weather.

Rip Van Winkle, however, was one of those happy mortals, of foolish, well-oiled dispositions, who take the world easy, eat white bread or brown, whichever can be got with least thought or trouble, and would rather starve on a penny than work for a pound. If left to himself, he would have whistled life away in perfect contentment; but his wife kept continually dinning in his ears about his idleness, his carelessness, and the ruin he was bringing on his family. Morning, noon, and night, her tongue was incessantly going, and everything he said or did was sure to produce a torrent of household eloquence. Rip had but one way of replying to all lectures of the kind, and that, by frequent use, had grown into a habit. He shrugged his shoulders, shook his head, cast up his eyes, but said nothing. This, however, always provoked a fresh volley from his wife; so that he was fain to draw off his forces, and take to the outside of the house—the only side which, in truth, belongs to a hen-pecked husband.

Rip's sole domestic adherent was his dog Wolf, who was as much hen-pecked as his master; for Dame Van Winkle regarded them as companions in idleness, and even looked upon Wolf with an evil eye, as the cause of his master's going so often astray. True it is, in all points of spirit befitting an honorable dog, he was as courageous an animal as ever scoured the woods; but what courage can withstand the ever-during and all-besetting terrors of a woman's tongue? The moment Wolf entered the house his crest fell, his tail drooped to the ground, or curled between his legs, he sneaked about with a gallows air, casting many a sidelong glance at Dame Van Winkle, and at the least flourish of a broomstick or ladle he would fly to the door with yelping precipitation.

Times grew worse and worse with Rip Van Winkle as years of matrimony rolled on; a tart temper never mellows with age, and a sharp tongue is the only edged tool that grows keener with constant use. For a long while he used to console himself, when driven from home, by frequenting a kind of perpetual club of the sages, philosophers, and other idle personages of the village, which held its sessions on a bench before a small inn, designated by a rubicund portrait of His Majesty George the Third. Here they used to sit in the shade through a long, lazy summer's day, talking listlessly over village gossip, or telling endless sleepy stories about nothing. But it would have been worth any statesman's money to have heard the profound discussions that sometimes took place, when by chance an old newspaper fell into their hands from some passing traveller. How solemnly they would listen to the contents, as drawled out by Derrick Van Bummel, the schoolmaster, a dapper learned little man, who was not to be daunted by the most gigantic word in the dictionary; and how sagely they would deliberate upon public events some months after they had taken place.

The opinions of this junto were completely controlled by Nicholas Vedder, a patriarch of the village, and landlord of the inn, at the door of which he took his seat from morning till night, just moving sufficiently to avoid the sun and keep in the shade of a large tree; so that the neighbors could tell the hour by his movements as accurately as by a sun-dial. It is true he was rarely heard to speak, but smoked his pipe incessantly. His adherents, however (for every great man has his adherents), perfectly understood him, and knew how to gather his opinions. When anything that was read or related displeased him, he was observed to smoke his pipe vehemently, and to send forth short, frequent, and angry puffs; but when pleased, he would inhale the smoke slowly and tranquilly, and emit it in light and placid clouds; and sometimes, taking the pipe from his mouth, and letting the fragrant vapor curl about his nose, would gravely nod his head in token of perfect approbation.

From even this stronghold the unlucky Rip was at length routed by his termagant wife, who would suddenly break in upon the tranquillity of the assemblage and call the members all to naught; nor was that august personage, Nicholas Vedder himself, sacred from the daring tongue of this terrible virago, who charged him outright with encouraging her husband in habits of idleness.

Poor Rip was at last reduced almost to despair; and his only alternative, to escape from the labor of the farm and clamor of his wife, was to take gun in hand and stroll away into the woods. Here he would sometimes seat himself at the foot of a tree, and share the contents of his wallet with Wolf, with whom he sympathized as a fellow-sufferer in persecution. "Poor Wolf," he would say, "thy mistress leads thee a dog's life of it; but never mind, my lad, whilst I live thou shalt never want a friend to stand by thee!" Wolf would wag his tail, look wistfully in his master's face; and if dogs can feel pity, I verily believe he reciprocated the sentiment with all his heart.

In a long ramble of the kind on a fine autumnal day, Rip had unconsciously scrambled to one of the highest parts of the Kaatskill mountains. He was after his favorite sport of squirrel-shooting, and the still solitudes had echoed and re-echoed with the reports of his gun. Panting and fatigued, he threw himself, late in the afternoon, on a green knoll, covered with mountain herbage, that crowned the brow of a precipice. From an opening between the trees he could overlook all the lower country for many a mile of rich woodland. He saw at a distance the lordly Hudson, far, far below him, moving on its silent but majestic course, with the reflection of a purple cloud, or the sail of a lagging bark, here and there sleeping on its glassy bosom, and at last losing itself in the blue highlands.

On the other side he looked down into a deep mountain glen, wild, lonely, and shagged, the bottom filled with fragments from the impending cliffs, and scarcely lighted by the reflected rays of the setting sun. For some time Rip lay musing on this scene; evening was gradually advancing; the mountains began to throw their long blue shadows over the valleys; he saw that it would be dark long before he could reach the village, and he heaved a heavy sigh when he thought of encountering the terrors of Dame Van Winkle.

As he was about to descend, he heard a voice from a distance, hallooing, "Rip Van Winkle! Rip Van Winkle!" He looked round, but could see nothing but a crow winging its solitary flight across the mountain. He thought his fancy must have deceived him, and turned again to

descend, when he heard the same cry ring through the
still evening air: "Rip Van Winkle! Rip Van Winkle!"
— at the same time Wolf bristled up his back, and giving
a low growl, skulked to his master's side, looking fearfully
down into the glen. Rip now felt a vague apprehension
stealing over him; he looked anxiously in the same direction, and perceived a strange figure slowly toiling up
the rocks, and bending under the weight of something
he carried on his back. He was surprised to see any
human being in this lonely and unfrequented place; but
supposing it to be some one of the neighborhood in
need of his assistance, he hastened down to yield it.

On nearer approach he was still more surprised at the
singularity of the stranger's appearance. He was a
short, square-built old fellow, with thick bushy hair, and
a grizzled beard. His dress was of the antique Dutch
fashion, — a cloth jerkin strapped round the waist —
several pairs of breeches, the outer one of ample volume,
decorated with rows of buttons down the sides, and
bunches at the knees. He bore on his shoulder a stout
keg, that seemed full of liquor, and made signs for Rip
to approach and assist him with the load. Though
rather shy and distrustful of this new acquaintance, Rip
complied with his usual alacrity; and mutually relieving
one another, they clambered up a narrow gully, apparently the dry bed of a mountain torrent. As they ascended, Rip every now and then heard long, rolling
peals, like distant thunder, that seemed to issue out of
a deep ravine, or rather cleft, between lofty rocks, toward
which their rugged path conducted. He paused for an
instant, but supposing it to be the muttering of one of
those transient thunder-showers which often take place
in mountain heights, he proceeded. Passing through the
ravine, they came to a hollow, like a small amphitheatre,

surrounded by perpendicular precipices, over the brinks of which impending trees shot their branches, so that you only caught glimpses of the azure sky and the bright evening cloud. During the whole time Rip and his companion had labored on in silence; for though the former marvelled greatly what could be the object of carrying a keg of liquor up this wild mountain, yet there was something strange and incomprehensible about the unknown, that inspired awe and checked familiarity.

On entering the amphitheatre, new objects of wonder presented themselves. On a level spot in the centre was a company of odd-looking personages playing at ninepins. They were dressed in a quaint, outlandish fashion; some wore short doublets, others jerkins, with long knives in their belts, and most of them had enormous breeches of similar style with that of the guide's. Their visages, too, were peculiar: one had a large beard, broad face, and small piggish eyes; the face of another seemed to consist entirely of nose, and was surmounted by a white sugarloaf hat, set off with a little red cock's tail. They all had beards, of various shapes and colors. There was one who seemed to be the commander. He was a stout old gentleman, with a weather-beaten countenance; he wore a laced doublet, broad belt and hanger, high-crowned hat and feather, red stockings, and high-heeled shoes, with roses in them. The whole group reminded Rip of the figures in an old Flemish painting, in the parlor of Dominie Van Shaick, the village parson, and which had been brought over from Holland at the time of the settlement.

What seemed particularly odd to Rip was, that, though these folks were evidently amusing themselves, yet they maintained the gravest faces, the most mysterious silence, and were, withal, the most melancholy party of pleasure he had ever witnessed. Nothing interrupted the stillness of the scene but the noise of the balls, which, whenever they were rolled, echoed along the mountains like rumbling peals of thunder.

As Rip and his companion approached them, they suddenly desisted from their play, and stared at him with such fixed, statue-like gaze, and such strange, uncouth, lack-lustre countenances, that his heart turned within him, and his knees smote together. His companion now emptied the contents of the keg into large flagons, and made signs to him to wait upon the company. He obeyed with fear and trembling; they quaffed the liquor in profound silence, and then returned to their game.

By degrees Rip's awe and apprehension subsided. He even ventured, when no eye was fixed upon him, to taste the beverage, which he found had much of the flavor of excellent Hollands. He was naturally a thirsty soul, and was soon tempted to repeat the draught. One taste provoked another; and he reiterated his visits to the flagon so often that at length his senses were overpowered, his eyes swam in his head, his head gradually declined, and he fell into a deep sleep.

On waking, he found himself on the green knoll whence he had first seen the old man of the glen. He rubbed his eyes — it was a bright sunny morning. The birds were hopping and twittering among the bushes, and the eagle was wheeling aloft, and breasting the pure mountain breeze. "Surely," thought Rip, "I have not slept here all night." He recalled the occurrences before he fell asleep. The strange man with a keg of liquor — the mountain ravine — the wild retreat among the rocks — the woe-begone party at ninepins — the flagon — "Oh! that flagon! that wicked flagon!" thought Rip, — "what excuse shall I make to Dame Van Winkle?"

He looked round for his gun, but in place of the clean, well-oiled fowling-piece, he found an old firelock lying by him, the barrel incrusted with rust, the lock falling off, and the stock worm-eaten. He now suspected that the grave roisters of the mountain had put a trick upon him, and, having dosed him with liquor, had robbed him of his gun. Wolf, too, had disappeared, but he might have strayed away after a squirrel or partridge. He whistled after him, and shouted his name, but all in vain; the echoes repeated his whistle and shout, but no dog was to be seen.

He determined to revisit the scene of the last evening's gambol, and if he met with any of the party, to demand his dog and gun. As he rose to walk, he found himself stiff in the joints, and wanting in his usual activity. "These mountain beds do not agree with me," thought Rip, "and if this frolic should lay me up with a fit of the rheumatism, I shall have a blessed time with Dame Van Winkle." With some difficulty he got down into the glen: he found the gully up which he and his companion had ascended the preceding evening; but to his astonishment a mountain stream was now foaming down it, leaping from rock to rock, and filling the glen with babbling murmurs. He, however, made shift to scramble up its sides, working his toilsome way through thickets of birch, sassafras, and witch-hazel, and sometimes tripped up or entangled by the wild grape-vines that twisted their coils or tendrils from tree to tree, and spread a kind of network in his path.

At length he reached to where the ravine had opened through the cliffs to the amphitheatre; but no traces of such opening remained. The rocks presented a high, impenetrable wall, over which the torrent came tumbling in a sheet of feathery foam, and fell into a broad, deep basin, black from the shadows of the surrounding forest. Here, then, poor Rip was brought to a stand. He again called and whistled after his dog: he was only answered by the cawing of a flock of idle crows, sporting high in air about a dry tree that overhung a sunny precipice; and who, secure in their elevation, seemed to look down and scoff at the poor man's perplexities. What was to be done? the morning was passing away, and Rip felt famished for want of his breakfast. He grieved to give up his dog and gun; he dreaded to meet his wife; but it would not do to starve among the mountains. He shook his head, shouldered the rusty firelock, and, with a heart full of trouble and anxiety, turned his steps homeward.

As he approached the village he met a number of people, but none whom he knew, which somewhat surprised him, for he had thought himself acquainted with every one in the country round. Their dress, too, was of a different fashion from that to which he was accustomed. They all stared at him with equal marks of surprise, and whenever they cast their eyes upon him, invariably stroked their chins. The constant recurrence of this gesture induced Rip, involuntarily, to do the same, when, to his astonishment, he found his beard had grown a foot long!

He had now entered the skirts of the village. A troop of strange children ran at his heels, hooting after him, and pointing at his gray beard. The dogs, too, not one of which he recognized for an old acquaintance, barked at him as he passed. The very village was altered; it was larger and more populous. There were rows of houses which he had never seen before, and those which had been his familiar haunts had disappeared. Strange names were over the doors — strange faces at the windows — everything was strange. His mind now misgave him; he began to doubt whether both he and the world around him were not bewitched. Surely this was his native village, which he had left but the day before. There stood the Kaatskill mountains — there ran the silver Hudson at a distance — there was every hill and dale precisely as it had always been. Rip was sorely perplexed. "That flagon last night," thought he, "has addled my poor head sadly!"

It was with some difficulty that he found the way to his own house, which he approached with silent awe, expecting every moment to hear the shrill voice of Dame Van Winkle. He found the house gone to decay — the roof fallen in, the windows shattered, and the doors off the hinges. A half-starved dog that looked like Wolf was skulking about it. Rip called him by name, but the cur snarled, showed his teeth, and passed on. This was an unkind cut indeed. "My very dog," sighed poor Rip, "has forgotten me!"

He entered the house, which, to tell the truth, Dame Van Winkle had always kept in neat order. It was empty, forlorn, and apparently abandoned. This desolateness overcame all his connubial fears — he called loudly for his wife and children — the lonely chambers rang for a moment with his voice, and then all again was silence.

He now hurried forth, and hastened to his old resort, the village inn — but it too was gone. A large rickety wooden building stood in its place with great gaping windows, some of them broken and mended with old hats and petticoats, and over the door was painted, "The Union Hotel, by Jonathan Doolittle." Instead of the great tree that used to shelter the quiet little Dutch inn of yore, there now was reared a tall naked pole, with something on the top that looked like a red nightcap, and from it was fluttering a flag, on which was a singular assemblage of stars and stripes; — all this was strange and incomprehensible. He recognized on the sign, however, the ruby face of King George, under which he had smoked so many a peaceful pipe; but even this was singularly metamorphosed. The red coat was changed for one of blue and buff, a sword was held in the hand instead of a sceptre, the head was decorated with a cocked hat, and underneath was painted in large characters, GENERAL WASHINGTON.

There was, as usual, a crowd of folk about the door, but none that Rip recollected. The very character of the people seemed changed. There was a busy, bustling, disputatious tone about it, instead of the accustomed phlegm and drowsy tranquillity. He looked in vain for the sage Nicholas Vedder, with his broad face, double chin, and fair long pipe, uttering clouds of tobacco smoke instead of idle speeches; or Van Bummel, the schoolmaster, doling forth the contents of an ancient newspaper. In place of these, a lean, bilious-looking fellow, with his pockets full of hand-bills, was haranguing vehemently about rights of citizens — elections — members of congress — liberty — Bunker's Hill — heroes of seventy-six — and other words, which were a perfect Babylonish jargon to the bewildered Van Winkle.

The appearance of Rip, with his long, grizzled beard, his rusty fowling-piece, his uncouth dress, and an army of women and children at his heels, soon attracted the attention of the tavern-politicians. They crowded round him, eying him from head to foot with great curiosity. The orator bustled up to him, and, drawing him partly aside, inquired "on which side he voted?" Rip stared in vacant stupidity. Another short but busy little fellow pulled him by the arm, and, rising on tiptoe, inquired in

his ear, " Whether he was Federal or Democrat ? "   Rip
was equally at a loss to comprehend the question ; when
a knowing, self-important old gentleman, in a sharp
cocked hat, made his way through the crowd, putting
them to the right and left with his elbows as he passed,
and planting himself before Van Winkle, with one arm
akimbo, the other resting on his cane, his keen eyes
and sharp hat penetrating, as it were, into his very
soul, demanded in an austere tone, " What brought
him to the election with a gun on his shoulder, and
a mob at his heels ; and whether he meant to breed
a riot in the village ? " — " Alas ! gentlemen," cried Rip,
somewhat dismayed, " I am a poor, quiet man, a native
of the place, and a loyal subject of the King, God
bless him ! "

Here a general shout burst from the by-standers —
" A tory ! a tory ! a spy ! a refugee ! hustle him ! away
with him ! "   It was with great difficulty that the self-
important man in the cocked hat restored order ; and,
having assumed a tenfold austerity of brow, demanded
again of the unknown culprit, what he came there for,
and whom he was seeking ? The poor man humbly
assured him that he meant no harm, but merely came
there in search of some of his neighbors, who used to
keep about the tavern.

" Well — who are they ? — name them."

Rip bethought himself a moment, and inquired,
" Where 's Nicholas Vedder ? "

There was a silence for a little while, when an old
man replied, in a thin piping voice, " Nicholas Vedder !
why, he is dead and gone these eighteen years ! There
was a wooden tombstone in the churchyard that used
to tell all about him, but that 's rotten and gone too."

" Where 's Brom Dutcher ? "

"Oh, he went off to the army in the beginning of the war; some say he was killed at the storming of Stony Point — others say he was drowned in a squall at the foot of Antony's Nose. I don't know — he never came back again."

"Where's Van Bummel, the schoolmaster?"

"He went off to the wars too, was a great militia general, and is now in Congress."

Rip's heart died away at hearing of these sad changes in his home and friends, and finding himself thus alone in the world. Every answer puzzled him too, by treating of such enormous lapses of time, and of matters which he could not understand: war — congress — Stony Point; — he had no courage to ask after any more friends, but cried out in despair, "Does nobody here know Rip Van Winkle?"

"Oh, Rip Van Winkle!" exclaimed two or three; "oh, to be sure! that's Rip Van Winkle yonder, leaning against the tree."

Rip looked, and beheld a precise counterpart of himself as he went up the mountain; apparently as lazy, and certainly as ragged. The poor fellow was now completely confounded. He doubted his own identity, and whether he was himself or another man. In the midst of his bewilderment, the man in the cocked hat demanded who he was, and what was his name.

"God knows," exclaimed he, at his wit's end; "I'm not myself — I'm somebody else — that's me yonder — no — that's somebody else got into my shoes — I was myself last night, but I fell asleep on the mountain, and they've changed my gun, and everything's changed, and I'm changed, and I can't tell what's my name, or who I am!"

The by-standers began now to look at each other, nod,

wink significantly, and tap their fingers against their foreheads. There was a whisper, also, about securing the gun, and keeping the old fellow from doing mischief, at the very suggestion of which the self-important man in the cocked hat retired with some precipitation. At this critical moment a fresh, comely woman pressed through the throng to get a peep at the gray-bearded man. She had a chubby child in her arms, which, frightened at his looks, began to cry. "Hush, Rip," cried she, "hush, you little fool; the old man won't hurt you." The name of the child, the air of the mother, the tone of her voice, all awakened a train of recollections in his mind. "What is your name, my good woman?" asked he.

"Judith Gardenier."

"And your father's name?"

"Ah, poor man, Rip Van Winkle was his name, but it's twenty years since he went away from home with his gun, and never has been heard of since,— his dog came home without him; but whether he shot himself, or was carried away by the Indians, nobody can tell. I was then but a little girl."

Rip had but one question more to ask; but he put it with a faltering voice:

"Where's your mother?"

"Oh, she too had died but a short time since; she broke a blood-vessel in a fit of passion at a New England peddler."

There was a drop of comfort, at least, in this intelligence. The honest man could contain himself no longer. He caught his daughter and her child in his arms. "I am your father!" cried he — "Young Rip Van Winkle once — old Rip Van Winkle now! Does nobody know poor Rip Van Winkle?"

All stood amazed, until an old woman, tottering out from among the crowd, put her hand to her brow, and peering under it in his face for a moment, exclaimed, "Sure enough! it is Rip Van Winkle — it is himself! Welcome home again, old neighbor! Why, where have you been these twenty long years?"

Rip's story was soon told, for the whole twenty years had been to him but as one night. The neighbors stared when they heard it; some were seen to wink at each other, and put their tongues in their cheeks: and the self-important man in the cocked hat, who, when the alarm was over, had returned to the field, screwed down the corners of his mouth, and shook his head — upon which there was a general shaking of the head throughout the assemblage.

It was determined, however, to take the opinion of old Peter Vanderdonk, who was seen slowly advancing up the road. He was a descendant of the historian of that name, who wrote one of the earliest accounts of the province. Peter was the most ancient inhabitant of the village, and well versed in all the wonderful events and traditions of the neighborhood. He recollected Rip at once, and corroborated his story in the most satisfactory manner. He assured the company that it was a fact, handed down from his ancestor the historian, that the Kaatskill mountains had always been haunted by strange beings; that it was affirmed that the great Hendrick Hudson, the first discoverer of the river and country, kept a kind of vigil there every twenty years, with his crew of the Half-moon, being permitted in this way to revisit the scenes of his enterprise, and keep a guardian eye upon the river and the great city called by his name; that his father had once seen them in their old Dutch dresses playing at ninepins in a hollow of the mountain;

and that he himself had heard, one summer afternoon, the sound of their balls, like distant peals of thunder.

To make a long story short, the company broke up and returned to the more important concerns of the election. Rip's daughter took him home to live with her; she had a snug, well-furnished house, and a stout, cheery farmer for a husband, whom Rip recollected for one of the urchins that used to climb upon his back. As to Rip's son and heir, who was the ditto of himself, seen leaning against the tree, he was employed to work on the farm; but evinced an hereditary disposition to attend to anything else but his business.

Rip now resumed his old walks and habits; he soon found many of his former cronies, though all rather the worse for the wear and tear of time; and preferred making friends among the rising generation, with whom he soon grew into great favor.

Having nothing to do at home, and being arrived at that happy age when a man can be idle with impunity, he took his place once more on the bench at the inn-door, and was reverenced as one of the patriarchs of the village, and a chronicle of the old times "before the war." It was some time before he could get into the regular track of gossip, or could be made to comprehend the strange events that had taken place during his torpor. How that there had been a revolutionary war, — that the country had thrown off the yoke of old England — and that, instead of being a subject of his Majesty George the Third, he was now a free citizen of the United States. Rip, in fact, was no politician; the changes of states and empires made but little impression on him; but there was one species of despotism under which he had long groaned, and that was — petticoat government. Happily that was at an end; he had got his neck out of the yoke of matrimony, and could go in and out whenever he pleased, without dreading the tyranny of Dame Van Winkle. Whenever her name was mentioned, however, he shook his head, shrugged his shoulders, and cast up his eyes; which might pass either for an expression of resignation to his fate, or joy at his deliverance.

He used to tell his story to every stranger that arrived at Mr. Doolittle's hotel. He was observed, at first, to vary on some points every time he told it, which was, doubtless, owing to his having so recently awaked. It at last settled down precisely to the tale I have related, and not a man, woman, or child in the neighborhood but knew it by heart. Some always pretended to doubt the reality of it, and insisted that Rip had been out of his head, and that this was one point on which he always remained flighty. The old Dutch inhabitants, however, almost universally gave it full credit. Even to this day they never hear a thunder-storm of a summer afternoon about the Kaatskill, but they say Hendrick Hudson and his crew are at their game of ninepins; and it is a common wish of all hen-pecked husbands in the neighborhood, when life hangs heavy on their hands, that they might have a quieting draught out of Rip Van Winkle's flagon.

NOTE. — The foregoing Tale, one would suspect, had been suggested to Mr. Knickerbocker by a little German superstition about the Emperor Frederick *der Rothbart*, and the Kypphäuser mountain: the subjoined note, however, which he had appended to the tale, shows that it is an absolute fact, narrated with his usual fidelity.

" The story of Rip Van Winkle may seem incredible to many, but nevertheless I give it my full belief, for I know the vicinity of our old Dutch settlements to have been very subject to marvellous events and appearances. Indeed, I have heard many stranger stories than this, in the villages along the Hudson; all of which were too well authenticated to admit of a doubt. I have even talked with Rip Van Winkle myself, who, when last I saw him, was a very venerable old man, and so perfectly rational and consistent on every other point, that I think no conscientious person could refuse to take this into the bargain; nay, I have seen a certificate on the subject taken before a country justice and signed with a cross, in the justice's own handwriting. The story, therefore, is beyond the possibility of doubt.

"D. K."

POSTSCRIPT. — The following are travelling notes from a memorandum-book of Mr. Knickerbocker.

The Kaatsberg, or Catskill Mountains, have always been a region full of fable. The Indians considered them the abode of spirits, who influenced the weather, spreading sunshine or clouds over the landscape, and sending good or bad hunting-seasons. They were ruled by an old squaw spirit, said to be their mother. She dwelt on the highest peak of the Catskills, and had charge of the doors of day and night to open and shut them at the proper hour. She hung up the new moons in the skies, and cut up the old ones into stars. In times of drought, if properly propitiated, she would spin light summer clouds out of cobwebs and morning dew, and send them off from the crest of the mountain, flake after flake, like flakes of carded cotton, to float in the air; until, dissolved by the heat of the sun, they would fall in gentle showers, causing the grass to spring, the fruits to ripen, and the corn to grow an inch an hour. If displeased, however, she would brew up clouds black as ink, sitting in the midst of them like a bottle-bellied spider in the midst of its web; and when these clouds broke, woe betide the valleys!

In old times, say the Indian traditions, there was a kind of Manitou or Spirit, who kept about the wildest recesses of the Catskill Mountains, and took a mischievous pleasure in wreaking all kinds of evils and vexations upon the red men. Sometimes he would assume the form of a bear, a panther, or a deer, lead the bewildered hunter a weary chase through tangled forests and among ragged rocks; and then spring off with a loud ho! ho! leaving him aghast on the brink of a beetling precipice or raging torrent.

The favorite abode of this Manitou is still shown. It is a great rock or cliff on the loneliest part of the mountains, and, from the flowering vines which clamber about it, and the wild flowers which abound in its neighborhood, is known by the name of the Garden Rock. Near the foot of it is a small lake, the haunt of the solitary bittern, with water-snakes basking in the sun on the leaves of the pond-lilies which lie on the surface. This place was held in great awe by the Indians, insomuch that the boldest hunter would not pursue his game within its precincts. Once upon a time, however, a hunter who had lost his way, penetrated to the Garden Rock, where he beheld a number of gourds placed in the crotches of trees. One of these he seized and made off with it, but in the hurry of his retreat he let it fall among the rocks, when a great stream gushed forth, which washed him away and swept him down precipices, where he was dashed to pieces, and the stream made its way to the Hudson, and continues to flow to the present day; being the identical stream known by the name of the Kaaters-kill.

9

IV

A PASSION IN THE DESERT

more than a series of short stories, and often a novel is a single short story developed and elaborated in detail. A well-known English critic is of the opinion that Thackeray was a short story writer gone wrong, and that "Vanity Fair" is in reality a short story which should have ended with the first of the three original volumes. The novels of Dickens make no pretence at cohesion, and short stories are frequently introduced. In these writers, description reaches a tropical luxuriance equalled nowhere else, and of course the minute study of character is the element of chief interest and value.

"A Passion in the Desert" is remarkable for two things. First, we find "atmosphere" in such perfection that we fairly feel oppressed by the hot, sultry air of the desert. And again, although there is no woman in the story, nevertheless we find an innocent and purified study of sexual passion and feminine caprice and character (by reflection in the tiger) which leaves the oftentimes bald vulgarity of the "Decameron" far behind in its essential interest. Though Balzac, in common with all French writers, goes much nearer the unveiled freedom of Boccaccio in others of his stories, in "A Passion in the Desert" we have what is to the English mind the ideal presentation of extreme passion. The passion of love between man and woman exceeds all others in its interest to readers of fiction, and is unsurpassed as a moving force in the imaginary affairs of men; but it must appear in its refined and higher attributes, as the fire which lights up all the nobler human faculties.

A PASSION IN THE DESERT

[Translated by the Editor]

"IT makes me shudder," she cried as she emerged from Monsieur Martin's menagerie. She had just been looking at that daring showman " working " with his hyena — to speak in the style of the handbills.

" By what means," she went on, "can he have tamed these animals to the point of being quite certain of their affection for — "

"What seems to you a problem," said I, interrupting her, " is nevertheless perfectly natural."

" Indeed ! " she cried, an incredulous smile playing over her lips.

"Do you think, then, these wild beasts are entirely devoid of passion?" I demanded. " Let me assure you, we can communicate to them all the vices of modern civilization."

She looked at me in astonishment.

" I admit," I went on, "that the first time I saw Monsieur Martin, I, like you, was betrayed into an exclamation of surpise. I found myself beside an old soldier who had lost a leg. He had entered with me, and his features had caught my eye. He had an intrepid countenance, seamed with the lines of war and written all over with the battles of Napoleon. Besides, he had an air of frankness and good humor which impressed me favorably. You could see by his looks that he was one of those troopers who are surprised at nothing, who see the humorous side even of the last agonies of a dying comrade, who bury or plunder with equal cheerfulness, and whose authoritative arguments are found in bullets: in short, he was one of those men who waste no time in deliberation, and would not hesitate to make friends with the devil on a moment's notice.

"After watching the proprietor of the menagerie out of his box, my companion looked about with an expression of contempt on his lips, — one of those mocking smiles peculiar to the person of superior knowledge, indicating that he is not among the dupes. When I expatiated on the courage of Monsieur Martin, he laughed, and, wagging his head in a knowing way, remarked, ' *Connu !* ' ' Easy !'

" ' How, *easy ?* ' I answered. ' If you can explain this mystery I shall be infinitely obliged to you.'

" After chatting a few minutes we went to dine at the nearest restaurant. At dessert a bottle of champagne revived the memory of this queer old soldier in all its clearness. He told me his story, and I realized that he had every reason to exclaim, ' *Connu !* ' "

When we got home, she teased me so much that I consented to relate to her the soldier's confidence. The next day she received this episode of an epic which we might entitle " The French in Egypt."

During the expedition undertaken by General Desaix into Upper Egypt, a Provençal soldier fell into the hands of the Maugrabins and was carried away by these Arabs into the desert beyond the cataracts of the Nile. In order to place a safe distance between themselves and the French army, the Maugrabins made a forced march, resting only by night. They camped about a well hidden by palm-trees, where they had previously concealed provisions. Not suspecting that the idea of escape would enter the mind of their prisoner, they merely tied his hands, and when they had eaten some dates and fed their horses, they went to sleep. When the courageous Frenchman saw that his enemies were no longer in a condition to watch him, he managed to use his teeth to get hold of a scimiter, and fixing the blade between his knees, cut the cord which restrained his hands, and in a moment found himself free. He then seized a carbine and a poniard, took the precaution of providing himself with some dry dates, a little sack of barley, and powder and balls. He buckled the scimiter about his waist, mounted a horse, and quickly spurred away in the direction in which he thought the French army must lie. So impatient was he to see the mess tent once more, that he urged on his already tired courser at such a speed that the poor animal, its flanks lacerated by the spurs, soon breathed its last and left its rider in the midst of the desert.

After walking on for some time in the sand with all the courage of an escaped convict, the soldier was obliged to stop, as the day was at an end. In spite of the beauty of an Oriental night, he felt that he had not the strength to continue his journey. He had been fortunate enough to gain an eminence on the top of which grew palms, whose foliage had been visible for a long time and had filled his heart with gentle hopes. His weariness was so great that he lay down on a granite boulder, by chance hollowed out like a camp-bed, and fell asleep without taking any precaution for his safety during the night. He had made the sacrifice of his life. His last thought was one of regret. He already repented of having left the Maugrabins, whose wandering life began to smile upon him, now that they were far away and he was helpless.

He was awakened by the sun, whose pitiless rays, beating straight down upon the granite rock, produced an unbearable heat; for this Frenchman had been awkward enough to place himself on the opposite side from the shade thrown by the verdant and majestic heads of the palm-trees.

He looked at these trees with a start. They reminded him of the graceful shafts crowned with long leaves which distinguished the Saracen columns of the cathedral at Arles. But when, after having counted the palms, he cast his eyes on the surrounding plain, the most frightful despair settled on his soul. He saw a limitless ocean. The dark sands of the desert extended as far as the eye could reach in every direction, and glittered like a steel blade in bright sunlight. It appeared to him like a sea of glass, or a succession of lakes united as a folding mirror. Borne upward in great billows, a fiery vapor seethed above the quivering earth. The sky had an Oriental brilliance and a provoking purity, which no power of imagination could surpass. The sky and earth were on fire. The silence was awful in its savage and terrible majesty. Infinite immensity in every direction weighed down upon the soul: not a cloud in the sky, not a breath in the air, not a speck on the bosom of the desert, heaving in almost invisible waves. The horizon ended, as it does at sea on a clear day, in one line of light as sharp as the cut of a sabre. The man hugged the trunk of one of the palms as if it had been the body of a friend; then, in the shelter of the narrow shadow which the tree threw upon the granite rock, he wept as he sat immovable, contemplating with profound sadness the relentless scene which presented itself to his eyes. He cried out, to try the solitude. His voice, lost in the hollows of the hill, returned a feeble sound far off without wakening an answering echo: the echo was in his own heart. The Frenchman was twenty-two years old. He loaded his carbine: "It will always be ready," he said to himself as he placed on the ground the means of his deliverance.

Looking now at the black expanse, now at the blue expanse, the soldier dreamed of France. He smelt with delight the gutters of Paris, he recalled the towns through which he had passed, the faces of his comrades, and the slightest circumstances of his life's history. Indeed, his tropical imagination made him behold the stones of his native Provence in the play of the heat which undulated over the limitless face of the desert.

Frightened at the danger which this cruel hallucination portended, he went down the opposite side of the hill from that he had come up the evening before. Great was his joy on discovering a kind of grotto, naturally shaped in the immense blocks of granite which formed the base of the tiny mountain. The remains of a mat announced that this retreat had once been inhabited. A few steps farther on, he saw some trees loaded with dates. Then the instinct which draws us to life re-awakened in his heart. He hoped he might live long enough to attract the notice of some passing Maugrabins, or, perhaps, hear once more the roar of cannon; for, at this moment, Bonaparte was overrunning Egypt.

Roused by this thought, he knocked down some ripe fruit to eat, for the date-trees seemed bending under the weight of it, and in the taste of this unhoped-for manna he found assurance that the inhabitant of the cave had cultivated the trees. The fresh, savory meat argued the care of his predecessor. The Frenchman suddenly passed from the shadow of despair to an almost idiotic joy. He remounted to the top of the hill, and occupied himself the remainder of the day in cutting one of the sterile palms which the night before had served him for shelter. A vague recollection made him think of the animals of the desert; and reflecting that they might come to drink at the spring which could be seen at the base of the rocks, but disappeared in the sands, he resolved to guard himself by placing a barrier at the entrance to his retreat. In spite of his toil, in spite of the strength given by the fear of being devoured in his sleep, he found it impossible to cut the palm into pieces that day; but he succeeded in felling it. When, toward evening, this king of the desert toppled over, the noise of its fall resounded far and wide, and it was like a moan uttered by the solitude. The soldier shuddered at it, as if he heard a voice predicting misery. But like an heir who does not long mourn the death of a parent, he despoiled the beautiful tree of the broad green leaves which are its poetic adornment, and made use of them to repair the mat on which he was to sleep.

Worn out by the heat and the labor, he fell asleep under the red roof of his damp cave.

In the middle of the night his sleep was disturbed by an unusual noise. He sat up, and the deep silence which reigned about him permitted him to recognize the alternating accents of a respiration whose savage energy could belong to no human creature. A profound fear, increased by the gloom, the silence, and the phantoms of imagination, froze his heart. He almost felt his hair stand on end when, dilating the pupils of his eyes, he perceived in the shadow two feeble yellow sparks. At first he attributed these lights to some reflection of his own eyeballs; but soon, as the brilliancy of the night assisted him gradually to distinguish the various objects within the cave, he perceived an enormous animal lying only two steps away.

Was it a lion, a tiger, or a crocodile? The Frenchman was unable to tell under what species his enemy should be classed, but his fright was all the greater because his lack of knowledge made him imagine every misfortune at once. He endured the cruel torture of listening, of catching every variation in that respiration and missing nothing, without daring to make the slightest movement. An odor as strong as that exhaled by foxes, but more penetrating, more serious, so to speak, filled the grotto; and when the Frenchman perceived this smell, his terror became overwhelming, for he could no longer regard with doubt the existence of a terrible companion, whose royal den served as his place of bivouac. Soon the reflection of the moon as it neared the horizon illumined the cave and by insensible degrees revealed the resplendent spotted coat of a panther.

This lion of Egypt was sleeping, curled up like a great dog, the peaceable possessor of a sumptuous corner at the door of this hostelry; its eyes opened for a moment, then closed again. Its face was turned toward the Frenchman. A thousand confused thoughts passed through the mind of the panther's prisoner. At first he thought of killing it with a shot from his gun, but he soon saw there was not room enough to take aim, and that the shot would fail to take effect. And if it should awake! The supposition made him stiff with fear. Listening to the beating of his own heart, clearly heard in the silence, he cursed the too strong pulsations which the rush of blood produced, fearing to disturb that sleep which allowed him time to think of some expedient to preserve his life. Twice he placed his hand on his scimiter with the design of cutting off the head of his enemy, but the difficulty of cutting through the stiff short hair obliged him to renounce this daring project. To fail? that would surely mean death, thought he. He preferred the chances of combat, and resolved to await the day.

And the day did not give him long to wait. The Frenchman could now examine the panther: its muzzle was smeared with blood. "She has had a good meal," he thought with no disquieting conjecture that she might have been feasting on human flesh. "She will not be hungry when she wakes up."

It was a female. The fur on the belly and thighs was a brilliant white. Several marks that looked like velvet formed pretty anklets. The muscular tail was also white, but terminated in black rings. The upper part of the coat, yellow as unburnished gold, but sleek and soft, bore the characteristic tufts shaded off like roses, which serve to distinguish panthers from other members of the feline family. This tranquil and redoubtable hostess breathed heavily as she lay in an attitude as graceful as that of a cat on a rug by the fire. Her blood-stained paws, nervous and well armed, extended in front of her head, which rested upon them, and from which extended her thin, straight whiskers, like threads of silver. If she had been in a cage, forsooth, the Frenchman would certainly have admired the grace of this beast, and the sharp contrasts of living colors which gave to her coat an imperial splendor; but at this moment his vision was troubled by this sinister apparition. The presence of the panther, even asleep, could not fail of the effect said to be produced by the magnetic eyes of the serpent on the nightingale. The soldier's courage vanished for a moment before this danger, though doubtless it would have risen at the mouth of a cannon belching forth grape-shot. However, one bold thought made daylight in his heart and sealed up the pores from which the cold sweat had been oozing out on his forehead. Hardy as those men who, driven to the last extremity, come to defy death and offer themselves to her fell blows, he resolved to view this adventure merely as a tragic drama, and play out his part with honor to the final scene.

"Day before yesterday, perhaps the Arabs would have killed me," said he to himself. Considering himself as dead, he awaited bravely and with anxious curiosity the awakening of his enemy.

When the sun appeared, the panther suddenly opened her eyes; then she violently stretched out her paws as if to get rid of the cramps; at last she yawned, and thereby displayed a frightful row of teeth and a slender tongue, as rough as a rasp.

"A regular little mistress!" thought the Frenchman, as he watched her roll about in the most graceful and coquettish movements. She licked off the blood which smeared her paws and muzzle, and scratched her head with repeated strokes full of prettiness. "Well! making a bit of a toilet!" he said to himself, recovering his spirits with the return of his courage. "We shall presently be wishing each other good morning." And he seized the short little dagger which he had taken from the Maugrabins.

At this moment the panther turned her head toward the Frenchman and looked at him steadily without moving. The fixity of her metallic eyes and their insupportable brightness made the man shudder, especially when the beast walked toward him; but he watched her with a caressing gaze, staring at her as if to hypnotize her, and let her come quite near him. Then, by a movement as gentle and as amorous as if he had been caressing the prettiest woman in the world, he passed his hand over her body from the head to the tail, scratching the flexible vertebræ which marked the panther's yellow back.

The beast voluptuously straightened her tail, and her eyes grew gentle. And when for the third time the Frenchman accomplished this effective flattery, she began to purr, as our cats do in expressing their pleasure; but this murmur proceeded from a throat so powerful and deep, that it resounded through the cave like the bass chords of a church organ.

The Frenchman, realizing the importance of these caresses, redoubled them in a way to surprise, to stupefy this imperious coquette. When he felt assured of having extinguished the ferocity of his capricious companion, whose hunger had so fortunately been satisfied the evening before, he rose to go out of the cave. The panther indeed let him pass; but when he had ascended the hill, she came bounding up with the lightness of a sparrow hopping from branch to branch, and began rubbing herself against the soldier's legs, putting up her back like all the race of cats. Then, regarding her guest with an eye whose brilliancy had become somewhat less inflexible, she uttered that savage cry which naturalists compare to the grating of a saw.

"She is exacting!" cried the Frenchman with a smile. He ventured to play with her ears, to caress her belly, and vigorously to scratch her head with his finger-nails; and, perceiving his success, he tickled the top of her head with the point of his dagger, watching for the propitious moment to kill her; but the hardness of the bone made him tremble lest he should not succeed.

The sultana of the desert indicated her acceptance of the attentions of her slave by raising her head, stretching her neck, displaying her infatuation by the tranquillity of her demeanor. The Frenchman suddenly fancied that to assassinate this savage princess at a single stroke, he must stab her in the throat, and he raised the blade, when the panther, doubtless surfeited, lay down at his feet, from time to time casting up glances at him, in which, in spite of their native fierceness, was mingled a confused goodwill. The poor fellow ate some dates, leaning against one of the palms, in turn casting a searching eye on the desert to see if he might discern a liberator, and on his terrible companion that he might watch her uncertain clemency. The panther kept looking at the place where the date stones fell, and each time he threw one down, her eyes expressed a certain mistrust and incredulity. She examined the Frenchman with the prudence of a merchant; but this examination was favorable to him, for when he had finished his meagre repast she licked his shoes, and, with a tongue rough and strong, she removed in a marvellous manner the dust that had hardened in the creases.

"But when she shall be hungry!" thought the Frenchman. In spite of the shudder which this thought caused him, the soldier began from curiosity to measure the proportions of the panther, certainly one of the most beautiful individuals of the species, for she was three feet high, and five feet long, without counting her tail. This powerful member, shaped like a cudgel, was almost three feet long. The head, almost as large as that of a lion, was distinguished by an expression of rare craftiness; the cold cruelty of the tiger dominated it, but there was also a vague resemblance to the face of an artful woman. The fact is, at this moment the face of this solitary queen revealed a gayety not unlike that of a drunken Nero: she had satiated herself with blood and she wished to play.

The soldier began to walk up and down; the panther left him free, contenting herself with following the movements of her master with her eyes, indeed resembling less a faithful dog, than a great restless angora. When he turned he saw by the spring the remains of his horse: the panther had dragged the carcass all that distance. About two thirds had been devoured. The sight gave reassurance. It was now easy to explain the absence of the panther, and why she had respected his slumbers. This first piece of good fortune emboldened him to tempt the future. He conceived the fond hope of living comfortably with the panther during the entire day, of course neglecting no means of taming her and conciliating her. He came back to her and had the unspeakable happiness of seeing her wag her tail in an almost imperceptible movement. He then sat down without fear beside her, and the two began to play; he fondled her paws, her muzzle; he pulled her ears; he rolled her over on her back, and vigorously scratched her warm, silky flanks. She allowed him to do as he would, and when he undertook to stroke the hair on her paws, she carefully drew in her claws, which were curved like damsons. The Frenchman, keeping his hand on his dagger, thought even of plunging it into the belly of the too trustful panther; but he feared being strangled in the last convulsion which would seize her. And besides, he felt in his heart a sort of compunction which cried out to him to respect an inoffensive creature. He seemed to have found a friend in this limitless desert. Involuntarily he called up the memory of his first mistress, whom he had named Mignonne, by opposition of phrase, because she was so insanely jealous that, during the entire time their passion lasted, he was in fear of the knife with which she continually threatened him. This memory of his youth suggested the idea of teaching this young panther to answer to the name, now that he strangely enough began to regard with less terror her agility, grace, and suppleness.

Toward the end of the day he had become accustomed
to his perilous situation, and he almost enjoyed the pain-
fulness of it. Indeed, his companion had come habitu-
ally to look at him when he cried out in a falsetto voice,
"Mignonne!" At sunset Mignonne uttered several
times a deep and melancholy cry.

"She has been well brought up!" thought the gay-
hearted soldier; "she says her prayers." But this
mental pleasantry came into his mind only after he had
remarked the quiet demeanor which his companion continued to preserve. "Come, my pretty blonde, I will let
you go to bed first," said he, counting on the activity of
his own legs to escape as quickly as possible when she
should be asleep, and find out another lodging during
the night.

The soldier awaited with impatience the hour of his
flight, and when it arrived he ran swiftly in the direction
of the Nile; but hardly had he made a quarter of a
league in the sand when he heard the panther bounding
after him, and uttering at intervals that rasping cry, more
frightening even than the sound of her leaping.

"Hello!" said he, "she has taken me into her affections. Perhaps this young panther has never before met
any one. It is flattering to have her first love." At
that moment the man fell into one of those quicksands
so dreaded by travellers, since it is impossible to escape from them. Feeling that he was fast, he gave forth
a cry of alarm. The panther seized him by the collar
with her teeth, and leaping backward with vigor, she
dragged him from the abyss as by magic.

"Ah, Mignonne!" cried the soldier, caressing her
with warmth, "it is now for life and for death between
us. But no tricks!" And he retraced his steps.

Thenceforth the desert seemed inhabited. It contained a being to whom the man could talk, whose ferocity had been softened for him, though he was unable to explain the reasons for this remarkable friendship. Powerful as was the soldier's desire to remain on his guard, he fell asleep. On awaking he could see Mignonne nowhere. He mounted the hill, and in the distance he discerned her bounding along, as is the habit of these animals, since running is prevented by the extreme flexibility of the spinal column.

Mignonne arrived, her lips covered with blood. She received the inevitable caresses that her companion gave her, testifying by much deep purring how happy it made her. Her eyes, filled with languor, turned on the Frenchman even more gently than the night before, and he spoke to her as to a domestic animal.

"Ah! ah! mademoiselle! why, you're a fine girl, aren't you? Just see! We like to be flattered, don't we! Aren't you ashamed of yourself? Have you eaten a Maugrabin? Oh, well! they are no better than animals like you. But don't go to eating Frenchmen, or I shan't like you any more!"

She played as a young dog plays with his master, letting herself be rolled over, slapped, and caressed by turns; and sometimes she would tempt the soldier, thrusting out her paw to him with a gesture of solicitation.

Some days passed in this manner. This companionship allowed the Frenchman to admire the sublime beauties of the desert. Now that he had found periods of fear and of tranquillity, food, and a creature to occupy his thoughts, life began to have variety for him. It was an existence full of contrasts. The solitude revealed to him all her secrets, and enveloped him with her charms. In the rising and the setting of the sun he found spectacles unknown to the civilized world. He knew what it was to tremble when he heard over his head the soft whirr of the wings of a bird — rare visitor, — or when he saw the clouds, those changing and many colored travellers, melting into one another. At night he studied the effect of the moon on the ocean of sand, in which the simoom produced quickly changing billows and undulations. He lived the life of the Orient, wondering at its marvellous pomps; and often, after having enjoyed the terrible spectacle of a hurricane on this plain, where the sands were lifted up and formed red, dry mists, death-bearing clouds, he watched with joy for the coming of night, for then a healing refreshment fell from the stars, to whose imaginary music he would listen. Then solitude taught him to unroll the treasures of dreams. He spent whole hours in the recollection of nothings, comparing his past life with his present. At last he conceived a passion for the panther; for it was absolutely necessary that he have some object of affection. Whether his will, powerfully projected, had modified the character of his companion, or she found abundant nourishment, thanks to the fighting then going on in the desert, she respected the life of the Frenchman, and he ended by abandoning his mistrust, so thoroughly tamed did she appear. He spent the greater part of his time in sleep, but he was obliged to watch, like a spider in the heart of her web, that the moment of his deliverance might not escape him, when some one should pass across the circle marked by the horizon. He had given up his shirt to make a flag, which he hoisted at the top of a palm branch stripped of its leaves. Taught by necessity, he found out how to keep it spread out by stretching it on little twigs, since the wind might not make it wave at the moment when some passing traveller in the desert was looking in that direction.

It was during the long hours in which hope abandoned him that he amused himself with the panther. He had come to know the varying inflections of her voice, and the expression of her eyes; he had studied every spot in the markings and shadings of her golden coat. Mignonne did not even snarl when he took hold of the tuft on her redoubtable tail, to count the black and white rings, those graceful ornaments which shone in the sunlight like jewels. He took pleasure in contemplating the delicate and fine lines of her contour, the whiteness of her belly, the grace of her head; but especially did he take delight in watching her at play, and he constantly wondered at her suppleness and youthfulness of movement; he could not but admire the graceful way in which she would leap, creep, slip, insinuate herself, seize upon anything, roll over, crouch down, and then spring away. However rapid her leap, or slippery the rock under her feet, she would stop in an instant at the word "Mignonne."

One day, when the sun was shining brightly, an immense bird cut through the air. The Frenchman left his panther, to examine this new visitor; but after a moment's waiting, the deserted sultana gave a harsh growl.

"My God, I believe she is jealous!" he cried, as he saw her eyes becoming hard again. "The soul of Virginia has passed into her body; that is quite evident."

The eagle disappeared in the upper air while the soldier admired the rounded back of the panther. Ah, there was such grace and youthful beauty in her contour! She was as pretty as a woman. The light fur of her coat harmonized perfectly with the fine tones of dull white which marked her flanks. The brilliant light of the sun made this living gold fairly to blaze round the dusky spots, lending an indefinable fascination. The Frenchman and the panther looked at each other with an air of perfect understanding. The coquette quivered when she felt the nails of her friend scratching her head, her eyes shone like two flashes of lightning, and then she shut them tightly.

"She has a soul," he said, as he studied the tranquillity of this queen of the sands, golden like them, white like them, solitary and burning like them.

"Well!" said she to me, "I have read your plea in favor of beasts; but how did it end with these two persons so well suited to comprehend each other?"

"Ah, you see, it ended for them, as in the case of all grand passions, with a misunderstanding. One suspects the other of treason; there is no explanation, because of pride; and they fall out through stubbornness."

"And sometimes, at a happy moment," said she, "a look, an exclamation is sufficient. But — come, finish the story."

"It is horribly difficult; but after what the old villain had already confided to me, you will understand, when he exclaimed, as he finished his bottle of champagne: 'I do not know what injury I had done her, but she turned as if enraged, and with her sharp teeth seized me by the leg, certainly with no great violence. But I, thinking she was about to devour me, plunged my dagger into her neck. She rolled over, uttering a cry which froze my heart. I saw her struggling, still watching me but without anger. I would have given the world, my cross (which I had not then received), to bring her back to life. It was as if I had assassinated a real person. And the soldiers, who had seen my signal and had hastened to my rescue, found me in tears.

"'Ah, well, monsieur,' he went on after a moment of silence, 'I have been a campaigner in Germany, in Spain, in Russia, in France; I have marched this carcass of mine about a good deal, but I have never seen anything to resemble the desert. Ah, yes! it is very beautiful.'

"'How did it affect you?' I inquired.

"'Oh! that is impossible to describe, young man. Besides, I am not always regretting my bunch of palms and my panther. I should be forever melancholy if I did that. In the desert, you see, there is everything, and there is nothing.'

"'But can't you explain?'

"'Well,' he replied, a gesture of impatience escaping him, 'it is God without man.'"

A CHILD'S DREAM OF A STAR

By CHARLES DICKENS

INTRODUCTORY

PATHETIC SENTIMENT

IN " Rip Van Winkle " we find the beginning
of humor, — not the serious humor of a
sea of sentiment, which rises alternately in
crested waves of pure fun, only to sink the next
instant into the depths of pathos, but the whimsical lightness of the essayist.   In Dickens we find
the humor of sentiment closely united with its
counterpart, the pathetic.   Sentiment is in Dickens a peculiar enveloping atmosphere of tenderness, — a mild and moist air quite different from
the heated breath of passion.   As a source of
popularity, it is to English fiction what passion
is to the French.   It is a soothing opiate, mildly
stimulating, and infinitely restful, and to the multitude it often excuses an endless catalogue of
sins.   We may almost say that no artist can be
permanently popular without it, — certainly no
artist of the strictly realistic school; and even
romance ceases to hold the throng of its admir-

ers, long before sentiment yields an iota of its popularity.

The master of sentiment is Dickens, and in no other writer can it be studied so effectively. In him we may find all kinds of sentiment, corresponding with the variety of life which he represents. Curiously enough pathetic sentiment seems to be better adapted to the short story than humorous sentiment. Perhaps this is because humor cannot be concentrated in a short space so easily as pathos can. In the short story intensity takes the place of variety, and the shorter the story the more intense it must be made in order to secure the reader's interest.

Until fiction appropriated it, sentiment, both pathetic and humorous, was the peculiar possession of the ballad and the song. It cannot be expressed in simple narrative prose, such as we found in "Patient Griselda" and "Aladdin," but requires a special structure which shall utilize some of the characteristics of verse, but in a free and untrammelled way. Verse is mechanical and fixed, while prose is perfectly pliant and adaptable. Modern writers have found means to produce all the effects of poetry in prose, and have even proved that in its possibilities of expression prose is vastly superior to verse. The effectiveness of the artist's personal skill is correspondingly greater with the increase of his opportunities and the removal from mechanical forms. In "A

Child's Dream of a Star" we find some of the devices of the prose poet, such as the chorus-like repetition, and the balanced and cumulative structures. But in the musical element Dickens was lacking.

A CHILD'S DREAM OF A STAR

THERE was once a child, and he strolled about a good deal, and thought of a number of things. He had a sister, who was a child too, and his constant companion. These two used to wonder all day long. They wondered at the beauty of the flowers; they wondered at the height and blueness of the sky; they wondered at the depth of the bright water; they wondered at the goodness and the power of God who made the lovely world.

They used to say to one another, sometimes, Supposing all the children upon earth were to die, would the flowers, and the water, and the sky be sorry? They believed they would be sorry. For, said they, the buds are the children of the flowers, and the little playful streams that gambol down the hillsides are the children of the water; and the smallest bright specks playing at hide-and-seek in the sky all night, must surely be the children of the stars; and they would all be grieved to see their playmates, the children of men, no more.

There was one clear shining star that used to come out in the sky before the rest, near the church-spire, above the graves. It was larger and more beautiful, they thought, than all the others, and every night they watched for it, standing hand in hand at the window.

Whoever saw it first, cried out, "I see the star!" And often they cried out both together, knowing so well when it would rise, and where. So they grew to be such friends with it, that before lying down in their beds, they always looked out once again, to bid it good night; and when they were turning round to sleep, they used to say, "God bless the star!"

But while she was still very young, O, very, very young, the sister drooped, and came to be so weak that she could no longer stand in the window at night; and then the child looked sadly out by himself, and when he saw the star, turned round and said to the patient pale face on the bed, "I see the star!" and then a smile would come upon the face, and a little weak voice used to say, "God bless my brother and the star!"

And so the time came, all too soon! when the child looked out alone, and when there was no face on the bed; and when there was a little grave among the graves, not there before; and when the star made long rays down towards him, as he saw it through his tears.

Now, these rays were so bright, and they seemed to make such a shining way from earth to heaven, that when the child went to his solitary bed, he dreamed about the star; and dreamed that, lying where he was, he saw a train of people taken up that sparkling road by angels. And the star, opening, showed him a great world of light, where many more such angels waited to receive them.

All these angels who were waiting turned their beaming eyes upon the people who were carried up into the star; and some came out from the long rows in which they stood, and fell upon the people's necks, and kissed them tenderly, and went away with them down avenues of light, and were so happy in their company, that lying in his bed he wept for joy.

But there were many angels who did not go with them, and among them one he knew. The patient face that once had lain upon the bed was glorified and radiant, but his heart found out his sister among all the host.

His sister's angel lingered near the entrance of the star, and said to the leader among those who had brought the people thither, —

"Is my brother come?"

And he said, "No."

She was turning hopefully away, when the child stretched out his arms, and cried, "O sister, I am here! Take me!" And then she turned her beaming eyes upon him and it was night; and the star was shining into the room, making long rays down towards him as he saw it through his tears.

From that hour forth the child looked out upon the star as on the home he was to go to, when his time should come; and he thought that he did not belong to the earth alone, but to the star too, because of his sister's angel gone before.

There was a baby born to be a brother to the child; and while he was so little that he never yet had spoken word, he stretched his tiny form out on his bed and died.

Again the child dreamed of the opened star, and of the company of angels, and the train of people, and the rows of angels with their beaming eyes all turned upon those people's faces.

Said his sister's angel to the leader.

"Is my brother come?"

And he said, "Not that one, but another."

As the child beheld his brother's angel in her arms,

he cried, "O sister, I am here! Take me!" And she turned and smiled upon him, and the star was shining.

He grew to be a young man, and was busy at his books when an old servant came to him and said,—

"Thy mother is no more. I bring her blessing on her darling son!"

Again at night he saw the star, and all that former company. Said his sister's angel to the leader,—

"Is my brother come?"

And he said, "Thy mother!"

A mighty cry of joy went forth through all the star, because the mother was reunited to her two children. And he stretched out his arms and cried, "O mother, sister, and brother, I am here! Take me!" And they answered him, "Not yet." And the star was shining.

He grew to be a man whose hair was turning gray, and he was sitting in his chair by the fireside, heavy with grief, and with his face bedewed with tears, when the star opened once again.

Said his sister's angel to the leader, "Is my brother come?"

And he said, "Nay, but his maiden daughter."

And the man who had been the child saw his daughter, newly lost to him, a celestial creature among those three, and he said, "My daughter's head is on my sister's bosom, and her arm is round my mother's neck, and at her feet there is the baby of old time, and I can bear the parting from her, God be praised!"

And the star was shining.

Thus the child came to be an old man, and his once smooth face was wrinkled, and his steps were slow and feeble, and his back was bent. And one night as he lay upon his bed, his children standing round, he cried, as he had cried so long ago,—

" I see the star ! "

They whispered one another, " He is dying."

And he said, " I am.   My age is falling from me like a garment, and I move towards the star as a child.   And O my Father, now I thank thee that it has so often opened to receive those dear ones who await me ! "

And the star was shining ; and it shines upon his grave.

11

VI

A CHRISTMAS CAROL

A CHRISTMAS CAROL

By CHARLES DICKENS

INTRODUCTORY

HUMOROUS SENTIMENT

IF the intensity of pathetic sentiment requires condensation, as we found in the case of "A Child's Dream of a Star," humorous sentiment requires expansion. In "A Christmas Carol" Dickens fairly floats on a sea of sentiment —humorous sentiment, good-humored sentiment. The Christmas season is a time of expansion. As the waistband enlarges the heart fills up, till it bubbles over like a glass of good ale. The language in this Christmas story is a series of expanding flowers, each idea being a centre, with words and phrases growing out in every direction, like petal laid on petal. Each scene is a perfect nosegay of scented blossoms; and to make the miracle more striking, Dickens brings all these blossoms out of a dried-up and half-dead old stalk, the miser Scrooge.

In no story that he ever wrote was Dickens more at home than in this, and in no story has he succeeded better in pouring out the full wealth of his sentimental nature. Harsh critics sometimes say that he quite bubbled over, and that sentiment, like butter, should not be thicker than the bread it covers. The story was originally written in fifty thousand words, and in that form attained its popularity. When he began his series of public readings in America, the author was called upon to give the "Carol," and to bring it within the limits of an evening's entertainment he was obliged to condense it to a quarter of its original length. In so doing he made a far better story of it, and it is in this rewritten form that we here present it.

Sentiment is without doubt the secret of wide popularity. If one would wish to know what a popular story is, let him study this little fantastic Christmas tale, for no more popular short story was ever written. We have compared Dickens's style to the song and the ballad. The higher poetic elements are lacking. "A Christmas Carol" is by no means highly artistic work. We must look elsewhere for the more refined and intellectual phases of prose poetry — in Hawthorne, for instance. But it is doubtful if ever a song or ballad, even when sung with all the appeal of a sympathetic human voice, ever touched the heart of the people so widely and so permanently as this "Carol," the very name of which indicates its literary affinities.

A CHRISTMAS CAROL

STAVE ONE

MARLEY'S GHOST

MARLEY was dead, to begin with. There is no doubt whatever about that. The register of his burial was signed by the clergyman, the clerk, the undertaker, and the chief mourner. Scrooge signed it. And Scrooge's name was good upon 'Change for anything he chose to put his hand to.

Old Marley was as dead as a door-nail.

Scrooge knew he was dead? Of course he did. How could it be otherwise? Scrooge and he were partners for I don't know how many years. Scrooge was his sole executor, his sole administrator, his sole assign, his sole residuary legatee, his sole friend, his sole mourner.

Scrooge never painted out old Marley's name, however. There it yet stood, years afterwards, above the warehouse door, — Scrooge and Marley. The firm was known as Scrooge and Marley. Sometimes people new to the business called Scrooge Scrooge, and sometimes Marley. He answered to both names. It was all the same to him.

Oh! But he was a tight-fisted hand at the grindstone, was Scrooge! a squeezing, wrenching, grasping, scraping, clutching, covetous old sinner! External heat and cold had little influence on him. No warmth could warm, no cold could chill him. No wind that blew was bitterer than he, no falling snow was more intent upon its purpose, no pelting rain less open to entreaty. Foul weather didn't know where to have him. The heaviest rain and snow and hail and sleet could boast of the advantage over him in only one respect, — they often "came down" handsomely, and Scrooge never did.

Nobody ever stopped him in the street to say, with gladsome looks, "My dear Scrooge, how are you? When will you come to see me?" No beggars implored him to bestow a trifle, no children asked him what it was o'clock, no man or woman ever once in all his life inquired the way to such and such a place, of Scrooge. Even the blind men's dogs appeared to know him; and when they saw him coming on, would tug their owners into doorways and up courts; and then would wag their tails as though they said, "No eye at all is better than an evil eye, dark master!"

But what did Scrooge care! It was the very thing he liked. To edge his way along the crowded paths of life, warning all human sympathy to keep its distance, was what the knowing ones call "nuts" to Scrooge.

Once upon a time — of all the good days in the year, upon a Christmas eve — old Scrooge sat busy in his counting-house. It was cold, bleak, biting, foggy weather; and the city clocks had only just gone three, but it was quite dark already.

The door of Scrooge's counting-house was open, that he might keep his eye upon his clerk, who, in a dismal little cell beyond, a sort of tank, was copying letters. Scrooge had a very small fire, but the clerk's fire was so very much smaller that it looked like one coal. But he couldn't replenish it, for Scrooge kept the coal-box in his own room; and so surely as the clerk came in with the shovel the master predicted that it would be necessary for them to part. Wherefore the clerk put on his white comforter, and tried to warm himself at the candle; in which effort, not being a man of a strong imagination, he failed.

"A merry Christmas, uncle! God save you!" cried a cheerful voice. It was the voice of Scrooge's nephew, who came upon him so quickly that this was the first intimation Scrooge had of his approach.

"Bah!" said Scrooge; "humbug!"

"Christmas a humbug, uncle! You don't mean that, I am sure?"

"I do. Out upon merry Christmas! What's Christmas time to you but a time for paying bills without money; a time for finding yourself a year older, and not an hour richer; a time for balancing your books and having every item in 'em through a round dozen of months presented dead against you? If I had my will, every idiot who goes about with 'Merry Christmas' on his lips should be boiled with his own pudding, and buried with a stake of holly through his heart! He should!"

"Uncle!"

"Nephew, keep Christmas in your own way, and let me keep it in mine."

"Keep it! But you don't keep it."

"Let me leave it alone, then. Much good may it do you! Much good it has ever done you!"

"There are many things from which I might have derived good, by which I have not profited, I dare say, Christmas among the rest. But I am sure I have always thought of Christmas time, when it has come round, — apart from the veneration due to its sacred origin, if anything belonging to it *can* be apart from that, — as a good time; a kind, forgiving, charitable, pleasant time; the only time I know of, in the long calendar of the year, when men and women seem by one consent to open their shut-up hearts freely, and to think of people below them as if they really were fellow-travellers to the grave, and not another race of creatures bound on other journeys. And therefore, uncle, though it has never put a scrap of gold or silver in my pocket, I believe that it *has* done me good, and *will* do me good; and I say, God bless it ! "

The clerk in the tank involuntarily applauded.

" Let me hear another sound from *you*," said Scrooge, " and you 'll keep your Christmas by losing your situation ! — You 're quite a powerful speaker, sir," he added, turning to his nephew. " I wonder you don't go into Parliament."

" Don't be angry, uncle. Come ! Dine with us, to-morrow."

Scrooge said that he would see him — yes, indeed he did. He went the whole length of the expression, and said that he would see him in that extremity first.

" But why ? " cried Scrooge's nephew. " Why ? "

" Why did you get married ? "

" Because I fell in love."

" Because you fell in love ! " growled Scrooge, as if that were the only one thing in the world more ridiculous than a merry Christmas. " Good afternoon ! "

" Nay, uncle, but you never came to see me before that happened. Why give it as a reason for not coming now ? "

" Good afternoon."

" I want nothing from you ; I ask nothing of you ; why cannot we be friends ? "

" Good afternoon."

" I am sorry, with all my heart, to find you so resolute. We have never had any quarrel, to which I have been a party. But I have made the trial in homage to Christmas, and I 'll keep my Christmas humor to the last. So, A Merry Christmas, uncle !"

"Good afternoon !"

"And A Happy New Year !"

"Good afternoon !"

His nephew left the room without an angry word, notwithstanding. The clerk, in letting Scrooge's nephew out, had let two other people in. They were portly gentlemen, pleasant to behold, and now stood, with their hats off, in Scrooge's office. They had books and papers in their hands, and bowed to him.

"Scrooge and Marley's, I believe," said one of the gentlemen, referring to his list. "Have I the pleasure of addressing Mr. Scrooge, or Mr. Marley?"

"Mr. Marley has been dead these seven years. He died seven years ago, this very night."

"At this festive season of the year, Mr. Scrooge," said the gentleman, taking up a pen, "it is more than usually desirable that we should make some slight provision for the poor and destitute, who suffer greatly at the present time. Many thousands are in want of common necessaries ; hundreds of thousands are in want of common comforts, sir."

"Are there no prisons?"

"Plenty of prisons. But under the impression that they scarcely furnish Christian cheer of mind or body to the unoffending multitude, a few of us are endeavoring to raise a fund to buy the poor some meat and drink, and means of warmth. We choose this time, because it is a time of all others when Want is keenly felt and Abundance rejoices. What shall I put you down for?"

"Nothing !"

"You wish to be anonymous?"

"I wish to be left alone. Since you ask me what I wish, gentlemen, that is my answer. I don't make merry myself at Christmas, and I can't afford to make idle people merry. I help to support the prisons and the workhouses, — they cost enough, — and those who are badly off must go there."

"Many can't go there; and many would rather die."

"If they would rather die, they had better do it, and decrease the surplus population."

At length the hour of shutting up the counting-house arrived. With an ill-will Scrooge, dismounting from his stool, tacitly admitted the fact to the expectant clerk in the Tank, who instantly snuffed his candle out, and put on his hat.

"You'll want all day to-morrow, I suppose?"

"If quite convenient, sir."

"It's not convenient, and it's not fair. If I was to stop half a crown for it, you'd think yourself mightily ill-used, I'll be bound?"

"Yes, sir."

"And yet you don't think *me* ill-used, when I pay a day's wages for no work."

"It's only once a year, sir."

"A poor excuse for picking a man's pocket every twenty-fifth of December! But I suppose you must have the whole day. Be here all the earlier *next* morning."

The clerk promised that he would; and Scrooge walked out with a growl. The office was closed in a twinkling, and the clerk, with the long ends of his white comforter dangling below his waist (for he boasted no great-coat), went down a slide, at the end of a lane of boys, twenty times, in honor of its being Christmas eve, and then ran home as hard as he could pelt, to play at blind-man's-buff.

Scrooge took his melancholy dinner in his usual melancholy tavern; and having read all the newspapers, and beguiled the rest of the evening with his banker's book, went home to bed. He lived in chambers which had once belonged to his deceased partner. They were a gloomy suite of rooms, in a lowering pile of building up a yard. The building was old enough now, and dreary enough; for nobody lived in it but Scrooge, the other rooms being all let out as offices.

Now it is a fact, that there was nothing at all particular about the knocker on the door of this house, except that it was very large; also, that Scrooge had seen it, night and morning, during his whole residence in that place; also, that Scrooge had as little of what is called fancy about him as any man in the city of London. And yet Scrooge, having his key in the lock·of the door, saw in the knocker, without its undergoing any intermediate process of change, not a knocker, but Marley's face.

Marley's face, with a dismal light about it, like a bad lobster in a dark cellar. It was not angry or ferocious, but it looked at Scrooge as Marley used to look,— with ghostly spectacles turned up upon its ghostly forehead.

As Scrooge looked fixedly at this phenomenon, it was a knocker again. He said, "Pooh, pooh!" and closed the door with a bang.

The sound resounded through the house like thunder. Every room above, and every cask in the wine-merchant's cellars below, appeared to have a separate peal of echoes of its own. Scrooge was not a man to be frightened by echoes. He fastened the door, and walked across the hall, and up the stairs. Slowly, too, trimming his candle as he went.

Up Scrooge went, not caring a button for its being very dark. Darkness is cheap, and Scrooge liked it. But before he shut his heavy door, he walked through his rooms to see that all was right. He had just enough recollection of the face to desire to do that.

Sitting-room, bedroom, lumber-room, all as they should be. Nobody under the table, nobody under the sofa; a small fire in the grate; spoon and basin ready; and the little saucepan of gruel (Scrooge had a cold in his head) upon the hob. Nobody under the bed; nobody in the closet; nobody in his dressing-gown, which was hanging up in a suspicious attitude against the wall. Lumber-room as usual. Old fire-guard, old shoes, two fish-baskets, washing-stand on three legs, and a poker.

Quite satisfied, he closed his door, and locked himself in; double-locked himself in, which was not his custom. Thus secured against surprise, he took off his cravat, put on his dressing-gown and slippers and his night-cap, and sat down before the very low fire to take his gruel.

As he threw his head back in the chair, his glance happened to rest upon a bell, a disused bell, that hung in the room, and communicated, for some purpose now forgotten, with a chamber in the highest story of the building. It was with great astonishment, and with a strange, inexplicable dread, that, as he looked, he saw this bell begin to swing. Soon it rang out loudly, and so did every bell in the house.

This was succeeded by a clanking noise, deep down below, as if some person were dragging a heavy chain over the casks in the wine-merchant's cellar.

Then he heard the noise much louder, on the floors

below; then coming up the stairs; then coming straight towards his door.

It came on through the heavy door, and a spectre passed into the room before his eyes. And upon its coming in, the dying flame leaped up, as though it cried, "I know him! Marley's ghost!"

The same face, the very same. Marley in his pigtail, usual waistcoat, tights, and boots. His body was transparent; so that Scrooge, observing him, and looking through his waistcoat, could see the two buttons on his coat behind.

Scrooge had often heard it said that Marley had no bowels, but he had never believed it until now.

No, nor did he believe it even now. Though he looked the phantom through and through, and saw it standing before him, — though he felt the chilling influence of its death-cold eyes, and noticed the very texture of the folded kerchief bound about its head and chin, — he was still incredulous.

"How now!" said Scrooge, caustic and cold as ever. "What do you want with me?"

"Much!" — Marley's voice, no doubt about it.

"Who are you?"

"Ask me who I *was*."

"Who *were* you, then?"

"In life I was your partner, Jacob Marley."

"Can you — can you sit down?"

"I can."

"Do it, then."

Scrooge asked the question, because he did n't know whether a ghost so transparent might find himself in a condition to take a chair; and felt that, in the event of its being impossible, it might involve the necessity of an embarrassing explanation. But the ghost sat down on the opposite side of the fireplace, as if he were quite used to it.

" You don't believe in me."

" I don't."

" What evidence would you have of my reality beyond that of your senses?"

" I don't know."

" Why do you doubt your senses?"

" Because a little thing affects them. A slight disorder of the stomach makes them cheats. You may be an undigested bit of beef, a blot of mustard, a crumb of cheese, a fragment of an underdone potato. There's more of gravy than of grave about you, whatever you are!"

Scrooge was not much in the habit of cracking jokes, nor did he feel in his heart by any means waggish then. The truth is, that he tried to be smart, as a means of distracting his own attention, and keeping down his horror.

But how much greater was his horror when, the phantom taking off the bandage round its head, as if it were too warm to wear in-doors, its lower jaw dropped down upon its breast!

" Mercy! Dreadful apparition, why do you trouble me? Why do spirits walk the earth, and why do they come to me?"

" It is required of every man, that the spirit within him should walk abroad among his fellow-men, and travel far and wide; and if that spirit goes not forth in life, it is condemned to do so after death. I cannot tell you all I would. A very little more is permitted to me. I cannot rest, I cannot stay, I cannot linger anywhere. My spirit never walked beyond our counting-house, — mark me! — in life my spirit never roved beyond the narrow limits of our money-changing hole; and weary journeys lie before me!"

"Seven years dead. And travelling all the time? You travel fast?"

"On the wings of the wind."

"You might have got over a great quantity of ground in seven years."

"O blind man, blind man! not to know that ages of incessant labor by immortal creatures for this earth must pass into eternity before the good of which it is susceptible is all developed. Not to know that any Christian spirit working kindly in its little sphere, whatever it may be, will find its mortal life too short for its vast means of usefulness. Not to know that no space of regret can make amends for one life's opportunities misused! Yet I was like this man; I once was like this man!"

"But you were always a good man of business, Jacob," faltered Scrooge, who now began to apply this to himself.

"Business!" cried the ghost, wringing its hands again. "Mankind was my business. The common welfare was my business; charity, mercy, forbearance, benevolence, were all my business. The dealings of my trade were but a drop of water in the comprehensive ocean of my business."

Scrooge was very much dismayed to hear the spectre going on at this rate, and began to quake exceedingly.

"Hear me! My time is nearly gone."

"I will. But don't be hard upon me! Don't be flowery, Jacob! Pray!"

"I am here to-night to warn you that you have yet a chance and hope of escaping my fate. A chance and hope of my procuring, Ebenezer."

"You were always a good friend to me. Thank'ee!"

"You will be haunted by Three Spirits."

"Is that the chance and hope you mentioned, Jacob? I — I think I'd rather not."

"Without their visits, you cannot hope to shun the path I tread. Expect the first to-morrow night, when the bell tolls One. Expect the second on the next night at the same hour. The third, upon the next night, when the last stroke of Twelve has ceased to vibrate. Look to see me no more; and look that, for your own sake, you remember what has passed between us!"

It walked backward from him; and at every step it took, the window raised itself a little, so that, when the apparition reached it, it was wide open.

Scrooge closed the window, and examined the door by which the Ghost had entered. It was double-locked, as he had locked it with his own hands, and the bolts were undisturbed. Scrooge tried to say, "Humbug!" but stopped at the first syllable. And being, from the emotion he had undergone, or the fatigues of the day, or his glimpse of the invisible world, or the dull conversation of the Ghost, or the lateness of the hour, much in need of repose, he went straight to bed, without undressing, and fell asleep on the instant.

STAVE TWO

THE FIRST OF THE THREE SPIRITS

WHEN Scrooge awoke, it was so dark, that, looking out of bed, he could scarcely distinguish the transparent window from the opaque walls of his chamber, until suddenly the church clock tolled a deep, dull, hollow, melancholy ONE.

Light flashed up in the room upon the instant, and

the curtains of his bed were drawn aside by a strange figure, — like a child: yet not so like a child as like an old man, viewed through some supernatural medium, which gave him the appearance of having receded from the view, and being diminished to a child's proportions. Its hair, which hung about its neck and down its back, was white as if with age; and yet the face had not a wrinkle in it, and the tenderest bloom was on the skin. It held a branch of fresh green holly in its hand; and, in singular contradiction of that wintry emblem, had its dress trimmed with summer flowers. But the strangest thing about it was, that from the crown of its head there sprung a bright clear jet of light, by which all this was visible; and which was doubtless the occasion of its using, in its duller moments, a great extinguisher for a cap, which it now held under its arm.

"Are you the Spirit, sir, whose coming was foretold to me?"

"I am!"

"Who and what are you?"

"I am the Ghost of Christmas Past."

"Long past?"

"No. Your past. The things that you will see with me are shadows of the things that have been; they will have no consciousness of us."

Scrooge then made bold to inquire what business brought him there.

"Your welfare. Rise, and walk with me!"

It would have been in vain for Scrooge to plead that the weather and the hour were not adapted to pedestrian purposes; that the bed was warm, and the thermometer a long way below freezing; that he was clad but lightly in his slippers, dressing-gown, and nightcap; and that he had a cold upon him at that time. The grasp, though gentle as a woman's hand, was not to be resisted. He rose ; but, finding that the Spirit made towards the window, clasped its robe in supplication.

" I am a mortal, and liable to fall."

" Bear but a touch of my hand *there*," said the Spirit, laying it upon his heart, " and you shall be upheld in more than this ! "

As the words were spoken, they passed through the wall, and stood in the busy thoroughfares of a city. It was made plain enough by the dressing of the shops that here, too, it was Christmas time.

The Ghost stopped at a certain warehouse door, and asked Scrooge if he knew it.

" Know it ! Was I apprenticed here ! "

They went in. At sight of an old gentleman in a Welsh wig, sitting behind such a high desk that, if he had been two inches taller, he must have knocked his head against the ceiling, Scrooge cried in great excitement, " Why, it 's old Fezziwig ! Bless his heart, it 's Fezziwig, alive again ! "

Old Fezziwig laid down his pen, and looked up at the clock, which pointed to the hour of seven. He rubbed his hands ; adjusted his capacious waistcoat ; laughed all over himself, from his shoes to his organ of benevolence ; and called out in a comfortable, oily, rich, fat, jovial voice, " Yo ho, there ! Ebenezer ! Dick ! "

A living and moving picture of Scrooge's former self, a young man, came briskly in, accompany by his fellow-'prentice.

" Dick Wilkins, to be sure ! " said Scrooge to the Ghost. " My old fellow-'prentice, bless me, yes. There he is. He was very much attached to me, was Dick. Poor Dick ! Dear, dear ! "

" Yo ho, my boys ! " said Fezziwig. " No more work

to-night. Christmas eve, Dick. Christmas, Ebenezer! Let's have the shutters up, before a man can say Jack Robinson! Clear away, my lads, and let's have lots of room here!"

Clear away! There was nothing they wouldn't have cleared away, or couldn't have cleared away, with old Fezziwig looking on. It was done in a minute. Every movable was packed off, as if it were dismissed from public life forevermore; the floor was swept and watered, the lamps were trimmed, fuel was heaped upon the fire; and the warehouse was as snug and warm and dry and bright a ball-room as you would desire to see upon a winter's night.

In came a fiddler with a music-book, and went up to the lofty desk, and made an orchestra of it, and tuned like fifty stomach-aches. In came Mrs. Fezziwig, one vast substantial smile. In came the three Miss Fezziwigs, beaming and lovable. In came the six young followers whose hearts they broke. In came all the young men and women employed in the business. In came the housemaid, with her cousin the baker. In came the cook, with her brother's particular friend the milkman. In they all came one after another; some shyly, some boldly, some gracefully, some awkwardly, some pushing, some pulling; in they all came, anyhow and everyhow. Away they all went, twenty couple at once; hands half round and back again the other way; down the middle and up again; round and round in various stages of affectionate grouping; old top couple always turning up in the wrong place; new top couple starting off again, as soon as they got there; all top couples at last, and not a bottom one to help them. When this result was brought about, old Fezziwig, clapping his hands to stop the dance, cried out, "Well done!" and the fiddler plunged his hot face into a pot of porter especially provided for that purpose.

There were more dances, and there were forfeits, and more dances, and there was cake, and there was negus, and there was a great piece of Cold Roast, and there was a great piece of Cold Boiled, and there were mince-pies, and plenty of beer. But the great effect of the evening came after the Roast and Boiled, when the fiddler struck up "Sir Roger de Coverley." Then old Fezziwig stood out to dance with Mrs. Fezziwig. Top couple, too; with a good stiff piece of work cut out for them; three or four and twenty pair of partners; people who were not to be trifled with; people who *would* dance, and had no notion of walking.

But if they had been twice as many, — four times, — old Fezziwig would have been a match for them, and so would Mrs. Fezziwig. As to *her*, she was worthy to be his partner in every sense of the term. A positive light appeared to issue from Fezziwig's calves. They shone in every part of the dance. You couldn't have predicted, at any given time, what would become of 'em next. And when old Fezziwig and Mrs. Fezziwig had gone all through the dance, — advance and retire, turn your partner, bow and courtesy, corkscrew, thread the needle, and back again to your place, — Fezziwig "cut," — cut so deftly, that he appeared to wink with his legs.

When the clock struck eleven this domestic ball broke up. Mr. and Mrs. Fezziwig took their stations, one on either side the door, and, shaking hands with every person individually as he or she went out, wished him or her a Merry Christmas. When everybody had retired but the two 'prentices, they did the same to them; and thus the cheerful voices died away, and the lads were left to their beds, which were under a counter in the back shop.

"A small matter," said the Ghost, "to make these silly folks so full of gratitude. He has spent but a few pounds of your mortal money, — three or four perhaps. Is that so much that he deserves this praise?"

"It is n't that," said Scrooge, heated by the remark, and speaking unconsciously like his former, not his latter self, — "it is n't that, Spirit. He has the power to render us happy or unhappy; to make our service light or burdensome, a pleasure or a toil. Say that his power lies in words and looks; in things so slight and insignificant that it is impossible to add and count 'em up: what then? The happiness he gives is quite as great as if it cost a fortune."

He felt the Spirit's glance, and stopped.

"What is the matter?"

"Nothing particular."

"Something, I think?"

"No, no. I should like to be able to say a word or two to my clerk just now. That 's all."

"My time grows short," observed the Spirit. "Quick!"

This was not addressed to Scrooge, or to any one whom he could see, but it produced an immediate effect. For again he saw himself. He was older now; a man in the prime of life.

He was not alone, but sat by the side of a fair young girl in a black dress, in whose eyes there were tears.

"It matters little," she said softly to Scrooge's former self. "To you, very little. Another idol has displaced me; and if it can comfort you in time to come, as I would have tried to do, I have no just cause to grieve."

"What Idol has displaced you?"

"A golden one. You fear the world too much. I

have seen your nobler aspirations fall off one by one, until the master-passion, Gain, engrosses you. Have I not?"

"What then? Even if I have grown so much wiser, what then? I am not changed towards you. Have I ever sought release from our engagement?"

"In words, no. Never."

"In what, then?"

"In a changed nature; in an altered spirit; in another atmosphere of life; another Hope as its great end. If you were free to-day, to-morrow, yesterday, can even I believe that you would choose a dowerless girl; or, choosing her, do I not know that your repentance and regret would surely follow? I do; and I release you. With a full heart, for the love of him you once were."

"Spirit! remove me from this place."

"I told you these were shadows of the things that have been," said the Ghost. "That they are what they are, do not blame me!"

"Remove me!" Scrooge exclaimed. "I cannot bear it! Leave me! Take me back. Haunt me no longer!"

As he struggled with the Spirit he was conscious of being exhausted, and overcome by an irresistible drowsiness; and, further, of being in his own bedroom. He had barely time to reel to bed before he sank into a heavy sleep.

STAVE THREE

THE SECOND OF THE THREE SPIRITS

SCROOGE awoke in his own bedroom. There was no doubt about that. But it and his own adjoining sitting-room, into which he shuffled in his slippers, attracted by a great light there, had undergone a surprising transformation. The walls and ceiling were so hung with living green, that it looked a perfect grove. The leaves of holly, mistletoe, and ivy reflected back the light, as if so many little mirrors had been scattered there; and such a mighty blaze went roaring up the chimney, as that petrifaction of a hearth had never known in Scrooge's time, or Marley's, or for many and many a winter season gone. Heaped upon the floor, to form a kind of throne, were turkeys, geese, game, brawn, great joints of meat, sucking pigs, long wreaths of sausages, mince-pies, plum-puddings, barrels of oysters, red-hot chestnuts, cherry-cheeked apples, juicy oranges, luscious pears, immense twelfth-cakes, and great bowls of punch. In easy state upon this couch there sat a Giant glorious to see; who bore a glowing torch, in shape not unlike Plenty's horn, and who raised it high to shed its light on Scrooge, as he came peeping round the door.

"Come in, — come in! and know me better, man! I am the Ghost of Christmas Present. Look upon me! You have never seen the like of me before!"

"Never."

"Have never walked forth with the younger members or my family; meaning (for I am very young) my elder brothers born in these later years?" pursued the Phantom.

"I don't think I have, I am afraid I have not. Have you had many brothers, Spirit?"

"More than eighteen hundred."

"A tremendous family to provide for! Spirit, conduct me where you will. I went forth last night on compulsion, and I learnt a lesson which is working now. To-night, if you have aught to teach me, let me profit by it."

"Touch my robe!"

Scrooge did as he was told, and held it fast.

The room and its contents all vanished instantly, and they stood in the city streets upon a snowy Christmas morning.

Scrooge and the Ghost passed on, invisible, straight to Scrooge's clerk's; and on the threshold of the door the Spirit smiled, and stopped to bless Bob Cratchit's dwelling with the sprinklings of his torch. Think of that! Bob had but fifteen "Bob"[1] a week himself; he pocketed on Saturdays but fifteen copies of his Christian name; and yet the Ghost of Christmas Present blessed his four-roomed house!

Then up rose Mrs. Cratchit, Cratchit's wife, dressed out but poorly in a twice-turned gown, but brave in ribbons, which are cheap and make a goodly show for sixpence; and she laid the cloth, assisted by Belinda Cratchit, second of her daughters, also brave in ribbons; while Master Peter Cratchit plunged a fork into the saucepan of potatoes, and, getting the corners of his monstrous shirt-collar (Bob's private property, conferred upon his son and heir in honor of the day) into his mouth, rejoiced to find himself so gallantly attired, and yearned to show his linen in the fashionable Parks. And now two smaller Cratchits, boy and girl, came tearing in, screaming that outside the baker's they had smelt the goose, and known it for their own; and, basking in luxurious thoughts of sage and onion, these young Cratchits danced about the table, and exalted Master Peter Cratchit to the skies, while he (not proud, although his collars nearly choked him) blew the fire, until the slow potatoes, bubbling up, knocked loudly at the saucepan-lid to be let out and peeled.

---

[1] "Bob" is English slang for "shilling."

"What has ever got your precious father, then?" said Mrs. Cratchit. "And your brother Tiny Tim! And Martha warn't as late last Christmas day by half an hour!"

"Here's Martha, mother!" said a girl, appearing as she spoke.

"Here's Martha, mother!" cried the two young Cratchits. "Hurrah! There's *such* a goose, Martha!"

"Why, bless your heart alive, my dear, how late you are?" said Mrs. Cratchit, kissing her a dozen times, and taking off her shawl and bonnet for her.

"We'd a deal of work to finish up last night," replied the girl, "and had to clear away this morning, mother!"

"Well! Never mind so long as you are come," said Mrs. Cratchit. "Sit ye down before the fire, my dear, and have a warm, Lord bless ye!"

"No, no! There's father coming," cried the two young Cratchits, who were everywhere at once. "Hide, Martha, hide!"

So Martha hid herself, and in came little Bob, the father, with at least three feet of comforter, exclusive of the fringe, hanging down before him; and his threadbare clothes darned up and brushed, to look seasonable; and Tiny Tim upon his shoulder. Alas for Tiny Tim, he bore a little crutch, and had his limbs supported by an iron frame!

"Why, where's our Martha?" cried Bob Cratchit, looking round.

"Not coming," said Mrs. Cratchit.

"Not coming!" said Bob, with a sudden declension in his high spirits; for he had been Tim's blood-horse all the way from church, and had come home rampant, — "not coming upon Christmas day!"

Martha didn't like to see him disappointed, if it were

only in joke; so she came out prematurely from behind the closet door, and ran into his arms, while the two young Cratchits hustled Tiny Tim, and bore him off into the wash-house that he might hear the pudding singing in the copper.

"And how did little Tim behave?" asked Mrs. Cratchit, when she had rallied Bob on his credulity, and Bob had hugged his daughter to his heart's content.

"As good as gold," said Bob, "and better. Somehow he gets thoughtful, sitting by himself so much, and thinks the strangest things you ever heard. He told me, coming home, that he hoped the people saw him in the church, because he was a cripple, and it might be pleasant to them to remember, upon Christmas day, who made lame beggars walk and blind men see."

Bob's voice was tremulous when he told them this, and trembled more when he said that Tiny Tim was growing strong and hearty.

His active little crutch was heard upon the floor, and back came Tiny Tim before another word was spoken, escorted by his brother and sister to his stool beside the fire; and while Bob, turning up his cuffs, — as if, poor fellow, they were capable of being made more shabby, — compounded some hot mixture in a jug with gin and lemons, and stirred it round and round and put it on the hob to simmer, Master Peter and the two ubiquitous young Cratchits went to fetch the goose, with which they soon returned in high procession.[1]

Mrs. Cratchit made the gravy (ready beforehand in a little saucepan) hissing hot; Master Peter mashed the potatoes with incredible vigor; Miss Belinda sweetened up the apple-sauce; Martha dusted the hot plates; Bob took Tiny Tim beside him in a tiny corner at the table;

[1] The goose had been cooked in the baker's oven, for economy.

the two young Cratchits set chairs for everybody, not forgetting themselves, and mounting guard upon their posts, crammed spoons into their mouths, lest they should shriek for goose before their turn came to be helped. At last the dishes were set on, and grace was said. It was succeeded by a breathless pause, as Mrs. Cratchit, looking slowly all along the carving-knife, prepared to plunge it in the breast; but when she did, and when the long-expected gush of stuffing issued forth, one murmur of delight arose all round the board, and even Tiny Tim, excited by the two young Cratchits, beat on the table with the handle of his knife, and feebly cried, Hurrah!

There never was such a goose. Bob said he did n't believe there ever was such a goose cooked. Its tenderness and flavor, size and cheapness, were the themes of universal admiration. Eked out by apple-sauce and mashed potatoes, it was a sufficient dinner for the whole family; indeed, as Mrs. Cratchit said with great delight (surveying one small atom of a bone upon the dish), they had n't ate it all at last! Yet every one had had enough, and the youngest Cratchits in particular were steeped in sage and onion to the eyebrows! But now, the plates being changed by Miss Belinda, Mrs. Cratchit left the room alone, — too nervous to bear witnesses, — to take the pudding up, and bring it in.

Suppose it should not be done enough! Suppose it should break in turning out! Suppose somebody should have got over the wall of the back yard, and stolen it, while they were merry with the goose, — a supposition at which the two young Cratchits became livid! All sorts of horrors were supposed.

Hallo! A great deal of steam! The pudding was out of the copper. A smell like a washing-day! That was the cloth. A smell like an eating-house and a pastry-cook's next door to each other, with a laundress's next door to that! That was the pudding! In half a minute Mrs. Cratchit entered, — flushed but smiling proudly, — with the pudding, like a speckled cannon-ball, so hard and firm, blazing in half of half a quartern of ignited brandy, and bedight with Christmas holly stuck into the top.

O, a wonderful pudding! Bob Cratchit said, and calmly, too, that he regarded it as the greatest success achieved by Mrs. Cratchit since their marriage. Mrs. Cratchit said that now the weight was off her mind, she would confess she had had her doubts about the quantity of flour. Everybody had something to say about it, but nobody said or thought it was at all a small pudding for a large family. Any Cratchit would have blushed to hint at such a thing.

At last the dinner was all done, the cloth was cleared, the hearth swept, and the fire made up. The compound in the jug being tasted and considered perfect, apples and oranges were put upon the table, and a shovelful of chestnuts on the fire.

Then all the Cratchit family drew round the hearth, in what Bob Cratchit called a circle, and at Bob Cratchit's elbow stood the family display of glass, — two tumblers, and a custard-cup without a handle.

These held the hot stuff from the jug, however, as well as golden goblets would have done; and Bob served it out with beaming looks, while the chestnuts on the fire sputtered and crackled noisily. Then Bob proposed : —

"A Merry Christmas to us all, my dears. God bless us!"

Which all the family re-echoed.

"God bless us every one!" said Tiny Tim, the last of all.

He sat very close to his father's side, upon his little stool. Bob held his withered little hand in his, as if he loved the child, and wished to keep him by his side, and dreaded that he might be taken from him.

Scrooge raised his head speedily, on hearing his own name.

"Mr. Scrooge!" said Bob; "I'll give you Mr. Scrooge, the Founder of the Feast!"

"The Founder of the Feast, indeed!" cried Mrs. Cratchit, reddening. "I wish I had him here. I'd give him a piece of my mind to feast upon, and I hope he'd have a good appetite for it."

"My dear," said Bob, "the children! Christmas day."

"It should be Christmas day, I am sure," said she, "on which one drinks the health of such an odious, stingy, hard, unfeeling man as Mr. Scrooge. You know he is, Robert! Nobody knows it better than you do, poor fellow!"

"My dear," was Bob's mild answer, "Christmas day."

"I'll drink his health for your sake and the day's," said Mrs. Cratchit, "not for his. Long life to him. A merry Christmas and a happy New Year! He'll be very merry and very happy, I have no doubt!"

The children drank the toast after her. It was the first of their proceedings which had no heartiness in it. Tiny Tim drank it last of all, but he didn't care two-pence for it. Scrooge was the Ogre of the family. The mention of his name cast a dark shadow on the party, which was not dispelled for full five minutes.

After it had passed away, they were ten times merrier than before, from the mere relief of Scrooge the Baleful being done with. Bob Cratchit told them how he had a situation in his eye for Master Peter, which would bring in, if obtained, full five and sixpence weekly,

The two young Cratchits laughed tremendously at the idea of Peter's being a man of business; and Peter himself looked thoughtfully at the fire from between his collars, as if he were deliberating what particular investments he should favor when he came into the receipt of that bewildering income. Martha, who was a poor apprentice at a milliner's, then told them what kind of work she had to do, and how many hours she worked at a stretch, and how she meant to lie abed to-morrow morning for a good long rest; to-morrow being a holiday she passed at home. Also how she had seen a countess and a lord some days before, and how the lord " was much about as tall as Peter "; at which Peter pulled up his collars so high that you couldn't have seen his head if you had been there. All this time the chestnuts and the jug went round and round; and by and by they had a song, about a lost child travelling in the snow, from Tiny Tim, who had a plaintive little voice, and sang it very well indeed.

There was nothing of high mark in this. They were not a handsome family; they were not well dressed; their shoes were far from being water-proof; their clothes were scanty; and Peter might have known, and very likely did, the inside of a pawnbroker's. But they were happy, grateful, pleased with one another, and contented with the time; and when they faded, and looked happier yet in the bright sprinklings of the Spirit's torch at parting, Scrooge had his eye upon them, and especially on Tiny Tim, until the last.

It was a great surprise to Scrooge, as this scene vanished, to hear a hearty laugh. It was a much greater surprise to Scrooge to recognize it as his own nephew's, and to find himself in a bright, dry, gleaming room, with the Spirit standing smiling by his side, and looking at that same nephew.

It is a fair, even-handed, noble adjustment of things, that while there is infection in disease and sorrow, there is nothing in the world so irresistibly contagious as laughter and good-humor. When Scrooge's nephew laughed, Scrooge's niece by marriage laughed as heartily as he. And their assembled friends, being not a bit behindhand, laughed out lustily.

" He said that Christmas was a humbug, as I live !" cried Scrooge's nephew. " He believed it too !"

" More shame for him, Fred !" said Scrooge's niece, indignantly. Bless those women ! they never do anything by halves. They are always in earnest.

She was very pretty, exceedingly pretty. With a dimpled, surprised-looking, capital face ; a ripe little mouth that seemed made to be kissed, — as no doubt it was ; all kinds of good little dots about her chin, that melted into one another when she laughed ; and the sunniest pair of eyes you ever saw in any little creature's head. Altogether she was what you would have called provoking, but satisfactory, too. O, perfectly satisfactory !

" He 's a comical old fellow," said Scrooge's nephew, " that 's the truth ; and not so pleasant as he might be. However, his offences carry their own punishment, and I have nothing to say against him. Who suffers by his ill whims ? Himself, always. Here he takes it into his head to dislike us, and he won't come and dine with us. What 's the consequence ? He don't lose much of a dinner."

" Indeed, I think he loses a very good dinner," interrupted Scrooge's niece. Everybody else said the same, and they must be allowed to have been competent judges, because they had just had dinner ; and, with the dessert upon the table, were clustered round the fire, by lamplight.

"Well, I am very glad to hear it," said Scrooge's nephew, "because I have n't any great faith in these young housekeepers. What do *you* say, Topper?"

Topper clearly had his eye on one of Scrooge's niece's sisters, for he answered that a bachelor was a wretched outcast, who had no right to express an opinion on the subject. Whereat Scrooge's niece's sister — the plump one with the lace tucker, not the one with the roses — blushed.

After tea they had some music. For they were a musical family, and knew what they were about, when they sung a Glee or Catch, I can assure you, — especially Topper, who could growl away in the bass like a good one, and never swell the large veins in his forehead, or get red in the face over it.

But they did n't devote the whole evening to music. After a while they played at forfeits; for it is good to be children sometimes, and never better than at Christmas, when its mighty Founder was a child himself. There was first a game at blind-man's-buff, though. And I no more believe Topper was really blinded than I believe he had eyes in his boots. Because the way in which he went after that plump sister in the lace tucker was an outrage on the credulity of human nature. Knocking down the fire-irons, tumbling over the chairs, bumping up against the piano, smothering himself among the curtains, wherever she went there went he! He always knew where the plump sister was. He would n't catch anybody else. If you had fallen up against him, as some of them did, and stood there, he would have made a feint of endeavoring to seize you, which would have been an affront to your understanding, and would instantly have sidled off in the direction of the plump sister.

"Here is a new game," said Scrooge. "One half-hour, Spirit, only one!"

It was a Game called Yes and No, where Scrooge's nephew had to think of something, and the rest must find out what; he only answering to their questions yes or no, as the case was. The fire of questioning to which he was exposed elicited from him that he was thinking of an animal, a live animal, rather a disagreeable animal, a savage animal, an animal that growled and grunted sometimes, and talked sometimes, and lived in London, and walked about the streets, and was n't made a show of, and was n't led by anybody, and did n't live in a menagerie, and was never killed in a market, and was not a horse, or an ass, or a cow, or a bull, or a tiger, or a dog, or a pig, or a cat, or a bear. At every new question put to him, this nephew burst into a fresh roar of laughter; and was so inexpressibly tickled, that he was obliged to get up off the sofa and stamp. At last the plump sister cried out,—

"I have found it out! I know what it is, Fred! I know what it is!"

"What is it?" cried Fred.

"It 's your uncle Scro-o-o-o-oge!"

Which it certainly was. Admiration was the universal sentiment, though some objected that the reply to "Is it a bear?" ought to have been "Yes."

Uncle Scrooge had imperceptibly become so gay and light of heart, that he would have drunk to the unconscious company in an inaudible speech. But the whole scene passed off in the breath of the last word spoken by his nephew; and he and the Spirit were again upon their travels.

Much they saw, and far they went, and many homes they visited, but always with a happy end. The Spirit

stood beside sick-beds, and they were cheerful; on foreign lands, and they were close at home; by struggling
men, and they were patient in their greater hope; by
poverty, and it was rich.   In almshouse, hospital, and
jail, in misery's every refuge, where vain man in his little
brief authority had not made fast the door, and barred
the Spirit out, he left his blessing, and taught Scrooge his
precepts.   Suddenly, as they stood together in an open
place; the bell struck twelve.

Scrooge looked about him for the Ghost, and saw it
no more.   As the last stroke ceased to vibrate, he remembered the prediction of old Jacob Marley, and, lifting up his eyes, beheld a solemn Phantom, draped and
hooded, coming like a mist along the ground towards
him.

STAVE FOUR

THE LAST OF THE SPIRITS

THE Phantom slowly, gravely, silently approached.
When it came near him, Scrooge bent down upon his
knee; for in the air through which this Spirit moved it
seemed to scatter gloom and mystery.

It was shrouded in a deep black garment, which concealed its head, its face, its form, and left nothing of it
visible save one outstretched hand.   He knew no more,
for the Spirit neither spoke nor moved.

"I am in the presence of the Ghost of Christmas Yet
To Come?   Ghost of the Future!   I fear you more
than any spectre I have seen.   But as I know your purpose is to do me good, and as I hope to live to be another man from what I was, I am prepared to bear you
company, and do it with a thankful heart.   Will you not
speak to me?"

It gave him no reply. The hand was pointed straight before them.

"Lead on! Lead on! The night is waning fast, and it is precious time to me, I know. Lead on, Spirit!"

They scarcely seemed to enter the city; for the city rather seemed to spring up about them. But there they were in the heart of it; on 'Change, amongst the merchants.

The Spirit stopped beside one little knot of business men. Observing that the hand was pointed to them, Scrooge advanced to listen to their talk.

"No," said a great fat man with a monstrous chin, "I don't know much about it either way. I only know he's dead."

"When did he die?" inquired another.

"Last night, I believe."

"Why, what was the matter with him? I thought he'd never die."

"God knows," said the first, with a yawn.

"What has he done with his money?" asked a red-faced gentleman.

"I have n't heard," said the man with the large chin. "Company, perhaps. He has n't left it to me. That's all I know. By, by!"

Scrooge was at first inclined to be surprised that the Spirit should attach importance to conversation apparently so trivial; but feeling assured that it must have some hidden purpose, he set himself to consider what it was likely to be. It could scarcely be supposed to have any bearing on the death of Jacob, his old partner, for that was Past, and this Ghost's province was the Future.

He looked about in that very place for his own image; but another man stood in his accustomed corner, and though the clock pointed to his usual time of day for being there, he saw no likeness of himself among the multitudes that poured in through the Porch. It gave him little surprise, however; for he had been revolving in his mind a change of life, and he thought and hoped he saw his new-born resolutions carried out in this.

They left this busy scene, and went into an obscure part of the town, to a low shop where iron, old rags, bottles, bones, and greasy offal were bought. A gray-haired rascal, of great age, sat smoking his pipe.

Scrooge and the Phantom came into the presence of this man, just as a woman with a heavy bundle slunk into the shop. But she had scarcely entered, when another woman, similarly laden, came in too; and she was closely followed by a man in faded black. After a short period of blank astonishment, in which the old man with the pipe had joined them, they all three burst into a laugh.

"Let the charwoman alone to be the first!" cried she who had entered first. "Let the laundress alone to be the second; and let the undertaker's man alone to be the third. Look here, old Joe, here's a chance! If we have n't all three met here without meaning it!"

"You could n't have met in better place. You were made free of it long ago, you know; and the other two ain't strangers. What have you got to sell? What have you got to sell?"

"Half a minute's patience, Joe, and you shall see."

"What odds then! What odds, Mrs. Dilber?" said the woman. "Every person has a right to take care of themselves. *He* always did! Who's the worse for the loss of a few things like these? Not a dead man, I suppose."

Mrs. Dilber, whose manner was remarkable for general propitiation, said, " No, indeed, ma'am."

" If he wanted to keep 'em after he was dead, a wicked old screw, why wasn't he natural in his lifetime? If he had been, he'd have had somebody to look after him when he was struck with Death, instead of lying gasping out his last there, alone by himself."

" It's the truest word that ever was spoke; it's a judgment on him."

" I wish it was a little heavier judgment, and it should have been, you may depend upon it, if I could have laid my hands on anything else. Open that bundle, old Joe, and let me know the value of it. Speak out plain. I'm not afraid to be the first, nor afraid for them to see it."

Joe went down on his knees for the greater convenience of opening the bundle, and dragged out a large and heavy roll of some dark stuff.

" What do you call this? Bed-curtains! "

" Ah! Bed-curtains! Don't drop that oil upon the blankets, now."

" *His* blankets? "

" Whose else's, do you think? He isn't likely to take cold without 'em, I dare say. Ah! You may look through that shirt till your eyes ache; but you won't find a hole in it, nor a threadbare place. It is the best he had, and a fine one too. They'd have wasted it by dressing him up in it, if it hadn't been for me."

Scrooge listened to this dialogue in horror.

" Spirit! I see, I see. The case of this unhappy man might be my own. My life tends that way now. Merciful Heaven, what is this? "

The scene had changed, and now he almost touched a bare, uncurtained bed. A pale light, rising in the outer air, fell straight upon this bed; and on it, unwatched, unwept, uncared for, was the body of this plundered unknown man.

"Spirit, let me see some tenderness connected with a death, or this dark chamber, Spirit, will be forever present to me."

The Ghost conducted him to poor Bob Cratchit's house, — the dwelling he had visited before, — and found the mother and the children seated round the fire.

Quiet. Very quiet. The noisy little Cratchits were as still as statues in one corner, and sat looking up at Peter, who had a book before him. The mother and her daughters were engaged in needlework. But surely they were very quiet!

"'And he took a child, and set him in the midst of them.'"

Where had Scrooge heard those words? He had not dreamed them. The boy must have read them out, as he and the Spirit crossed the threshold. Why did he not go on?

The mother laid her work upon the table, and put her hand up to her face.

"The color hurts my eyes," she said.

The color? Ah, poor Tiny Tim!

"They're better now again. It makes them weak by candle-light; and I wouldn't show weak eyes to your father when he comes home, for the world. It must be near his time."

"Past it, rather," Peter answered, shutting up his book. "But I think he has walked a little slower than he used, these few last evenings, mother."

"I have known him walk with — I have known him walk with Tiny Tim upon his shoulder, very fast indeed."

"And so have I," cried Peter. "Often."

"And so have I," exclaimed another. So had all.

"But he was very light to carry, and his father loved him so, that it was no trouble, — no trouble. And there is your father at the door!"

She hurried out to meet him; and little Bob in his comforter — he had need of it, poor fellow — came in. His tea was ready for him on the hob, and they all tried who should help him to it most. Then the two young Cratchits got upon his knees and laid, each child, a little cheek against his face, as if they said, "Don't mind it, father. Don't be grieved!"

Bob was very cheerful with them, and spoke pleasantly to all the family. He looked at the work upon the table, and praised the industry and speed of Mrs. Cratchit and the girls. They would be done long before Sunday, he said.

"Sunday! You went to-day, then, Robert?"

"Yes, my dear," returned Bob. "I wish you could have gone. It would have done you good to see how green a place it is. But you'll see it often. I promised him that I would walk there on a Sunday. My little, little child! My little child!"

He broke down all at once. He couldn't help it. If he could have helped it, he and the child would have been farther apart, perhaps, than they were.

"Spectre," said Scrooge, "something informs me that our parting moment is at hand. I know it, but I know not how. Tell me what man that was, with the covered face, whom we saw lying dead?"

The Ghost of Christmas Yet To Come conveyed him to a dismal, wretched, ruinous churchyard.

The Spirit stood among the graves, and pointed down to One.

"Before I draw nearer to that stone to which you

point, answer me one question. Are these the shadows of the things that Will be, or are they shadows of the things that May be only?"

Still the Ghost pointed downward to the grave by which it stood.

"Men's courses will foreshadow certain ends, to which, if persevered in, they must lead. But if the courses be departed from, the ends will change. Say it is thus with what you show me!"

The Spirit was immovable as ever.

Scrooge crept towards it, trembling as he went; and, following the finger, read upon the stone of the neglected grave his own name,— EBENEZER SCROOGE.

"Am *I* that man who lay upon the bed? No, Spirit! O no, no! Spirit! hear me! I am not the man I was. I will not be the man I must have been but for this intercourse. Why show me this, if I am past all hope? Assure me that I yet may change these shadows you have shown me by an altered life."

For the first time the kind hand faltered.

"I will honor Christmas in my heart, and try to keep it all the year. I will live in the Past, the Present, and the Future. The Spirits of all three shall strive within me. I will not shut out the lessons that they teach. O, tell me I may sponge away the writing on this stone!"

Holding up his hands in one last prayer to have his fate reversed, he saw an alteration in the Phantom's hood and dress. It shrunk, collapsed, and dwindled down into a bedpost.

Yes, and the bedpost was his own. The bed was his own, the room was his own. Best and happiest of all, the Time before him was his own, to make amends in!

He was checked in his transports by the churches ringing out the lustiest peals he had ever heard.

Running to the window, he opened it, and put out his head. No fog, no mist, no night; clear, bright, stirring, golden day!

"What's to-day?" cried Scrooge, calling downward to a boy in Sunday clothes, who perhaps had loitered in to look about him.

"Eh?"

"What's to-day, my fine fellow?"

"To-day! Why, CHRISTMAS DAY."

"It's Christmas day! I haven't missed it. Hallo, my fine fellow!"

"Hallo!"

"Do you know the Poulterer's, in the next street but one, at the corner?"

"I should hope I did."

"An intelligent boy! A remarkable boy! Do you know whether they've sold the prize Turkey that was hanging up there? Not the little prize Turkey, — the big one?"

"What, the one as big as me?"

"What a delightful boy! It's a pleasure to talk to him. Yes, my buck!"

"It's hanging there now."

"Is it? Go and buy it."

"Walk-ER!" exclaimed the boy.

"No, no, I am in earnest. Go and buy it, and tell 'em to bring it here, that I may give them the direction where to take it. Come back with the man, and I'll give you a shilling. Come back with him in less than five minutes, and I'll give you half a crown!"

The boy was off like a shot.

"I'll send it to Bob Cratchit's! He sha'n't know who sends it. It's twice the size of Tiny Tim. Joe Miller never made such a joke as sending it to Bob's will be!"

The hand in which he wrote the address was not a steady one; but write it he did, somehow, and went down stairs to open the street door, ready for the coming of the poulterer's man.

It *was* a Turkey! He never could have stood upon his legs, that bird. He would have snapped 'em short off in a minute, like sticks of sealing-wax.

Scrooge dressed himself "all in his best," and at last got out into the streets. The people were by this time pouring forth, as he had seen them with the Ghost of Christmas Present; and, walking with his hands behind him, Scrooge regarded every one with a delighted smile. He looked so irresistibly pleasant, in a word, that three or four good-humored fellows said, "Good morning, sir! A merry Christmas to you!" and Scrooge said often afterwards, that, of all the blithe sounds he had ever heard, those were the blithest in his ears.

In the afternoon, he turned his steps towards his nephew's house.

He passed the door a dozen times, before he had the courage to go up and knock. But he made a dash, and did it.

"Is your master at home, my dear?" said Scrooge to the girl. Nice girl! Very.

"Yes, sir."

"Where is he, my love?"

"He's in the dining-room, sir, along with mistress."

"He knows me," said Scrooge, with his hand already on the dining-room lock. "I'll go in here, my dear."

"Fred!"

"Why, bless my soul!" cried Fred, "who's that?"

"It's I. Your uncle Scrooge. I have come to dinner. Will you let me in, Fred?"

Let him in! It is a mercy he did n't shake his arm

off. He was at home in five minutes. Nothing could be heartier. His niece looked just the same. So did Topper when *he* came. So did the plump sister when *she* came. So did every one when *they* came. Wonderful party, wonderful games, wonderful unanimity, won-der-ful happiness!

But he was early at the office next morning. O, he was early there! If he could only be there first, and catch Bob Cratchit coming late! That was the thing he had set his heart upon.

And he did it. The clock struck nine. No Bob. A quarter past. No Bob. Bob was full eighteen minutes and a half behind his time. Scrooge sat with his door wide open, that he might see him come into the Tank.

Bob's hat was off before he opened the door; his comforter too. He was on his stool in a jiffy; driving away with his pen, as if he were trying to overtake nine o'clock.

"Hallo!" growled Scrooge in his accustomed voice, as near as he could feign it. "What do you mean by coming here at this time of day?"

"I am very sorry, sir. I *am* behind my time."

"You are? Yes. I think you are. Step this way, if you please."

"It's only once a year, sir. It shall not be repeated. I was making rather merry yesterday, sir."

"Now, I'll tell you what, my friend. I am not going to stand this sort of thing any longer. And therefore," Scrooge continued, leaping from his stool, and giving Bob such a dig in the waistcoat that he staggered back into the Tank again, — "and therefore I am about to raise your salary!"

Bob trembled, and got a little nearer to the ruler.

"A merry Christmas, Bob!" said Scrooge, with an

earnestness that could not be mistaken, as he clapped him on the back. " A merrier Christmas, Bob, my good fellow, than I have given you for many a year! I'll raise your salary, and endeavor to assist your struggling family, and we will discuss your affairs this very afternoon, over a Christmas bowl of smoking bishop, Bob! Make up the fires, and buy a second coal-scuttle before you dot another i, Bob Cratchit! "

Scrooge was better than his word. He did it all, and infinitely more; and to Tiny Tim, who did NOT die, he was a second father. He became as good a friend, as good a master, and as good a man as the good old city knew, or any other good old city, town, or borough in the good old world. Some people laughed to see the alteration in him; but his own heart laughed, and that was quite enough for him.

He had no further intercourse with spirits, but lived in that respect upon the total-abstinence principle ever afterward; and it was always said of him, that he knew how to keep Christmas well, if any man alive possessed the knowledge. May that be truly said of us, and all of us! And so, as Tiny Tim observed, God bless us, every one!

VII

A PRINCESS'S TRAGEDY

Each succeeding section of his work seems to bloom forth, opening in a splendid flower, like an expanding rose. His methods are mechanical to a considerable extent, like the methods of verse; but he attains great variety, and holds the reader by the tender feeling that is ever springing up afresh in his heart, to be poured into his characters. With Thackeray, all is refinement and polish, all is graceful, easy movement; his humor is whimsical, like that of the essayists, never sentimental; and he is ever restrained, as a gentleman should be. "A Princess's Tragedy" is as free from exaggeration as "Patient Griselda" or "Aladdin;" but Thackeray is deliberate in his withholding, while the earlier writers were ignorant of the art of expansion. As a result, we seem to see all that is left unexpressed and much more. This is because Thackeray saw it, and that which he did not describe still left its impress upon what he did. In Thackeray, words seemed to gain atmospheres and aromas of their own, due to the delicate and suggestive turning of his phrases. Dickens's method was more obvious, more striking, and hence more attractive, except to the judicious few. The refinements of Thackeray's style are more difficult to describe, and can be mastered and imitated only by those who are especially sensitive to delicate shades of meanings in words.

In "A Princess's Tragedy" we find none of the light and winning humor which characterizes "Vanity Fair," for example; and if we compare the two we shall easily perceive the quality which made that book so much more popular than "Barry Lyndon." The story has all the elements of the blood-and-thunder dime novel, but Thackeray's reserve, as well as his art, raises it into a drama awful and majestic.

A PRINCESS'S TRAGEDY

ROSINA of Liliengarten it was, indeed — such a full blown Rosina I have seldom seen. I found her in a decent first-floor in Leicester Fields (the poor soul fell much lower afterwards) drinking tea, which had somehow a very strong smell of brandy in it; and after salutations, which would be more tedious to recount than they were to perform, and after further straggling conversation, she gave me briefly the following narrative of the events in X——, which I may well entitle the "Princess's Tragedy."

"You remember Monsieur de Geldern, the Police Minister. He was of Dutch extraction, and, what is more, of a family of Dutch Jews. Although everybody was aware of this blot in his scutcheon, he was mortally angry if ever his origin was suspected; and made up for his father's errors by outrageous professions of religion, and the most austere practices of devotion. He visited church every morning, confessed once a week, and hated Jews and Protestants as much as an inquisitor could do. He never lost an opportunity of proving his sincerity, by persecuting one or the other whenever occasion fell in his way.

"He hated the princess mortally; for her highness in

some whim had insulted him with his origin, caused pork
to be removed from before him at table, or injured him
in some such silly way; and he had a violent animosity
to the old Baron de Magny, both in his capacity of
Protestant, and because the latter in some haughty mood
had publicly turned his back upon him as a sharper and
a spy. Perpetual quarrels were taking place between
them in council; where it was only the presence of his
august masters that restrained the baron from publicly
and frequently expressing the contempt which he felt for
the officer of police.

"Thus Geldern had hatred as one reason for ruining
the princess, and it is my belief he had a stronger motive
still — interest. You remember whom the duke married,
after the death of his first wife? — a princess of the
house of F——. Geldern built his fine palace two
years after, and, as I feel convinced, with the money which
was paid to him by the F—— family for forwarding the
match.

"To go to Prince Victor, and report to his highness a
case which everybody knew, was not by any means
Geldern's desire. He knew the man would be ruined
forever in the prince's estimation who carried him intelligence so disastrous. His aim, therefore, was, to leave
the matter to explain itself to his highness; and, when
the time was ripe, he cast about for a means of carrying
his point. He had spies in the houses of the elder and
younger Magny; but this you know, of course, from your
experience of Continental customs. We had all spies
over each other. Your black (Zamor, I think, was his
name) used to give me reports every morning; and I
used to entertain the dear old duke with stories of you
and your uncle practising piquet and dice in the morning, and with your quarrels and intrigues. We levied

similar contributions on everybody in X——, to amuse
the dear old man.   Monsieur de Magny's valet used to
report both to me and Monsieur de Geldern.

"I knew of the fact of the emerald being in pawn;
and it was out of my exchequer that the poor princess
drew the funds which were spent upon the odious Löwe,
and the still more worthless young chevalier.   How the
princess could trust the latter as she persisted in doing,
is beyond my comprehension; but there is no infatuation like that of a woman in love, and you will remark,
my dear Monsieur de Balibari, that our sex generally fix
upon a bad man."

"Not always, Madam," I interposed; "your humble
servant has created many such attachments."

"I do not see that that affects the truth of the proposi-
tion," said the old lady dryly, and continued her narrative.
"The Jew who held the emerald had had many dealings
with the princess, and at last was offered a bribe of such
magnitude, that he determined to give up the pledge.
He committed the inconceivable imprudence of bringing
the emerald with him to X——, and waited on Magny,
who was provided by the princess with the money to re-
deem the pledge, and was actually ready to pay it.

"Their interview took place in Magny's own apartments, when his valet overheard every word of their
conversation.   The young man, who was always utterly
careless of money when it was in his possession, was so
easy in offering it, that Löwe rose in his demands, and
had the conscience to ask double the sum for which he
had previously stipulated.

"At this the chevalier lost all patience, fell on the
wretch, and was for killing him; when the opportune
valet rushed in and saved him.   The man had heard
every word of the conversation between the disputants,

and the Jew ran flying with terror into his arms; and Magny, a quick and passionate but not a violent man, bade the servant lead the villain down stairs, and thought no more of him.

"Perhaps he was not sorry to be rid of him, and to have in his possession a large sum of money, four thousand ducats, with which he could tempt fortune once more; as you know he did at your table that night."

"Your ladyship went halves, Madam," said I; "and you know how little I was the better for my winnings."

"The man conducted the trembling Israelite out of the palace, and no sooner had seen him lodged at the house of one of his brethren, where he was accustomed to put up, than he went away to the office of his Excellency the Minister of Police, and narrated every word of the conversation which had taken place between the Jew and his master.

"Geldern expressed the greatest satisfaction at his spy's prudence and fidelity. He gave him a purse of twenty ducats, and promised to provide for him handsomely: as great men do sometimes promise to reward their instruments; but you, Monsieur de Balibari, know how seldom those promises are kept. 'Now, go and find out,' said Monsieur de Geldern, 'at what time the Israelite proposes to return home again, or whether he will repent and take the money.' The man went on this errand. Meanwhile, to make matters sure, Geldern arranged a play-party at my house, inviting you thither with your bank, as you may remember; and finding means, at the same time, to let Maxime de Magny know that there was to be faro at Madame de Liliengarten's. It was an invitation the poor fellow never neglected."

I remembered the facts, and listened on, amazed at the artifice of the infernal Minister of Police.

"The spy came back from his message to Löwe, and stated that he had made inquiries among the servants of the house where the Heidelberg banker lodged, and that it was the latter's intention to leave X——that afternoon. He travelled by himself, riding an old horse, exceedingly humbly attired, after the manner of his people.

"'Johann,' said the Minister, clapping the pleased spy upon the shoulder, 'I am more and more pleased with you. I have been thinking, since you left me, of your intelligence, and the faithful manner in which you have served me; and shall soon find an occasion to place you according to your merits. Which way does this Israelitish scoundrel take?'

"'He goes to R—— to-night.'

"'And must pass by the Kaiserwald. Are you a man of courage, Johann Kerner?'

"'Will your Excellency try me?' said the man, his eyes glittering: 'I served through the Seven Years' War, and was never known to fail there.'

"'Now, listen. The emerald must be taken from that Jew: in the very keeping it the scoundrel has committed high treason. To the man who brings me that emerald I swear I will give five hundred louis. You understand why it is necessary that it should be restored to her highness. I need say no more.'

"'You shall have it to-night, sir,' said the man. 'Of course your Excellency will hold me harmless in case of accident.'

"'Psha!' answered the Minister; 'I will pay you half the money beforehand; such is my confidence in you. Accident's impossible, if you take your measures properly. There are four leagues of wood; the Jew rides slowly. It will be night before he can reach, let us say, the old Powder-Mill in the wood. What's to prevent you from putting a rope across the road, and dealing with him there? Be back with me this evening at supper. If you meet any of the patrol, say "Foxes are loose," — that's the word for to-night. They will let you pass them without questions.'

"The man went off quite charmed with his commission; and when Magny was losing his money at our faro-table, his servant waylaid the Jew at the spot named the Powder-Mill in the Kaiserwald. The Jew's horse stumbled over a rope which had been placed across the road; and, as the rider fell groaning to the ground, Johann Kerner rushed out on him, masked, and pistol in hand, and demanded his money. He had no wish to kill the Jew, I believe, unless his resistance should render extreme measures necessary.

"Nor did he commit any such murder; for, as the yelling Jew roared for mercy, and his assailant menaced him with a pistol, a squad of patrol came up, and laid hold of the robber and the wounded man.

"Kerner swore an oath. 'You have come too soon,' said he to the sergeant of the police. 'Foxes are loose.' 'Some are caught,' said the sergeant, quite unconcerned; and bound the fellow's hands with the rope which he had stretched across the road to entrap the Jew. He was placed behind a policeman on a horse; Löwe was similarly accommodated, and the party thus came back into the town as the night fell.

"They were taken forthwith to the police quarter; and, as the chief happened to be there, they were examined by his Excellency in person. Both were rigorously searched; the Jew's papers and cases taken from him: the jewel was found in a private pocket. As for the spy, the Minister, looking at him angrily, said, 'Why, this is the servant of the Chevalier de Magny, one of her highness's equerries!' and without hearing a word in exculpation from the poor frightened wretch, ordered him into close confinement.

"Calling for his horse, he then rode to the prince's apartments at the palace, and asked for an instant audience. When admitted, he produced the emerald. 'This jewel,' said he, 'has been found on the person of a Heidelberg Jew, who has been here repeatedly of late, and has had many dealings with her highness's equerry, the Chevalier de Magny. This afternoon the chevalier's servant came from his master's lodgings, accompanied by the Hebrew; was heard to make inquiries as to the route the man intended to take on his way homewards; followed him, or preceded him rather, and was found in the act of rifling his victim by my police in the Kaiserwald. The man will confess nothing; but, on being searched, a large sum in gold was found on his person; and though it is with the utmost pain that I can bring myself to entertain such an opinion, and to implicate a gentleman of the character and name of Monsieur de Magny, I do submit that our duty is to have the chevalier examined relative to the affair. As Monsieur de Magny is in her highness's private service, and in her confidence, I have heard, I would not venture to apprehend him without your highness's permission.'

"The prince's master of the horse, a friend of the old Baron de Magny, who was present at the interview, no sooner heard the strange intelligence, than he hastened away to the old general, with the dreadful news of his grandson's supposed crime. Perhaps his highness himself was not unwilling that his old friend and tutor in arms should have the chance of saving his family from disgrace ; at all events, Monsieur de Hengst, the Master of the Horse, was permitted to go off to the baron undisturbed, and break to him the intelligence of the accusation pending over the unfortunate chevalier.

"It is possible that he expected some such dreadful catastrophe, for, after hearing Hengst's narrative (as the latter afterwards told me), he only said, ' Heaven's will be done ! ' for some time refused to stir a step in the matter, and then only by the solicitation of his friend, was induced to write the letter which Maxime de Magny received at our play-table.

"Whilst he was there, squandering the princess's money, a police visit was paid to his apartments, and a hundred proofs, not of his guilt with respect to the robbery, but of his guilty connection with the princess, were discovered there, — tokens of her giving, passionate letters from her, copies of his own correspondence to his young friends at Paris, — all of which the Police Minister perused, and carefully put together under seal for his highness, Prince Victor. I have no doubt he perused them, for, on delivering them to the hereditary prince, Geldern said that *in obedience to his highness's orders*, he had collected the chevalier's papers ; but he need not say that, on his honor, he (Geldern) himself had never examined the documents. His difference with Messieurs de Magny was known ; he begged his highness to employ any other official person in the judgment of the accusation brought against the young chevalier.

"All these things were going on while the chevalier was at play. A run of luck — you had great luck in those days, Monsieur de Balibari — was against him. He stayed and lost his four thousand ducats. He received his uncle's note, and, such was the infatuation of the wretched gambler, that, on receipt of it, he went down to the courtyard, where the horse was in waiting, absolutely took the money which the poor old gentleman had placed in the saddle-holsters, brought it up stairs, played it and lost it; and when he issued from the room to fly, it was too late: he was placed in arrest at the bottom of my staircase, as you were upon entering your own home.

"Even when he came in under the charge of the soldiery sent to arrest him, the old general, who was waiting, was overjoyed to see him, and flung himself into the lad's arms, and embraced him: it was said, for the first time in many years. 'He is here, gentlemen,' he sobbed out, — 'thank God he is not guilty of the robbery!' and then sank back in a chair in a burst of emotion, painful, it was said by those present, to witness on the part of a man so brave, and known to be so cold and stern.

"'Robbery!' said the young man. 'I swear before Heaven I am guilty of none!' and a scene of almost touching reconciliation passed between them, before the unhappy young man was led from the guard-house into the prison which he was destined never to quit.

"That night the duke looked over the papers which Geldern had brought to him. It was at a very early stage of the perusal, no doubt, that he gave orders for your arrest; for you were taken at midnight, Magny at ten o'clock; after which time the old Baron de Magny had seen his highness, protesting of his grandson's innocence, and the prince had received him most graciously and kindly. His highness said he had no doubt the young man was innocent; his birth and his blood rendered such a crime impossible; but suspicion was too strong against him: he was known to have been that day closeted with the Jew; to have received a very large sum of money which he squandered at play, and of which the Hebrew had, doubtless, been the lender, — to have despatched his servant after him, who inquired the hour of the Jew's departure, lay in wait for him, and rifled him. Suspicion was so strong against the chevalier, that common justice required his arrest ; and, meanwhile, until he cleared himself, he should be kept in not dishonorable durance, and every regard had for his name, and the services of his honorable grandfather. With this assurance, and with a warm grasp of the hand, the prince left old General de Magny that night ; and the veteran retired to rest, almost consoled and confident in Maxime's eventual and immediate release.

"But in the morning, before daybreak, the prince, who had been reading papers all night, wildly called to the page, who slept in the next room across the door, bade him get horses, which were always kept in readiness in the stables, and, flinging a parcel of letters into a box, told the page to follow him on horseback with these. The young man (Monsieur de Weissenborn) told this to a young lady who was then of my household, and who is now Madame de Weissenborn, and mother of a score of children.

"The page described that never was such a change seen as in his august master in the course of that single night. His eyes were bloodshot, his face livid, his clothes were hanging loose about him, and he who had always made his appearance on parade as precisely dressed as any sergeant of his troops, might have been seen galloping through the lonely streets at early dawn without a hat, his unpowdered hair streaming behind him like a madman.

"The page, with the box of papers, clattered after his master, — it was no easy task to follow him ; and they rode from the palace to the town, and through it to the general's quarter. The sentinels at the door were scared at the strange figure that rushed up to the general's gate, and, not knowing him, crossed bayonets, and refused him admission. 'Fools,' said Weissenborn, 'it is the prince!' And, jangling at the bell as if for an alarm of fire, the door was at length opened by the porter, and his highness ran up to the general's bedchamber, followed by the page with the box.

"'Magny — Magny,' roared the prince, thundering at the closed door, 'get up!' And to the queries of the old man from within, answered, 'It is I — Victor — the prince! — get up!' And presently the door was opened by the general in his *robe-de-chambre*, and the prince entered. The page brought in the box, and was bidden to wait without, which he did; but there led from Monsieur de Magny's bedroom into his ante-chamber two doors, the great one which formed the entrance into his room, and a smaller one which led, as the fashion is with our houses abroad, into the closet which communicates with the alcove where the bed is. The door of this was found by M. de Weissenborn to be open, and the young man was thus enabled to hear and see everything which occurred within the apartment.

"The general, somewhat nervously, asked what was the reason of so early a visit from his highness; to which the prince did not for a while reply, farther than by staring at him rather wildly, and pacing up and down the room.

"At last he said, 'Here is the cause!' dashing his fist on the box; and, as he had forgotten to bring the key with him, he went to the door for a moment, saying, 'Weissenborn perhaps has it;' but, seeing over the stove one of the general's *couteaux de chasse*, he took it down, and said, 'That will do,' and fell to work to burst the red trunk open with the blade of the forest-knife. The point broke, and he gave an oath, but continued haggling on with the broken blade, which was better suited to his purpose than the long, pointed knife, and finally succeeded in wrenching open the lid of the chest.

"'What is the matter?' said he, laughing. 'Here's the matter; — read that! — here's more matter, read that! — here's more — no, not that; that's somebody else's picture — but here's hers! Do you know that, Magny? My wife's — the princess's! Why did you and your cursed race ever come out of France, to plant your infernal wickedness wherever your feet fell, and to ruin honest German homes? What have you and yours ever had from my family but confidence and kindness? We gave you a home when you had none, and here's our reward!' and he flung a parcel of papers down before the old general, who saw the truth at once: — he had known it long before, probably, and sunk down on his chair, covering his face.

"The prince went on gesticulating, and shrieking almost. 'If a man injured you so, Magny, before you begot the father of that gambling, lying villain yonder, you would have known how to revenge yourself. You would have killed him! Yes, would have killed him. But who's to help me to my revenge? I've no equal. I can't meet that dog of a Frenchman, — that pimp from Versailles, and kill him, as if he had played the traitor to one of his own degree.'

"'The blood of Maxime de Magny,' said the old gentleman, proudly, 'is as good as that of any prince in Christendom.'

"'Can I take it?' cried the prince: 'you know I can't. I can't have the privilege of any other gentleman of Europe. What am I to do? Look here, Magny: I was wild when I came here: I didn't know what to do.

You 've served me for thirty years; you 've saved my life twice: they are all knaves and harlots about my poor old father here — no honest men or women — you are the only one — you saved my life: tell me what am I to do?' Thus, from insulting Monsieur de Magny, the poor distracted prince fell to supplicating him; and, at last, fairly flung himself down, and burst out in an agony of tears.

"Old Magny, one of the most rigid and cold of men on common occasions, when he saw this outbreak of passion on the prince's part, became, as my informant has described to me, as much affected as his master. The old man from being cold and high, suddenly fell, as it were, into the whimpering querulousness of extreme old age. He lost all sense of dignity: he went down on his knees, and broke out into all sorts of wild, incoherent attempts at consolation; so much so, that Weissenborn said he could not bear to look at the scene, and actually turned away from the contemplation of it.

"But, from what followed in a few days, we may guess the results of the long interview. The prince, when he came away from the conversation with his old servant, forgot his fatal box of papers and sent the page back for them. The general was on his knees praying in the room when the young man entered, and only stirred and looked round wildly as the other removed the packet. The prince rode away to his hunting-lodge at three leagues from X——, and three days after that Maxime de Magny died in prison; having made a confession that he was engaged in an attempt to rob the Jew, and that he had made away with himself, ashamed of his dishonor.

"But it is not known that it was the general himself who took his grandson poison: it was said even that he shot him in the prison. This, however, was not the case.

General de Magny carried his grandson the draught which was to carry him out of the world; represented to the wretched youth that his fate was inevitable; that it would be public and disgraceful unless he chose to anticipate the punishment, and so left him. But *it was not of his own accord* and not until he had used *every* means of escape, as you shall hear, that the unfortunate being's life was brought to an end.

"As for General de Magny, he quite fell into imbecility a short time after his nephew's death, and my honored duke's demise. After his highness the prince married the Princess Mary of F——, as they were walking in the English park together they once met old Magny riding in the sun in the easy chair, in which he was carried commonly abroad after his paralytic fits. 'This is my wife, Magny,' said the Prince, affectionately, taking the veteran's hand: and he added, turning to his princess, 'General de Magny saved my life during the Seven Years' War.'

"'What, you've taken her back again?' said the old man. 'I wish you'd send me back my poor Maxime.' He had quite forgotten the death of the poor princess Olivia, and the prince, looking very dark indeed, passed away.

"And now," said Madame de Liliengarten, "I have only one more gloomy story to relate to you — the death of the Princess Olivia. It is even more horrible than the tale I have just told you." With which preface the old lady resumed her narrative.

"The kind, weak princess's fate was hastened, if not occasioned by the cowardice of Magny. He found means to communicate with her from his prison, and her highness, who was not in open disgrace yet (for the duke, out of regard to the family, persisted in charging Magny with only robbery), made the most desperate efforts to relieve him, and to bribe the jailers to effect his escape. She was so wild that she lost all patience and prudence in the conduct of any schemes she may have had for Magny's liberation; for her husband was inexorable, and caused the chevalier's prison to be too strictly guarded for escape to be possible. She offered the state jewels in pawn to the court banker; who of course was obliged to decline the transaction. She fell down on her knees, it is said, to Geldern, the Police Minister, and offered him Heaven knows what as a bribe. Finally, she came screaming to my poor dear duke, who, with his age, diseases, and easy habits, was quite unfit for scenes of so violent a nature; and who, in consequence of the excitement created in his august bosom by frantic violence and grief, had a fit in which I very nigh lost him. That his dear life was brought to an untimely end by these transactions I have not the slightest doubt; for the Strasbourg pie, of which they said he died, never, I am sure, could have injured him, but for the injury which his dear gentle heart received from the unusual occurrences in which he was forced to take a share.

"All her highness's movements were carefully, though not ostensibly, watched by her husband, Prince Victor; who waiting upon his august father, sternly signified to him that if his highness (*my* duke) should dare to aid the princess in her efforts to release Magny, he, Prince Victor, would publicly accuse the princess and her paramour of high treason, and take measures with the Diet for removing his father from the throne, as incapacitated to reign. Hence interposition on our part was vain, and Magny was left to his fate.

"It came, as you are aware, very suddenly. Geldern, Police Minister, Hengst, Master of the Horse, and the Colonel of the Prince's guard, waited upon the young man in his prison two days after his grandfather had visited him there and left behind him the phial of poison which the criminal had not the courage to use. And Geldern signified to the young man that unless he took of his own accord the laurel-water provided by the elder Magny, more violent means of death would be instantly employed upon him, and that a file of grenadiers was in waiting in the courtyard to despatch him. Seeing this, Magny, with the most dreadful self-abasement, after dragging himself round the room on his knees from one officer to another, weeping and screaming with terror, at last desperately drank off the potion, and was a corpse in a few minutes. Thus ended this wretched young man.

"His death was made public in the 'Court Gazette' two days after, the paragraph stating that Monsieur de M——, struck with remorse for having attempted the murder of the Jew, had put himself to death by poison in prison; and a warning was added to all young noblemen of the duchy to avoid the dreadful sin of gambling, which had been the cause of the young man's ruin, and had brought upon the gray hairs of one of the noblest and most honorable of the servants of the duke irretrievable sorrow.

"The funeral was conducted with decent privacy, the General de Magny attending it. The carriage of the two dukes and all the first people of the court made their calls upon the general afterwards. He attended parade as usual the next day on the Arsenal-Place, and Duke Victor, who had been inspecting the building, came out of it leaning on the brave old warrior's arm. He was particularly gracious to the old man, and told his officers the oft-repeated story how at Rosbach, when the

X—— contingent served with the troops of the unlucky Soubise, the general had thrown himself in the way of a French dragoon who was pressing hard upon his highness in the rout, had received the blow intended for his master, and killed the assailant. And he alluded to the family motto of ' Magny sans tache,' and said 'It had been always so with his gallant friend and tutor in arms.' This speech affected all present very much; with the exception of the old general, who only bowed and did not speak: but when he went home he was heard muttering ' Magny sans tache, Magny sans tache !' and was attacked with paralysis that night, from which he never more than partially recovered.

"The news of Maxime's death had somehow been kept from the princess until now: a ' Gazette ' even being printed without the paragraph containing the account of his suicide ; but it was at length, I know not how, made known to her. And when she heard it, her ladies tell me, she screamed and fell, as if struck dead ; then sat up wildly and raved like a madwoman, and was then carried to her bed, where her physician attended her, and where she lay of a brain-fever. All this while the prince used to send to make inquiries concerning her ; and from his giving orders that his Castle of Schlangenfels should be prepared and furnished, I make no doubt it was his intention to send her into confinement thither : as had been done with the unhappy sister of his Britannic Majesty at Zell.

"She sent repeatedly to demand an interview with his highness ; which the latter declined, saying that he would communicate with her highness when her health was sufficiently recovered. To one of her passionate letters he sent back for reply a packet, which, when opened, was found to contain the emerald that had been the cause round which all this dark intrigue moved.

" Her highness at this time became quite frantic; vowed in the presence of all her ladies that one lock of her darling Maxime's hair was more precious to her than all the jewels in the world ; rang for her carriage, and said she would go and kiss his tomb ; proclaimed the murdered martyr's innocence, and called down the punishment of Heaven, the wrath of her family, upon his assassin. The prince, on hearing these speeches (they were all, of course, regularly brought to him), is said to have given one of his dreadful looks (which I remember now), and to have said, 'This cannot last much longer.'

" All that day and the next the Princess Olivia passed in dictating the most passionate letters to the prince her father, to the Kings of France, Naples, and Spain, her kinsmen, and to all other branches of her family, calling upon them in the most incoherent terms to protect her against the butcher and assassin her husband, assailing his person in the maddest terms of reproach, and at the same time confessing her love for the murdered Magny. It was in vain that those ladies who were faithful to her pointed out to her the inutility of these letters, the dangerous folly of the confessions which they made ; she insisted upon writing them, and used to give them to her second robe-woman, a Frenchwoman (her highness always affectioned persons of that nation) who had the key of her cassette, and carried every one of these epistles to Geldern.

" With the exception that no public receptions were held, the ceremony of the princess's establishment went on as before. Her ladies were allowed to wait upon her and perform their usual duties about her person. The only men admitted were, however, her servants, her physician and chaplain; and one day when she wished to go into the garden, a heyduc, who kept the door, intimated to her highness that the prince's orders were that she should keep her apartments.

"They abut, as you remember, upon the landing of the marble staircase of Schloss X——; the entrance to Prince Victor's suite of rooms being opposite the princess's on the same landing. This space is large, filled with sofas and benches, and the gentlemen and officers who waited upon the duke used to make a sort of ante-chamber of the landing-place, and pay their court to his highness there, as he passed out, at eleven o'clock, to parade. At such a time, the heyducs within the princess's suite of rooms used to turn out with their halberts and present to Prince Victor — the same ceremony being performed on his own side, when pages came out and announced the approach of his highness. The pages used to come out and say, 'The prince, gentlemen!' and the drums beat in the hall, and the gentlemen rose, who were waiting on the benches that ran along the balustrade.

"As if fate impelled her to her death, one day the princess, as her guards turned out, and she was aware that the prince was standing, as was his wont, on the landing, conversing with his gentlemen (in the old days he used to cross to the princess's apartment and kiss her hand) — the princess, who had been anxious all the morning, complaining of heat, insisting that all the doors of the apartments should be left open; and giving tokens of an insanity which I think was now evident, rushed wildly at the doors when the guards passed out, flung them open, and before a word could be said, or her ladies could follow her, was in presence of Duke Victor, who was talking as usual on the landing : placing herself between him and the stair, she began apostrophizing him with frantic vehemence : —

" ' Take notice, gentlemen ! ' she screamed out, ' that this man is a murderer and a liar ; that he lays plots for honorable gentlemen, and kills them in prison ! Take notice, that I too am in prison, and fear the same fate : the same butcher who killed Maxime de Magny, may, any night, put the knife to my throat. I appeal to you, and to all the kings of Europe, my royal kinsmen. I demand to be set free from this tyrant and villain, this liar and traitor ! I adjure you all, as gentlemen of honor, to carry these letters to my relatives, and say from whom you had them ! ' and with this the unhappy lady began scattering letters about the astonished crowd.

" ' *Let no man stoop !* ' cried the prince, in a voice of thunder. ' Madame de Gleim, you should have watched your patient better. Call the princess's physicians : her highness's brain is affected. Gentlemen, have the goodness to retire.' And the prince stood on the landing as the gentlemen went down the stairs, saying fiercely to the guard, ' Soldier, if she moves, strike with your halbert ! ' on which the man brought the point of his weapon to the princess's breast ; and the lady, frightened, shrank back and reëntered her apartments. ' Now, Monsieur de Weissenborn,' said the prince, ' pick up all those papers ; ' and the prince went into his own apartments, preceded by his pages, and never quitted them until he had seen every one of the papers burned.

" The next day the ' Court Gazette ' contained a bulletin signed by the three physicians, stating that ' Her highness the hereditary princess labored under inflammation of the brain, and had passed a restless and disturbed night.' Similar notices were issued day after day.

The services of all her ladies, except two, were dispensed with. Guards were placed within and without her doors; her windows were secured, so that escape from them was impossible: and you know what took place ten days after. The church-bells were ringing all night, and the prayers of the faithful asked for a person *in extremis.* A 'Gazette' appeared in the morning, edged with black, and stating that the high and mighty Princess Olivia Maria Ferdinanda, consort of His Serene Highness Victor Louis Emanuel, Hereditary Prince of X——, had died in the evening of the 24th of January, 1769.

"But do you know *how* she died, sir? That, too, is a mystery. Weissenborn, the page, was concerned in this dark tragedy; and the secret was so dreadful, that never, believe me, till Prince Victor's death did I reveal it.

"After the fatal *esclandre* which the princess had made, the prince sent for Weissenborn, and binding him by the most solemn adjuration to secrecy (he only broke it to his wife many years after: indeed there is no secret in the world that women cannot know if they will), despatched him on the following mysterious commission.

"'There lives,' said his highness, 'on the Kehl side of the river, opposite to Strasbourg, a man whose residence you will easily find out from his name, which is *Monsieur de Strasbourg.* You will make your inquiries concerning him quietly, and without occasioning any remark; perhaps you had better go into Strasbourg for the purpose, where the person is quite well known. You will take with you any comrade on whom you can perfectly rely: the lives of both, remember, depend on your secrecy. You will find out some period when Monsieur de Strasbourg is alone, or only in company of the domestic who lives with him (I myself visited the man by accident on my return from Paris five years since, and hence am induced to send for him now, in my present emergency). You will have your carriage waiting at his door at night; and you and your comrade will enter his house masked; and present him with a purse of a hundred louis; promising him double that sum on his return from his expedition. If he refuse, you must use force and bring him; menacing him with instant death should he decline to follow you. You will place him in the carriage with the blinds drawn, one or other of you never losing sight of him the whole way, and threatening him with death if he discover himself or cry out. You will lodge him in the old Tower here, where a room shall be prepared for him; and his work being done, you will restore him to his home in the same speed and secrecy with which you brought him from it.'

"Such were the mysterious orders Prince Victor gave his page; and Weissenborn, selecting for his comrade in the expedition Lieutenant Bartenstein, set out on his strange journey.

"All this while the palace was hushed, as if in mourning; the bulletins in the 'Court Gazette' appeared, announcing the continuance of the princess's malady; and though she had but few attendants, strange and circumstantial stories were told regarding the progress of her complaint. She was quite wild. She had tried to kill herself. She had fancied herself to be I don't know how many different characters. Expresses were sent to her family informing them of her state, and couriers despatched *publicly* to Vienna and Paris to procure the attendance of physicians skilled in treating diseases of the brain. That pretended anxiety was all a feint : it was never intended that the princess should recover.

"The day on which Weissenborn and Bartenstein returned from their expedition, it was announced that her highness the princess was much worse ; that night the report through the town was that she was at the agony : and that night the unfortunate creature was endeavoring to make her escape.

"She had unlimited confidence in the French chamber-woman who attended her, and between her and this woman the plan of escape was arranged. The princess took her jewels in a casket ; a private door, opening from one of her rooms and leading into the outer gate, it was said, of the palace, was discovered for her : and a letter was brought to her, purporting to be from the duke her father-in-law, and stating that a carriage and horses had been provided, and would take her to B—— : the territory where she might communicate with her family and be safe.

"The unhappy lady, confiding in her guardian, set out on the expedition. The passages wound through the walls of the modern part of the palace and abutted in effect at the old Owl Tower, as it was called, on the outer wall : the tower was pulled down afterwards, and for good reason.

"At a certain place the candle, which the chamber-woman was carrying, went out ; and the princess would have screamed with terror, but her hand was seized, and a voice cried, 'Hush !' The next minute a man in a mask (it was the duke himself) rushed forward, gagged her with a handkerchief, her hands and legs were bound, and she was carried swooning with terror into a vaulted room, where she was placed by a person there waiting, and tied in an arm-chair. The same mask who had gagged her, came and bared her neck and said, ' It had best be done now she has fainted.'

" Perhaps it would have been as well; for though she recovered from her swoon, and her confessor, who was present, came forward and endeavored to prepare her for the awful deed which was about to be done upon her, and for the state into which she was about to enter, when she came to herself it was only to scream like a maniac, to curse the duke as a butcher and tyrant, and to call upon Magny, her dear Magny.

" At this the duke said, quite calmly, ' May God have mercy on her sinful soul!' He, the confessor, and Geldern, who were present, went down on their knees; and, as his highness dropped his handkerchief, Weissenborn fell down in a fainting fit; while *Monsieur de Strasbourg*, taking the back hair in his hand, separated the shrieking head of Olivia from the miserable, sinful body. May Heaven have mercy upon her soul ! "

This was the story told by Madame de Liliengarten.

VIII

THE GOLD–BUG

THE GOLD-BUG

By EDGAR ALLAN POE

INTRODUCTORY

PLOT CONSTRUCTION

IT would be impossible to say that any of the short stories so far examined show the slightest progress in the special art of short story construction. In "Rip Van Winkle" we found perfection in descriptive character-drawing; in "A Passion in the Desert," atmosphere; in "A Child's Dream of a Star," sentiment; in "A Princess's Tragedy," the power of suggestiveness inherent in polished restraint: but it would be folly to pretend that any one of these stories is even equal in interest, as a story, to the two first presented, which were written more than six hundred years ago.

In Poe, however, we find a master of the short story who towers above even the anonymous author of the "Arabian Nights," and above Boccaccio. "The Gold-Bug" is as good a story as "Aladdin," and it wears better because it is so much more finely wrought. It is just as romantic as the "Arabian Nights," yet involves no assumption of the obviously absurd. Moreover, Poe invented it — created it, — while all the stories we have yet examined are based on plots (so far as they had plots of any value) which came to the authors ready made. The author was only the recorder or the "dresser up." But Poe made his story, and he made a good one; and since he showed the world how to do it, the best stories have been invented, not discovered.

Not only did Poe consciously invent the stories he wrote, but in his "Philosophy of Composition" he told us something of the way he went about doing it. Of course not all that he says there can be taken seriously, but much may be; and what he says of the construction of "The Raven" applies equally well, if not better, to the construction of a short story.

The first thing to be noted is that the writer starts with his conclusion. If he is to write a detective story, he begins in his mind with the solution of the mystery, and from that works back to the mystery. Once the plot is worked out, the author leads the reader from the mystery to the solution, and since he has so arranged it, everything works out to a nicety, to the wonder and amazement of the reader, and to the satisfaction of the author.

Second, in developing the details of a story, every act must have its adequate motive, and every fact its just reason. It is clear, therefore, that the story-writer must have a far-reaching knowledge of the springs of human action and the secrets of human life, for in his story he plays the " god in the machine," and unless he does his work well, the easy comparison that may be made with the real thing is so much to his disadvantage that he is compelled to retire from the field in disgrace.

The problem in " The Gold-Bug " is purely intellectual. Sentiment and descriptive character-drawing are absent, and we detect no special atmosphere. Poe concentrated his attention on the problem of constructing his story; but he shows that he understood something of the larger art, for in another class of his tales he created perfectly the atmosphere of horror, and did it so well that no one since has surpassed him. He was also a poet, and his prose and his poetry find themselves curiously linked in his work. We have already noted that he was a critic as well as a poet and a story writer, and told us much of the philosophy of his literary discoveries.

Poe was not accepted by his contemporaries in America, partly because he was constitutionally unfortunate and was unjustly maligned even after his death, partly because the discoveries of genius cannot be fully comprehended by the generation which gives them birth.

Poe's stories were translated into excellent French by Charles Baudelaire, an intense admirer of the American inventor; and in these translations the stories at once produced a marked effect on the French art, for it was much better prepared for Poe's discoveries than the English. A crop of conscious short story artists immediately sprung up, who absorbed and greatly improved Poe's principles. These French writers in turn influenced later English and American writers, who in this roundabout way came to know and appreciate Poe. So, although Poe's own stories are not sufficiently varied and profound to be great literature in themselves, they are the crude models of nearly all the best that was to follow, and in justice we must consider Poe the father of the modern art of short story writing.

THE GOLD–BUG

What ho! what ho! this fellow is dancing mad!
He hath been bitten by the Tarantula.
All in the Wrong.

MANY years ago I contracted an intimacy with a Mr. William Legrand. He was of an ancient Huguenot family, and had once been wealthy; but a series of misfortunes had reduced him to want. To avoid the mortification consequent upon his disasters, he left New Orleans, the city of his forefathers, and took up his residence at Sullivan's Island, near Charleston, South Carolina.

This island is a very singular one. It consists of little else than the sea-sand, and is about three miles long. Its breadth at no point exceeds a quarter of a mile. It is separated from the mainland by a scarcely perceptible creek oozing its way through a wilderness of reeds and slime, a favorite resort of the marsh-hen. The vegetation, as might be supposed, is scant, or at least dwarfish. No trees of any magnitude are to be seen. Near the western extremity, where Fort Moultrie stands, and where are some miserable frame buildings, tenanted, during summer, by the fugitives from Charleston dust and fever, may be found, indeed, the bristly palmetto; but the whole island, with the exception of this western point, and a line of hard, white beach on the sea-coast, is covered with a dense undergrowth of the sweet myrtle, so much prized by the horticulturists of England. The shrub here often attains the height of fifteen or twenty feet, and forms an almost impenetrable coppice, burdening the air with its fragrance.

In the inmost recesses of this coppice, not far from the eastern or more remote end of the island, Legrand had built himself a small hut, which he occupied when I first, by mere accident, made his acquaintance. This soon ripened into friendship, — for there was much in the recluse to excite interest and esteem. I found him well educated, with unusual powers of mind, but infected with misanthropy, and subject to perverse moods of alternate enthusiasm and melancholy. He had with him many books, but rarely employed them. His chief amusements were gunning and fishing, or sauntering along the beach and through the myrtles, in quest of shells or entomological specimens; — his collection of the latter might have been envied by a Swammerdam. In these excursions he was usually accompanied by an old negro, called Jupiter, who had been manumitted before the reverses of the family, but who could be induced, neither by threats nor by promises, to abandon what he considered his right of attendance upon the footsteps of his young "Massa Will." It is not improbable that the relatives of Legrand, conceiving him to be somewhat unsettled in intellect, had contrived to instil this obstinacy into Jupiter, with a view to the supervision and guardianship of the wanderer.

The winters in the latitude of Sullivan's Island are seldom very severe, and in the fall of the year it is a rare event indeed when a fire is considered necessary. About the middle of October, 18—, there occurred, however, a day of remarkable chilliness. Just before sunset I scrambled my way through the evergreens to the hut of my friend, whom I had not visited for several weeks, — my residence being, at that time, in Charleston, a distance of nine miles from the island, while the facilities of passage and re-passage were very far behind those of the present day. Upon reaching the hut I rapped, as was my custom, and getting no reply, sought for the key where I knew it was secreted, unlocked the door, and went in. A fine fire was blazing upon the hearth. It was a novelty, and by no means an ungrateful one. I threw off an overcoat, took an arm-chair by the crackling logs, and awaited patiently the arrival of my hosts.

Soon after dark they arrived, and gave me a most cordial welcome. Jupiter, grinning from ear to ear, bustled about to prepare some marsh-hens for supper. Legrand was in one of his fits — how else shall I term them? — of enthusiasm. He had found an unknown bivalve, forming a new genus, and, more than this, he had hunted down and secured, with Jupiter's assistance, a *scarabæus* which he believed to be totally new, but in respect to which he wished to have my opinion on the morrow.

"And why not to-night?" I asked, rubbing my hands over the blaze, and wishing the whole tribe of *scarabæi* at the devil.

"Ah, if I had only known you were here!" said Legrand, "but it's so long since I saw you; and how could I foresee that you would pay me a visit this very night of all others? As I was coming home I met Lieutenant G——, from the fort, and, very foolishly, I lent him the bug; so it will be impossible for you to see it until the morning. Stay here to-night, and I will send Jup down for it at sunrise. It is the loveliest thing in creation!"

"What? — sunrise?"

"Nonsense! no! — the bug. It is of a brilliant gold color, — about the size of a large hickory-nut, — with two jet-black spots near one extremity of the back, and another, somewhat longer, at the other. The *antennæ* are —— "

"Dey ain't *no* tin in him, Massa Will, I keep a tellin' on you," here interrupted Jupiter; "de bug is a goole-bug, solid, ebery bit of him, inside and all, sep him wing, — neber feel half so hebby a bug in my life."

"Well, suppose it is, Jup," replied Legrand, somewhat more earnestly, it seemed to me, than the case demanded, "is that any reason for your letting the birds burn? The color" — here he turned to me — "is really almost enough to warrant Jupiter's idea. You never saw a more brilliant metallic lustre than the scales emit, — but of this you cannot judge till to-morrow. In the meantime I can give you some idea of the shape." Saying this, he seated himself at a small table, on which were a pen and ink, but no paper. He looked for some in a drawer, but found none.

"Never mind," said he at length, "this will answer"; and he drew from his waistcoat-pocket a scrap of what I took to be very dirty foolscap, and made upon it a rough drawing with the pen. While he did this, I retained my seat by the fire, for I was still chilly. When the design was complete, he handed it to me without rising. As

I received it, a loud growl was heard, succeeded by a scratching at the door. Jupiter opened it, and a large Newfoundland, belonging to Legrand, rushed in, leaped upon my shoulders, and loaded me with caresses; for I had shown him much attention during previous visits. When his gambols were over, I looked at the paper, and, to speak the truth, found myself not a little puzzled at what my friend had depicted.

"Well!" I said, after contemplating it for some minutes, "this *is* a strange *scarabæus*, I must confess: new to me: never saw anything like it before, — unless it was a skull, or a death's-head, — which it more nearly resembles than anything else that has come under *my* observation."

"A death's-head!" echoed Legrand— "Oh — yes — well, it has something of that appearance upon paper, no doubt. The two upper black spots look like eyes, eh? and the longer one at the bottom like a mouth, — and then the shape of the whole is oval."

"Perhaps so," said I; "but, Legrand, I fear you are no artist. I must wait until I see the beetle itself, if I am to form any idea of its personal appearance."

"Well, I don't know," said he, a little nettled, "I draw tolerably, — *should* do it at least, — have had good masters, and flatter myself that I am not quite a blockhead."

"But, my dear fellow, you are joking, then," said I; "this is a very passable *skull*, — indeed, I may say that it is a very *excellent* skull, according to the vulgar notions about such specimens of physiology, — and your *scarabæus* must be the queerest *scarabæus* in the world if it resembles it. Why, we may get up a very thrilling bit of superstition upon this hint. I presume you will call the bug *scarabæus caput hominis,* or something of that kind, — there are many similar titles in the Natural Histories. But where are the *antennæ* you spoke of?"

"The *antennæ!*" said Legrand, who seemed to be getting unaccountably warm upon the subject; "I am sure you must see the *antennæ.* I made them as distinct as they are in the original insect, and I presume that is sufficient."

"Well, well," I said, "perhaps you have, — still I don't see them"; and I handed him the paper without additional remark, not wishing to ruffle his temper. But I was much surprised at the turn affairs had taken; his ill-humor puzzled me; and, as for the drawing of the beetle, there were positively *no antennæ* visible, and the whole *did* bear a very close resemblance to the ordinary cuts of a death's-head.

He received the paper very peevishly, and was about to crumple it, apparently to throw it in the fire, when a casual glance at the design seemed suddenly to rivet his attention. In an instant his face grew violently red, — in another as excessively pale. For some minutes, he continued to scrutinize the drawing minutely where he sat. At length he arose, took a candle from the table, and proceeded to seat himself upon a sea-chest in the farthest corner of the room. Here again he made an anxious examination of the paper, turning it in all directions. He said nothing, however, and his conduct greatly astonished me; yet I thought it prudent not to exacerbate the growing moodiness of his temper by any comment. Presently he took from his coat-pocket a wallet, placed the paper carefully in it, and deposited both in a writing-desk, which he locked. He now grew more composed in his demeanor; but his original air of enthusiasm had quite disappeared. Yet he seemed not so much sulky as abstracted. As the evening wore away he became more and more absorbed in revery, from which no sallies of mine could arouse him. It had been my intention to pass the night at the hut, as I had frequently done before, but seeing my host in this mood, I deemed it proper to take leave. He did not press me to remain, but, as I departed, he shook my hand with even more than his usual cordiality.

It was about a month after this (and during the interval I had seen nothing of Legrand) when I received a visit, at Charleston, from his man, Jupiter. I had never seen the good old negro look so dispirited, and I feared that some serious disaster had befallen my friend.

"Well, Jup," said I, "what is the matter now? — how is your master?"

"Why, to speak de troof, massa, him not so berry well as mought be."

"Not well! I am truly sorry to hear it. What does he complain of?"

"Dar! dat's it! — him neber 'plain of notin, — but him berry sick for all dat."

"Very sick, Jupiter! — why did n't you say so at once? Is he confined to bed?"

"No, dat he ain't! — he ain't 'fin'd nowhar, — dat's just whar de shoe pinch, — my mind is got to be berry hebby 'bout poor Massa Will."

"Jupiter, I should like to understand what it is you are talking about. You say your master is sick. Has n't he told you what ails him?"

"Why, massa, 't ain't worf while for to git mad about de matter, — Massa Will say noffin at all ain't de matter wid him, — but den what make him go about looking dis here way, wid he head down and he soldiers up, and as

white as a gose? And den he keep a syphon all de
time —— "

" Keeps a what, Jupiter? "

" Keeps a syphon wid de figgurs on de slate, — de
queerest figgurs I ebber did see. I's gittin' to be
skeered, I tell you. Hab for to keep mighty tight eye
'pon him 'noovers. T' odder day he gib me slip 'fore de
sun up and was gone de whole ob de blessed day. I
had a big stick ready cut for to gib him deuced good
beating when he did come, — but I's sich a fool dat I
had n't de heart arter all, — he look so berry poorly."

" Eh? — what? — ah, yes ! — upon the whole I think
you had better not be too severe with the poor fellow,
— don't flog him, Jupiter, — he can't very well stand it,
— but can you form no idea of what has occasioned
this illness, or rather this change of conduct? Has any
thing unpleasant happened since I saw you? "

" No, massa, dey ain't bin noffin onpleasant *since* den,
— 't was *fore* den, I'm feared, — 't was de berry day
you was dare."

" How? what do you mean? "

" Why, massa, I mean de bug — dare now."

" The what? "

" De bug, — I'm berry sartain dat Massa Will bin
bit somewhere 'bout de head by dat goole-bug."

" And what cause have you, Jupiter, for such a
supposition? "

" Claws enuff, massa, and mouff too. I nebber did
see sich a deuced bug, — he kick and he bite ebery
ting what cum near him. Massa Will cotch him fuss,
but had for to let him go gin mighty quick, I tell you
— den was de time he must ha' got de bite. I did n't
like de look ob de bug mouff, myself, nohow, so
I would n't take hold ob him wid my finger, but I

cotch him wid a piece ob paper dat I found. I rap him up in de paper and stuff piece ob it in he mouff, — dat was de way."

"And you think, then, that your master was really bitten by the beetle, and that the bite made him sick?"

"I don't tink noffin about it, — I nose it. What make him dream 'bout de goole so much, if 't ain't cause he bit by de goole-bug? I's heerd 'bout dem goole-bugs 'fore dis."

"But how do you know he dreams about gold?"

"How I know? why, cause he talk about it in he sleep, — dat's how I nose."

"Well, Jup, perhaps you are right; but to what fortunate circumstance am I to attribute the honor of a visit from you to-day?"

"What de matter, massa?"

"Did you bring any message from Mr. Legrand?"

"No, massa, I bring dis here pissel"; and here Jupiter handed me a note which ran thus:

MY DEAR ——: Why have I not seen you for so long a time? I hope you have not been so foolish as to take offence at any little *brusquerie* of mine; but no, that is improbable.

Since I saw you I have had great cause for anxiety. I have something to tell you, yet scarcely know how to tell it, or whether I should tell it at all.

I have not been quite well for some days past, and poor old Jup annoys me, almost beyond endurance, by his well-meant attentions. Would you believe it? — he had prepared a huge stick, the other day, with which to chastise me for giving him the slip, and spending the day, *solus*, among the hills on the mainland. I verily believe that my ill looks alone saved me a flogging.

I have made no addition to my cabinet since we met.

If you can in any way make it convenient, come over with

Jupiter. *Do* come. I wish to see you *to-night*, upon business of importance. I assure you that it is of the *highest* importance. Ever yours,

WILLIAM LEGRAND.

There was something in the tone of this note which gave me great uneasiness. Its whole style differed materially from that of Legrand. What could he be dreaming of? What new crotchet possessed his excitable brain? What " business of the highest importance " could *he* possibly have to transact? Jupiter's account of him boded no good. I dreaded lest the continued pressure of misfortune had, at length, fairly unsettled the reason of my friend. Without a moment's hesitation, therefore, I prepared to accompany the negro.

Upon reaching the wharf, I noticed a scythe and three spades, all apparently new, lying in the bottom of the boat in which we were to embark.

" What is the meaning of all this Jup? " I inquired.

" Him syfe, massa, and spade."

" Very true; but what are they doing here? "

" Him de syfe and de spade what Massa Will sis 'pon my buying for him in de town, and de debbil's own lot of money I had to gib for 'em."

" But what, in the name of all that is mysterious, is your ' Massa Will ' going to do with scythes and spades? "

" Dat 's more dan *I* know, and debbil take me if I don't b'lieve 't is more dan he know too. But it 's all cum ob de bug."

Finding that no satisfaction was to be obtained of Jupiter, whose whole intellect seemed to be absorbed by " de bug," I now stepped into the boat and made sail. With a fair and strong breeze we soon ran into the little cove to the northward of Fort Moultrie, and a walk of some two miles brought us to the hut. It was about three in the afternoon when we arrived. Legrand had been awaiting us in eager expectation. He grasped my hand with a nervous *empressement* which alarmed me and strengthened the suspicions already entertained. His countenance was pale even to ghastliness, and his deep-set eyes glared with unnatural lustre. After some inquiries respecting his health, I asked him, not knowing what better to say, if he had yet obtained the *scarabæus* from Lieutenant G——.

"Oh, yes," he replied, coloring violently, "I got it from him the next morning. Nothing should tempt me to part with that *scarabæus*. Do you know that Jupiter is quite right about it?"

"In what way?" I asked, with a sad foreboding at heart.

"In supposing it to be a bug of *real gold*." He said this with an air of profound seriousness, and I felt inexpressibly shocked.

"This bug is to make my fortune," he continued, with a triumphant smile, "to reinstate me in my family possessions. Is it any wonder, then, that I prize it? Since Fortune has thought fit to bestow it upon me, I have only to use it properly and I shall arrive at the gold of which it is the index. Jupiter, bring me that *scarabæus!*"

"What! de bug, massa? I'd rudder not go fer trubble dat bug, — you mus' git him for your own self."

Hereupon Legrand arose, with a grave and stately air, and brought me the beetle from a glass case in which it was enclosed. It was a beautiful *scarabæus*, and, at that time, unknown to naturalists, — of course a great prize in a scientific point of view. There were two round black spots near one extremity of the back, and a long one near the other. The scales were exceedingly hard and glossy, with all the appearance of burnished gold. The weight of the insect was very remarkable, and, taking all things into consideration, I could hardly blame Jupiter for his opinion respecting it; but what to make of Legrand's concordance with that opinion I could not for the life of me tell.

"I sent for you," said he, in a grandiloquent tone, when I had completed my examination of the beetle, — "I sent for you, that I might have your counsel and assistance in furthering the views of Fate and of the bug —— "

"My dear Legrand," I cried, interrupting him, "you are certainly unwell, and had better use some little precautions. You shall go to bed, and I will remain with you a few days, until you get over this. You are feverish and —— "

"Feel my pulse," said he.

I felt it, and, to say the truth, found not the slightest indication of fever.

"But you may be ill and yet have no fever. Allow me this once to prescribe for you. In the first place, go to bed. In the next —— "

"You are mistaken," he interposed; "I am as well as I can expect to be under the excitement which I suffer. If you really wish me well, you will relieve this excitement."

"And how is this to be done?"

"Very easily. Jupiter and myself are going upon an expedition into the hills, upon the mainland, and in this expedition we shall need the aid of some person in whom we can confide. You are the only one we can trust. Whether we succeed or fail, the excitement which you now perceive in me will be equally allayed."

"I am anxious to oblige you in any way," I replied;

"but do you mean to say that this infernal beetle has any connection with your expedition into the hills?"

"It has."

"Then, Legrand, I can become a party to no such absurd proceeding."

"I am sorry — very sorry, — for we shall have to try it by ourselves."

"Try it by yourselves! The man is surely mad! — but stay! — how long do you propose to be absent?"

"Probably all night. We shall start immediately, and be back, at all events, by sunrise."

"And will you promise me, upon your honor, that when this freak of yours is over, and the bug business (good God!) settled to your satisfaction, you will then return home and follow my advice implicitly, as that of your physician?"

"Yes; I promise; and now let us be off, for we have no time to lose."

With a heavy heart I accompanied my friend. We started about four o'clock, — Legrand, Jupiter, the dog, and myself. Jupiter had with him the scythe and spades, the whole of which he insisted upon carrying, — more through fear, it seemed to me, of trusting either of the implements within reach of his master, than from any excess of industry or complaisance. His demeanor was dogged in the extreme, and "dat deuced bug" were the sole words which escaped his lips during the journey. For my own part, I had charge of a couple of dark-lanterns, while Legrand contented himself with the *scarabæus*, which he carried attached to the end of a bit of whipcord; twirling it too and fro, with the air of a conjurer, as he went. When I observed this last plain evidence of my friend's aberration of mind, I could scarcely refrain from tears. I thought it best, however, to humor his fancy, at least for the present, or until I could adopt some more energetic measures with a chance of success. In the meantime I endeavored, but all in vain, to sound him in regard to the object of the expedition. Having succeeded in inducing me to accompany him, he seemed unwilling to hold conversation upon any topic of minor importance, and to all my questions vouchsafed no other reply than " We shall see ! "

We crossed the creek at the head of the island by means of a skiff, and, ascending the high grounds on the shore of the mainland, proceeded in a northwesterly direction, through a tract of country excessively wild and desolate, where no trace of a human footstep was to be seen. Legrand led the way with decision, pausing only for an instant, here and there, to consult what appeared to be certain landmarks of his own contrivance upon a former occasion.

In this manner we journeyed for about two hours, and the sun was just setting when we entered a region infinitely more dreary than any yet seen. It was a species of table-land, near the summit of an almost inaccessible hill, densely wooded from base to pinnacle, and interspersed with huge crags that appeared to lie loosely upon the soil, and in many cases were prevented from precipitating themselves into the valleys below, merely by the support of the trees against which they reclined. Deep ravines, in various directions, gave an air of still sterner solemnity to the scene.

The natural platform to which we had clambered was thickly overgrown with brambles, through which we soon discovered that it would have been impossible to force our way but for the scythe ; and Jupiter, by direction of his master, proceeded to clear for us a path to the foot of an enormously tall tulip-tree, which stood, with some eight or ten oaks, upon the level, and far surpassed them all, and all other trees which I had then ever seen, in the beauty of its foliage and form, in the wide spread of its branches, and in the general majesty of its appearance. When we reached this tree, Legrand turned to Jupiter, and asked him if he thought he could climb it. The old man seemed a little staggered by the question, and for some moments made no reply. At length he approached the huge trunk, walked slowly around it, and examined it with minute attention. When he had completed his scrutiny, he merely said:

"Yes, massa, Jup climb any tree he ebber see in he life."

"Then up with you as soon as possible, for it will soon be too dark to see what we are about."

"How far mus' go up, massa?" inquired Jupiter.

"Get up the main trunk first, and then I will tell you which way to go — and here — stop! take this beetle with you."

"De bug, Massa Will! — de goole-bug!" cried the negro, drawing back in dismay — "what for mus' tote de bug way up de tree? — d—n if I do!"

"If you are afraid, Jup, a great big negro like you, to take hold of a harmless little dead beetle, why you can carry it up by this string; but, if you do not take it up with you in some way, I shall be under the necessity of breaking your head with this shovel."

"What de matter now, massa?" said Jup, evidently shamed into compliance; "always want for to raise fuss wid old nigger. Was only funnin anyhow. *Me* feered de bug! what I keer for de bug?" Here he took cautiously hold of the extreme end of the string, and, maintaining the insect as far from his person as circumstances would permit, prepared to ascend the tree.

In youth, the tulip-tree, or *Liriodendron tulipiferum*,

the most magnificent of American foresters, has a trunk peculiarly smooth, and often rises to a great height without lateral branches; but, in its riper age, the bark becomes gnarled and uneven, while many short limbs make their appearance on the stem. Thus the difficulty of ascension, in the present case, lay more in semblance than in reality. Embracing the huge cylinder, as closely as possible, with his arms and knees, seizing with his hands some projections, and resting his naked toes upon others, Jupiter, after one or two narrow escapes from falling, at length wriggled himself into the first great fork, and seemed to consider the whole business as virtually accomplished. The *risk* of the achievement was, in fact, now over, although the climber was some sixty or seventy feet from the ground.

"Which way mus' go now, Massa Will?" he asked.

"Keep up the largest branch,—the one on this side," said Legrand. The negro obeyed him promptly, and apparently with but little trouble; ascending higher and higher, until no glimpse of his squat figure could be obtained through the dense foliage which enveloped it. Presently his voice was heard in a sort of halloo.

"How much fudder is got for go?"

"How high up are you?" asked Legrand.

"Ebber so fur," replied the negro; "can see de sky fru de top ob de tree."

"Never mind the sky, but attend to what I say. Look down the trunk and count the limbs below you on this side. How many limbs have you passed?"

"One, two, tree, four, fibe,—I done pass fibe big limb, massa, 'pon dis side."

"Then go one limb higher."

In a few minutes the voice was heard again, announcing that the seventh limb was attained.

"Now, Jup," cried Legrand, evidently much excited, "I want you to work your way out upon that limb as far as you can. If you see anything strange, let me know."

By this time what little doubt I might have entertained of my poor friend's insanity was put finally at rest. I had no alternative but to conclude him stricken with lunacy, and I became seriously anxious about getting him home. While I was pondering upon what was best to be done, Jupiter's voice was again heard.

"'Mos' feerd for to ventur 'pon dis limb berry far, — 't is dead limb putty much all de way."

"Did you say it was a *dead* limb, Jupiter?" cried Legrand, in a quavering voice.

"Yes, massa, him dead as de door-nail — done up for sartain — done departed dis here life."

"What in the name of Heaven shall I do?" asked Legrand, seemingly in the greatest distress.

"Do!" said I, glad of an opportunity to interpose a word; "why, come home and go to bed. Come, now! — that's a fine fellow. It's getting late, and, besides, you remember your promise."

"Jupiter," cried he, without heeding me in the least, "do you hear me?"

"Yes, Massa Will, hear you ebber so plain."

"Try the wood well, then, with your knife, and see if you think it *very* rotten."

"Him rotten, massa, sure nuff," replied the negro in a few moments, "but not so berry rotten as mought be. Mought ventur out leetle way 'pon de limb by myself, dat's true."

"By yourself! — What do you mean?"

"Why I mean de bug. 'T is *berry* hebby bug. S'pose I drop him down fuss, and den de limb won't break wid just de weight ob one nigger."

"You infernal scoundrel!" cried Legrand, apparently much relieved, "what do you mean by telling me such nonsense as that? As sure as you drop that beetle I 'll break your neck. Look here, Jupiter, do you hear me?"

"Yes, massa, need n't hollo at poor nigger dat style."

"Well! now listen! — if you will venture out on the limb as far as you think safe, and not let go the beetle, I 'll make you a present of a silver dollar as soon as you get down."

"I 'm gwine, Massa Will, — 'deed I is," replied the negro very promptly, — "mos' out to the eend now."

"*Out to the end!*" here fairly screamed Legrand; "do you say you are out to the end of that limb?"

"Soon be to de eend, massa, — o-o-o-o-oh! Lor-gol-a-marcy! what *is* dis here 'pon de tree?"

"Well!" cried Legrand, highly delighted, "what is it?"

"Why, 't ain't noffin but a skull — somebody bin lef' him head up de tree, and de crows done gobble ebery bit ob de meat off."

"A skull, you say! very well! — how is it fastened to the limb? — what holds it on?"

"Sure nuff, massa; mus' look. Why dis berry curous sarcumstance, 'pon my word, — dare 's a great big nail in de skull, what fastens ob it on to de tree."

"Well, now, Jupiter, do exactly as I tell you, — do you hear?"

"Yes, massa."

"Pay attention, then! — find the left eye of the skull."

"Hum! hoo! dat 's good! why, dare ain't no eye lef' at all."

"Curse your stupidity! do you know your right hand from your left?"

"Yes, I nose dat, — nose all 'bout dat, — 't is my lef' hand what I chops de wood wid."

"To be sure! you are left-handed; and your left eye is on the same side as your left hand. Now, I suppose, you can find the left eye of the skull, or the place where the left eye has been. Have you found it?"

Here was a long pause. At length the negro asked:

"Is de lef' eye of de skull 'pon de same side as de lef' hand of de skull too? — 'cause de skull ain't not got a bit ob a hand at all, — nebber mind! I got de lef' eye now, — here de lef' eye! what mus' do wid it?"

"Let the beetle drop through it, as far as the string will reach, — but be careful and not let go your hold of the string."

"All dat done, Massa Will; mighty easy ting for to put de bug fru de hole, — look out for him dare below!"

During this colloquy no portion of Jupiter's person could be seen; but the beetle, which he had suffered to descend, was now visible at the end of the string, and glistened, like a globe of burnished gold, in the last rays of the setting sun, some of which still faintly illumined the eminence upon which we stood. The *scarabæus* hung quite clear of any branches, and, if allowed to fall, would have fallen at our feet. Legrand immediately took the scythe, and cleared with it a circular space, three or four yards in diameter, just beneath the insect, and having accomplished this, ordered Jupiter to let go the string and come down from the tree.

Driving a peg, with great nicety, into the ground, at the precise spot where the beetle fell, my friend now produced from his pocket a tape-measure. Fastening one end of this at that point of the trunk of the tree which was nearest the peg, he unrolled it till it reached the peg, and thence farther unrolled it, in the direction already established by the two points of the tree and the peg, for the distance of fifty feet, — Jupiter clearing away the brambles with the scythe. At the spot thus attained a second peg was driven, and about this, as a centre, a rude circle, about four feet in diameter, described. Taking now a spade himself, and giving one to Jupiter and one to me, Legrand begged us to set about digging as quickly as possible.

To speak the truth, I had no especial relish for such amusement at any time, and, at that particular moment, would most willingly have declined it; for the night was coming on, and I felt much fatigued with the exercise already taken; but I saw no mode of escape, and was fearful of disturbing my poor friend's equanimity by a refusal. Could I have depended, indeed, upon Jupiter's aid, I would have had no hesitation in attempting to get the lunatic home by force; but I was too well assured of the old negro's disposition, to hope that he would assist me, under any circumstances, in a personal contest with his master. I made no doubt that the latter had been infected with some of the innumerable Southern superstitions about money buried, and that his fantasy had received confirmation by the finding of the *scarabæus*, or, perhaps, by Jupiter's obstinacy in maintaining it to be " a bug of real gold." A mind disposed to lunacy would readily be led away by such suggestions, — especially if chiming in with favorite preconceived ideas, — and then I called to mind the poor fellow's speech about the beetle's being "the index of his fortune." Upon the whole, I was sadly vexed and puzzled, but, at length, I concluded to make a virtue of necessity, — to dig with a good will, and thus the sooner to convince the visionary, by ocular demonstration, of the fallacy of the opinions he entertained.

The lanterns having been lit, we all fell to work with a zeal worthy a more rational cause ; and, as the glare fell upon our persons and implements, I could not help thinking how picturesque a group we composed, and how strange and suspicious our labors must have appeared to any interloper who, by chance, might have stumbled upon our whereabouts.

We dug very steadily for two hours. Little was said ; and our chief embarrassment lay in the yelpings of the dog, who took exceeding interest in our proceedings. He at length became so obstreperous that we grew fearful of his giving the alarm to some stragglers in the vicinity, — or, rather, this was the apprehension of Legrand ; — for myself, I should have rejoiced at any interruption which might have enabled me to get the wanderer home. The noise was, at length, very effectually silenced by Jupiter, who, getting out of the hole with a dogged air of deliberation, tied the brute's mouth up with one of his suspenders, and then returned, with a grave chuckle, to his task.

When the time mentioned had expired, we had reached a depth of five feet, and yet no signs of any treasure became manifest. A general pause ensued, and I began to hope that the farce was at an end. Legrand, however, although evidently much disconcerted, wiped his brow thoughtfully, and recommenced. We had excavated the entire circle of four feet diameter, and now we slightly enlarged the limit, and went to the farther depth of two feet. Still nothing appeared. The gold-seeker, whom I sincerely pitied, at length clambered from the pit, with the bitterest disappointment imprinted upon every feature, and proceeded, slowly and reluctantly, to put on his coat, which he had thrown off at the beginning of his labor. In the meantime I made no remark. Jupiter, at a signal from his master, began to gather up his tools. This done, and the dog having been unmuzzled, we turned in profound silence towards home.

We had taken, perhaps, a dozen steps in this direction, when, with a loud oath, Legrand strode up to Jupiter, and seized him by the collar. The astonished negro opened his eyes and mouth to the fullest extent, let fall the spades, and fell upon his knees.

"You scoundrel," said Legrand, hissing out the syllables from between his clenched teeth, — "you infernal black villain! — speak, I tell you! — answer me this instant, without prevarication! — which — which is your left eye?"

"Oh, my golly, Massa Will! ain't dis here my lef eye for sartain?" roared the terrified Jupiter, placing his hand upon his *right* organ of vision, and holding it there with a desperate pertinacity, as if in immediate dread of his master's attempt at a gouge.

"I thought so! — I knew it! hurrah!" vociferated Legrand, letting the negro go, and executing a series of curvets and caracoles, much to the astonishment of his valet, who, arising from his knees, looked, mutely, from his master to myself, and then from myself to his master.

"Come! we must go back," said the latter, "the game's not up yet." And he again led the way to the tulip-tree.

"Jupiter," said he, when we reached its foot, "come here! Was the skull nailed to the limb with the face outwards, or with the face to the limb?"

"De face was out, massa, so dat de crows could get at de eyes good, widout any trouble."

"Well, then, was it this eye or that through which you

dropped the beetle?" — here Legrand touched each of Jupiter's eyes.

" 'T was dis eye, massa, — de lef' eye, — jis as you tell me," and here it was his right eye that the negro indicated.

" That will do, — we must try it again."

Here my friend, about whose madness I now saw, or fancied that I saw, certain indications of method, removed the peg which marked the spot where the beetle fell, to a spot about three inches to the westward of its former position. Taking, now, the tape-measure from the nearest point of the trunk to the peg, as before, and continuing the extension in a straight line to the distance of fifty feet, a spot was indicated, removed, by several yards, from the point at which we had been digging.

Around the new position a circle, somewhat larger than in the former instance, was now described, and we again set to work with the spades. I was dreadfully weary, but, scarcely understanding what had occasioned the change in my thoughts, I felt no longer any great aversion from the labor imposed. I had become most unaccountably interested, — nay, even excited. Perhaps there was something, amid all the extravagant demeanor of Legrand, — some air of forethought, or of deliberation, — which impressed me. I dug eagerly, and now and then caught myself actually looking, with something that very much resembled expectation, for the fancied treasure, the vision of which had demented my unfortunate companion. At a period when such vagaries of thought most fully possessed me, and when we had been at work perhaps an hour and a half, we were again interrupted by the violent howlings of the dog. His uneasiness, in the first instance, had been, evidently, but the result of playfulness or caprice, but he now assumed a bitter and serious tone. Upon Jupiter's again attempting to muzzle him, he made furious resistance, and, leaping into the hole, tore up the mould frantically with his claws. In a few seconds he had uncovered a mass of human bones, forming two complete skeletons, intermingled with several buttons of metal, and what appeared to be the dust of decayed woollen. One or two strokes of a spade upturned the blade of a large Spanish knife, and, as we dug farther, three or four loose pieces of gold and silver coin came to light.

At sight of these, the joy of Jupiter could scarcely be restrained, but the countenance of his master wore an air of extreme disappointment. He urged us, however, to continue our exertions, and the words were hardly uttered, when I stumbled and fell forward, having caught the toe of my boot in a large ring of iron that lay half buried in the loose earth.

We now worked in earnest, and never did I pass ten minutes of more intense excitement. During this interval we had fairly unearthed an oblong chest of wood, which, from its perfect preservation and wonderful hardness, had plainly been subjected to some mineralizing process, — perhaps that of the bichloride of mercury. This box was three feet and a half long, three feet broad, and two and a half feet deep. It was firmly secured by bands of wrought-iron, riveted, and forming a kind of open trellis-work over the whole. On each side of the chest, near the top, were three rings of iron, — six in all, — by means of which a firm hold could be obtained by six persons. Our utmost united endeavors served only to disturb the coffer very slightly in its bed. We at once saw the impossibility of removing so great a weight. Luckily, the sole fastenings of the lid consisted of two sliding bolts. These we drew back, — trembling and panting with anxiety. In an instant, a treasure of incalculable value lay gleaming before us. As the rays of the lanterns fell within the pit, there flashed upwards a glow and a glare, from a confused heap of gold and of jewels, that absolutely dazzled our eyes.

I shall not pretend to describe the feelings with which I gazed. Amazement was, of course, predominant. Legrand appeared exhausted with excitement, and spoke very few words. Jupiter's countenance wore, for some minutes, as deadly a pallor as it is possible, in the nature of things, for any negro's visage to assume. He seemed stupefied, — thunder-stricken. Presently he fell upon his knees in the pit, and, burying his naked arms up to the elbows in gold, let them there remain, as if enjoying the luxury of a bath. At length, with a deep sigh, he exclaimed, as if in a soliloquy:

" And dis all cum ob de goole-bug! de putty goole-bug! de poor little goole-bug, what I boosed in dat sabage kind ob style! Ain't you 'shamed ob yourself, nigger? — Answer me dat!"

It became necessary, at last, that I should arouse both master and valet to the expediency of removing the treasure. It was growing late, and it behooved us to make exertion, that we might get everything housed before daylight. It was difficult to say what should be done, and much time was spent in deliberation, — so confused were the ideas of all. We finally lightened the box by removing two-thirds of its contents, when we were enabled, with some trouble, to raise it from the hole. The articles taken out were deposited among the brambles, and the dog left to guard them, with strict orders from Jupiter neither, upon any pretence, to stir from the spot, nor to open his mouth, until our return. We then hurriedly made for home with the chest; reaching the hut in safety, but after excessive toil, at one o'clock in the morning. Worn out as we were, it was not in human nature to do more immediately. We rested until two, and had supper; starting for the hills immediately afterwards, armed with three stout sacks, which, by good luck, were upon the premises. A little before four we arrived at the pit, divided the remainder of the booty, as equally as might be, among us, and, leaving the holes unfilled, again set out for the hut, at which, for the second time, we deposited our golden burdens, just as the first faint streaks of the dawn gleamed from over the tree-tops in the east.

We were now thoroughly broken down; but the intense excitement of the time denied us repose. After an unquiet slumber of some three or four hours' duration, we arose, as if by preconcert, to make examination of our treasure.

The chest had been full to the brim, and we spent the whole day and the greater part of the next night in a scrutiny of its contents. There had been nothing like order or arrangement. Everything had been heaped in promiscuously. Having assorted all with care, we found ourselves possessed of even vaster wealth than we had at first supposed. In coin there was rather more than four hundred and fifty thousand dollars, — estimating the value of the pieces, as accurately as we could, by the tables of the period. There was not a particle of silver. All was gold of antique date and of great variety, — French, Spanish, and German money, with a few English guineas, and some counters, of which we had never seen specimens before. There were several very large and heavy coins, so worn that we could make nothing of their inscriptions. There was no American money. The value of the jewels we found more difficulty in estimating. There were diamonds, — some of them exceedingly large and fine, — a hundred and ten in all, and not one of them small; eighteen rubies of remarkable brilliancy; three hundred and ten emeralds, all very beautiful; and twenty-one sapphires, with an opal. These stones had all been broken from their settings and thrown loose in the chest. The settings themselves, which we picked out from among the other gold, appeared to have been beaten up with hammers as if to prevent identification. Besides all this, there was a vast quantity of solid gold ornaments; — nearly two hundred massive finger and ear rings; — rich chains, — thirty of these, if I remember; — eighty-three very large and heavy crucifixes; — five gold censers of great value; — a prodigious golden punch-bowl, ornamented with richly chased vine-leaves and Bacchanalian figures; with two sword-handles exquisitely embossed, and many other smaller articles which I cannot recollect. The weight of these valuables exceeded three hundred and fifty pounds avoirdupois; and in this estimate I have not included one hundred and ninety-seven superb gold watches; three of the number being worth each five hundred dollars, if one. Many of them were very old, and as time-keepers valueless; the works having suffered, more or less, from corrosion; but all were richly jewelled and in cases of great worth. We estimated the entire contents of the chest, that night, at a million and a half of dollars; and, upon the subsequent disposal of the trinkets and jewels (a few being retained for our own use), it was found that we had greatly undervalued the treasure.

When, at length, we had concluded our examination, and the intense excitement of the time had in some measure subsided, Legrand, who saw that I was dying with

impatience for a solution of this most extraordinary rid-
dle, entered into a full detail of all the circumstances
connected with it.

" You remember," said he, " the night when I handed
you the rough sketch I had made of the *scarabæus*.
You recollect, also, that I became quite vexed at you
for insisting that my drawing resembled a death's-head.
When you first made this assertion I thought you were
jesting ; but afterwards I called to mind the peculiar spots
on the back of the insect, and admitted to myself that
your remark had some little foundation in fact. Still, the
sneer at my graphic powers irritated me, — for I am considered a good artist, — and, therefore, when you handed
me the scrap of parchment, I was about to crumple it up
and throw it angrily into the fire."

" The scrap of paper, you mean," said I.

" No ; it had much of the appearance of paper, and at
first I supposed it to be such, but when I came to draw
upon it, I discovered it, at once, to be a piece of very thin
parchment. It was quite dirty, you remember. Well, as
I was in the very act of crumpling it up, my glance fell
upon the sketch at which you had been looking, and you
may imagine my astonishment when I perceived, in fact,
the figure of a death's-head, just where, it seemed to me,
I had made the drawing of the beetle. For a moment I
was too much amazed to think with accuracy. I knew
that my design was very different in detail from this, —
although there was a certain similarity in general outline.
Presently I took a candle, and seating myself at the other
end of the room, proceeded to scrutinize the parchment
more closely. Upon turning it over, I saw my own sketch
upon the reverse, just as I had made it. My first idea,
now, was mere surprise at the really remarkable similarity of
outline, — at the singular coincidence involved in the fact

that, unknown to me, there should have been a skull upon the other side of the parchment, immediately beneath my figure of the *scarabæus*, and that this skull, not only in outline, but in size, should so closely resemble my drawing. I say the singularity of this coincidence absolutely stupefied me for a time. This is the usual effect of such coincidences. The mind struggles to establish a connection, — a sequence of cause and effect, — and, being unable to do so, suffers a species of temporary paralysis. But, when I recovered from this stupor, there dawned upon me gradually a conviction which startled me even far more than the coincidence. I began distinctly, positively, to remember that there had been *no* drawing upon the parchment when I made my sketch of the *scarabæus*. I became perfectly certain of this; for I recollected turning up first one side and then the other, in search of the cleanest spot. Had the skull been there then, of course I could not have failed to notice it. Here was indeed a mystery which I felt it impossible to explain; but, even at that early moment, there seemed to glimmer, faintly, within the most remote and secret chambers of my intellect, a glowworm-like conception of that truth which last night's adventure brought to so magnificent a demonstration. I arose at once, and putting the parchment securely away, dismissed all further reflection until I should be alone.

" When you had gone, and when Jupiter was fast asleep, I betook myself to a more methodical investigation of the affair. In the first place I considered the manner in which the parchment had come into my possession. The spot where we discovered the *scarabæus* was on the coast of the mainland, about a mile eastward of the island, and but a short distance above high-water mark. Upon my taking hold of it, it gave me a sharp bite, which caused me to let it drop. Jupiter, with his accustomed caution, before seizing the insect, which had flown towards him, looked about him for a leaf, or something of that nature, by which to take hold of it. . It was at this moment that his eyes, and mine also, fell upon the scrap of parchment, which I then supposed to be paper. It was lying half buried in the sand, a corner sticking up. Near the spot where we found it, I observed the remnants of the hull of what appeared to have been a ship's long-boat. The wreck seemed to have been there for a very great while ; for the resemblance to boat timbers could scarcely be traced.

" Well, Jupiter picked up the parchment, wrapped the beetle in it, and gave it to me. Soon afterwards we turned to go home, and on the way met Lieutenant G——. I showed him the insect, and he begged me to let him take it to the fort. Upon my consenting, he thrust it forthwith into his waistcoat-pocket, without the parchment in which it had been wrapped, and which I had continued to hold in my hand during his inspection. Perhaps he dreaded my changing my mind, and thought it best to make sure of the prize at once,—you know how enthusiastic he is on all subjects connected with natural history. At the same time, without being conscious of it, I must have deposited the parchment in my own pocket.

" You remember that when I went to the table, for the purpose of making a sketch of the beetle, I found no paper where it was usually kept. I looked in the drawer, and found none there. I searched my pockets, hoping to find an old letter, when my hand fell upon the parchment. I thus detail the precise mode in which it came into my possession ; for the circumstances impressed me with peculiar force.

" No doubt you will think me fanciful, — but I had already established a kind of *connection*. I had put together two links of a great chain. There was a boat lying upon a sea-coast, and not far from the boat was a parchment — *not a paper* — with a skull depicted upon it. You will, of course, ask: 'Where is the connection?' I reply that the skull, or death's-head, is the well-known emblem of the pirate. The flag of the death's-head is hoisted in all engagements.

" I have said that the scrap was parchment, and not paper. Parchment is durable, — almost imperishable. Matters of little moment are rarely consigned to parchment; since, for the mere ordinary purposes of drawing or writing, it is not nearly so well adapted as paper. This reflection suggested some meaning — some relevancy — in the death's-head. I did not fail to observe, also, the *form* of the parchment. Although one of its corners had been, by some accident, destroyed, it could be seen that the original form was oblong. It was just such a slip, indeed, as might have been chosen for a memorandum, — for a record of something to be long remembered and carefully preserved."

" But," I interposed, you say that the skull was *not* upon the parchment when you made the drawing of the beetle. How then do you trace any connection between the boat and the skull, — since this latter, according to your own admission, must have been designed (God only knows how or by whom) at some period subsequent to your sketching the *scarabæus*?"

" Ah, hereupon turns the whole mystery; although the secret, at this point, I had comparatively little difficulty in solving. My steps were sure, and could afford but a single result. I reasoned, for example, thus: When I drew the *scarabæus*, there was no skull apparent upon the parchment. When I had completed the drawing I gave it to you, and observed you narrowly until you returned it. *You*, therefore, did not design the skull, and no one else was present to do it. Then it was not done by human agency. And nevertheless it was done.

"At this stage of my reflections I endeavored to remember, and *did* remember, with entire distinctness, every incident which occurred about the period in question. The weather was chilly (O rare and happy accident!), and a fire was blazing upon the hearth. I was heated with exercise, and sat near the table. You, however, had drawn a chair close to the chimney. Just as I placed the parchment in your hand, and as you were in the act of inspecting it, Wolf, the Newfoundland, entered, and leaped upon your shoulders. With your left hand you caressed him and kept him off, while your right, holding the parchment, was permitted to fall listlessly between your knees, and in close proximity to the fire. At one moment I thought the blaze had caught it, and was about to caution you, but, before I could speak, you had withdrawn it, and were engaged in its examination. When I considered all these particulars, I doubted not for a moment that *heat* had been the agent in bringing to light, upon the parchment, the skull which I saw designed upon it. You are well aware that chemical preparations exist, and have existed time out of mind, by means of which it is possible to write upon either paper or vellum, so that the characters shall become visible only when subjected to the action of fire. Zaffre, digested in *aqua regia*, and diluted with four times its weight of water, is sometimes employed; a green tint results. The regulus of cobalt, dissolved in spirit of nitre, gives a red. These colors disappear at longer or shorter intervals after the material written upon cools, but again become apparent upon the re-application of heat.

"I now scrutinized the death's-head with care. Its

outer edges — the edges of the drawing nearest the edge of the vellum — were far more *distinct* than the others. It was clear that the action of the caloric had been imperfect or unequal. I immediately kindled a fire, and subjected every portion of the parchment to a glowing heat. At first, the only effect was the strengthening of the faint lines in the skull; but, upon persevering in the experiment, there became visible, at the corner of the slip, diagonally opposite to the spot in which the death's-head was delineated, the figure of what I at first supposed to be a goat. A closer scrutiny, however, satisfied me that it was intended for a kid."

"Ha! ha!" said I, "to be sure I have no right to laugh at you, — a million and a half of money is too serious a matter for mirth, — but you are not about to establish a third link in your chain, — you will not find any especial connection between your pirates and a goat, — pirates, you know, have nothing to do with goats; they appertain to the farming interest."

"But I have just said that the figure was *not* that of a goat."

"Well, a kid then, — pretty much the same thing."

"Pretty much, but not altogether," said Legrand. "You may have heard of one *Captain* Kidd. I at once looked upon the figure of the animal as a kind of punning or hieroglyphical signature. I say signature, because its position upon the vellum suggested this idea. The death's-head at the corner diagonally opposite had, in the same manner, the air of a stamp, or seal. But I was sorely put out by the absence of all else — of the body to my imagined instrument — of the text for my context."

"I presume you expected to find a letter between the stamp and the signature."

"Something of that kind. The fact is, I felt irresistibly impressed with a presentiment of some vast good-fortune impending. I can scarcely say why. Perhaps, after all, it was rather a desire than an actual belief; — but do you know that Jupiter's silly words, about the bug being of solid gold, had a remarkable effect upon my fancy? And then the series of accidents and coincidences, — these were so *very* extraordinary. Do you observe how mere an accident it was that these events should have occurred upon the *sole* day of all the year in which it has been, or may be, sufficiently cool for fire, and that without the fire, or without the intervention of the dog at the precise moment in which he appeared, I should never have become aware of the death's-head, and so never the possessor of the treasure?"

"But proceed, — I am all impatience."

"Well; you have heard, of course, the many stories current — the thousand vague rumors afloat about money buried, somewhere upon the Atlantic coast, by Kidd and his associates. These rumors must have had some foundation in fact. And that the rumors have existed so long and so continuously could have resulted, it appeared to me, only from the circumstance of the buried treasure still *remaining* entombed. Had Kidd concealed his plunder for a time, and afterwards reclaimed it, the rumors would scarcely have reached us in their present unvarying form. You will observe that the stories told are all about money-seekers, not about money-finders. Had the pirate recovered his money, there the affair would have dropped. It seemed to me that some accident — say the loss of a memorandum indicating its locality — had deprived him of the means of recovering it, and that this accident had become known to his followers, who otherwise might never have heard that treasure had been concealed at all, and who, busying themselves in

vain, because unguided, attempts to regain it, had given
first birth, and then universal currency, to the reports
which are now so common. Have you ever heard of any
important treasure being unearthed along the coast? "

" Never."

" But that Kidd's accumulations were immense, is
well known. I took it for granted, therefore, that the
earth still held them ; and you will scarcely be surprised
when I tell you that I felt a hope, nearly amounting to
certainty, that the parchment so strangely found involved
a lost record of the place of deposit."

" But how did you proceed ? "

" I held the vellum again to the fire, after increasing
the heat ; but nothing appeared. I now thought it
possible that the coating of dirt might have something to
do with the failure ; so I carefully rinsed the parchment
by pouring warm water over it, and, having done this,
I placed it in a tin pan, with the skull downwards,
and put the pan upon a furnace of lighted charcoal.
In a few minutes, the pan having become thoroughly
heated, I removed the slip, and, to my inexpressible joy,
found it spotted, in several places, with what appeared
to be figures arranged in lines. Again I placed it in the
pan, and suffered it to remain another minute. Upon
taking it off, the whole was just as you see it now."

Here Legrand, having re-heated the parchment, sub-
mitted it to my inspection. The following characters
were rudely traced, in a red tint, between the death's-
head and the goat :

53‡‡†305))6*;4826)4‡.)4‡);806*;48†8¶60))85;1‡
(;:‡*8†83(88)5*†;46(;88*96*?;8)*‡(;485);5*†2:*‡(;
4956*2(5*—4)8¶8*;4069285);)6†8)4‡‡;1(‡9;48081
;8:8‡1;48†85;4)485†528806*81(‡9;48;8)8;4(‡?34;48)
4‡;161;:188;‡?;

"But," said I, returning him the slip, "I am as much in the dark as ever. Were all the jewels of Golconda awaiting me upon my solution of this enigma, I am quite sure that I should be unable to earn them."

"And yet," said Legrand, "the solution is by no means so difficult as you might be led to imagine from the first hasty inspection of the characters. These characters, as any one might readily guess, form a cipher — that is to say, they convey a meaning; but then, from what is known of Kidd, I could not suppose him capable of constructing any of the more abstruse cryptographs. I made up my mind, at once, that this was of a simple species, — such, however, as would appear, to the crude intellect of the sailor, absolutely insoluble without the key."

"And you really solved it?"

"Readily; I have solved others of an abstruseness ten thousand times greater. Circumstances, and a certain bias of mind, have led me to take interest in such riddles, and it may well be doubted whether human ingenuity can construct an enigma of the kind which human ingenuity may not, by proper application, resolve. In fact, having once established connected and legible characters, I scarcely gave a thought to the mere difficulty of developing their import.

"In the present case, — indeed in all cases of secret writing, — the first question regards the *language* of the cipher; for the principles of solution, so far, especially, as the more simple ciphers are concerned, depend upon, and are varied by, the genius of the particular idiom. In general, there is no alternative but experiment (directed by probabilities) of every tongue known to him who attempts the solution, until the true one be attained. But, with the cipher now before us, all difficulty was removed by the signature. The pun upon the word

' Kidd ' is appreciable in no other language than the
English.   But for this consideration I should have begun
my attempts with the Spanish and French, as the tongues
in which a secret of this kind would most naturally have
been written by a pirate of the Spanish main.   As it was,
I assumed the cryptograph to be English.

"You observe there are no divisions between the
words.   Had there been divisions, the task would have
been comparatively easy.   In such case I should have
commenced with a collation and analysis of the shorter
words, and, had a word of a single letter occurred, as is
most likely (*a* or *I*, for example), I should have considered
the solution as assured.   But, there being no division,
my first step was to ascertain the predominant letters, as
well as the least frequent.   Counting all, I constructed
a table, thus :

Of the character 8 there are 33.

;	"	26.
4	"	19.
‡)	"	16.
*	"	13.
5	"	12.
6	"	11.
† 1	"	8.
0	"	6.
9 2	"	5.
: 3	"	4.
?	"	3.
¶	"	2.
— .	"	1.

"Now, in English, the letter which most frequently
occurs is *e*.   Afterwards, the succession runs thus : *a o i*

d h n r s t u y c f g l m w b k p q x z. *E* predominates so remarkably, that an individual sentence of any length is rarely seen in which it is not the prevailing character.

"Here, then, we have, in the very beginning, the groundwork for something more than a mere guess. The general use which may be made of the table is obvious; but, in this particular cipher, we shall only very partially require its aid. As our predominant character is 8, we will commence by assuming it as the *e* of the natural alphabet. To verify the supposition, let us observe if the 8 be seen often in couples, — for *e* is doubled with great frequency in English, — in such words, for example, as 'meet,' 'fleet,' 'speed,' 'seen,' 'been,' 'agree,' etc. In the present instance we see it doubled no less than five times, although the cryptograph is brief.

"Let us assume 8, then, as *e*. Now, of all *words* in the language, 'the' is most usual; let us see, therefore, whether there are not repetitions of any three characters, in the same order of collocation, the last of them being 8. If we discover repetitions of such letters, so arranged, they will most probably represent the word 'the.' Upon inspection, we find no less than seven such arrangements, the characters being ;48. We may, therefore, assume that ; represents *t*, 4 represents *h*, and 8 represents *e*, — the last being now well confirmed. Thus a great step has been taken.

"But, having established a single word, we are enabled to establish a vastly important point; that is to say, several commencements and terminations of other words. Let us refer, for example, to the last instance but one, in which the combination ;48 occurs, — not far from the end of the cipher. We know that the ; immediately ensuing is the commencement of a word,

and, of the six characters succeeding this 'the,' we are
cognizant of no less than five. Let us set these characters down, thus, by the letters we know them to represent, leaving a space for the unknown —

t eeth.

"Here we are enabled, at once, to discard the *th*, as
forming no portion of the word commencing with the
first *t;* since, by experiment of the entire alphabet for a
letter adapted to the vacancy, we perceive that no word
can be formed of which this *th* can be a part. We are
thus narrowed into

t ee,

and, going through the alphabet, if necessary, as before,
we arrive at the word 'tree,' as the sole possible reading. We thus gain another letter, *r*, represented by (,
with the words 'the tree' in juxtaposition.

"Looking beyond these words, for a short distance,
we again see the combination ;48, and employ it by
way of *termination* to what immediately precedes. We
have thus this arrangement :

the tree ;4(‡?34 the,

or, substituting the natural letters, where known, it reads
thus :

the tree thr‡?3h the.

"Now, if, in place of the unknown characters, we
leave blank spaces, or substitute dots, we read thus :

the tree thr...h the,

when the word 'through' makes itself evident at once.
But this discovery gives us three new letters, *o*, *u*, and *g*,
represented by ‡, ?, and 3.

"Looking, now, narrowly, through the cipher for
combinations of known characters, we find, not very far
from the beginning, this arrangement,

$$83(88, \text{ or } egree,$$

which, plainly, is the conclusion of the word 'degree,'
and gives us another letter *d*, represented by †.

"Four letters beyond the word 'degree,' we perceive
the combination

$$;46(;88*.$$

"Translating the known characters, and representing
the unknown by dots, as before, we read thus:

$$th.rtee.,$$

an arrangement immediately suggestive of the word
'thirteen,' and again furnishing us with two new characters, *i* and *n*, represented by 6 and *.

"Referring, now, to the beginning of the cryptograph, we find the combination,

$$53\ddagger\ddagger\dagger.$$

"Translating, as before, we obtain

$$.good,$$

which assures us that the first letter is *A*, and that the
first two words are 'A good.'

"It is now time that we arrange our key, as far as

discovered, in a tabular form, to avoid confusion. It will stand thus:

5	represents	a
†	"	d
8	"	e
3	"	g
4	"	h
6	"	i
*	"	n
‡	"	o
(	"	r
;	"	t
?	"	u

"We have, therefore, no less than eleven of the most important letters represented, and it will be unnecessary to proceed with the details of the solution. I have said enough to convince you that ciphers of this nature are readily soluble, and to give you some insight into the *rationale* of their development. But be assured that the specimen before us appertains to the very simplest species of cryptograph. It now only remains to give you the full translation of the characters upon the parchment, as unriddled. Here it is:

" '*A good glass in the bishop's hostel in the devil's seat forty-one degrees and thirteen minutes northeast and by north main branch seventh limb east side shoot from the left eye of the death's-head a bee line from the tree through the shot fifty feet out.*' "

"But," said I, "the enigma seems still in as bad a condition as ever. How is it possible to extort a meaning from all this jargon about 'devil's seats,' 'death's-heads,' and 'bishop's hotels'?"

"I confess," replied Legrand, "that the matter still wears a serious aspect, when regarded with a casual glance. My first endeavor was to divide the sentence into the natural division intended by the cryptographist."

"You mean, to punctuate it?"

"Something of that kind."

"But how was it possible to effect this?"

"I reflected that it had been a *point* with the writer to run his words together without division, so as to increase the difficulty of solution. Now, a not over-acute man, in pursuing such an object, would be nearly certain to overdo the matter. When, in the course of his composition, he arrived at a break in his subject which would naturally require a pause, or a point, he would be exceedingly apt to run his characters, at this place, more than usually close together. If you will observe the manuscript in the present instance, you will easily detect five such cases of unusual crowding. Acting upon this hint, I made the division thus:

" ' *A good glass in the bishop's hostel in the devils' seat —forty-one degrees and thirteen minutes — northeast and by north — main branch seventh limb east side — shoot from the left eye of the death's-head — a bee-line from the tree through the shot fifty feet out.*' "

"Even this division," said I, "leaves me still in the dark."

"It left me also in the dark," replied Legrand, "for a few days; during which I made diligent inquiry, in the neighborhood of Sullivan's Island, for any building which went by the name of the 'Bishop's Hotel'; for, of course, I dropped the obsolete word 'hostel.' Gain-

ing no information on the subject, I was on the point of
extending my sphere of search, and proceeding in a
more systematic manner, when, one morning, it entered
into my head, quite suddenly, that this 'Bishop's Hostel' might have some reference to an old family, of the
name of Bessop, which, time out of mind, had held
possession of an ancient manor-house, about four miles
to the northward of the island. I accordingly went over
to the plantation, and reinstituted my inquiries among
the older negroes of the place. At length one of the
most aged of the women said that she had heard of
such a place as *Bessop's Castle*, and thought that she
could guide me to it, but that it was not a castle, nor a
tavern, but a high rock.

"I offered to pay her well for her trouble, and, after
some demur, she consented to accompany me to the
spot. We found it without much difficulty, when, dis-
missing her, I proceeded to examine the place. The
'castle' consisted of an irregular assemblage of cliffs
and rocks, — one of the latter being quite remarkable
for its height as well as for its insulated and artificial
appearance. I clambered to its apex, and then felt
much at a loss as to what should be next done.

"While I was busied in reflection, my eyes fell upon
a narrow ledge in the eastern face of the rock, perhaps
a yard below the summit upon which I stood. This
ledge projected about eighteen inches, and was not more
than a foot wide, while a niche in the cliff just above it
gave it a rude resemblance to one of the hollow-backed
chairs used by our ancestors. I made no doubt that
here was the 'devil's seat' alluded to in the manuscript,
and now I seemed to grasp the whole secret.

"The 'good glass,' I knew, could have reference to
nothing but a telescope; for the word 'glass' is rarely

employed in any other sense by seamen. Now here, I at once saw, was a telescope to be used, and a definite point of view, *admitting no variation,* from which to use it. Nor did I hesitate to believe that the phrases, 'forty-one degrees and thirteen minutes,' and 'northeast and by north,' were intended as directions for the levelling of the glass. Greatly excited by these discoveries, I hurried home, procured a telescope, and returned to the rock.

"I let myself down to the ledge, and found that it was impossible to retain a seat upon it except in one particular position. This fact confirmed my preconceived idea. I proceeded to use the glass. Of course, the 'forty-one degrees and thirteen minutes' could allude to nothing but elevation above the visible horizon, since the horizontal direction was clearly indicated by the words, 'northeast and by north.' This latter direction I at once established by means of a pocket-compass; then, pointing the glass as nearly at an angle of forty-one degrees of elevation as I could do it by guess, I moved it cautiously up or down, until my attention was arrested by a circular rift or opening in the foliage of a large tree that overtopped its fellows in the distance. In the centre of this rift I perceived a white spot, but could not, at first, distinguish what it was. Adjusting the focus of the telescope, I again looked, and now made it out to be a human skull.

"Upon this discovery I was so sanguine as to consider the enigma solved; for the phrase, 'main branch, seventh limb, east side,' could refer only to the position of the skull upon the tree, while 'shoot from the left eye of the death's-head' admitted, also, of but one interpretation, in regard to a search for buried treasure. I perceived that the design was to drop a bullet from the left eye of the skull, and that a bee-line, or, in other words, a straight line, drawn from the nearest point of the trunk through 'the shot' (or the spot where the bullet fell), and thence extended to a distance of fifty feet, would indicate a definite point, — and beneath this point I thought it at least *possible* that a deposit of value lay concealed."

"All this," I said, "is exceedingly clear, and, although ingenious, still simple and explicit. When you left the 'Bishop's Hotel,' what then?"

"Why, having carefully taken the bearings of the tree, I turned homewards. The instant that I left 'the devil's seat,' however, the circular rift vanished, nor could I get a glimpse of it afterwards, turn as I would. What seems to me the chief ingenuity in this whole business is the fact (for repeated experiment has convinced me it *is* a fact) that the circular opening in question is visible from no other attainable point of view than that afforded by the narrow ledge upon the face of the rock.

"In this expedition to the 'Bishop's Hotel' I had been attended by Jupiter, who had, no doubt, observed, for some weeks past, the abstraction of my demeanor, and took especial care not to leave me alone. But, on the next day, getting up very early, I contrived to give him the slip, and went into the hills in search of the tree. After much toil I found it. When I came home at night my valet proposed to give me a flogging. With the rest of the adventure I believe you are as well acquainted as myself."

"I suppose," said I, "you missed the spot, in the first attempt at digging, through Jupiter's stupidity in letting the bug fall through the right instead of through the left eye of the skull."

"Precisely. This mistake made a difference of about two inches and a half in 'the shot' — that is to say, in the position of the peg nearest the tree; and had the treasure been *beneath* 'the shot,' the error would have been of little moment; but 'the shot,' together with the nearest point of the tree, were merely two points for the establishment of a line of direction; of course the error, however trivial in the beginning, increased as we proceeded with the line, and by the time we had gone fifty feet threw us quite off the scent. But for my deep-seated impressions that treasure was here somewhere actually buried, we might have had all our labor in vain."

"But your grandiloquence, and your conduct in swinging the beetle, — how excessively odd! I was sure you were mad. And why did you insist upon letting fall the bug, instead of a bullet, from the skull?"

"Why, to be frank, I felt somewhat annoyed by your evident suspicions touching my sanity, and so resolved to punish you quietly, in my own way, by a little bit of sober mystification. For this reason I swung the beetle, and for this reason I let it fall from the tree. An observation of yours about its great weight suggested the latter idea."

"Yes, I perceive; and now there is only one point which puzzles me. What are we to make of the skeletons found in the hole?"

"That is a question I am no more able to answer than yourself. There seems, however, only one plausible way of accounting for them, — and yet it is dreadful to believe in such atrocity as my suggestion would imply. It is clear that Kidd, — if Kidd indeed secreted this treasure, which I doubt not, — it is clear that he must have had assistance in the labor. But, this labor con-

IX

THE GREAT STONE FACE

seems to have entered but slightly into the progress of the short story; but he took it up and made it the keynote of nearly all he wrote. His stories are all intended to illustrate a moral of some kind, just as Poe's were intended to illustrate an intellectual principle or problem.

We have already referred to the influence of the ballad and song on the short story, and have spoken of them as the source of the sentiment in Dickens. Hawthorne was to add to the short story also an element from the lyric and the poetic tale (so closely akin to the ballad and song), namely, beauty. Hawthorne even went further, and appropriated characteristics of the painter and the sculptor. A short story as Hawthorne tells it is a perfect canvas. The subject is arranged with a view to light and shade, and it is treated with perfect sense of color. Every line is a line of beauty, and the atmosphere is ethereal and æsthetic. In "The Great Stone Face" we also see the same lofty sentiment that we found in Dickens, the same intimate treatment of that which, but for fiction, must remain forever hidden from the world's eye, and the same succession of emotion following upon emotion. Poetry has always been apt in blending the noble and lofty in moral sentiment with the element of beauty; and in Hawthorne we find the ancient fable clothed most naturally and gracefully with the poet's clouds of fancy and splendor of color. Had Hawthorne possessed also Poe's masterful intellect, he would no doubt have proved to be the supreme genius of the short story. Poe, we shall find, has had many successors, but Hawthorne none.

THE GREAT STONE FACE.

ONE afternoon, when the sun was going down, a mother and her little boy sat at the door of their cottage, talking about the Great Stone Face. They had but to lift their eyes, and there it was plainly to be seen, though miles away, with the sunshine brightening all its features.

And what was the Great Stone Face?

Embosomed amongst a family of lofty mountains, there was a valley so spacious that it contained many thousand inhabitants. Some of these good people dwelt in log-huts, with the black forest all around them, on the steep and difficult hillsides. Others had their homes in comfortable farm-houses, and cultivated the rich soil on the gentle slopes or level surfaces of the valley. Others, again, were congregated into populous villages, where some wild, highland rivulet, tumbling down from its birth-place in the upper mountain region, had been caught and tamed by human cunning, and compelled to turn the machinery of cotton-factories. The inhabitants of this valley, in short, were numerous, and of many modes of life. But all of them, grown people and children, had a kind of familiarity with the Great Stone Face, although some possessed the gift of distinguishing this grand natural phenomenon more perfectly than many of their neighbors.

The Great Stone Face, then, was a work of Nature in her mood of majestic playfulness, formed on the perpendicular side of a mountain by some immense rocks, which had been thrown together in such a position as, when viewed at a proper distance, precisely to resemble the features of the human countenance. It seemed as if an enormous giant, or a Titan, had sculptured his own likeness on the precipice. There was the broad arch of the forehead, a hundred feet in height ; the nose, with its long bridge ; and the vast lips, which, if they could have spoken, would have rolled their thunder accents from one end of the valley to the other. True it is, that if the spectator approached too near, he lost the outline of the gigantic visage, and could discern only a heap of ponderous and gigantic rocks, piled in chaotic ruin one upon another. Retracing his steps, however, the wondrous features would again be seen ; and the farther he withdrew from them, the more like a human face, with all its original divinity intact, did they appear ; until, as it grew dim in the distance, with the clouds and glorified vapor of the mountains clustering about it, the Great Stone Face seemed positively to be alive.

It was a happy lot for children to grow up to manhood or womanhood with the Great Stone Face before their eyes, for all the features were noble, and the expression was at once grand and sweet, as if it were the glow of a vast, warm heart, that embraced all mankind in its affections, and had room for more. It was an education only to look at it. According to the belief of many people, the valley owed much of its fertility to this benign aspect that was continually beaming over it, illuminating the clouds, and infusing its tenderness into the sunshine.

As we began with saying, a mother and her little boy sat at their cottage-door, gazing at the Great Stone Face, and talking about it. The child's name was Ernest.

"Mother," said he, while the Titanic visage smiled on him, "I wish that it could speak, for it looks so very kindly that its voice must needs be pleasant. If I were to see a man with such a face, I should love him dearly."

"If an old prophecy should come to pass," answered his mother, "we may see a man, some time or other, with exactly such a face as that."

"What prophecy do you mean, dear mother?" eagerly inquired Ernest. "Pray tell me all about it!"

So his mother told him a story that her own mother had told to her, when she herself was younger than little Ernest; a story, not of things that were past, but of what was yet to come; a story, nevertheless, so very old, that even the Indians, who formerly inhabited this valley, had heard it from their forefathers, to whom, as they affirmed, it had been murmured by the mountain streams, and whispered by the wind among the tree-tops. The purport was, that, at some future day, a child should be born hereabouts, who was destined to become the greatest and noblest personage of his time, and whose countenance, in manhood, should bear an exact resemblance to the Great Stone Face. Not a few old-fashioned people, and young ones likewise, in the ardor of their hopes, still cherished an enduring faith in this old prophecy. But others, who had seen more of the world, had watched and waited till they were weary, and had beheld no man with such a face, nor any man that proved to be much greater or nobler than his neighbors, concluded it to be nothing but an idle tale. At all events, the great man of the prophecy had not yet appeared.

"O mother, dear mother!" cried Ernest, clapping his hands above his head, "I do hope that I shall live to see him!"

His mother was an affectionate and thoughtful woman, and felt that it was wisest not to discourage the generous hopes of her little boy. So she only said to him, "Perhaps you may."

And Ernest never forgot the story that his mother told him. It was always in his mind, whenever he looked upon the Great Stone Face. He spent his childhood in the log-cottage where he was born, and was dutiful to his mother, and helpful to her in many things, assisting her much with his little hands, and more with his loving heart. In this manner, from a happy yet often pensive child, he grew up to be a mild, quiet, unobtrusive boy, and sun-browned with labor in the fields, but with more intelligence brightening his aspect than is seen in many lads who have been taught at famous schools. Yet Ernest had had no teacher, save only that the Great Stone Face became one to him. When the toil of the day was over, he would gaze at it for hours, until he began to imagine that those vast features recognized him, and gave him a smile of kindness and encouragement, responsive to his own look of veneration. We must not take upon us to affirm that this was a mistake, although the Face may have looked no more kindly at Ernest than at all the world besides. But the secret was, that the boy's tender and confiding simplicity discerned what other people could not see ; and thus the love, which was meant for all, became his peculiar portion.

About this time, there went a rumor throughout the valley, that the great man, foretold from ages long ago, who was to bear a resemblance to the Great Stone Face, had appeared at last. It seems that, many years before, a young man had migrated from the valley and settled at a distant seaport, where, after getting together a little money, he had set up as a shopkeeper. His name — but I could never learn whether it was his real one, or a nickname that had grown out of his habits and success in life — was Gathergold. Being shrewd and active, and endowed by Providence with that inscrutable faculty which develops itself in what the world calls luck, he became an exceedingly rich merchant, and owner of a whole fleet of bulky-bottomed ships. All the countries of the globe appeared to join hands for the mere purpose of adding heap after heap to the mountainous accumulation of this one man's wealth. The cold regions of the north, almost within the gloom and shadow of the Arctic Circle, sent him their tribute in the shape of furs; hot Africa sifted for him the golden sands of her rivers, and gathered up the ivory tusks of her great elephants out of the forests; the East came bringing him the rich shawls, and spices, and teas, and the effulgence of diamonds, and the gleaming purity of large pearls; the ocean, not to be behindhand with the earth, yielding up her mighty whales, that Mr. Gathergold might sell their oil, and make a profit on it. Be the original commodity what it might, it was gold within his grasp. It might be said of him, as of Midas in the fable, that whatever he touched with his finger immediately glistened, and grew yellow, and was changed at once into sterling metal, or, which suited him still better, into piles of coin. And, when Mr. Gathergold had become so very rich that it would have taken him a hundred years only to count his wealth, he bethought himself of his native valley, and resolved to go back thither, and end his days where he was born. With this purpose in view, he sent a skilful architect to build him such a palace as should be fit for a man of his vast wealth to live in.

As I have said above, it had already been rumored in the valley that Mr. Gathergold had turned out to be the prophetic personage so long and vainly looked for, and that his visage was the perfect and undeniable similitude

of the Great Stone Face. People were the more ready
to believe that this must needs be the fact, when they beheld the splendid edifice that rose, as if by enchantment,
on the site of his father's old weather-beaten farm-house.
The exterior was of marble, so dazzlingly white that it
seemed as though the whole structure might melt away
in the sunshine, like those humbler ones which Mr. Gathergold, in his young play-days, before his fingers were
gifted with the touch of transmutation, had been accustomed to build of snow. It had a richly ornamented
portico, supported by tall pillars, beneath which was a
lofty door, studded with silver knobs, and made of a kind
of variegated wood that had been brought from beyond
the sea. The windows, from the floor to the ceiling of
each stately apartment, were composed, respectively, of
but one enormous pane of glass, so transparently pure
that it was said to be a finer medium than even the vacant atmosphere. Hardly anybody had been permitted
to see the interior of this palace; but it was reported,
and with good semblance of truth, to be far more gorgeous than the outside, insomuch that whatever was iron
or brass in other houses was silver or gold in this; and
Mr. Gathergold's bedchamber, especially, made such a
glittering appearance that no ordinary man would have
been able to close his eyes there. But, on the other
hand, Mr. Gathergold was now so inured to wealth, that
perhaps he could not have closed his eyes unless where
the gleam of it was certain to find its way beneath his
eyelids.

In due time, the mansion was finished; next came the
upholsterers, with magnificent furniture; then, a whole
troop of black and white servants, the harbingers of Mr.
Gathergold, who, in his own majestic person, was expected to arrive at sunset. Our friend Ernest, mean-

while, had been deeply stirred by the idea that the great man, the noble man, the man of prophecy, after so many ages of delay, was at length to be made manifest to his native valley. He knew, boy as he was, that there were a thousand ways in which Mr. Gathergold, with his vast wealth, might transform himself into an angel of benefi-cence, and assume a control over human affairs as wide and benignant as the smile of the Great Stone Face. Full of faith and hope, Ernest doubted not that what the people said was true, and that now he was to behold the living likeness of those wondrous features on the moun-tain-side. While the boy was still gazing up the valley, and fancying, as he always did, that the Great Stone Face returned his gaze and looked kindly at him, the rumbling of wheels was heard, approaching swiftly along the winding road.

"Here he comes!" cried a group of people who were assembled to witness the arrival. "Here comes the great Mr. Gathergold!"

A carriage, drawn by four horses, dashed round the turn of the road. Within it, thrust partly out of the window, appeared the physiognomy of a little old man, with a skin as yellow as if his own Midas-hand had transmuted it. He had a low forehead, small, sharp eyes, puckered about with innumerable wrinkles, and very thin lips, which he made still thinner by pressing them forcibly together.

"The very image of the Great Stone Face!" shouted the people. "Sure enough, the old prophecy is true; and here we have the great man come, at last!"

And, what greatly perplexed Ernest, they seemed act-ually to believe that here was the likeness which they spoke of. By the roadside there chanced to be an old beggar-woman and two little beggar-children, stragglers from some far-off region, who, as the carriage rolled onward, held out their hands and lifted up their doleful voices, most piteously beseeching charity. A yellow claw — the very same that had clawed together so much wealth — poked itself out of the coach-window, and dropped some copper coins upon the ground; so that, though the great man's name seems to have been Gathergold, he might just as suitably have been nicknamed Scattercopper. Still, nevertheless, with an earnest shout, and evidently with as much good faith as ever, the people bellowed, —

"He is the very image of the Great Stone Face!"

But Ernest turned sadly from the wrinkled shrewdness of that sordid visage, and gazed up the valley, where, amid a gathering mist, gilded by the last sunbeams, he could still distinguish those glorious features which had impressed themselves into his soul. Their aspect cheered him. What did the benign lips seem to say?

"He will come! Fear not, Ernest; the man will come!"

The years went on, and Ernest ceased to be a boy. He had grown to be a young man now. He attracted little notice from the other inhabitants of the valley; for they saw nothing remarkable in his way of life, save that, when the labor of the day was over, he still loved to go apart and gaze and meditate upon the Great Stone Face. According to their idea of the matter, it was a folly, indeed, but pardonable, inasmuch as Ernest was industrious, kind, and neighborly, and neglected no duty for the sake of indulging this idle habit. They knew not that the Great Stone Face had become a teacher to him, and that the sentiment which was expressed in it would enlarge the young man's heart, and fill it with wider and deeper sympathies than other hearts. They knew not that thence would come a better wisdom than could be learned from books, and a better life than could be moulded on the defaced example of other human lives. Neither did Ernest know that the thoughts and affections which came to him so naturally, in the fields and at the fireside, and wherever he communed with himself, were of a higher tone than those which all men shared with him. A simple soul, — simple as when his mother first taught him the old prophecy, — he beheld the marvellous features beaming adown the valley, and still wondered that their human counterpart was so long in making his appearance.

By this time poor Mr. Gathergold was dead and buried; and the oddest part of the matter was, that his wealth, which was the body and spirit of his existence, had disappeared before his death, leaving nothing of him but a living skeleton, covered over with a wrinkled, yellow skin. Since the melting away of his gold, it had been very generally conceded that there was no such striking resemblance, after all, betwixt the ignoble features of the ruined merchant and that majestic face upon the mountain-side. So the people ceased to honor him during his lifetime, and quietly consigned him to forgetfulness after his decease. Once in a while, it is true, his memory was brought up in connection with the magnificent palace which he had built, and which had long ago been turned into a hotel for the accommodation of strangers, multitudes of whom came, every summer, to visit that famous natural curiosity, the Great Stone Face. Thus, Mr. Gathergold being discredited and thrown into the shade, the man of prophecy was yet to come.

It so happened that a native-born son of the valley, many years before, had enlisted as a soldier, and, after a great deal of hard fighting, had now become an illustrious commander. Whatever he may be called in history, he was known in camps and on the battle-field under the nickname of Old Blood-and-Thunder. This war-worn veteran, being now infirm with age and wounds, and weary of the turmoil of a military life, and of the roll of the drum and the clangor of the trumpet, that had so long been ringing in his ears, had lately signified a purpose of returning to his native valley, hoping to find repose where he remembered to have left it. The inhabitants, his old neighbors and their grown-up children, were resolved to welcome the renowned warrior with a salute of cannon and a public dinner; and all the more enthusiastically, it being affirmed that now, at last, the likeness of the Great Stone Face had actually appeared. An aid-de-camp of Old Blood-and-Thunder, travelling through the valley, was said to have been struck with the resemblance. Moreover the schoolmates and early acquaintances of the general were ready to testify, on oath, that, to the best of their recollection, the aforesaid general had been exceedingly like the majestic image, even when a boy, only that the idea had never occurred to them at that period. Great, therefore, was the excitement throughout the valley; and many people, who had never once thought of glancing at the Great Stone Face for years before, now spent their time in gazing at it, for the sake of knowing exactly how General Blood-and-Thunder looked.

On the day of the great festival, Ernest, with all the other people of the valley, left their work, and proceeded to the spot where the sylvan banquet was prepared. As he approached, the loud voice of the Rev. Dr. Battleblast was heard, beseeching a blessing on the good things set before them, and on the distinguished friend of peace in whose honor they were assembled. The tables were arranged in a cleared space of the woods, shut in by the surrounding trees, except where a vista opened eastward, and afforded a distant view of the Great Stone Face. Over the general's chair, which was a relic from the home of Washington, there was an arch of verdant boughs, with the laurel profusely intermixed, and surmounted by his country's banner, beneath which he had won his victories. Our friend Ernest raised himself on his tiptoes, in hopes to get a glimpse of the celebrated guest; but there was a mighty crowd about the tables anxious to hear the toasts and speeches, and to catch any word that might fall from the general in reply; and a volunteer company, doing duty as a guard, pricked ruthlessly with their bayonets at any particularly quiet person among the throng. So Ernest, being of an unobtrusive character, was thrust quite into the background, where he could see no more of Old Blood-and-Thunder's physiognomy than if it had been still blazing on the battle-field. To console himself, he turned towards the Great Stone Face, which, like a faithful and long-remembered friend, looked back and smiled upon him through the vista of the forest. Meantime, however, he could overhear the remarks of various individuals, who were comparing the features of the hero with the face on the distant mountain-side.

"'T is the same face, to a hair!" cried one man, cutting a caper for joy.

"Wonderfully like, that's a fact!" responded another.

"Like! why, I call it Old Blood-and-Thunder himself, in a monstrous looking-glass!" cried a third. "And why not? He's the greatest man of this or any other age, beyond a doubt."

And then all three of the speakers gave a great shout,

which communicated electricity to the crowd, and called forth a roar from a thousand voices, that went reverberating for miles among the mountains, until you might have supposed that the Great Stone Face had poured its thunder-breath into the cry. All these comments, and this vast enthusiasm, served the more to interest our friend; nor did he think of questioning that now, at length, the mountain-visage had found its human counterpart. It is true, Ernest had imagined that this long-looked-for personage would appear in the character of a man of peace, uttering wisdom, and doing good, and making people happy. But, taking an habitual breadth of view, with all his simplicity, he contended that Providence should choose its own method of blessing mankind, and could conceive that this great end might be effected even by a warrior and a bloody sword, should inscrutable wisdom see fit to order matters so.

"The general! the general!" was now the cry. "Hush! silence! Old Blood-and-Thunder's going to make a speech."

Even so; for, the cloth being removed, the general's health had been drunk amid shouts of applause, and he now stood upon his feet to thank the company. Ernest saw him. There he was, over the shoulders of the crowd, from the two glittering epaulets and embroidered collar upward, beneath the arch of green boughs with intertwined laurel, and the banner drooping as if to shade his brow! And there, too, visible in the same glance, through the vista of the forest, appeared the Great Stone Face! And was there, indeed, such a resemblance as the crowd had testified? Alas, Ernest could not recognize it! He beheld a war-worn and weather-beaten countenance, full of energy, and expressive of an iron will; but the gentle wisdom, the deep, broad, tender sympathies, were altogether wanting in Old Blood-and-Thunder's visage; and even if the Great Stone Face had assumed his look of stern command, the milder traits would still have tempered it.

"This is not the man of prophecy," sighed Ernest, to himself, as he made his way out of the throng. "And must the world wait longer yet?"

The mists had congregated about the distant mountain-side, and there were seen the grand and awful features of the Great Stone Face, awful but benignant, as if a mighty angel were sitting among the hills, and enrobing himself in a cloud-vesture of gold and purple. As he looked, Ernest could hardly believe but that a smile beamed over the whole visage, with a radiance still brightening, although without motion of the lips. It was probably the effect of the western sunshine, melting through the thinly diffused vapors that had swept between him and the object that he gazed at. But — as it always did — the aspect of his marvellous friend made Ernest as hopeful as if he had never hoped in vain.

"Fear not, Ernest," said his heart, even as if the Great Face were whispering him, — "fear not, Ernest; he will come."

More years sped swiftly and tranquilly away. Ernest still dwelt in his native valley, and was now a man of middle age. By imperceptible degrees, he had become known among the people. Now, as heretofore, he labored for his bread, and was the same simple-hearted man that he had always been. But he had thought and felt so much, he had given so many of the best hours of his life to unworldly hopes for some great good to mankind, that it seemed as though he had been talking with the angels, and had imbibed a portion of their wisdom unawares. It was visible in the calm and well-considered beneficence of his daily life, the quiet stream of which had made a wide green margin all along its course. Not a day passed by, that the world was not the better because this man, humble as he was, had lived. He never stepped aside from his own path, yet would always reach a blessing to his neighbor. Almost involuntarily, too, he had become a preacher. The pure and high simplicity of his thought, which, as one of its manifestations, took shape in the good deeds that dropped silently from his hand, flowed also forth in speech. He uttered truths that wrought upon and moulded the lives of those who heard him. His auditors, it may be, never suspected that Ernest, their own neighbor and familiar friend, was more than an ordinary man; least of all did Ernest himself suspect it; but, inevitably as the murmur of a rivulet, came thoughts out of his mouth that no other human lips had spoken.

When the people's minds had had a little time to cool, they were ready enough to acknowledge their mistake in imagining a similarity between General Blood-and-Thunder's truculent physiognomy and the benign visage on the mountain-side. But now, again, there were reports and many paragraphs in the newspapers, affirming that the likeness of the Great Stone Face had appeared upon the broad shoulders of a certain eminent statesman. He, like Mr. Gathergold and Old Blood-and-Thunder, was a native of the valley, but had left it in his early days, and taken up the trades of law and politics. Instead of the rich man's wealth and the warrior's sword, he had but a tongue, and it was mightier than both together. So wonderfully eloquent was he, that whatever he might choose to say, his auditors had no choice but to believe him; wrong looked like right, and right like wrong; for when it pleased him, he could make a kind of illuminated fog with his mere breath, and obscure the natural daylight with it. His tongue, indeed, was a magic instrument: sometimes it rumbled like the thunder; sometimes it warbled like the sweetest music. It was the blast of war, — the song of peace; and it seemed to have a heart in it, when there was no such matter. In good truth, he was a wondrous man; and when his tongue had acquired him all other imaginable success, — when it had been heard in halls of state, and in the courts of princes and potentates, — after it had made him known all over the world, even as a voice crying from shore to shore, — it finally persuaded his countrymen to select him for the Presidency. Before this time, — indeed, as soon as he began to grow celebrated, — his admirers had found out the resemblance between him and the Great Stone Face; and so much were they struck by it, that throughout the country this distinguished gentleman was known by the name of Old Stony Phiz. The phrase was considered as giving a highly favorable aspect to his political prospects; for, as is likewise the case with the Popedom, nobody ever becomes President without taking a name other than his own.

While his friends were doing their best to make him President, Old Stony Phiz, as he was called, set out on a visit to the valley where he was born. Of course, he had no other object than to shake hands with his fellow-citizens, and neither thought nor cared about any effect which his progress through the country might have upon the election. Magnificent preparations were made to receive the illustrious statesman; a cavalcade of horse-men set forth to meet him at the boundary line of the State, and all the people left their business and gathered along the wayside to see him pass. Among these was Ernest. Though more than once disappointed, as we have seen, he had such a hopeful and confiding nature, that he was always ready to believe in whatever seemed beautiful and good. He kept his heart continually open, and thus was sure to catch the blessing from on high, when it should come. So now again, as buoyantly as ever, he went forth to behold the likeness of the Great Stone Face.

The cavalcade came prancing along the road, with a great clattering of hoofs and a mighty cloud of dust, which rose up so dense and high that the visage of the mountain-side was completely hidden from Ernest's eyes. All the great men of the neighborhood were there on horseback: militia officers, in uniform; the member of Congress; the sheriff of the county; the editors of newspapers; and many a farmer, too, had mounted his patient steed, with his Sunday coat upon his back. It really was a very brilliant spectacle, especially as there were numerous banners flaunting over the cavalcade, on some of which were gorgeous portraits of the illustrious statesman and the Great Stone Face, smiling familiarly at one another, like two brothers. If the pictures were to be trusted, the mutual resemblance, it must be confessed, was marvellous. We must not forget to mention that there was a band of music, which made the echoes of the mountains ring and reverberate with the loud triumph of its strains; so that airy and soul-thrilling melodies broke out among all the heights and hollows, as if every nook of his native valley had found a voice, to welcome the distinguished guest. But the grandest effect was when the far-off mountain precipice flung back the music; for then the Great Stone Face itself seemed to be swelling the triumphant chorus, in acknowledgment that, at length, the man of prophecy was come.

All this while the people were throwing up their hats and shouting, with enthusiasm so contagious that the heart of Ernest kindled up, and he likewise threw up his hat, and shouted, as loudly as the loudest, "Huzza for the great man! Huzza for Old Stony Phiz!" But as yet he had not seen him.

"Here he is, now!" cried those who stood near Ernest. "There! There! Look at Old Stony Phiz and then at the Old Man of the Mountain, and see if they are not as like as two twin-brothers!"

In the midst of all this gallant array, came an open barouche, drawn by four white horses; and in the barouche, with his massive head uncovered, sat the illustrious statesman, Old Stony Phiz himself.

"Confess it," said one of Ernest's neighbors to him, "the Great Stone Face has met its match at last!"

Now, it must be owned that, at his first glimpse of the countenance which was bowing and smiling from the barouche, Ernest did fancy that there was a resemblance between it and the old familiar face upon the mountainside. The brow, with its massive depth and loftiness, and all the other features, indeed, were boldly and strongly hewn, as if in emulation of a more than heroic, of a Titanic model. But the sublimity and stateliness, the grand expression of a divine sympathy, that illuminated the mountain visage, and etherealized its ponderous granite substance into spirit, might here be sought in vain. Something had been originally left out, or had departed. And therefore the marvellously gifted statesman had always a weary gloom in the deep caverns of his eyes, as of a child that has outgrown its playthings, or a man of mighty faculties and little aims, whose life, with all its high performances, was vague and empty, because no high purpose had endowed it with reality.

Still, Ernest's neighbor was thrusting his elbow into his side, and pressing him for an answer.

"Confess! confess! Is not he the very picture of your Old Man of the Mountain?"

"No!" said Ernest, bluntly, "I see little or no likeness."

"Then so much the worse for the Great Stone Face!" answered his neighbor; and again he set up a shout for Old Stony Phiz.

But Ernest turned away, melancholy, and almost despondent: for this was the saddest of his disappointments, to behold a man who might have fulfilled the prophecy, and had not willed to do so. Meantime, the cavalcade, the banners, the music, and the barouches swept past him, with the vociferous crowd in the rear, leaving the dust to settle down, and the Great Stone Face to be revealed again, with the grandeur that it had worn for untold centuries.

"Lo, here I am, Ernest!" the benign lips seemed to say. "I have waited longer than thou, and am not yet weary. Fear not; the man will come."

The years hurried onward, treading in their haste on one another's heels. And now they began to bring white hairs, and scatter them over the head of Ernest; they made reverend wrinkles across his forehead, and furrows in his cheeks. He was an aged man. But not in vain had he grown old: more than the white hairs on his head were the sage thoughts in his mind; his wrinkles and furrows were inscriptions that Time had graved, and in which he had written legends of wisdom that had been tested by the tenor of a life. And Ernest had ceased to be obscure. Unsought for, undesired, had come the fame which so many seek, and made him known in the great world, beyond the limits of the valley in which he had dwelt so quietly. College professors, and even the active men of cities, came from far to see and converse with Ernest; for the report had gone abroad that this simple husbandman had ideas unlike those of other men, not gained from books, but of a higher tone, — a tranquil and familiar majesty, as if he had been talking with the angels as his daily friends. Whether it were sage, statesman, or philanthropist, Ernest received these visitors with the gentle sincerity that had characterized him from boyhood, and spoke freely with them of whatever came uppermost, or lay deepest in his heart or their own. While they talked together, his face would kindle, unawares, and shine upon them, as with a mild evening light. Pensive with the fulness of such discourse, his guests took leave and went their way; and passing up the valley, paused to look at the Great Stone Face, imagining that they had seen its likeness in a human countenance, but could not remember where.

While Ernest had been growing up and growing old, a bountiful Providence had granted a new poet to this earth. He, likewise, was a native of the valley, but had spent the greater part of his life at a distance from that romantic region, pouring out his sweet music amid the bustle and din of cities. Often, however, did the mountains which had been familiar to him in his childhood lift their snowy peaks into the clear atmosphere of his poetry. Neither was the Great Stone Face forgotten, for the poet had celebrated it in an ode, which was grand enough to have been uttered by its own majestic lips. This man of genius, we may say, had come down from heaven with wonderful endowments. If he sang of a mountain, the eyes of all mankind beheld a mightier grandeur reposing on its breast, or soaring to its summit, than had before been seen there. If his theme were a lovely lake, a celestial smile had now been thrown over it, to gleam forever on its surface. If it were the vast old sea, even the deep immensity of its dread bosom seemed to swell the higher, as if moved by the emotions of the song. Thus the world assumed another and a better aspect from the hour that the poet blessed it with his happy eyes. The Creator had bestowed him, as the last best touch to his own handiwork. Creation was not finished till the poet came to interpret, and so complete it.

The effect was no less high and beautiful, when his human brethren were the subject of his verse. The man or woman, sordid with the common dust of life, who crossed his daily path, and the little child who played in it, were glorified if he beheld them in his mood of poetic faith. He showed the golden links of the great chain that intertwined them with an angelic kindred; he brought out the hidden traits of a celestial birth that made them worthy of such kin. Some, indeed, there were, who thought to show the soundness of their judgment by affirming that all the beauty and dignity of the natural world existed only in the poet's fancy. Let such men speak for themselves, who undoubtedly appear to have been spawned forth by Nature with a contemptuous bitterness; she having plastered them up out of her refuse stuff, after all the swine were made. As respects all things else, the poet's ideal was the truest truth.

The songs of this poet found their way to Ernest. He read them after his customary toil, seated on the bench before his cottage-door, where for such a length of time he had filled his repose with thought, by gazing at the Great Stone Face. And now as he read stanzas that

caused the soul to thrill within him, he lifted his eyes
to the vast countenance beaming on him so benignantly.

"O majestic friend," he murmured, addressing the
Great Stone Face, "is not this man worthy to resemble
thee?"

The Face seemed to smile, but answered not a word.

Now it happened that the poet, though he dwelt so
far away, had not only heard of Ernest, but had medi-
tated much upon his character, until he deemed nothing
so desirable as to meet this man, whose untaught wisdom walked hand in hand with the noble simplicity of
his life. One summer morning, therefore, he took passage by the railroad, and, in the decline of the afternoon,
alighted from the cars at no great distance from Ernest's
cottage. The great hotel, which had formerly been the
palace of Mr. Gathergold, was close at hand, but the
poet, with his carpet-bag on his arm, inquired at once
where Ernest dwelt, and was resolved to be accepted
as his guest.

Approaching the door, he there found the good old
man, holding a volume in his hand, which alternately he
read, and then, with a finger between the leaves, looked
lovingly at the Great Stone Face.

"Good evening," said the poet. "Can you give a
traveller a night's lodging?"

"Willingly," answered Ernest; and then he added,
smiling, "Methinks I never saw the Great Stone Face
look so hospitably at a stranger."

The poet sat down on the bench beside him, and he
and Ernest talked together. Often had the poet held
intercourse with the wittiest and the wisest, but never
before with a man like Ernest, whose thoughts and feelings gushed up with such a natural freedom, and who
made great truths so familiar by his simple utterance of

them. Angels, as had been so often said, seemed to have wrought with him at his labor in the fields; angels seemed to have sat with him by the fireside; and, dwelling with angels as friend with friends, he had imbibed the sublimity of their ideas, and imbued it with the sweet and lowly charm of household words. So thought the poet. And Ernest, on the other hand, was moved and agitated by the living images which the poet flung out of his mind, and which peopled all the air about the cottage-door with shapes of beauty, both gay and pensive. The sympathies of these two men instructed them with a profounder sense than either could have attained alone. Their minds accorded into one strain, and made delightful music which neither of them could have claimed as all his own, nor distinguished his own share from the other's. They led one another, as it were, into a high pavilion of their thoughts, so remote, and hitherto so dim, that they had never entered it before, and so beautiful that they desired to be there always.

As Ernest listened to the poet, he imagined that the Great Stone Face was bending forward to listen too. He gazed earnestly into the poet's glowing eyes.

"Who are you, my strangely gifted guest?" he said.

The poet laid his finger on the volume that Ernest had been reading.

"You have read these poems," said he. "You know me, then, — for I wrote them."

Again, and still more earnestly than before, Ernest examined the poet's features; then turned towards the Great Stone Face; then back, with an uncertain aspect, to his guest. But his countenance fell; he shook his head, and sighed.

"Wherefore are you sad?" inquired the poet.

"Because," replied Ernest, "all through life I have

awaited the fulfilment of a prophecy; and, when I read these poems, I hoped that it might be fulfilled in you."

"You hoped," answered the poet, faintly smiling, "to find in me the likeness of the Great Stone Face. And you are disappointed, as formerly with Mr. Gathergold, and Old Blood-and-Thunder, and Old Stony Phiz. Yes, Ernest, it is my doom. You must add my name to the illustrious three, and record another failure of your hopes. For — in shame and sadness do I speak it, Ernest — I am not worthy to be typified by yonder benign and majestic image."

"And why?" asked Ernest. He pointed to the volume. "Are not those thoughts divine?"

"They have a strain of the Divinity," replied the poet. "You can hear in them the far-off echo of a heavenly song. But my life, dear Ernest, has not corresponded with my thought. I have had grand dreams, but they have been only dreams, because I have lived — and that, too, by my own choice — among poor and mean realities. Sometimes even — shall I dare to say it? — I lack faith in the grandeur, the beauty, and the goodness, which my own works are said to have made more evident in nature and in human life. Why, then, pure seeker of the good and true, shouldst thou hope to find me, in yonder image of the divine?"

The poet spoke sadly, and his eyes were dim with tears. So, likewise, were those of Ernest.

At the hour of sunset, as had long been his frequent custom, Ernest was to discourse to an assemblage of the neighboring inhabitants in the open air. He and the poet, arm in arm, still talking together as they went along, proceeded to the spot. It was a small nook among the hills, with a gray precipice behind, the stern front of which was relieved by the pleasant foliage of many creeping plants, that made a tapestry for the naked rock, by hanging their festoons from all its rugged angles. At a small elevation above the ground, set in a rich framework of verdure, there appeared a niche, spacious enough to admit a human figure, with freedom for such gestures as spontaneously accompany earnest thought and genuine emotion. Into this natural pulpit Ernest ascended, and threw a look of familiar kindness around upon his audience. They stood, or sat, or reclined upon the grass, as seemed good to each, with the departing sunshine falling obliquely over them, and mingling its subdued cheerfulness with the solemnity of a grove of ancient trees, beneath and amid the boughs of which the golden rays were constrained to pass. In another direction was seen the Great Stone Face, with the same cheer, combined with the same solemnity, in its benignant aspect.

Ernest began to speak, giving to the people of what was in his heart and mind. His words had power, because they accorded with his thoughts; and his thoughts had reality and depth, because they harmonized with the life which he had always lived. It was not mere breath that this preacher uttered; they were the words of life, because a life of good deeds and holy love was melted into them. Pearls, pure and rich, had been dissolved into this precious draught. The poet, as he listened, felt that the being and character of Ernest were a nobler strain of poetry than he had ever written. His eyes glistening with tears, he gazed reverentially at the venerable man, and said within himself that never was there an aspect so worthy of a prophet and a sage as that mild, sweet, thoughtful countenance, with the glory of white hair diffused about it. At a distance, but distinctly to be seen, high up in the golden light of the setting sun, appeared the Great Stone Face, with hoary mists around it, like the white hairs around the brow of Ernest. Its look of grand beneficence seemed to embrace the world.

At that moment, in sympathy with a thought which he was about to utter, the face of Ernest assumed a grandeur of expression, so imbued with benevolence, that the poet, by an irresistible impulse, threw his arms aloft, and shouted, —

"Behold! Behold! Ernest is himself the likeness of the Great Stone Face!"

Then all the people looked, and saw that what the deep-sighted poet said was true. The prophecy was fulfilled. But Ernest, having finished what he had to say, took the poet's arm, and walked slowly homeward, still hoping that some wiser and better man than himself would by and by appear, bearing a resemblance to the GREAT STONE FACE.

X

THE NECKLACE. THE STRING

THE NECKLACE. THE STRING

By GUY DE MAUPASSANT

INTRODUCTORY

THE WELL–BALANCED SHORT STORY

THE legitimate successor of Poe as an inventor and constructor of short stories is Guy de Maupassant, who carried the art well-nigh to perfection. It is said that he received a most careful training at the hands of Flaubert, his uncle, and was not allowed to publish anything for the space of seven years, when "Boule de Suif" made its appearance in a volume of short stories by the younger French writers, edited by Zola. This single story made Maupassant's reputation, and in only one or two cases did he surpass or even equal it in his subsequent work. His two masterpieces are this story and "La Maison Tellier," but both are the stories of prostitutes and unsuitable for English translation. Not far behind them stands "The String;" and no story illustrates Maupassant's art better than "The Necklace." Both are very short, and so better illustrative of his most striking characteristic than either of the stories mentioned above. Had Maupassant possessed Hawthorne's loftiness of character and Poe's breadth of understanding he would unquestionably have been our supreme artist in the short story. As it is he illustrates the possibilities of art triumphant over littleness of soul and narrowness of mind. He deliberately chooses the most insignificant incidents and the slightest possible problems of life, and makes them supremely interesting. It is difficult to conceive of any greater triumph of mere art.

It is true that Maupassant's method is artificial, and any attempt at direct imitation of him would no doubt prove disastrous. But for the critical student seeking to penetrate the principles which govern the art of short story writing, no stories will so well repay careful study as his.

It will be of interest to state briefly the characteristics of a short story as we find them in Maupassant.

First, in order to construct a short story we must have a central idea which comes to us from real life. Formerly the whole story, nearly, was taken from life: in Maupassant very little of it is a mere discovery, but on that little a great deal depends. That a woman should lose a diamond necklace, work ten years to pay for it, and then discover that it was paste, is but a new form of a very old situation, and one that is constantly recurring in everyday life; but it is striking.

Given our central idea, how shall we develop it? Maupassant begins "The Necklace" thus: "She was one of those pretty and charming girls who are sometimes, as if by a mistake of destiny, born in a family of clerks." We must choose a character best adapted to illustrating, by his or her life, the effect of our central idea. It is not necessary here to give all the reasons why Maupassant chose the particular character he did for this story, for many of them are sufficiently obvious. In writing the story he begins by describing her, and devotes fully three hundred of his brief eighteen hundred words to this description. He tells how she dressed, what sort of things she had in the house, what sort of man her husband was, what they had for dinner, her dreams and hopes. And all the rest of the story is about this woman, what happened to her, how she was delighted and disappointed. Her husband is hardly mentioned after the first. It is a story about this woman who has interested you, and everything is omitted but that which affects her life.

In the course of the story we note that the event permanently changes the course of the life of the central character. Here we may note that in every story that is technically a " short story " the interest centres on but one character, and the event of the story must permanently alter the course of life of that character. The lives of other persons also may be altered, but they are referred to in the story only so far as they have relations to the central character, and are necessary to a proper presentation of that character. Herein is the difference between a novel and a short story, — at least between a short story and a novel developed according to the laws of the drama: a short story has but one character whose life (either physical or mental) is materially altered by the event, while a novel represents the collision of several characters who alter each other's lives.

The event is highly dramatic, and though fore-shadowed and prepared for throughout, comes as a surprise. Much of the interest and effect of the story depends on this surprise, which nevertheless appears to be the most natural and logical outcome of the story. An unnatural event produces no effect. An unexpected catastrophe, which at the same time appears perfectly natural, forces the mind to reflect on the moral or intellectual problem presented. After reading "The Necklace" we spontaneously ejaculate, "Oh, the irony of fate!" and this ejaculation, unexpressed in the story, but inevitable on the part of the reader, constitutes the moral of the tale. The reader will observe the superior art which points the moral without expressing it. In order to have interest, a story must have some relation to the reflections or experiences of the reader. Success depends largely on understanding the reader's life, and nicely adapting the story to the solution of the reader's doubts or stimulating the mind to new reflections.

One point remains to be noted. Dramatic strength is always attained by sudden and striking contrasts. In "The Necklace," notice the striking contrast in the latter part of the story between what Madame Loisel actually did and what in the first part of the story she wanted to do. She wanted luxuries, servants, a fine house; but she dismissed the servant she had, and rented a garret under the roof. Each fact in the last part is matched with a corresponding dream in the first part. Then at the end of the story her friend, who is rich and still remains young, with smooth, white hands, is brought face to face with madame, who has grown coarse and rough. The use of contrast is constant and extreme, and the dramatic strength gained is corresponding.

The reader will take interest in analyzing " The String " in the same way, and noting how closely similar is the method of its construction. The elements pointed out above will be found in varying proportions in all completely artistic short stories.

THE NECKLACE

SHE was one of those pretty and charming girls who, as if by a mistake of destiny, are born in a family of clerks. She had no dowry, no expectations, no means of becoming known, understood, loved, wedded by any rich and distinguished man; and so she let herself be married to a petty clerk in the Bureau of Public Instruction.

She was simple in her dress because she could not be elaborate, but she was as unhappy as if she had fallen from a higher rank, for with women there is no distinction of higher and lower: their beauty, their grace, and their natural charm fill the place of birth and family. Natural delicacy, instinctive elegance, a lively wit, are the ruling forces in the social realm, and make daughters of the common people the equals of the finest ladies.

She suffered ceaselessly, feeling herself born for all the refinements and luxuries of life. She suffered from the poverty of her home as she looked at the dirty walls, the worn-out chairs, the ugly curtains. All those things of which another woman of her station would have been quite unconscious tortured her and made her indignant. The sight of the country girl who was maid-of-all-works in her humble household filled her almost with desperation.

She dreamed of echoing halls hung with Oriental draperies and lighted by tall bronze candelabra, while two tall footmen in knee-breeches drowsed in great armchairs by reason of the heating stove's oppressive warmth. She dreamed of splendid parlors furnished in rare old silks, of carved cabinets loaded with priceless curiosities, and of entrancing little boudoirs just right for afternoon chats with bosom friends — men famous and sought after, the envy and the desire of all the other women.

When she sat down to dinner at a little table covered with a cloth three days old, and looked across at her husband as he uncovered the soup and exclaimed with an air of rapture, "Oh, the delicious stew! I know nothing better than that," she dreamed of dainty dinners, of shining silverware, of tapestries which peopled the walls with antique figures and strange birds in fairy forests; she dreamed of delicious viands served in wonderful dishes, of whispered gallantries heard with a sphinx-like smile as you eat the pink flesh of a trout or the wing of a bird.

She had no dresses, no jewels, nothing; and she loved only that, she felt made for that. She was filled with a desire to please, to be envied, to be bewitching and sought after. She had a rich friend, a former schoolmate at the convent, whom she no longer wished to visit because she suffered so much when she came home. For whole days at a time she wept without ceasing in bitterness and hopeless misery.

.   .   .   .   .   .

Now, one evening her husband came home with a triumphant air, holding in his hand a large envelope.

"There," said he, "there is something for you."

She quickly tore open the paper and drew out a printed card, bearing these words: —

"The Minister of Public Instruction and Mme. Georges Rampouneau request the honor of M. and Mme. Loisel's company at the palace of the Ministry, Monday evening, January 18th."

Instead of being overcome with delight, as her husband expected, she threw the invitation on the table with disdain, murmuring:

"What do you wish me to do with that?"

"Why, my dear, I thought you would be pleased. You never go out, and it is such a fine opportunity, this! I had awful trouble in getting it. Every one wants to go; it is very select, and they are not giving many invitations to clerks. You will see the whole official world."

She looked at him with irritation, and said, impatiently:

"What do you wish me to put on my back if I go?"

He had not thought of that. He stammered:

"Why, the dress you go to the theatre in. It seems all right to me."

He stopped, stupefied, distracted, on seeing that his

wife was crying. Two great tears descended slowly from the corners of her eyes toward the corners of her mouth. He stuttered:

"What's the matter? What's the matter?"

By a violent effort she subdued her feelings and replied in a calm voice, as she wiped her wet cheeks:

"Nothing. Only I have no dress and consequently I cannot go to this ball. Give your invitation to some friend whose wife is better equipped than I."

He was in despair. He replied:

"Let us see, Mathilde. How much would it cost, a suitable dress, which you could wear again on future occasions, something very simple?"

She reflected for some seconds, computing the cost, and also wondering what sum she could ask without bringing down upon herself an immediate refusal and an astonished exclamation from the economical clerk.

At last she answered hesitatingly:

"I don't know exactly, but it seems to me that with four hundred francs I could manage."

He turned a trifle pale, for he had been saving just that sum to buy a gun and treat himself to a little hunting the following summer, in the country near Nanterre, with a few friends who went there to shoot larks of a Sunday.

However, he said:

"Well, I think I can give you four hundred francs. But see that you have a pretty dress."

.   .   .   .   .   .

The day of the ball drew near, and Madame Loisel seemed sad, unhappy, anxious. Her dress was ready, however. Her husband said to her one evening:

"What is the matter? Come, you've been looking queer these last three days."

And she replied:

"It worries me that I have no jewels, not a single stone, nothing to put on. I shall look wretched enough. I would almost rather not go to this party."

He answered:

"You might wear natural flowers. They are very fashionable this season. For ten francs you can get two or three magnificent roses."

She was not convinced.

"No; there is nothing more humiliating than to look poor among women who are rich."

But her husband cried:

"How stupid of you! Go and find your friend Madame Forestier and ask her to lend you some jewels. You are intimate enough with her for that."

She uttered a cry of joy.

"Of course. I had not thought of that."

The next day she went to her friend's house and told her distress.

Madame Forestier went to her handsome wardrobe, took out a large casket, brought it back, opened it, and said to Madame Loisel:

"Choose, my dear."

She saw first of all some bracelets, then a pearl necklace, then a Venetian cross, gold and precious stones of wonderful workmanship. She tried on the ornaments before the glass, hesitated, could not make up her mind to part with them, to give them back. She kept asking:

"You have nothing else?"

"Why, yes. See, I do not know what will please you."

All at once she discovered, in a black satin box, a splendid diamond necklace, and her heart began to beat with immoderate desire. Her hands trembled as she took it. She fastened it around her throat, over her high-necked dress, and stood lost in ecstasy as she looked at herself.

Then she asked, hesitating, full of anxiety:

" Would you lend me that, — only that? "

" Why, yes, certainly."

She sprang upon the neck of her friend, embraced her rapturously, then fled with her treasure.

.   .   .   .   .   .

The day of the ball arrived. Madame Loisel was a success. She was prettier than all the others, elegant, gracious, smiling, and crazy with joy. All the men stared at her, asked her name, tried to be introduced. All the cabinet officials wished to waltz with her. The minister noticed her.

She danced with intoxication, with passion, made drunk with pleasure, forgetting all in the triumph of her beauty, in the glory of her success, in a sort of mist of happiness, the result of all this homage, all this admiration, all these awakened desires, this victory so complete and so sweet to the heart of woman.

She left about four o'clock in the morning. Her husband had been sleeping since midnight in a little deserted anteroom with three other gentlemen, whose wives were having a good time.

He threw about her shoulders the wraps which he had brought for her to go out in, the modest wraps of common life, whose poverty contrasted sharply with the elegance of the ballroom toilet. She felt this and wished to escape, that she might not be noticed by the other women who were enveloping themselves in costly furs.

Loisel held her back.

" Wait here, you will catch cold outside. I will go and find a cab."

But she would not listen to him, and rapidly descended the stairs. When they were at last in the street, they could find no carriage, and began to look for one, crying after the cabmen they saw passing at a distance.

They walked down toward the Seine in despair, shivering with the cold. At last they found on the quay one of those ancient nocturnal coupés that one sees in Paris only after dark, as if they were ashamed to display their wretchedness during the day.

They were put down at their door in the Rue des Martyrs, and sadly mounted the steps to their apartments. It was all over, for her. And as for him, he reflected that he must be at his office at ten o'clock.

She took off the wraps which enveloped her shoulders before the glass, to take a final look at herself in all her glory. But suddenly she uttered a cry. She no longer had the necklace about her neck !

Her husband, already half undressed, inquired :

" What is the matter ? "

She turned madly toward him.

" I have — I have — I no longer have Madame Forestier's necklace."

He stood up, distracted.

" What ! — how ! — it is impossible ! "

They looked in the folds of her dress, in the folds of her cloak, in the pockets, everywhere. They could not find a trace of it.

He asked :

" You are sure you still had it when you left the ball ? "

" Yes. I felt it in the vestibule at the palace."

" But if you had lost it in the street we should have heard it fall. It must be in the cab."

" Yes. That 's probably it. Did you take the number ? "

" No.   And you, you did not notice it?"

" No."

They looked at each other thunderstruck.   At last Loisel put on his clothes again.

" I am going back," said he, " over every foot of the way we came, to see if I shall not find it."

So he started.   She remained in her ball dress without strength to go to bed, sitting on a chair, with no fire, her mind a blank.

Her husband returned about seven o'clock.   He had found nothing.

He went to police headquarters, to the newspapers to offer a reward, to the cab companies, everywhere, in short, where a suspicion of hope led him.

She watched all day, in the same state of blank despair before this frightful disaster.

Loisel returned in the evening with cheeks hollow and pale ; he had found nothing.

" You must write to your friend," said he, " that you have broken the clasp of her necklace and that you are having it repaired.   It will give us time to turn around."

She wrote at his dictation.

.   .   .   .   .   .

At the end of a week they had lost all hope.

And Loisel, looking five years older, declared :

" We must consider how to replace the ornament."

The next day they took the box which had contained it, and went to the place of the jeweller whose name they found inside.   He consulted his books.

" It was not I, madame, who sold the necklace ; I must simply have furnished the casket."

Then they went from jeweller to jeweller, looking for an ornament like the other, consulting their memories, both sick with chagrin and anguish.

They found, in a shop at the Palais-Royal, a string of diamonds which seemed to them exactly what they were looking for. It was worth forty thousand francs. They could have it for thirty-six thousand.

So they begged the jeweller not to sell it for three days. And they made an arrangement that he should take it back for thirty-four thousand francs if the other were found before the end of February.

Loisel had eighteen thousand francs which his father had left him. He would borrow the rest.

He did borrow, asking a thousand francs of one, five hundred of another, five louis here, three louis there. He gave notes, made ruinous engagements, dealt with usurers, with all the tribe of money-lenders. He compromised the rest of his life, risked his signature without knowing if he might not be involving his honor, and, terrified by the anguish yet to come, by the black misery about to fall upon him, by the prospect of every physical privation and every mental torture, he went to get the new necklace, and laid down on the dealer's counter thirty-six thousand francs.

When Madame Loisel took the ornament back to Madame Forestier, the latter said coldly:

"You should have returned it sooner, for I might have needed it."

She did not open the case, to the relief of her friend. If she had detected the substitution, what would she have thought? What would she have said? Would she have taken her friend for a thief?

.   .   .   .   .   .

Madame Loisel now knew the horrible life of the needy; moreover, all at once she took her part heroically. They must pay this frightful debt. She would pay it. They dismissed their maid, they gave up their apartment, they rented another under the roof.

She came to know the drudgery of housework, the odious cares of the kitchen. She washed the dishes, using her rosy nails on the greasy pots and the bottoms of the saucepans. She washed the dirty linen, the shirts and the dishcloths, which she hung to dry on a line; she carried the garbage down to the street every morning, and carried up the water, stopping at each landing to rest. And, dressed like a woman of the people, she went to the fruiterer's, the grocer's, the butcher's, her basket on her arm, bargaining, abusing, defending sou by sou her miserable money.

Each month they had to pay some notes, renew others, obtain more time.

The husband worked evenings neatly footing up the account books of some tradesman, and often far into the night he sat copying manuscript at five sous a page.

And this life lasted ten years.

At the end of ten years they had paid everything, — everything, with the exactions of usury and the accumulations of compound interest.

Madame Loisel seemed old now. She had become the woman of impoverished households, — strong and hard and rough. With hair half combed, with skirts awry, and reddened hands, she talked loud as she washed the floor with great swishes of water. But sometimes, when her husband was at the office, she sat down near the window and thought of that evening at the ball so long ago, when she had been so beautiful and so fêted.

What would have happened if she had not lost that necklace? Who knows, who knows? How strange life is, how changeful! How little a thing is needed for us to be lost or to be saved!

.   .   .   .   .   .

But one Sunday, as she was going for a walk in the Champs Élysées to refresh herself after the labors of the week, all at once she saw a woman walking with a child. It was Madame Forestier, still young, still beautiful, still charming.

Madame Loisel was agitated. Should she speak to her? Why, of course. And now that she had paid, she would tell her all. Why not?

She went up.

"Bonjour, Jeanne."

The other, astonished to be addressed so familiarly by this woman of the people, did not recognize her. She stammered:

"But — madame — I do not know you. You must have made a mistake."

"No, I am Mathilde Loisel."

Her friend uttered a cry.

"Oh! my poor Mathilde, how changed you are!"

"Yes, I have had days hard enough since I saw you, days wretched enough — and all because of you!"

"Me? How so?"

"You remember that necklace of diamonds that you lent me to wear to the ministerial ball?"

"Yes. Well?"

"Well, I lost it."

"How? But you returned it to me."

"I returned to you another exactly like it. These ten years we've been paying for it. You know it was not easy for us, who had nothing. At last it is over, and I am very glad."

Madame Forestier stood staring at her.

"You say that you bought a necklace of diamonds to replace mine?"

"Yes; you did not notice it, then? They were very like."

And she smiled with a proud and naïve pleasure.

Madame Forestier, deeply moved, took both her hands.

"Oh, my poor Mathilde! Why, my necklace was paste. It was worth five hundred francs at most."

THE STRING

BY every road round Goderville the countrymen with their wives were coming toward the town, for it was market-day. The men plodded on, their bodies lurching forward at every movement of their long twisted limbs, which were deformed by hard work, — by holding the plough, which throws up the left shoulder and twists the figure; by mowing grain, which forces out the knees in the effort to stand quite steady; in short, by all the tedious and painful toil of the fields. Their blue blouses, starched and shining as if they had been varnished, with collar and cuffs stitched in a neat design, were inflated about their bony forms, exactly like balloons ready to soar, but putting forth a head, two arms, and two legs.

Some were leading a cow or a calf by a rope; and, just behind, their wives lashed the animal over the back with a leafy branch, to hasten its pace. On their arms the women carried large baskets, whence protruded the heads of chickens or of ducks; and they walked with shorter, quicker steps than the men, their withered, upright figures wrapped in scanty little shawls pinned over their flat breasts, their hair closely done up in white cloths, with a cap above.

Now a cart passed by, jerked along by an ambling nag; and queerly it shook up the two men sitting side by side and a woman at the bottom of the vehicle, who held on to the sides to ease the heavy jolting.

In the market-place at Goderville a crowd had gathered, a mingled multitude of men and beasts. The horns of the cattle, the tall, long-napped hats of the rich peasants, and the head-dresses of the peasant women rose above the surface of that living sea; and the harsh, shrill, squeaking voices made a continuous and savage roar; while at times there rose above it a burst of laughter from the husky throat of an amused country fellow, or the long-drawn moo of a cow tied to a wall.

It all smelled of the stable, of milk and dung, of hay and sweat, emitting that pungent and disagreeable odor of man and beast, which is peculiar to the inhabitants of the fields.

Master Hauchecorne, of Bréauté, had just arrived at Goderville, and was making his way toward the market-place when he saw on the ground a little piece of string. Master Hauchecorne, economical like all true Normans, considered everything worth picking up which might be of use; so he stooped painfully down, — for he suffered from rheumatism, — took the bit of twine from the ground, and was preparing to roll it up with care, when he noticed Master Malandain the harness-maker on his doorstep, looking at him. They had once had a difference in regard to a halter, and they remained angry, with ill will on both sides. Master Hauchecorne was seized with a feeling of shame at being caught thus by his enemy looking in the dirt for a piece of string. He hastily concealed his find under his blouse, then in the pocket of his trousers; then he pretended still to be looking on the ground for something he failed to find, and at last went away toward the market-place, his head thrust forward, his body doubled up by his pains.

In a moment he was lost in the clamorous and slow-moving crowd, agitated by its interminable bargains. The peasants felt of the cows, went away, came back, perplexed and forever afraid of being cheated, never daring to decide, eying the seller, always searching to discover the tricks of the man and the defects of the beast.

The women had placed their great baskets at their feet; and they drew out their poultry and placed it on the ground, where it lay with legs tied, scared eye, and scarlet comb.

They listened to offers, dryly maintaining their price with impassive countenance; or, all at once deciding to accept the proposed reduction, they cried out to the customer who was slowly moving away:

" Oh, say, Mas' Anthime, I 'll let you have it."

Then little by little the market-place was emptied, and when the Angelus sounded noon, those who lived at a distance scattered to the inns.

At Jourdain's the great dining-room was filled with eaters, just as the vast court was filled with vehicles of every kind — carts, gigs, wagons, tilburies, nameless tilt-carts, yellow with mud, misshapen, patched, their shafts pointing to the skies like two arms, or else their noses to the ground and their tails in the air.

Opposite the diners as they sat at table the fire burned freely in the huge chimney, throwing out a lively warmth upon the backs of the row upon the right. On three spits chickens, pigeons, and legs of lamb were turning before the fire; and a savory odor of roast meat, and of gravy streaming over its crisp, browned surface, floated up from the hearth, kindling the appetite till the mouth watered for the viands.

All the aristocracy of the plough were eating there with Master Jourdain, innkeeper and horse-dealer, a knave whose pockets were well lined.

The plates went round, and were emptied, as were the jugs of yellow cider. Each told of his affairs, his bargains, and his sales ; and all discussed the crops. The season was good for vegetables, but a little wet for grain.

All at once the rub-a-dub of the drum sounded in the court before the house. In a moment every man was on his feet (save some of the more indifferent) and rushed to door or windows, his mouth still full, and his napkin in his hand.

After he had finished his tattoo, the public crier raised his voice, launching his jerky phrases with pauses quite out of place :

" Be it known to the inhabitants of Goderville, and in general to all — persons present at the market, that there has been lost this morning, on the road from Beuzeville, between — nine and ten o'clock, a black leather pocketbook, containing five hundred francs and business papers. You are requested to return it — to the mayor's office, without delay, or to Master Fortuné Houlbrèque, of Manneville. There will be twenty francs reward."

Then the man went away. Far down the street the muffled beating of the drum might have been heard, and the faint voice of the crier repeating his announcement.

In a moment every one was talking of the incident, discussing the chances Master Houlbrèque had of recovering or not recovering his pocketbook.

So the meal went on.

As they were draining their coffee cups, a police officer appeared on the threshold.

He asked :

" Is Master Hauchecorne, of Bréauté, here ? "

Master Hauchecorne, who was seated at the opposite end of the table, answered :

"That's me."

The officer replied :

"Master Hauchecorne, will you have the kindness to accompany me to the office of the mayor? His honor, the mayor, wishes to speak with you."

The farmer, surprised, disturbed, finished his glass at a gulp, rose, and, even more bent than in the morning, since the first steps after each period of rest were particularly difficult, he started along, saying over and over :

"That's me, that's me."

So he followed the officer.

The mayor was waiting for him, seated in an armchair. He was the notary of the district, a big, severe man, pompous in his speech.

"Master Hauchecorne," said he, "you were seen this morning to pick up, on the road from Beuzeville, the pocketbook lost by Master Houlbrèque, of Manneville."

The old fellow stood looking at the mayor, speechless, already terrified by the suspicion that rested upon him, without in the least knowing why.

"Me, me ! I picked up that pocketbook?"

"Yes, you."

"Word of honor, I don't know nothing about it at all."

"You were seen."

"Seen? Me? Who says he saw me?"

"M. Malandain, the harness-maker."

Then the old man remembered, understood ; and, reddening with anger, he said :

"Uh ! 'e saw me, did 'e, the rat ! 'E saw me pick up this string here ; see here, your honor."

And, fumbling at the bottom of his pocket, he drew out a little piece of twine.

But the mayor incredulously shook his head.

"You will not make me believe, Master Hauchecorne, that M. Malandain, who is a man of his word, has mistaken this string for a pocketbook."

The farmer, furious, raising his hand and spitting [1] to attest his good faith, repeated:

"Nevertheless, it is the truth of the good God, the solemn truth, your honor. There! on my soul and salvation, I swear it."

The mayor replied:

"After you had picked up the object, you even hunted about a long time in the dust, to see if some piece of money had not slipped out of it."

The good man was stifled with indignation and fear.

"How can they tell! — how can they tell! — such lies as that to libel an honest man! How can they tell!"

He might protest: no one believed him.

He was confronted with M. Malandain, who repeated and sustained his declaration. They abused one another for an hour. At his request, Master Hauchecorne was searched. Nothing was found on him.

At last the mayor, much perplexed, sent him away, warning him that he would lay the matter before the court and ask for instructions.

The news had spread. On his leaving the mayor's office, the old man was surrounded and questioned with a curiosity that was serious or jesting, but into which no indignation entered. And he proceeded to tell the story of the string.

They did not believe him. They laughed.

He went along, stopped by every one, stopping his acquaintances again and again, going all over his story

[1] In England peasants spit on their hands and say, "S' 'elp me Gawd."

and repeating his protestations, showing his pockets turned inside out to prove there was nothing in them.

They said to him:

"Go on, you old rogue!"

And he grew angry, working himself into a fever, desperate at not being believed, for he did not know what to do, and kept telling his story over and over.

Night came on. It was time to go home. He set out along the road with three of his neighbors, to whom he showed the place where he had picked up the bit of cord; and all along the road he kept talking of the incident.

That evening he made the round in the village of Bréauté, to let everybody know. He told his story only to the incredulous.

He was ill of it all night.

The next day, about one o'clock in the afternoon, Marius Paumelle, a laborer on the farm of Master Breton, gardener at Ymauville, returned the pocket-book and its contents to Master Houlbrèque of Manneville.

This man's statement was to the effect that he had found the thing on the road, but not knowing how to read, he had carried it home and given it to his master.

The news spread. Master Hauchecorne was informed of it. He started off at once, and immediately began to retell the story as completed by the *dénouement*. He was triumphant.

"I di'n' care so much for the thing itself, you understand," said he, "but it was the lie. There is nothing nastier than being set down for a liar."

All day he talked of his adventure; he told it on the road to the people who passed, at the public house to the

people who drank, and the next Sunday to those who
gathered at the church. He even stopped strangers to
tell them about it. Now he felt easy, and yet something
troubled him, without his knowing exactly what. People
seemed to smile as they listened. They did not appear
convinced. He felt as if they babbled behind his
back.

On Tuesday of the following week he turned up at the
market at Goderville, sent there only by the need of telling his tale.

Malandain, standing in his doorway, began to laugh as
he saw him pass. Why?

He accosted a farmer of Criquetot, who did not allow
him to finish, but, giving him a tap in the pit of the
stomach, cried in his face:

" Go on, you old rogue ! " Then the fellow turned on
his heel.

Master Hauchecorne stood speechless, more unhappy
than ever. Why did every one call him " old rogue " ?

When he sat down at the table at Jourdain's, he proceeded to explain the affair.

A horse-dealer of Montivilliers cried at him:

" Come, come, now, you old scamp, we know all about
you and your piece of string."

" But they found the pocketbook ! "

The other went on:

" Don't speak of it, daddy ; there is one who finds it
and one who takes it back. No one sees, no one knows ;
but you give yourself away."

The peasant sat dumbfounded ; he understood at last.
They accused him of having sent the pocketbook back
by a confederate, by an accomplice.

He tried to protest. Every one at the table began to
laugh.

He could not eat his dinner, and went away amid their ridicule.

He went home, ashamed and indignant, choking with rage, overcome with confusion, all the more in despair that he was capable, with his Norman artfulness, of doing that of which they accused him, and even of pluming himself on it as a good trick. His innocence dimly seemed to him impossible to prove, his trickiness being so well known, and he felt struck to the heart by the injustice of the suspicion.

Then he began again to tell of his adventure, adding new arguments each time, more energetic protests, and more solemn oaths which he thought out in his hours of solitude, his mind being occupied with the story of the string. People believed him the less, the more subtle and complicated his argument became.

"Ha! liar's proofs, those!" they said behind his back.

He felt it; it gnawed at his vitals; he wore himself out with useless efforts.

The jokers now made him tell "The Story of the String" for their amusement, as a soldier who has been on a campaign is made to tell of the battle.

His mind, deeply affected, grew weak.

Toward the end of December he took to his bed.

He died early in January, and in the delirium of his death agony he protested his innocence, repeating:

"A li'l' string, a li'l' string, — see, here it is, your honor."

XI

THE MAN WHO WOULD BE KING

THE MAN WHO WOULD BE KING

By RUDYARD KIPLING

INTRODUCTORY

STRENGTH IN CONTRAST

IN spite of the greatness of Poe and Hawthorne, and the rise of the short story in
France, it was not until the advent of
Kipling in 1889 that the short story in English
became a recognized and popular vehicle for
presenting an author's special knowledge of life.
While short stories have always been indispens-
able to the magazines, a volume of short stories
on a variety of topics and kinds of life did not
have sufficient unity to hold the public interest
permanently. Kipling's success was due to the
fact that his stories presented a series of pictures
of a fresh and interesting kind of life. To some
extent they resembled chapters in a novel, and the
most popular volume, that of "Soldiers Three,"
was confined to incidents in the lives of three men.
Such a unity in the subject-matter of the stories is

essential to the large success of any volume of short stories.

Kipling's artistic originality is confined almost entirely to the style in which he writes. In our study of Maupassant it was pointed out that the secret of strength is contrast. Kipling uses this not only in the construction of his stories, but in the wording of every sentence; almost every phrase represents a striking, yet reasonable, incongruity, which acts as a continual stimulus upon the imagination of the reader. Though a method, a conscious device, it requires originality and force of mind to prevent the incongruities from becoming absurd, and to keep them perpetually suggestive, as Kipling does. In this particular device Kipling remains unsurpassed, though he has had many imitators.

In spite of the presence of Carnehan, "The Man Who Would Be King" is the story of one man, namely Dravot. These personages were selected because of the violent contrast between their characters as presented in the early part of the story and their ambition to be kings. The central idea, that such men may reasonably come so near to being kings, is a great and striking one. The moral is suggested in the motto, " Brother to a Prince and fellow to a beggar if he be found worthy." In the matter of final success, character (personal worth) is all; social position (prince or beggar), nothing. Dravot failed because of a weakness in his character, not because chance had made him an outcast.

THE MAN WHO WOULD BE KING

Brother to a Prince and fellow to a beggar if he be found worthy.

THE Law, as quoted, lays down a fair conduct of life, and one not easy to follow. I have been fellow to a beggar again and again under circumstances which prevented either of us finding out whether the other was worthy. I have still to be brother to a Prince, though I once came near to kinship with what might have been a veritable King and was promised the reversion of a Kingdom—army, law-courts, revenue and policy all complete. But, to-day, I greatly fear that my King is dead, and if I want a crown I must go hunt it for myself.

The beginning of everything was in a railway train upon the road to Mhow from Ajmir. There had been a Deficit in the Budget, which necessitated travelling, not Second-class, which is only half as dear as First-class, but by Intermediate, which is very awful indeed. There are no cushions in the Intermediate class, and the population are either Intermediate, which is Eurasian, or native, which for a long night journey is nasty, or Loafer, which is amusing though intoxicated. Intermediates do not buy from refreshment-rooms. They carry their food in bundles and pots, and buy sweets from the native sweetmeat-sellers, and drink the roadside water. That is why in hot weather Intermediates are taken out of the carriages dead, and in all weathers are most properly looked down upon.

My particular Intermediate happened to be empty till I reached Nasirabad, when a big black-browed gentleman in shirt-sleeves entered, and, following the custom of Intermediates, passed the time of day. He was a wanderer and a vagabond like myself, but with an educated taste for whiskey. He told tales of things he had seen and done, of out-of-the-way corners of the Empire into which he had penetrated, and of adventures in which he risked his life for a few days' food.

"If India was filled with men like you and me, not knowing more than the crows where they'd get their next day's rations, it isn't seventy millions of revenue the land would be paying — it's seven hundred millions," said he ; and as I looked at his mouth and chin I was disposed to agree with him.

We talked politics — the politics of Loaferdom that sees things from the underside where the lath and plaster is not smoothed off — and we talked postal arrangements because my friend wanted to send a telegram back from the next station to Ajmir, the turning-off place from the Bombay to the Mhow line as you travel westward. My friend had no money beyond eight annas which he wanted for dinner, and I had no money at all, owing to the hitch in the Budget before mentioned. Further, I was going into a wilderness where, though I should resume touch with the Treasury, there were no telegraph offices. I was, therefore, unable to help him in any way.

"We might threaten a Station-master, and make him send a wire on tick," said my friend, "but that'd mean enquiries for you and for me, and *I*'ve got my hands full these days. Did you say you were travelling back along this line within any days?"

"Within ten," I said.

"Can't you make it eight?" said he. "Mine is rather urgent business."

" I can send your telegram within ten days if that will serve you," I said.

" I could n't trust the wire to fetch him now I think of it. It's this way. He leaves Delhi on the 23rd for Bombay. That means he'll be running through Ajmir about the night of the 23rd."

" But I'm going into the Indian Desert," I explained.

" Well *and* good," said he. " You'll be changing at Marwar Junction to get into Jodhpore territory — you must do that — and he'll be coming through Marwar Junction in the early morning of the 24th by the Bombay Mail. Can you be at Marwar Junction on that time? 'T won't be inconveniencing you because I know that there's precious few pickings to be got out of these Central India States — even though you pretend to be correspondent of the *Backwoodsman*."

" Have you ever tried that trick?" I asked.

" Again and again, but the Residents find you out, and then you get escorted to the Border before you've time to get your knife into them. But about my friend here. I *must* give him a word o' mouth to tell him what's come to me or else he won't know where to go. I would take it more than kind of you if you was to come out of Central India in time to catch him at Marwar Junction, and say to him: ' He has gone South for the week.' He'll know what that means. He's a big man with a red beard, and a great swell he is. You'll find him sleeping like a gentleman with all his luggage round him in a Second-class apartment. But don't you be afraid. Slip down the window and say: ' He has gone South for the week,' and he'll tumble. It's only cutting your time of stay in those parts by two days. I ask you as a stranger — going to the West," he said with emphasis.

"Where have *you* come from?" said I.

"From the East," said he, "and I am hoping that you will give him the message on the Square — for the sake of my Mother as well as your own."

Englishmen are not usually softened by appeals to the memory of their mothers; but for certain reasons, which will be fully apparent, I saw fit to agree.

"It's more than a little matter," said he, "and that's why I asked you to do it — and now I know that I can depend on you doing it. A Second-class carriage at Marwar Junction, and a red-haired man asleep in it. You'll be sure to remember. I get out at the next station, and I must hold on there till he comes or sends me what I want."

"I'll give the message if I catch him," I said, "and for the sake of your Mother as well as mine I'll give you a word of advice. Don't try to run the Central India States just now as the correspondent of the *Backwoodsman*. There's a real one knocking about here, and it might lead to trouble."

"Thank you," said he simply, "and when will the swine be gone? I can't starve because he's ruining my work. I wanted to get hold of the Degumber Rajah down here about his father's widow, and give him a jump."

"What did he do to his father's widow, then?"

"Filled her up with red pepper and slippered her to death as she hung from a beam. I found that out myself and I'm the only man that would dare going into the State to get hush-money for it. They'll try to poison me, same as they did in Chortumna when I went on the loot there. But you'll give the man at Marwar Junction my message?"

He got out at a little roadside station, and I reflected.

I had heard, more than once, of men personating correspondents of newspapers and bleeding small Native States with threats of exposure, but I had never met any of the caste before. They lead a hard life, and generally die with great suddenness. The Native States have a wholesome horror of English newspapers, which may throw light on their peculiar methods of government, and do their best to choke correspondents with champagne, or drive them out of their mind with four-in-hand barouches. They do not understand that nobody cares a straw for the internal administration of Native States so long as oppression and crime are kept within decent limits, and the ruler is not drugged, drunk, or diseased from one end of the year to the other. They are the dark places of the earth, full of unimaginable cruelty, touching the Railway and the Telegraph on one side, and, on the other, the days of Harun-al-Raschid. When I left the train I did business with divers Kings, and in eight days passed through many changes of life. Sometimes I wore dress-clothes and consorted with Princes and Politicals, drinking from crystal and eating from silver. Sometimes I lay out upon the ground and devoured what I could get, from a plate made of leaves, and drank the running water, and slept under the same rug as my servant. It was all in the day's work.

Then I headed for the Great Indian Desert upon the proper date, as I had promised, and the night Mail set me down at Marwar Junction, where a funny little, happy-go-lucky, native-managed railway runs to Jodhpore. The Bombay Mail from Delhi makes a short halt at Marwar. She arrived as I got in, and I had just time to hurry to her platform and go down the carriages. There was only one Second-class on the train. I slipped the window and looked down upon a flaming red beard, half covered by a railway rug. That was my man, fast asleep, and I dug him gently in the ribs. He woke with a grunt and I saw his face in the light of the lamps. It was a great and shining face.

"Tickets again?" said he.

"No," said I. "I am to tell you that he is gone South for the week. He has gone South for the week!"

The train had begun to move out. The red man rubbed his eyes. "He has gone South for the week," he repeated. "Now that's just like his impidence. Did he say that I was to give you anything? 'Cause I won't."

"He didn't," I said and dropped away, and watched the red lights die out in the dark. It was horribly cold because the wind was blowing off the sands. I climbed into my own train — not an Intermediate carriage this time — and went to sleep.

If the man with the beard had given me a rupee I should have kept it as a memento of a rather curious affair. But the consciousness of having done my duty was my only reward.

Later on I reflected that two gentlemen like my friends could not do any good if they forgathered and personated correspondents of newspapers, and might, if they blackmailed one of the little rat-trap states of Central India or Southern Rajputana, get themselves into serious difficulties. I therefore took some trouble to describe them as accurately as I could remember to people who would be interested in deporting them: and succeeded, so I was later informed, in having them headed back from the Degumber borders.

Then I became respectable, and returned to an Office where there were no Kings and no incidents outside the daily manufacture of a newspaper. A newspaper office seems to attract every conceivable sort of person, to the prejudice of discipline. Zenana-mission ladies arrive, and beg that the Editor will instantly abandon all his duties to describe a Christian prize-giving in a back-slum of a perfectly inaccessible village; Colonels who have been overpassed for command sit down and sketch the outline of a series of ten, twelve, or twenty-four leading articles on Seniority *versus* Selection; missionaries wish to know why they have not been permitted to escape from their regular vehicles of abuse and swear at a brother-missionary under special patronage of the editorial We; stranded theatrical companies troop up to explain that they cannot pay for their advertisements, but on their return from New Zealand or Tahiti will do so with interest; inventors of patent punkah-pulling machines, carriage couplings and unbreakable swords and axle-trees call with specifications in their pockets and hours at their disposal; tea-companies enter and elaborate their prospectuses with the office pens; secretaries of ball-committees clamor to have the glories of their last dance more fully described; strange ladies rustle in and say: "I want a hundred lady's cards printed *at once*, please," which is manifestly part of an Editor's duty; and every dissolute ruffian that ever tramped the Grand Trunk Road makes it his business to ask for employment as a proof-reader. And, all the time, the telephone-bell is ringing madly, and Kings are being killed on the Continent, and Empires are saying — "You're another," and Mister Gladstone is calling down brimstone upon the British Dominions, and the little black copy-boys are whining, " *kaa-pi chay-ha-yeh* " (copy wanted) like tired bees, and most of the paper is as blank as Modred's shield.

But that is the amusing part of the year. There are

six other months when none ever come to call, and the thermometer walks inch by inch up to the top of the glass, and the office is darkened to just above reading-light, and the press-machines are red-hot of touch, and nobody writes anything but accounts of amusements in the Hill-stations or obituary notices. Then the tele-phone becomes a tinkling terror, because it tells you of the sudden deaths of men and women that you knew intimately, and the prickly-heat covers you with a gar-ment, and you sit down and write : "A slight increase of sickness is reported from the Khuda Janta Khan District. The outbreak is purely sporadic in its nature, and, thanks to the energetic efforts of the District authorities, is now almost at an end. It is, however, with deep regret we record the death," etc.

Then the sickness really breaks out, and the less recording and reporting the better for the peace of the subscribers. But the Empires and the Kings continue to divert themselves as selfishly as before, and the Foreman thinks that a daily paper really ought to come out once in twenty-four hours, and all the people at the Hill-stations in the middle of their amusements say : "Good gracious ! Why can't the paper be sparkling? I 'm sure there 's plenty going on up here."

That is the dark half of the moon, and, as the adver-tisements say, " must be experienced to be appreciated."

It was in that season, and a remarkably evil season, that the paper began running the last issue of the week on Saturday night, which is to say Sunday morning, after the custom of a London paper. This was a great con-venience, for immediately after the paper was put to bed, the dawn would lower the thermometer from 96° to almost 84° for half an hour, and in that chill — you have no idea how cold is 84° on the grass until you begin to pray for it — a very tired man could get off to sleep ere the heat roused him.

One Saturday night it was my pleasant duty to put the paper to bed alone. A King or courtier or a courtesan or a Community was going to die or get a new Constitution, or do something that was important on the other side of the world, and the paper was to be held open till the latest possible minute in order to catch the telegram.

It was a pitchy black night, as stifling as a June night can be, and the *loo*, the red-hot wind from the westward, was booming among the tinder-dry trees and pretending that the rain was on its heels. Now and again a spot of almost boiling water would fall on the dust with the flop of a frog, but all our weary world knew that was only pretence. It was a shade cooler in the press-room than the office, so I sat there, while the type ticked and clicked, and the night-jars hooted at the windows, and the all but naked compositors wiped the sweat from their foreheads, and called for water. The thing that was keeping us back, whatever it was, would not come off, though the *loo* dropped and the last type was set, and the whole round earth stood still in the choking heat, with its finger on its lip, to wait the event. I drowsed, and wondered whether the telegraph was a blessing, and whether this dying man, or struggling people, might be aware of the inconvenience the delay was causing. There was no special reason beyond the heat and worry to make tension, but, as the clock-hands crept up to three o'clock and the machines spun their fly-wheels two and three times to see that all was in order, before I said the word that would set them off, I could have shrieked aloud.

Then the roar and rattle of the wheels shivered the quiet into little bits. I rose to go away, but two men in white clothes stood in front of me. The first one said : " It 's him ! " The second said : " So it is ! " And they both laughed almost as loudly as the machinery roared, and mopped their foreheads. " We seed there was a light burning across the road and we were sleeping in that ditch there for coolness, and I said to my friend here, The office is open. Let 's come along and speak to him as turned us back from the Degumber State," said the smaller of the two. He was the man I had met in the Mhow train, and his fellow was the red-bearded man of Marwar Junction. There was no mistaking the eye-brows of the one or the beard of the other.

I was not pleased, because I wished to go to sleep, not to squabble with loafers. " What do you want ? " I asked.

" Half an hour's talk with you, cool and comfortable, in the office," said the red-bearded man. " We 'd *like* some drink — the Contrack does n't begin yet, Peachey, so you need n't look — but what we really want is advice. We don't want money. We ask you as a favor, because we found out you did us a bad turn about Degumber State."

I led from the press-room to the stifling office with the maps on the walls, and the red-haired man rubbed his hands. " That 's something like," said he. " This was the proper shop to come to. Now, Sir, let me introduce to you Brother Peachey Carnehan, that 's him, and Brother Daniel Dravot, that is *me*, and the less said about our professions the better, for we have been most things in our time. Soldier, sailor, compositor, photographer, proof-reader, street-preacher, and correspondents of the *Backwoodsman* when we thought the paper wanted one. Carnehan is sober, and so am I. Look at us first, and see that 's sure. It will save you cutting into my talk.

We'll take one of your cigars apiece, and you shall see us light up."

I watched the test. The men were absolutely sober, so I gave them each a tepid whiskey and soda.

"Well *and* good," said Carnehan of the eyebrows, wiping the froth from his moustache. "Let me talk now, Dan. We have been all over India, mostly on foot. We have been boiler-fitters, engine-drivers, petty contractors, and all that, and we have decided that India is n't big enough for such as us."

They certainly were too big for the office. Dravot's beard seemed to fill half the room and Carnehan's shoulders the other half, as they sat on the big table. Carnehan continued: "The country is n't half worked out because they that governs it won't let you touch it. They spend all their blessed time in governing it, and you can't lift a spade, nor chip a rock, nor look for oil, nor anything like that without all the Government saying — 'Leave it alone, and let us govern.' Therefore, such *as* it is, we will let it alone, and go away to some other place where a man is n't crowded and can come to his own. We are not little men, and there is nothing that we are afraid of except Drink, and we have signed a Contrack on that. *Therefore*, we are going away to be Kings."

"Kings in our own right," muttered Dravot.

"Yes, of course," I said. "You've been tramping in the sun, and it's a very warm night, and had n't you better sleep over the notion? Come to-morrow."

"Neither drunk nor sunstruck," said Dravot. "We have slept over the notion half a year, and require to see Books and Atlases, and we have decided that there is only one place now in the world that two strong men can Sar-a-*whack*. They call it Kafiristan. By my reckoning it's the top right-hand corner of Afghanistan, not more than three hundred miles from Peshawar. They have two-and-thirty heathen idols there, and we 'll be the thirty-third and fourth. It 's a mountaineous country, and the women of those parts are very beautiful."

"But that is provided against in the Contrack," said Carnehan. "Neither Woman nor Liqu-or, Daniel."

"And that 's all we know, except that no one has gone there, and they fight, and in any place where they fight a man who knows how to drill men can always be a King. We shall go to those parts and say to any King we find — 'D' you want to vanquish your foes?' and we will show him how to drill men; for that we know better than anything else. Then we will subvert that King and seize his Throne and establish a Dy-nasty."

"You 'll be cut to pieces before you 're fifty miles across the Border," I said. "You have to travel through Afghanistan to get to that country. It 's one mass of mountains and peaks and glaciers, and no Englishman has been through it. The people are utter brutes, and even if you reached them you could n't do anything."

"That 's more like," said Carnehan. "If you could think us a little more mad we would be more pleased. We have come to you to know about this country, to read a book about it, and to be shown maps. We want you to tell us that we are fools and to show us your books." He turned to the book-cases.

"Are you at all in earnest?" I said.

"A little," said Dravot sweetly. "As big a map as you have got, even if it 's all blank where Kafiristan is, and any books you 've got. We can read, though we are n't very educated."

I uncased the big thirty-two-miles-to-the-inch map of India, and two smaller Frontier maps, hauled down volume INF–KAN of the *Encyclopædia Britannica,* and the men consulted them.

"See here !" said Dravot, his thumb on the map. "Up to Jagdallak, Peachey and me know the road. We was there with Roberts's Army. We'll have to turn off to the right at Jagdallak through Laghmann territory. Then we get among the hills — fourteen thousand feet — fifteen thousand — it will be cold work there, but it don't look very far on the map."

I handed him Wood on the *Sources of the Oxus.* Carnehan was deep in the *Encyclopædia.*

"They're a mixed lot," said Dravot reflectively ; "and it won't help us to know the names of their tribes. The more tribes the more they'll fight, and the better for us. From Jagdallak to Ashang. H'mm !"

"But all the information about the country is as sketchy and inaccurate as can be," I protested. "No one knows anything about it really. Here's the file of the *United Services' Institute.* Read what Bellew says."

"Blow Bellew !" said Carnehan. "Dan, they're a stinkin' lot of heathens, but this book here says they think they're related to us English."

I smoked while the men pored over *Raverty, Wood,* the maps, and the *Encyclopædia.*

"There is no use your waiting," said Dravot politely. "It's about four o'clock now. We'll go before six o'clock if you want to sleep, and we won't steal any of the papers. Don't you sit up. We're two harmless lunatics, and if you come to-morrow evening down to the Serai we'll say good-bye to you."

"You *are* two fools," I answered. "You'll be turned back at the Frontier or cut up the minute you set foot in Afghanistan. Do you want any money or a recommendation down-country? I can help you to the chance of work next week."

" Next week we shall be hard at work ourselves, thank you," said Dravot. " It is n't so easy being a King as it looks. When we 've got our Kingdom in going order we 'll let you know, and you can come up and help us to govern it."

" Would two lunatics make a Contrack like that? " said Carnehan, with subdued pride, showing me a greasy half-sheet of notepaper on which was written the following. I copied it, then and there, as a curiosity —

This Contract between me and you persuing witnesseth in the name of God — Amen and so forth.

> *(One)*   *That me and you will settle this matter to-gether; i. e., to be Kings of Kafiristan.*
>
> *(Two)*   *That you and me will not, while this matter is being settled, look at any Liquor, nor any Woman black, white, or brown, so as to get mixed up with one or the other harmful.*
>
> *(Three)*   *That we conduct ourselves with Dignity and Discretion, and if one of us gets into trouble the other will stay by him.*
>
> *Signed by you and me this day.*
> *Peachey Taliaferro Carnehan.*
> *Daniel Dravot.*
> *Both Gentlemen at Large.*

" There was no need for the last article," said Carnehan, blushing modestly ; " but it looks regular. Now you know the sort of men that loafers are — we *are* loafers, Dan, until we get out of India — and *do* you think that we would sign a Contrack like that unless we was in earnest?

We have kept away from the two things that make life worth having."

"You won't enjoy your lives much longer if you are going to try this idiotic adventure. Don't set the office on fire," I said, "and go away before nine o'clock."

I left them still poring over the maps and making notes on the back of the "Contrack." "Be sure to come down to the Serai to-morrow," were their parting words.

The Kumharsen Serai is the great four-square sink of humanity where the strings of camels and horses from the North load and unload. All the nationalities of Central Asia may be found there, and most of the folk of India proper. Balkh and Bokhara there meet Bengal and Bombay, and try to draw eye-teeth. You can buy ponies, turquoises, Persian pussy-cats, saddle-bags, fat-tailed sheep and musk in the Kumharsen Serai, and get many strange things for nothing. In the afternoon I went down to see whether my friends intended to keep their word or were lying there drunk.

A priest attired in fragments of ribbons and rags stalked up to me, gravely twisting a child's paper whirli-gig. Behind him was his servant bending under the load of a crate of mud toys. The two were loading up two camels, and the inhabitants of the Serai watched them with shrieks of laughter.

"The priest is mad," said a horse-dealer to me. "He is going up to Kabul to sell toys to the Amir. He will either be raised to honor or have his head cut off. He came in here this morning and has been behaving madly ever since."

"The witless are under the protection of God," stammered a flat-cheeked Usbeg in broken Hindi. "They foretell future events."

"Would they could have foretold that my caravan

would have been cut up by the Shinwaris almost within shadow of the Pass!" grunted the Eusufzai agent of a Rajputana trading-house whose goods had been diverted into the hands of other robbers just across the Border, and whose misfortunes were the laughing-stock of the bazar. "Ohé, priest, whence come you and whither do you go?"

"From Roum have I come," shouted the priest, waving his whirligig; "from Roum, blown by the breath of a hundred devils across the sea! O thieves, robbers, liars, the blessing of Pir Khan on pigs, dogs, and perjurers! Who will take the Protected of God to the North to sell charms that are never still to the Amir? The camels shall not gall, the sons shall not fall sick, and the wives shall remain faithful while they are away, of the men who give me place in their caravan. Who will assist me to slipper the King of the Roos with a golden slipper with a silver heel? The protection of Pir Khan be upon his labors!" He spread out the skirts of his gaberdine and pirouetted between the lines of tethered horses.

"There starts a caravan from Peshawar to Kabul in twenty days, *Huzrut*," said the Eusufzai trader. "My camels go therewith. Do thou also go and bring us good-luck."

"I will go even now!" shouted the priest. "I will depart upon my winged camels, and be at Peshawar in a day! Ho! Hazar Mir Khan," he yelled to his servant, "drive out the camels, but let me first mount my own."

He leaped on the back of his beast as it knelt, and, turning round to me, cried: "Come thou also, Sahib, a little along the road, and I will sell thee a charm — an amulet that shall make thee King of Kafiristan."

Then the light broke upon me, and I followed the two

camels out of the Serai till we reached open road and the priest halted.

"What d' you think o' that?" said he in English. "Carnehan can't talk their patter, so I 've made him my servant. He makes a handsome servant. 'T is n't for nothing that I 've been knocking about the country for fourteen years. Did n't I do that talk neat? We 'll hitch on to a caravan at Peshawar till we get to Jagdallak, and then we 'll see if we can get donkeys for our camels, and strike into Kafiristan. Whirligigs for the Amir, O Lor! Put your hand under the camel-bags and tell me what you feel."

I felt the butt of a Martini, and another and another.

"Twenty of 'em," said Dravot placidly. "Twenty of 'em and ammunition to correspond, under the whirligigs and the mud dolls."

"Heaven help you if you are caught with those things!" I said. "A Martini is worth her weight in silver among the Pathans."

"Fifteen hundred rupees of capital — every rupee we could beg, borrow, or steal — are invested on these two camels," said Dravot. "We won't get caught. We 're going through the Khaiber with a regular caravan. Who 'd touch a poor mad priest?"

"Have you got everything you want?" I asked, overcome with astonishment.

"Not yet, but we shall soon. Give us a memento of your kindness, *Brother*. You did me a service, yesterday, and that time in Marwar. Half my Kingdom shall you have, as the saying is." I slipped a small charm compass from my watch chain and handed it up to the priest.

"Good-bye," said Dravot, giving me hand cautiously. "It 's the last time we 'll shake hands with an Englishman these many days. Shake hands with him, Carne-han," he cried, as the second camel passed me.

Carnehan leaned down and shook hands. Then the camels passed away along the dusty road, and I was left alone to wonder. My eye could detect no failure in the disguises. The scene in the Serai proved that they were complete to the native mind. There was just the chance, therefore, that Carnehan and Dravot would be able to wander through Afghanistan without detection. But, beyond, they would find death — certain and awful death.

Ten days later a native correspondent giving me the news of the day from Peshawar, wound up his letter with : " There has been much laughter here on account of a certain mad priest who is going in his estimation to sell petty gauds and insignificant trinkets which he ascribes as great charms to H.H. the Amir of Bokhara. He passed through Peshawar and associated himself to the Second Summer caravan that goes to Kabul. The merchants are pleased because through superstition they imagine that such mad fellows bring good-fortune."

The two, then, were beyond the Border. I would have prayed for them, but, that night, a real King died in Europe, and demanded an obituary notice.

. . . . . .

The wheel of the world swings through the same phases again and again. Summer passed and winter thereafter, and came and passed again. The daily paper continued and I with it, and upon the third summer there fell a hot night, a night-issue, and a strained waiting for something to be telegraphed from the other side of the world, exactly as had happened before. A few great men had died in the past two years, the machines worked with more clatter, and some of the trees in the Office garden were a few feet taller. But that was all the difference.

I passed over to the press-room, and went through just such a scene as I have already described. The nervous tension was stronger than it had been two years before, and I felt the heat more acutely. At three o'clock I cried, "Print off," and turned to go, when there crept to my chair what was left of a man. He was bent into a circle, his head was sunk between his shoulders, and he moved his feet one over the other like a bear. I could hardly see whether he walked or crawled — this rag-wrapped, whining cripple who addressed me by name, crying that he was come back. "Can you give me a drink?" he whimpered. "For the Lord's sake, give me a drink!"

I went back to the office, the man following with groans of pain, and I turned up the lamp.

"Don't you know me?" he gasped, dropping into a chair, and he turned his drawn face, surmounted by a shock of gray hair, to the light.

I looked at him intently. Once before had I seen eyebrows that met over the nose in an inch-broad black band, but for the life of me I could not tell where.

"I don't know you," I said, handing him the whiskey. "What can I do for you?"

He took a gulp of the spirit raw, and shivered in spite of the suffocating heat.

"I've come back," he repeated; "and I was the King of Kafiristan — me and Dravot — crowned Kings we was! In this office we settled it — you setting there and giving us the books. I am Peachey — Peachey Taliaferro Carnehan, and you've been setting here ever since — O Lord!"

I was more than a little astonished, and expressed my feelings accordingly.

"It's true," said Carnehan, with a dry cackle, nursing his feet, which were wrapped in rags. "True as gospel. Kings we were, with crowns upon our heads — me and Dravot — poor Dan — oh, poor, poor Dan, that would never take advice, not though I begged of him!"

"Take the whiskey," I said, "and take your own time. Tell me all you can recollect of everything from beginning to end. You got across the border on your camels, Dravot dressed as a mad priest and you his servant. Do you remember that?"

"I ain't mad — yet, but I shall be that way soon. Of course I remember. Keep looking at me, or maybe my words will go all to pieces. Keep looking at me in my eyes and don't say anything."

I leaned forward and looked into his face as steadily as I could. He dropped one hand upon the table and I grasped it by the wrist. It was twisted like a bird's claw, and upon the back was a ragged, red, diamond-shaped scar.

"No, don't look there. Look at *me*," said Carnehan. "That comes afterwards, but for the Lord's sake don't distrack me. We left with that caravan, me and Dravot playing all sorts of antics to amuse the people we were with. Dravot used to make us laugh in the evenings when all the people was cooking their dinners — cooking their dinners, and . . . what did they do then? They lit little fires with sparks that went into Dravot's beard, and we all laughed — fit to die. Little red fires they was, going into Dravot's big red beard — so funny." His eyes left mine and he smiled foolishly.

"You went as far as Jagdallak with that caravan," I said at a venture, "after you had lit those fires. To

Jagdallak, where you turned off to try to get into Kafiristan."

"No, we did n't neither. What are you talking about? We turned off before Jagdallak, because we heard the roads was good. But they was n't good enough for our two camels — mine and Dravot's. When we left the caravan, Dravot took off all his clothes and mine too, and said we would be heathen, because the Kafirs did n't allow Mohammedans to talk to them. So we dressed betwixt and between, and such a sight as Daniel Dravot I never saw yet nor expect to see again. He burned half his beard, and slung a sheep-skin over his shoulder, and shaved his head into patterns. He shaved mine, too, and made me wear outrageous things to look like a heathen. That was in a most mountaineous country, and our camels could n't go along any more because of the mountains. They were tall and black, and coming home I saw them fight like wild goats — there are lots of goats in Kafiristan. And these mountains, they never keep still, no more than the goats. Always fighting they are, and don't let you sleep at night."

"Take some more whiskey," I said very slowly. "What did you and Daniel Dravot do when the camels could go no further because of the rough roads that led into Kafiristan?"

"What did which do? There was a party called Peachey Taliaferro Carnehan that was with Dravot. Shall I tell you about him? He died out there in the cold. Slap from the bridge fell old Peachey, turning and twisting in the air like a penny whirligig that you can sell to the Amir. — No; they was two for three ha'pence, those whirligigs, or I am much mistaken and woeful sore. . . . And then these camels were no use, and Peachey said to Dravot — 'For the Lord's sake let's get out of this before our heads are chopped off,' and with that they killed the camels all among the mountains, not having anything in particular to eat, but first they took off the boxes with the guns and the ammunition, till two men came along driving four mules. Dravot up and dances in front of them, singing — ' Sell me four mules.' Says the first man — 'If you are rich enough to buy, you are rich enough to rob;' but before ever he could put his hand to his knife, Dravot breaks his neck over his knee, and the other party runs away. So Carnehan loaded the mules with the rifles that was taken off the camels, and together we starts forward into those bitter cold mountaineous parts, and never a road broader than the back of your hand."

He paused for a moment, while I asked him if he could remember the nature of the country through which he had journeyed.

" I am telling you as straight as I can, but my head isn't as good as it might be. They drove nails through it to make me hear better how Dravot died. The country was mountaineous and the mules were most contrary, and the inhabitants was dispersed and solitary. They went up and up, and down and down, and that other party, Carnehan, was imploring of Dravot not to sing and whistle so loud, for fear of bringing down the tremenjus avalanches. But Dravot says that if a King couldn't sing it wasn't worth being King, and whacked the mules over the rump, and never took no heed for ten cold days. We came to a big level valley all among the mountains, and the mules were near dead, so we killed them, not having anything in special for them or us to eat. We sat upon the boxes, and played odd and even with the cartridges that was jolted out.

"Then ten men with bows and arrows ran down that valley, chasing twenty men with bows and arrows, and the row was tremenjus. They was fair men — fairer than you or me — with yellow hair and remarkable well built. Says Dravot, unpacking the guns — 'This is the beginning of the business. We 'll fight for the ten men,' and with that he fires two rifles at the twenty men, and drops one of them at two hundred yards from the rock where he was sitting. The other men began to run, but Carnehan and Dravot sits on the boxes picking them off at all ranges, up and down the valley. Then we goes up to the ten men that had run across the snow too, and they fires a footy little arrow at us. Dravot he shoots above their heads and they all falls down flat. Then he walks over them and kicks them, and then he lifts them up and shakes hands all round to make them friendly like. He calls them and gives them the boxes to carry, and waves his hand for all the world as though he was King already. They takes the boxes and him across the valley and up the hill into a pine wood on the top, where there was half a dozen big stone idols. Dravot he goes to the biggest — a fellow they call Imbra — and lays a rifle and a cartridge at his feet, rubbing his nose respectful with his own nose, patting him on the head, and saluting in front of it. He turns round to the men and nods his head, and says — 'That's all right. I'm in the know too, and all these old jim-jams are my friends.' Then he opens his mouth and points down it, and when the first man brings him food, he says — 'No;' and when the second man brings him food, he says — 'No;' but when one of the old priests and the boss of the village brings him food, he says — 'Yes,' very haughty, and eats it slow. That was how we came to our first village, without any trouble, just as though we had tumbled from the skies. But we tumbled from one of those damned rope-bridges, you see, and — you couldn't expect a man to laugh much after that?"

"Take some more whiskey and go on," I said. "That was the first village you came into. How did you get to be King?"

"I wasn't King," said Carnehan. "Dravot, he was the King, and a handsome man he looked with the gold crown on his head and all. Him and the other party stayed in that village, and every morning Dravot sat by the side of old Imbra, and the people came and worshipped. That was Dravot's order. Then a lot of men came into the valley, and Carnehan and Dravot picks them off with the rifles before they knew where they was, and runs down into the valley and up again the other side and finds another village, same as the first one, and the people all falls down flat on their faces, and Dravot says — ' Now what is the trouble between you two villages?' and the people points to a woman, as fair as you or me, that was carried off, and Dravot takes her back to the first village and counts up the dead — eight there was. For each dead man Dravot pours a little milk on the ground and waves his arms like a whirligig and ' That's all right,' says he. Then he and Carnehan takes the big boss of each village by the arm and walks them down into the valley, and shows them how to scratch a line with a spear right down the valley, and gives each a sod of turf from both sides of the line. Then all the people comes down and shouts like the devil and all, and Dravot says — ' Go and dig the land, and be fruitful and multiply,' which they did, though they didn't understand. Then we asks the names of things in their lingo — bread and water and fire and idols and such, and Dravot leads the priest of each village up to the idol, and says he must sit there and judge the people, and if anything goes wrong he is to be shot.

"Next week they was all turning up the land in the valley as quiet as bees and much prettier, and the priests heard all the complaints and told Dravot in dumb show what it was about. 'That's just the beginning,' says Dravot. 'They think we're Gods.' He and Carnehan picks out twenty good men and shows them how to click off a rifle, and form fours, and advance in line, and they was very pleased to do so, and clever to see the hang of it. Then he takes out his pipe and his baccy-pouch and leaves one at one village, and one at the other, and off we two goes to see what was to be done in the next valley. That was all rock, and there was a little village there, and Carnehan says — 'Send 'em to the old valley to plant,' and takes 'em there and gives 'em some land that was n't took before. They were a poor lot, and we blooded 'em with a kid before letting 'em into the new Kingdom. That was to impress the people, and then they settled down quiet, and Carnehan went back to Dravot who had got into another valley, all snow and ice and most mountaineous. There was no people there and the Army got afraid, so Dravot shoots one of them, and goes on till he finds some people in a village, and the Army explains that unless the people wants to be killed they had better not shoot their little matchlocks; for they had matchlocks. We makes friends with the priest and I stays there alone with two of the Army, teaching the men how to drill, and a thundering big Chief comes across the snow with kettle-drums and horns twanging, because he heard there was a new God kicking about. Carnehan sights for the brown of the men half a mile across the snow and wings one of them. Then he sends a message to the Chief that, unless he wished to be killed, he must come and shake hands with me and leave his arms behind. The Chief comes alone first, and Carnehan shakes hands with him and whirls his arms about, same as Dravot used, and very much surprised that Chief was, and strokes my eyebrows. Then Carnehan goes alone to the Chief, and asks him in dumb show if he had an enemy he hated. 'I have,' says the Chief. So Carnehan weeds out the pick of his men, and sets the two of the Army to show them drill and at the end of two weeks the men can manoeuvre about as well as Volunteers. So he marches with the Chief to a great big plain on the top of a mountain, and the Chief's men rushes into a village and takes it ; we three Martinis firing into the brown of the enemy. So we took that village too, and I gives the Chief a rag from my coat and says, ' Occupy till I come ; ' which was scriptural. By way of a reminder, when me and the Army was eighteen hundred yards away, I drops a bullet near him standing on the snow, and all the people falls flat on their faces. Then I sends a letter to Dravot wherever he be by land or by sea."

At the risk of throwing the creature out of train I interrupted — " How could you write a letter up yonder? "

"The letter? — Oh ! — The letter ! Keep looking at me between the eyes, please. It was a string-talk letter, that we 'd learned the way of it from a blind beggar in the Punjab."

I remember that there had once come to the office a blind man with a knotted twig and a piece of string which he wound round the twig according to some cipher of his own. He could, after the lapse of days or hours, repeat the sentence which he had reeled up. He had reduced the alphabet to eleven primitive sounds ; and tried to teach me his method, but I could not understand.

" I sent that letter to Dravot," said Carnehan; " and told him to come back because this Kingdom was growing too big for me to handle, and then I struck for the first valley, to see how the priests were working. They called the village we took along with the Chief, Bashkai, and the first village we took, Er-Heb. The priests at Er-Heb was doing all right, but they had a lot of pending cases about land to show me, and some men from another village had been firing arrows at night. I went out and looked for that village, and fired four rounds at it from a thousand yards. That used all the cartridges I cared to spend, and I waited for Dravot, who had been away two or three months, and I kept my people quiet.

" One morning I heard the devil's own noise of drums and horns, and Dan Dravot marches down the hill with his Army and a tail of hundreds of men, and, which was the most amazing, a great gold crown on his head. ' My Gord, Carnehan,' says Daniel, ' this is a tremenjus business, and we 've got the whole country as far as it 's worth having. I am the son of Alexander by Queen Semiramis, and you 're my younger brother and a God too! It 's the biggest thing we 've ever seen. I 've been marching and fighting for six weeks with the Army, and every footy little village for fifty miles has come in rejoiceful; and more than that, I 've got the key of the whole show, as you 'll see, and I 've got a crown for you! I told 'em to make two of 'em at a place called Shu, where the gold lies in the rock like suet in mutton. Gold I 've seen, and turquoise I 've kicked out of the cliffs, and there 's garnets in the sands of the river, and here 's a chunk of amber that a man brought me. Call up all the priests and, here, take your crown.'

" One of the men opens a black hair bag, and I slips the crown on. It was too small and too heavy, but I wore it for the glory. Hammered gold it was — five pound weight, like a hoop of a barrel.

"'Peachey,' says Dravot, 'we don't want to fight no more. The Craft's the trick, so help me!' and he brings forward that same Chief that I left at Bashkai — Billy Fish we called him afterwards, because he was so like Billy Fish that drove the big tank-engine at Mach on the Bolan in the old days. 'Shake hands with him,' says Dravot, and I shook hands and nearly dropped, for Billy Fish gave me the Grip. I said nothing, but tried him with the Fellow Craft Grip. He answers, all right, and I tried the Master's Grip, but that was a slip. 'A Fellow Craft he is!' I says to Dan. 'Does he know the word?' — 'He does,' says Dan, 'and all the priests know. It's a miracle! The Chiefs and the priests can work a Fellow Craft Lodge in a way that's very like ours, and they've cut the marks on the rocks, but they don't know the Third Degree, and they've come to find out. It's Gord's Truth. I've known these long years that the Afghans knew up to the Fellow Craft Degree, but this is a miracle. A God and a Grand-Master of the Craft am I, and a Lodge in the Third Degree I will open, and we'll raise the head priests and the Chiefs of the villages.'

"'It's against all the law,' I says, 'holding a Lodge without warrant from any one; and you know we never held office in any Lodge.'

"'It's a master-stroke o' policy,' says Dravot. 'It means running the country as easy as a four-wheeled bogie on a down grade. We can't stop to inquire now, or they'll turn against us. I've forty Chiefs at my heel, and passed and raised according to their merit they shall be. Billet these men on the villages, and see that we run up a Lodge of some kind. The temple of Imbra will do for the Lodge-room. The women must make aprons as you show them. I'll hold a levee of Chiefs to-night and Lodge to-morrow.'

"I was fair run off my legs, but I wasn't such a fool as not to see what a pull this Craft business gave us. I showed the priests' families how to make aprons of the degrees, but for Dravot's apron the blue border and marks was made of turquoise lumps on white hide, not cloth. We took a great square stone in the temple for the Master's chair, and little stones for the officers' chairs, and painted the black pavement with white squares, and did what we could to make things regular.

"At the levee which was held that night on the hillside with big bonfires, Dravot gives out that him and me were Gods and sons of Alexander, and Past Grand-masters in the Craft, and was come to make Kafiristan a country where every man should eat in peace and drink in quiet, and specially obey us. Then the Chiefs come round to shake hands, and they were so hairy and white and fair it was just shaking hands with old friends. We gave them names according as they was like men we had known in India — Billy Fish, Holly Dilworth, Pikky Kergan, that was Bazar-master when I was at Mhow, and so on, and so on.

"*The* most amazing miracles was at Lodge next night. One of the old priests was watching us continuous, and I felt uneasy, for I knew we'd have to fudge the Ritual, and I didn't know what the men knew. The old priest was a stranger come in from beyond the village of Bash-kai. The minute Dravot puts on the Master's apron that the girls had made for him, the priest fetches a whoop and a howl, and tries to overturn the stone that Dravot was sitting on. 'It's all up now,' I says. 'That comes of meddling with the Craft without warrant!' Dravot never winked an eye, not when ten priests took and tilted over the Grand-master's chair — which was to say the stone of Imbra. The priest begins rubbing the bottom end of it to clear away the black dirt, and presently he shows all the other priests the Master's Mark, same as was on Dravot's apron, cut into the stone. Not even the priests of the temple of Imbra knew it was there. The old chap falls flat on his face at Dravot's feet and kisses 'em. 'Luck again,' says Dravot, across the Lodge to me, 'they say it 's the missing Mark that no one could understand the why of. We 're more than safe now.' Then he bangs the butt of his gun for a gavel and says: 'By virtue of the authority vested in me by my own right hand and the help of Peachey, I declare myself Grand-Master of all Freemasonry in Kafiristan in this the Mother Lodge o' the country, and King of Kafiristan equally with Peachey!' At that he puts on his crown and I puts on mine — I was doing Senior Warden — and we opens the Lodge in most ample form. It was a amazing miracle! The priests moved in Lodge through the first two degrees almost without telling, as if the memory was coming back to them. After that, Peachey and Dravot raised such as was worthy — high priests and Chiefs of far-off villages. Billy Fish was the first, and I can tell you we scared the soul out of him. It was not in any way according to Ritual, but it served our turn. We did n't raise more than ten of the biggest men, because we did n't want to make the Degree common. And they was clamoring to be raised.

"'In another six months,' says Dravot, 'we 'll hold another Communication, and see how you are working.' Then he asks them about their villages, and learns that they was fighting one against the other, and were sick and tired of it. And when they was n't doing that they was fighting with the Mohammedans. 'You can fight those when they come into our country,' says Dravot, 'Tell off every tenth man of your tribes for a Frontier guard, and send two hundred at a time to this valley to be drilled. Nobody is going to be shot or speared any more so long as he does well, and I know that you won't cheat me, because you 're white people — sons of Alexander — and not like common, black Mohammedans. You are *my* people, and by God,' says he, running off into English at the end — 'I 'll make a damned fine Nation of you, or I 'll die in the making!'

"I can't tell all we did for the next six months, because Dravot did a lot I could n't see the hang of, and he learned their lingo in a way I never could. My work was to help the people plough, and now and again go out with some of the Army and see what the other villages were doing, and make 'em throw rope-bridges across the ravines which cut up the country horrid. Dravot was very kind to me, but when he walked up and down in the pine wood pulling that bloody red beard of his with both fists I knew he was thinking plans I could not advise about, and I just waited for orders.

"But Dravot never showed me disrespect before the people. They were afraid of me and the Army, but they loved Dan. He was the best of friends with the priests and the Chiefs; but any one could come across the hills with a complaint, and Dravot would hear him out fair, and call four priests together and say what was to be done. He used to call in Billy Fish from Bashkai, and Pikky Kergan from Shu, and an old Chief we call Kafuzelum — it was like enough to his real name — and hold councils with 'em when there was any fighting to be done in small villages. That was his Council of War, and the four priests of Bashkai, Shu, Khawak, and Madora was his Privy Council. Between the lot of 'em they sent me, with forty men and twenty rifles, and sixty men carrying turquoises, into the Ghorband country to buy those hand-made Martini rifles, that come out of the Amir's workshops at Kabul, from one of the Amir's Herati regiments that would have sold the very teeth out of their mouths for turquoises.

"I stayed in Ghorband a month, and gave the Governor there the pick of my baskets for hush-money, and bribed the Colonel of the regiment some more, and, between the two and the tribes-people, we got more than a hundred hand-made Martinis, a hundred good Kohat Jezails that 'll throw to six hundred yards, and forty man-loads of very bad ammunition for the rifles. I came back with what I had, and distributed 'em among the men that the Chiefs sent in to me to drill. Dravot was too busy to attend to those things, but the old Army that we first made helped me, and we turned out five hundred men that could drill, and two hundred that knew how to hold arms pretty straight. Even those cork-screwed, hand-made guns was a miracle to them. Dravot talked big about powder-shops and factories, walking up and down in the pine wood when the winter was coming on.

"'I won't make a Nation,' says he. 'I 'll make an Empire! These men are n't niggers; they 're English! Look at their eyes — look at their mouths. Look at the way they stand up. They sit on chairs in their own houses. They 're the Lost Tribes, or something like it, and they 've grown to be English. I 'll take a census in the spring if the priests don't get frightened. There must be a fair two million of 'em in these hills. The villages are full o' little children. Two million people

— two hundred and fifty thousand fighting men — and
all English! They only want the rifles and a little drill-
ing. Two hundred and fifty thousand men, ready to cut
in on Russia's right flank when she tries for India!
Peachey, man,' he says, chewing his beard in great
hunks, 'we shall be Emperors — Emperors of the
Earth! Rajah Brooke will be a suckling to us. I'll
treat with the Viceroy on equal terms. I'll ask him to
send me twelve picked English — twelve that I know of
— to help us govern a bit. There's Mackray, Sergeant-
pensioner at Segowli — many's the good dinner he's given
me, and his wife a pair of trousers. There's Donkin, the
Warder of Tounghoo Jail; there's hundreds that I could
lay my hand on if I was in India. The Viceroy shall do
it for me, I'll send a man through in the spring for those
men, and I'll write for a dispensation from the Grand
Lodge for what I've done as Grand-Master. That —
and all the Sniders that'll be thrown out when the native troops in India take up the Martini. They'll be
worn smooth, but they'll do for fighting in these hills.
Twelve English, a hundred thousand Sniders run through
the Amir's country in dribblets — I'd be content with
twenty thousand in one year — and we'd be an Empire.
When everything was shipshape, I'd hand over the crown
— this crown I'm wearing now — to Queen Victoria on
my knees, and she'd say: "Rise up, Sir Daniel Dravot."
Oh, it's big! It's big, I tell you! But there's so much
to be done in every place — Bashkai, Khawak, Shu, and
everywhere else.'

"'What is it?' I says. 'There are no more men
coming in to be drilled this autumn. Look at those
fat black clouds. They're bringing the snow.'

"'It isn't that,' says Daniel, putting his hand very
hard on my shoulder; 'and I don't wish to say any-

thing that's against you, for no other living man would have followed me and made me what I am as you have done. You're a first-class Commander-in-Chief, and the people know you; but — it's a big country, and somehow you can't help me, Peachey, in the way I want to be helped.'

" 'Go to your blasted priests, then!' I said, and I was sorry when I made that remark, but it did hurt me sore to find Daniel talking so superior when I'd drilled all the men, and done all he told me.

" 'Don't let's quarrel, Peachey,' says Daniel without cursing. 'You're a King too, and the half of this Kingdom is yours; but can't you see, Peachey, we want cleverer men than us now — three or four of 'em, that we can scatter about for our Deputies. It's a hugeous great State, and I can't always tell the right thing to do, and I haven't time for all I want to do, and here's the winter coming on and all.' He put half his beard into his mouth, all red like the gold of his crown.

" 'I'm sorry, Daniel,' says I. 'I've done all I could. I've drilled the men and shown the people how to stack their oats better; and I've brought in those tin-ware rifles from Ghorband — but I know what you're driving at. I take it Kings always feel oppressed that way.'

" 'There's another thing too,' says Dravot, walking up and down. 'The winter's coming and these people won't be giving much trouble, and if they do we can't move about. I want a wife.'

" 'For Gord's sake leave the women alone!' I says. 'We've both got all the work we can, though I *am* a fool. Remember the Contrack, and keep clear o' women.'

" 'The Contrack only lasted till such time as we was

Kings; and Kings we have been these months past,' says Dravot, weighing his crown in his hand. 'You go get a wife too, Peachey—a nice, strappin', plump girl that'll keep you warm in the winter. They're prettier than English girls, and we can take the pick of 'em. Boil 'em once or twice in hot water, and they'll come out like chicken and ham.'

"'Don't tempt me!' I says. 'I will not have any dealings with a woman not till we are a dam' side more settled than we are now. I've been doing the work o' two men, and you've been doing the work o' three. Let's lie off a bit, and see if we can get some better tobacco from Afghan country and run in some good liquor; but no women.'

"'Who's talking o' *women*?' says Dravot. 'I said *wife*—a Queen to breed a King's son for the King. A Queen out of the strongest tribe, that'll make them your blood-brothers, and that'll lie by your side and tell you all the people thinks about you and their own affairs. That's what I want.'

"'Do you remember that Bengali woman I kept at Mogul Serai when I was a plate-layer?' says I. 'A fat lot o' good she was to me. She taught me the lingo and one or two other things; but what happened? She ran away with the Station Master's servant and half my month's pay. Then she turned up at Dadur Junction in tow of a half-caste, and had the impidence to say I was her husband—all among the drivers in the running-shed too!'

"'We've done with that,' says Dravot, 'these women are whiter than you or me, and a Queen I will have for the winter months.'

"'For the last time o' asking, Dan, do *not*,' I says. 'It'll only bring us harm. The Bible says that Kings ain't to waste their strength on women, 'specially when they 've got a new raw Kingdom to work over.'

"'For the last time of answering I will,' said Dravot, and he went away through the pine-trees looking like a big red devil, the sun being on his crown and beard and all.

"But getting a wife was not as easy as Dan thought. He put it before the Council, and there was no answer till Billy Fish said that he 'd better ask the girls. Dravot damned them all round. 'What 's wrong with me?' he shouts, standing by the idol Imbra. 'Am I a dog or am I not enough of a man for your wenches? Have n't I put the shadow of my hand over this country? Who stopped the last Afghan raid?' It was me really, but Dravot was too angry to remember. 'Who bought your guns? Who repaired the bridges? Who 's the Grand-Master of the sign cut in the stone?' says he, and he thumped his hand on the block that he used to sit on in Lodge, and at Council, which opened like Lodge always. Billy Fish said nothing and no more did the others. 'Keep your hair on, Dan,' said I; 'and ask the girls. That 's how it 's done at Home, and these people are quite English.'

"'The marriage of the King is a matter of State,' says Dan, in a white-hot rage, for he could feel, I hope, that he was going against his better mind. He walked out of the Council-room, and the others sat still, looking at the ground.

"'Billy Fish,' says I to the Chief of Bashkai, 'what 's the difficulty here? A straight answer to a true friend.'

"'You know,' says Billy Fish. 'How should a man tell you who knows everything? How can daughters of men marry Gods or Devils? It 's not proper.'

"I remembered something like that in the Bible; but

if, after seeing us as long as they had, they still believed we were Gods, it was n't for me to undeceive them.

"'A God can do anything,' says I. 'If the King is fond of a girl he 'll not let her die.' — 'She 'll have to,' said Billy Fish. 'There are all sorts of Gods and Devils in these mountains, and now and again a girl marries one of them and is n't seen any more. Besides, you two know the Mark cut in the stone. Only the Gods know that. We thought you were men till you showed the sign of the Master.'

"I wished then that we had explained about the loss of the genuine secrets of a Master-Mason at the first go-off; but I said nothing. All that night there was a blowing of horns in a little dark temple half-way down the hill, and I heard a girl crying fit to die. One of the priests told us that she was being prepared to marry the King.

"'I 'll have no nonsense of that kind,' says Dan. 'I don't want to interfere with your customs, but I 'll take my own wife.' — 'The girl 's a little bit afraid,' says the priest. 'She thinks she 's going to die, and they are a-heartening of her up down in the temple.'

"'Hearten her very tender, then,' says Dravot, 'or I 'll hearten you with the butt of a gun so you 'll never want to be heartened again.' He licked his lips, did Dan, and stayed up walking about more than half the night, thinking of the wife that he was going to get in the morning. I was n't by any means comfortable, for I knew that dealings with a woman in foreign parts, though you was a crowned King twenty times over, could not but be risky. I got up very early in the morning while Dravot was asleep, and I saw the priests talking together in whispers, and the Chiefs talking together too, and they looked at me out of the corners of their eyes.

"'What is up, Fish?' I say to the Bashkai man,

who was wrapped up in his furs and looking splendid to behold.

" ' I can't rightly say,' says he ; ' but if you can make the King drop all this nonsense about marriage, you 'll be doing him and me and yourself a great service.'

" ' That I do believe,' says I. ' But sure, you know, Billy, as well as me, having fought against and for us, that the King and me are nothing more than two of the finest men that God Almighty ever made. Nothing more, I do assure you.'

" ' That may be,' says Billy Fish, ' and yet I should be sorry if it was.' He sinks his head upon his great fur cloak for a minute and thinks. ' King,' says he, ' be you man or God or Devil, I 'll stick by you to-day. I have twenty of my men with me, and they will follow me. We 'll go to Bashkai until the storm blows over.'

" A little snow had fallen in the night, and everything was white except the greasy fat clouds that blew down and down from the north. Dravot came out with his crown on his head, swinging his arms and stamping his feet, and looking more pleased than Punch.

" ' For the last time, drop it, Dan,' says I in a whisper, ' Billy Fish here says that there will be a row.'

" ' A row among my people !' says Dravot. ' Not much. Peachey, you 're a fool not to get a wife too. Where 's the girl?' says he with a voice as loud as the braying of a jackass. ' Call up all the Chiefs and priests, and let the Emperor see if his wife suits him.'

" There was no need to call any one. They were all there leaning on their guns and spears round the clearing in the centre of the pine wood. A lot of priests went down to the little temple to bring up the girl, and the horns blew fit to wake the dead. Billy Fish saunters round and gets as close to Daniel as he could, and behind him stood his twenty men with matchlocks. Not a man of them under six feet. I was next to Dravot, and behind me was twenty men of the regular Army. Up comes the girl, and a strapping wench she was, covered with silver and turquoises but white as death, and looking back every minute at the priests.

"'She'll do,' said Dan, looking her over. 'What's to be afraid of, lass? Come and kiss me.' He puts his arm round her. She shuts her eyes, gives a bit of a squeak, and down goes her face in the side of Dan's flaming red beard.

"'The slut's bitten me!' says he, clapping his hand to his neck, and, sure enough, his hand was red with blood. Billy Fish and two of his matchlock-men catches hold of Dan by the shoulders and drags him into the Bashkai lot, while the priests howls in their lingo, — 'Neither God nor Devil but a man!' I was all taken aback, for a priest cut at me in front, and the Army behind began firing into the Bashkai men.

"'God A'mighty!' says Dan. 'What is the meaning o' this?'

"'Come back! Come away!' says Billy Fish. 'Ruin and Mutiny is the matter. We'll break for Bashkai if we can.'

"I tried to give some sort of orders to my men — the men o' the regular Army — but it was no use, so I fired into the brown of 'em with an English Martini and drilled three beggars in a line. The valley was full of shouting, howling creatures, and every soul was shrieking, 'Not a God nor a Devil but only a man!' The Bashkai troops stuck to Billy Fish all they were worth, but their matchlocks wasn't half as good as the Kabul breech-loaders, and four of them dropped. Dan was bellowing like a bull, for he was very wrathy; and Billy

25

Fish had a hard job to prevent him running out at the crowd.

" 'We can't stand,' says Billy Fish. 'Make a run for it down the valley! The whole place is against us.' The matchlock-men ran, and we went down the valley in spite of Dravot. He was swearing horrible and crying out he was a King. The priests rolled great stones on us, and the regular Army fired hard, and there wasn't more than six men, not counting Dan, Billy Fish, and Me, that came down to the bottom of the valley alive.

" Then they stopped firing and the horns in the temple blew again. 'Come away — for Gord's sake come away!' says Billy Fish. 'They'll send runners out to all the villages before ever we get to Bashkai. I can protect you there, but I can't do anything now.'

" My own notion is that Dan began to go mad in his head from that hour. He stared up and down like a stuck pig. Then he was all for walking back alone and killing the priests with his bare hands; which he could have done. 'An Emperor am I,' says Daniel, 'and next year I shall be a Knight of the Queen.'

" 'All right, Dan,' says I; 'but come along now while there's time.'

" 'It's your fault,' says he, 'for not looking after your Army better. There was mutiny in the midst, and you didn't know — you damned engine-driving, plate-laying, missionary's-pass-hunting hound!' He sat upon a rock and called me every foul name he could lay tongue to. I was too heart-sick to care, though it was all his foolishness that brought the smash.

" 'I'm sorry, Dan,' says I, 'but there's no accounting for natives. This business is our Fifty-Seven. Maybe we'll make something out of it yet, when we've got to Bashkai.'

"'Let's get to Bashkai, then,' says Dan, 'and, by God, when I come back here again I'll sweep the valley so there isn't a bug in a blanket left!'

"We walked all that day, and all that night Dan was stumping up and down on the snow, chewing his beard and muttering to himself.

"'There's no hope o' getting clear,' said Billy Fish. 'The priests will have sent runners to the villages to say that you are only men. Why didn't you stick on as Gods till things was more settled? I'm a dead man,' says Billy Fish, and he throws himself down on the snow and begins to pray to his Gods.

"Next morning we was in a cruel bad country — all up and down, no level ground at all, and no food either. The six Bashkai men looked at Billy Fish hungryway as if they wanted to ask something, but they said never a word. At noon we came to the top of a flat mountain all covered with snow, and when we climbed up into it, behold, there was an Army in position waiting in the middle!

"'The runners have been very quick,' says Billy Fish, with a little bit of a laugh. 'They are waiting for us.'

"Three or four men began to fire from the enemy's side, and a chance shot took Daniel in the calf of the leg. That brought him to his senses. He looks across the snow at the Army, and sees the rifles that we had brought into the country.

"'We're done for,' says he. 'They are Englishmen, these people, — and it's my blasted nonsense that has brought you to this. Get back, Billy Fish, and take your men away; you've done what you could, and now cut for it. Carnehan,' says he, 'shake hands with me and go along with Billy. Maybe they won't kill you. I'll go and meet 'em alone. It's me that did it. Me, the King!'

" ' Go ! ' says I.   ' Go to Hell, Dan.   I am with you here.   Billy Fish, you clear out, and we two will meet those folk.'

" ' I'm a Chief,' says Billy Fish, quite quiet.   ' I stay with you.   My men can go.'

" The Bashkai fellows did n't wait for a second word but ran off, and Dan and Me and Billy Fish walked across to where the drums were drumming and the horns were horning.   It was cold — awful cold.   I 've got that cold in the back of my head now.   There 's a lump of it there."

The punkah-coolies had gone to sleep.   Two kerosene lamps were blazing in the office, and the perspiration poured down my face and splashed on the blotter as I leaned forward.   Carnehan was shivering, and I feared that his mind might go.   I wiped my face, took a fresh grip of the piteously mangled hands, and said : " What happened after that ? "

The momentary shift of my eyes had broken the clear current.

" What was you pleased to say ? " whined Carnehan. " They took them without any sound.   Not a little whisper all along the snow, not though the King knocked down the first man that set hand on him — not though old Peachey fired his last cartridge into the brown of 'em. Not a single solitary sound did those swines make.   They just closed up tight, and I tell you their furs stunk. There was a man called Billy Fish, a good friend of us all, and they cut his throat, Sir, then and there, like a pig ; and the King kicks up the bloody snow and says : ' We 've had a dashed fine run for our money. What 's coming next ? '   But Peachey, Peachey Taliaferro, I tell you, Sir, in confidence as betwixt two friends, he lost his head, Sir.   No, he did n't neither.   The King lost his head, so he did, all along o' one of those cunning rope-bridges. Kindly let me have the paper-cutter, Sir. It tilted this way. They marched him a mile across that snow to a rope-bridge over a ravine with a river at the bottom. You may have seen such. They prodded him behind like an ox. 'Damn your eyes!' says the King. 'D' you suppose I can't die like a gentleman?' He turns to Peachey — Peachey that was crying like a child. 'I've brought you to this, Peachey,' says he. 'Brought you out of your happy life to be killed in Kafiristan, where you was late Commander-in-Chief of the Emperor's forces. Say you forgive me, Peachey.' — 'I do,' says Peachey. 'Fully and freely do I forgive you, Dan.' — 'Shake hands, Peachey,' says he. 'I'm going now.' Out he goes, looking neither right nor left, and when he was plumb in the middle of those dizzy dancing ropes, — 'Cut, you beggars,' he shouts; and they cut, and old Dan fell, turning round and round and round, twenty thousand miles, for he took half an hour to fall till he struck the water, and I could see his body caught on a rock with the gold crown close beside.

" But do you know what they did to Peachey between two pine-trees? They crucified him, Sir, as Peachey's hand will show. They used wooden pegs for his hands and his feet; and he didn't die. He hung there and screamed, and they took him down next day, and said it was a miracle that he wasn't dead. They took him down — poor old Peachey that hadn't done them any harm — that hadn't done them any —— "

He rocked to and fro and wept bitterly, wiping his eyes with the back of his scarred hands and moaning like a child for some ten minutes.

" They was cruel enough to feed him up in the temple, because they said he was more of a God than old Daniel that was a man. Then they turned him out on the snow, and told him to go home, and Peachey came home in about a year, begging along the roads quite safe; for Daniel Dravot he walked before and said: 'Come along, Peachey. It's a big thing we're doing.' The mountains they danced at night, and the mountains they tried to fall on Peachey's head, but Dan he held up his hand, and Peachey came along bent double. He never let go of Dan's hand, and he never let go of Dan's head. They gave it to him as a present in the temple, to remind him not to come again, and though the crown was pure gold, and Peachey was starving, never would Peachey sell the same. You knew Dravot, Sir! You knew Right Worshipful Brother Dravot! Look at him now!"

He fumbled in the mass of rags round his bent waist; brought out a black horsehair bag embroidered with silver thread; and shook therefrom on to my table — the dried, withered head of Daniel Dravot! The morning sun that had long been paling the lamps struck the red beard and blind sunken eyes; struck, too, a heavy circlet of gold studded with raw turquoises, that Carnehan placed tenderly on the battered temples.

"You be'old now," said Carnehan, "the Emperor in his 'abit as he lived — the King of Kafiristan with his crown upon his head. Poor old Daniel that was a monarch once!"

I shuddered, for, in spite of defacements manifold, I recognized the head of the man of Marwar Junction. Carnehan rose to go. I attempted to stop him. He was not fit to walk abroad. "Let me take away the whiskey, and give me a little money," he gasped. "I was a King once. I'll go to the Deputy Commissioner and ask to set in the Poorhouse till I get my health. No, thank you, I can't wait till you get a carriage for me. I've urgent private affairs — in the south — at Marwar."

He shambled out of the office and departed in the direction of the Deputy Commissioner's house. That day at noon I had occasion to go down the blinding hot Mall, and I saw a crooked man crawling along the white dust of the roadside, his hat in his hand, quavering dolorously after the fashion of street singers at Home. There was not a soul in sight, and he was out of all possible earshot of the houses. And he sang through his nose, turning his head from right to left : —

> " The Son of Man goes forth to war,
>   A golden crown to gain ;
> His blood-red banner streams afar —
>   Who follows in his train ? "

I waited to hear no more, but put the poor wretch into my carriage and drove him off to the nearest missionary for eventual transfer to the Asylum. He repeated the hymn twice while he was with me whom he did not in the least recognize, and I left him singing it to the missionary.

Two days later I inquired after his welfare of the Superintendent of the Asylum.

" He was admitted suffering from sun-stroke. He died early yesterday morning," said the Superintendent. " Is it true that he was half an hour bare-headed in the sun at midday ? "

" Yes," said I, " but do you happen to know if he had anything upon him by any chance when he died ? "

" Not to my knowledge," said the Superintendent.

And there the matter rests.

XII

HOW GAVIN BIRSE PUT IT TO MAG LOWNIE

HOW GAVIN BIRSE PUT IT TO MAG LOWNIE

ROM

A WINDOW IN THRUMS

By J. M. BARRIE

INTRODUCTORY

REALISM AS A LITERARY METHOD

THE word *realism* has come to have two meanings. Primarily it signified a study of phases of life which had come under the direct observation of the author. The so-called realists argued that this was the only scientific and trustworthy method of presenting life, namely, offering to the world only that which a man had seen with his own eyes. To this the idealists replied that the essential things of life pertained to the mind and heart, which no man hath seen, and that the imaginary forms of romance often represent these unseen essentials better than any description of exterior customs or physical surroundings.

As a matter of fact, however, realism was used by its advocates (perhaps unconsciously) merely as a literary method. The ordinary man comes to believe in what he has not seen, largely by the confidence he gains in recognizing that which he knows very well. Therefore if we mingle much that is commonplace and very well known in a story with that which we wish to teach, the reader is likely to accept the whole with avidity, because he recognizes so much that he knows to be actual and true.

One of the devices of realism is dialect. It gives an impression of actual and living men and women. Few readers have any interest in dialect as such, and it may easily be carried to excess, for the essential thing after all is the revelation of the mind and heart of man which the story-writer has to make.

Among the professed realists of recent times, none has been more successful than J. M. Barrie. Nothing so wins upon us as sympathetic understanding of all kinds and conditions of men, for it promotes the chief principle of universal religion, brotherly love. In stories such as those we find in "A Window in Thrums," the actual characters and events are insignificant; but indirectly they reveal our own relative lack of importance to powers higher than we are; and the genial humor and affection which pervades these studies of insignificant lives wins us to a kindred love. Humor is the saving salt of sane existence, the corrective to the natural tendency toward depression and morbidity; and humor is Barrie's constant weapon.

In a story like this of Barrie's, we may discover all the essential principles of the artistic short story, but united in such different proportions from any we have met before that we see the possibilities of the greatest variety, in a seemingly strictly limited art.   All art really gains power and loses nothing by its limitations.

HOW GAVIN BIRSE PUT IT TO MAG LOWNIE.

IN a wet day the rain gathered in blobs on the road that passed our garden.   Then it crawled into the cart-tracks until the road was streaked with water. Lastly, the water gathered in heavy yellow pools.   If the on-ding still continued, clods of earth toppled from the garden dyke into the ditch.

On such a day, when even the dulseman had gone into shelter, and the women scudded by with their wrappers over their heads, came Gavin Birse to our door.   Gavin, who was the Glen Quharity post, was still young, but had never been quite the same man since some amateurs in the glen ironed his back for rheumatism.   I thought he had called to have a crack with me.   He sent his compliments up to the attic, however, by Leeby, and would I come and be a witness?

Gavin came up and explained.   He had taken off his scarf and thrust it into his pocket, lest the rain should take the color out of it.   His boots cheeped, and his shoulders had risen to his ears.   He stood steaming before my fire.

"If it's no ower muckle to ask ye," he said, "I would like ye for a witness."

"A witness! But for what do you need a witness, Gavin?"

"I want ye," he said, "to come wi' me to Mag's, and be a witness."

Gavin and Mag Lownie had been engaged for a year or more. Mag was the daughter of Janet Ogilvy, who was best remembered as the body that took the hill (that is, wandered about it) for twelve hours on the day Mr. Dishart, the Auld Licht minister, accepted a call to another church.

"You don't mean to tell me, Gavin," I asked, "that your marriage is to take place to-day?"

By the twist of his mouth I saw that he was only deferring a smile.

"Far frae that," he said.

"Ah, then, you have quarrelled, and I am to speak up for you?"

"Na, na," he said, "I dinna want ye to do that above all things. It would be a favor if ye could gie me a bad character."

This beat me, and, I dare say, my face showed it.

"I'm no juist what ye would call anxious to marry Mag noo," said Gavin, without a tremor.

I told him to go on.

"There's a lassie oot at Craigiebuckle," he explained, "workin' on the farm — Jeanie Luke by name. Ye may hae seen her?"

"What of her?" I asked, severely.

"Weel," said Gavin, still unabashed, "I'm thinkin' noo 'at I would rather hae her."

Then he stated his case more fully.

"Ay, I thocht I liked Mag oncommon till I saw Jeanie, an' I like her fine yet, but I prefer the other ane. That state o' matters canna gang on for ever, so I came into Thrums the day to settle 't one wy or another."

"And how," I asked, "do you propose going about it? It is a somewhat delicate business."

"Ou, I see nae great difficulty in 't. I 'll speir at Mag, blunt oot, if she 'll let me aff. Yes, I 'll put it to her plain."

"You 're sure Jeanie would take you?"

"Ay; oh, there 's nae fear o' that."

"But if Mag keeps you to your bargain?"

"Weel, in that case there 's nae harm done."

"You are in a great hurry, Gavin?"

"Ye may say that; but I want to be married. The wifie I lodge wi' canna last lang, an' I would like to settle doon in some place."

"So you are on your way to Mag's now?"

"Ay, we 'll get her in atween twal' and ane."

"Oh, yes; but why do you want me to go with you?"

"I want ye for a witness. If she winna let me aff, weel and guid; and if she will, it 's better to hae a witness in case she should go back on her word."

Gavin made his proposal briskly, and as coolly as if he were only asking me to go fishing; but I did not accompany him to Mag's. He left the house to look for another witness, and about an hour afterwards Jess saw him pass with Tammas Haggart. Tammas cried in during the evening to tell us how the mission prospered.

"Mind ye," said Tammas, a drop of water hanging to the point of his nose, "I disclaim all responsibility in the business. I ken Mag weel for a thrifty, respectable woman, as her mither was afore her, and so I said to Gavin when he came to speir me."

"Ay, mony a pirn has 'Lisbeth filled to me," said Hendry, settling down to a reminiscence.

" No to be ower hard on Gavin," continued Tammas, forestalling Hendry, " he took what I said in guid part ; but aye when I stopped speakin' to draw breath, he says, ' The queistion is, will ye come wi' me ?' He was michty made up in 's mind."

" Weel, ye went wi' him," suggested Jess, who wanted to bring Tammas to the point.

" Ay," said the stone-breaker, " but no in sic a hurry as that."

He worked his mouth round and round, to clear the course, as it were, for a sarcasm.

" Fowk often say," he continued, " 'at am quick beyond the ord'nar' in seeing the humorous side o' things."

Here Tammas paused, and looked at us.

" So ye are, Tammas," said Hendry. " Losh, ye mind hoo ye saw the humorous side o' me wearin' a pair o' boots 'at wisna marrows ! No, the ane had a toe-piece on, an' the other hadna."

" Ye juist wore them sometimes when ye was delvin'," broke in Jess, " ye have as guid a pair o' boots as ony in Thrums."

" Ay, but I had worn them," said Hendry, " at odd times for mair than a year, an' I had never seen the humorous side o' them. Weel, as fac as death (here he addressed me), Tammas had juist seen them twa or three times when he saw the humorous side o' them. Syne I saw their humorous side, too, but no till Tammas pointed it oot."

" That was naething," said Tammas, " naething ava to some things I 've done."

" But what aboot Mag ? " said Leeby.

" We wasna that length, was we ? " said Tammas. " Na, we was speakin' aboot the humorous side. Ay, wait a wee, I didna mention the humorous side for naething."

He paused to reflect.

"Oh, yes," he said at last, brightening up, "I was sayin' to ye hoo quick I was to see the humorous side o' onything. Ay, then, what made me say that was 'at in a clink (flash) I saw the humorous side o' Gavin's position."

"Man, man," said Hendry, admiringly, "and what is 't?"

"Oh, it 's this, there 's something humorous in speirin' a woman to let ye aff so as ye can be married to another woman."

"I daursay there is," said Hendry, doubtfully.

"Did she let him aff?" asked Jess, taking the words out of Leeby's mouth.

"I 'm comin' to that," said Tammas. "Gavin proposes to me after I had ha'en my laugh——"

"Yes," cried Hendry, banging the table with his fist, "it has a humorous side. Ye 're richt again, Tammas."

"I wish ye wadna blatter (beat) the table," said Jess, and then Tammas proceeded.

"Gavin wanted me to tak' paper an' ink an' a pen wi' me, to write the proceedin's doon, but I said, 'Na, na, I 'll tak' paper, but no nae ink nor nae pen, for there 'll be ink an' a pen there.' That was what I said."

"An' did she let him aff?" asked Leeby.

"Weel," said Tammas, "aff we goes to Mag's hoose, an' sure enough Mag was in. She was alone, too; so Gavin, no to waste time, juist sat doon for politeness' sake, an' syne rises up again; an' says he, 'Marget Lownie, I hae a solemn question to speir at ye, namely this, Will you, Marget Lownie, let me, Gavin Birse, aff?'"

"Mag would start at that?"

"Sal, she was braw an' cool. I thocht she maun hae got wind o' his intentions aforehand, for she juist replies, quiet-like, 'Hoo do ye want aff, Gavin?'

"'Because,' says he, like a book, 'my affections has undergone a change.'

"'Ye mean Jean Luke,' says Mag.

"'That is wha I mean,' says Gavin, very straitforrard."

"But she didna let him aff, did she?"

"Na, she wasna the kind. Says she, 'I wonder to hear ye, Gavin, but am no goin' to agree to naething o' that sort.'

"'Think it ower,' says Gavin.

"'Na, my mind's made up,' said she.

"'Ye would sune get anither man,' he says, earnestly.

"'Hoo do I ken that?' she speirs, rale sensibly, I thocht, for men's no sae easy to get.

"'Am sure o't,' Gavin says, wi' michty conviction in his voice, 'for ye're bonny to look at, an' weel kent for bein' a guid body.'

"'Ay,' says Mag, 'I'm glad ye like me, Gavin, for ye have to tak me.'"

"That put a clincher on him," interrupted Hendry.

"He was loth to gie in," replied Tammas, "so he says, 'Ye think am a fine character, Marget Lownie, but ye're very far mista'en. I wouldna wonder but what I was loosin' my place some o' thae days, an' syne whaur would ye be?—Marget Lownie,' he goes on, 'am nat'rally lazy an' fond o' the drink. As sure as ye stand there, am a reg'lar deevil!'"

"That was strong language," said Hendry, "but he would be wantin' to fleg (frighten) her?"

"Juist so, but he didna manage 't, for Mag says, 'We a' hae oor faults, Gavin, an' deevil or no deevil, ye're the man for me!'

"Gavin thocht a bit," continued Tammas, "an' syne he tries her on a new tack. 'Marget Lownie,' he says, 'yer father's an auld man noo, an' he has naebody but yersel to look after him. I'm thinkin' it would be kind o' cruel o' me to tak ye awa' frae him?'"

"Mag wouldna be ta'en wi' that; she wasna born on a Sawbath," said Jess, using one of her favorite sayings.

"She wasna," answered Tammas. "Says she, 'Hae nae fear on that score, Gavin; my father's fine willin' to spare me!'"

"An' that ended it?"

"Ay, that ended it."

"Did ye tak it doun in writin'?" asked Hendry.

"There was nae need," said Tammas, handing round his snuff-mull. "No, I never touched paper. When I saw the thing was settled, I left them to their coortin'. They're to tak a look at Snecky Hobart's auld hoose the nicht. It's to let."

XIII

ON THE STAIRS

ON THE STAIRS

FROM

"TALES OF MEAN STREETS"

BY ARTHUR MORRISON

INTRODUCTORY

SLIGHTNESS AND SUGGESTION

IN the study of Thackeray's "A Princess's Tragedy," we have already noticed the artistic value of restraint, and the power of suggestion; but in the case of Thackeray this was only the natural self-repression of a gentleman on painful topics. Suggestion as a literary method in short story writing was reserved for later writers. We saw something of it in the unexpressed moral of Maupassant's "Necklace." In many of Kipling's stories, especially his very short ones, such as "The Story of Muhammad Din," we may find still further development of the method. The editor knows of no better example, however, than that afforded by Arthur Morrison's "On the Stairs." A whole drama is revealed in the most simple and unpromising realistic details.

The story is not a great one in itself, but its cleverness is fascinating to the student of literary art.

ON THE STAIRS

THE house had been "genteel." When trade was prospering in the East End, and the ship-fitter or block-maker thought it no shame to live in the parish where his workshop lay, such a master had lived here. Now, it was a tall, solid, well-bricked, ugly house, grimy and paintless in the joinery, cracked and patched in the windows : where the front door stood open all day long ; and the womankind sat on the steps, talking of sickness and deaths and the cost of things ; and treacherous holes lurked in the carpet of road-soil on the stairs and in the passage.   For when eight families live in a house, nobody buys a door-mat, and the street was one of those streets that are always muddy.   It smelt, too, of many things, none of them pleasant (one was fried fish) ; but for all that it was not a slum.

Three flights up, a gaunt woman with bare forearms stayed on her way to listen at a door which, opening, let out a warm, fetid waft from a close sick-room.   A bent and tottering old woman stood on the threshold, holding the door behind her.

"An' is 'e no better now, Mrs. Curtis ? " the gaunt woman asked, with a nod at the opening.

The old woman shook her head, and pulled the door closer.   Her jaw waggled loosely in her withered chaps : "Nor won't be ; till 'e 's gone."   Then after a certain pause, " 'E 's goin'," she said.

" Don't doctor give no 'ope ? "

" Lor' bless ye, I don't want to ast no doctors," Mrs.

Curtis replied, with something not unlike a chuckle.
"I've seed too many on 'em. The boy's a-goin', fast;
I can see that. An' then " — she gave the handle another
tug, and whispered — " he's been called." She nodded
amain. "Three seprit knocks at the bed-head las'
night; an' I know what *that* means!"

The gaunt woman raised her brows, and nodded.
"Ah, well," she said, "we all on us comes to it some
day, sooner or later. An' it's often a 'appy release."

The two looked into space beyond each other, the
elder with a nod and a croak. Presently the other pursued, " 'E's been a very good son, ain't 'e? "

"Ay, ay, well enough son to me," responded the old
woman, a little peevishly; " an' I'll 'ave 'im put away
decent, though there's on'y the Union for me after. I
can do that, thank Gawd!" she added, meditatively, as
chin on fist she stared into the thickening dark over the
stairs.

"When I lost my pore 'usband," said the gaunt
woman, with a certain brightening, "I give 'im a
'ansome funeral. 'E was a Oddfeller, an' I got twelve
pound. I 'ad a oak caufin an' a open 'earse. There
was a kerridge for the fam'ly an' one for 'is mates —
two 'orses each, an' feathers, an' mutes; an' it went the
furthest way round to the cimitry. 'Wotever 'appens,
Mrs. Manders,' says the undertaker, 'you'll feel as
you've treated 'im proper; nobody can't reproach you
over that.' An' they couldn't. 'E was a good 'usband
to me, an' I buried 'im respectable."

The gaunt woman exulted. The old, old story of
Manders's funeral fell upon the other one's ears with a
freshened interest, and she mumbled her gums rumi-
nantly. "Bob'll 'ave a 'ansome buryin', too," she
said. "I can make it up, with the insurance money,

an' this, an' that. On'y I dunno about mutes. It's a expense."

In the East End, when a woman has not enough money to buy a thing much desired, she does not say so in plain words; she says the thing is an "expense," or a "great expense." It means the same thing, but it sounds better. Mrs. Curtis had reckoned her resources, and found that mutes would be an "expense." At a cheap funeral mutes cost half-a-sovereign and their liquor. Mrs. Manders said as much.

"Yus, yus, 'arf-a-sovereign," the old woman assented. Within, the sick man feebly beat the floor with a stick. "I'm a-comin'," she cried shrilly; "yus, 'arf-a-sovereign, but it's a lot, an' I don't see 'ow I'm to do it —not at present." She reached for the door-handle again, but stopped and added, by after-thought, "Unless I don't 'ave no plooms."

"It 'ud be a pity not to 'ave plooms. I 'ad—"

There were footsteps on the stairs: then a stumble and a testy word. Mrs. Curtis peered over into the gathering dark. "Is it the doctor, sir?" she asked. It was the doctor's assistant; and Mrs. Manders tramped up to the next landing as the door of the sick-room took him in.

For five minutes the stairs were darker than ever. Then the assistant, a very young man, came out again, followed by the old woman with a candle. Mrs. Manders listened in the upper dark. "He's sinking fast," said the assistant. "He *must* have a stimulant. Dr. Mansell ordered port wine. Where is it?" Mrs. Curtis mumbled dolorously. "I tell you he *must* have it," he averred with unprofessional emphasis (his qualification was only a month old). "The man can't take solid food, and his strength must be kept up somehow.

Another day may make all the difference. Is it because you can't afford it?" "It's a expense — sich a expense, doctor," the old woman pleaded. "An' wot with 'arf-pints o' milk an' —" She grew inarticulate, and mumbled dismally.

"But he must have it, Mrs. Curtis, if it's your last shilling: it's the only way. If you mean you absolutely have n't the money —" and he paused a little awkwardly. He was not a wealthy young man — wealthy young men do not devil for East End doctors — but he was conscious of a certain haul of sixpences at nap the night before; and, being inexperienced, he did not foresee the career of persecution whereon he was entering at his own expense and of his own motion. He produced five shillings: "If you absolutely have n't the money, why — take this and get a bottle — good: not at a public-house. But mind, *at once*. He should have had it before."

It would have interested him, as a matter of coincidence, to know that his principal had been guilty of the selfsame indiscretion — even the amount was identical — on that landing the day before. But, as Mrs. Curtis said nothing of this, he floundered down the stair and out into the wetter mud, pondering whether or not the beloved son of a Congregational minister might take full credit for a deed of charity on the proceeds of sixpenny nap. But Mrs. Curtis puffed her wrinkles, and shook her head sagaciously as she carried in her candle. From the room came a clink as of money falling into a teapot. And Mrs. Manders went about her business.

The door was shut, and the stair a pit of blackness. Twice a lodger passed down, and up and down, and still it did not open. Men and women walked on the lower flights, and out at the door, and in again. From the street a shout or a snatch of laughter floated up the pit.

On the pavement footsteps rang crisper and fewer, and from the bottom passage there were sounds of stagger and sprawl. A demented old clock buzzed divers hours at random, and was rebuked every twenty minutes by the regular tread of a policeman on his beat. Finally, somebody shut the street-door with a great bang, and the street was muffled. A key turned inside the door on the landing, but that was all. A feeble light shone for hours along the crack below, and then went out. The crazy old clock went buzzing on, but nothing left that room all night. Nothing that opened the door. . . .

When next the key turned, it was to Mrs. Manders's knock, in the full morning; and soon the two women came out on the landing together, Mrs. Curtis with a shapeless clump of bonnet. " Ah, 'e 's a lovely corpse," said Mrs. Manders. " Like wax. So was my 'usband."

" I must be stirrin'," croaked the old woman, " an' go about the insurance an' the measurin' an' that. There 's lots to do."

" Ah, there is. 'Oo are you goin' to 'ave, — Wilkins? I 'ad Wilkins. Better than Kedge, *I* think : Kedge's mutes dresses rusty, an' their trousis is frayed. If you was thinkin' of 'avin' mutes — "

" Yus, yus," — with a palsied nodding, — " I 'm a-goin' to 'ave mutes : I can do it respectable, thank Gawd ! "

" And the plooms ? "

" Ay, yus, and the plooms too. They ain't sich a great expense, after all."

PRINTED FOR A. C. McCLURG & CO. BY
THE UNIVERSITY PRESS, JOHN WILSON
& SON (INC.), CAMBRIDGE, U.S.A.

A SELECTION FROM
The Best English Essays

ILLUSTRATIVE OF THE HISTORY
OF ENGLISH PROSE STYLE

CHOSEN AND ARRANGED WITH HISTORICAL AND CRITICAL INTRODUCTIONS

By SHERWIN CODY

EDITOR OF "THE WORLD'S GREATEST SHORT STORIES," AND AUTHOR OF
"THE ART OF WRITING AND SPEAKING THE ENGLISH LANGUAGE"

MR. CODY'S "Selection of the World's Greatest Short Stories" has met with much approval by students of literature, and it is expected that this new book, which is a companion volume to the earlier work in every respect, will be quite as successful. He has included essays by Addison, Swift, De Quincey, Lamb, Carlyle, Emerson, Macaulay, Ruskin, Arnold, and Bacon, as illustrative of the history of English prose style; and his historical and critical introductions to each essay give the book its practical value.

$1.00 net

A. C. McCLURG & COMPANY
PUBLISHERS · · CHICAGO